LT
DEA

Deaver, Jeffery.

The kill room.

Also by Jeffery Deaver

*Featuring Lincoln Rhyme and Amelia Sachs
**Featuring Kathryn Dance

THE KILL
ROOM

A LINCOLN RHYME NOVEL

JEFFERY DEAVER

GRAND CENTRAL
PUBLISHING
LARGE PRINT

Grand Central Publishing
Hachette Book Group
237 Park Avenue
New York, NY 10017
www.HachetteBookGroup.com

Printed in the United States of America

RRD-C and RRD-H

First Edition: June 2013
10 9 8 7 6 5 4 3 2 1

Grand Central Publishing is a division of Hachette Book Group, Inc.
The Grand Central Publishing name and logo is a trademark of Hachette Book Group, Inc.

The Hachette Speakers Bureau provides a wide range of authors for speaking events. To find out more, go to www.hachettespeakersbureau.com or call (866) 376-6591.

The publisher is not responsible for websites (or their content) that are not owned by the publisher.

Library of Congress Cataloging-in-Publication Data
Deaver, Jeffery.
    The Kill Room : A Lincoln Rhyme Novel / Jeffery Deaver. — First Edition.
        pages cm
    ISBN 978-1-4555-1706-0 (hardcover) — ISBN 978-1-4555-2957-5 (large print hardcover) — ISBN 978-1-4555-1707-7 (ebook) 1. Rhyme, Lincoln (Fictitious character)—Fiction. 2. Police—New York (State)—New York—Fiction. I. Title.
    PS3554.E1755K55 2013
    813'.54—dc23
                                                                    2012041911

ISBN 978-1-4555-7348-6 (international paperback)

For Judy, Fred and Dax

THE KILL ROOM

I disapprove of what you say, but I will defend to the death your right to say it.

—EVELYN BEATRICE HALL,
THE FRIENDS OF VOLTAIRE, 1906

I

THE POISONWOOD TREE

CHAPTER 1

THE FLASH OF LIGHT TROUBLED HIM.

A glint, white or pale yellow, in the distance.

From the water? From the strip of land across the peaceful turquoise bay?

But here, there could be no danger. Here, he was in a beautiful and isolated resort. Here, he was out of the glare of media and the gaze of enemies.

Roberto Moreno squinted out the window. He was merely in his late thirties but his eyes were not good and he pushed the frames higher on his nose and scanned the vista—the garden outside the suite's window, the narrow white beach, the pulsing blue-green sea. Beautiful, isolated...and protected. No vessels bobbed within sight. And even if an enemy with a rifle could have learned he was here and made his way unseen through the industrial plants on that spit of land a mile away across the water, the distance and the pollution clouding the view would have made a shot impossible.

No more flashes, no more glints.

You're safe. Of course you are.

But still Moreno remained wary. Like Martin Luther King, like Gandhi, he was always at risk. This was the way of his life. He wasn't afraid of death. But he was afraid of dying before his work was done. And at this young age he still had much to do. For instance, the event he'd just finished organizing an hour or so ago—a significant one, sure to get a lot of people's attention—was merely one of a dozen planned for the next year.

And beyond, an abundant future loomed.

Dressed in a modest tan suit, a white shirt and royal blue tie—oh, so Caribbean—the stocky man now filled two cups from the coffeepot that room service had just delivered and returned to the couch. He handed one to the reporter, who was setting up a tape recorder.

"Señor de la Rua. Some milk? Sugar?"

"No, thank you."

They were speaking in Spanish, in which Moreno was fluent. He hated English and only spoke it when he needed to. He'd never quite shucked the New Jersey accent when he was speaking in his native tongue, "hehr" for "her," "mirrah" for "mirror," "gun" for "gone." The tones of his own voice took him right back to his early days in the States—his father working long hours and living life sober, his mother spending long hours not. Bleak landscapes, bullies from a nearby high school. Until salvation. the family's move to a place far kinder than South Hills, a place where even the language was softer and more elegant.

The reporter said, "But call me Eduardo. Please."

"And I'm Roberto."

The name was really "Robert" but that smacked of lawyers on Wall Street and politicians in Washington and generals on the battlefields sowing foreign ground with the bodies of the locals like cheap seeds.

Hence, *Roberto.*

"You live in Argentina," Moreno said to the journalist, who was a slight man, balding and dressed in a tie-less blue shirt and threadbare black suit. "Buenos Aires?"

"That's right."

"Do you know about the name of the city?"

De la Rua said no; he wasn't a native.

"The meaning is 'good air,' of course," Moreno said. He read extensively—several books a week, much of it Latin American literature and history. "But the air referred to was in *Sardinia*, Italy, not Argentina. So called after a settlement on top of a hill in Cagliari. The settlement was above the, let us say, pungent smells of the old city and was accordingly named *Buen Ayre*. The Spanish explorer who discovered what became Buenos Aires named it after that settlement. Of course that was the *first* settlement of the city. They were wiped out by the natives, who didn't enjoy the exploitation by Europe."

De la Rua said, "Even your anecdotes have a decidedly anti-colonial flavor."

Moreno laughed. But the humor vanished and he looked quickly out the window again.

That damn glint of light. Still, though, he could see nothing but trees and plants in the garden and that hazy line of land a mile away. The inn was on the largely deserted southwest coast of New Providence, the island in the Bahamas where Nassau was located. The grounds were fenced and guarded. And the garden was reserved for this suite alone and protected by a high fence to the north and south, with the beach to the west.

No one was there. No one could be there.

A bird, perhaps. A flutter of leaf.

Simon had checked the grounds not long ago. Moreno glanced at him now, a large, quiet Brazilian, dark-complected, wearing a nice suit—Moreno's guard dressed better than he did, though not flashy. Simon, in his thirties, looked appropriately dangerous, as one would expect, and want, in this profession but he wasn't a thug. He'd been an officer in the army, before going civilian as a security expert.

He was also very good at his job. Simon's head swiveled; he'd become aware of his boss's gaze and immediately stepped to the window, looking out.

"Just a flash of light," Moreno explained.

The bodyguard suggested drawing the shades.

"I think not."

Moreno had decided that Eduardo de la Rua, who'd flown here coach class at his own expense from the city of good air, deserved to enjoy the beautiful view. He wouldn't get to experience much luxury, as a hardworking journalist known for reporting the truth, rather than producing puff pieces for corporate officials and politicians. Moreno also decided to take the man to a very nice meal at the South Cove Inn's fine restaurant for lunch.

Simon gazed outside once more, returned to his chair and picked up a magazine.

De la Rua clicked on the tape recorder. "Now, may I?"

"Please." Moreno turned his full attention to the journalist.

"Mr. Moreno, your Local Empowerment Movement has just opened an office in Argentina, the first in the country. Could you tell me how you conceived the idea? And what your group does?"

Moreno had given this lecture dozens of times. It varied, based on the particular journalist or audience, but the core was simple: to encourage indigenous people to reject U.S. government and corporate influence by becoming self-sufficient, notably through microlending, microagriculture and microbusiness.

He now told the reporter, "We resist American corporate development. And the government's aid and social programs, whose purpose, after all, is simply to addict us to their values. We are not viewed as human beings; we are viewed as a source of cheap labor and a market for American goods. Do you see the vicious cycle? Our people are exploited in American-owned factories and then seduced into buying products from those same companies."

The journalist said, "I've written much about business investment in Argentina and other South American countries. And I know about your movement, which also makes such investments. One could argue you rail against capitalism yet you embrace it."

Moreno brushed his longish hair, black and prematurely gray. "No, I rail against the *misuse* of capitalism—the *American* misuse of capitalism in particular. I am using business as a weapon. Only fools rely on ideology exclusively for change. Ideas are the rudder. Money is the propeller."

The reporter smiled. "I will use that as my lead. Now, some people say, I've read some people say you are a revolutionary."

"Ha, I'm a loudmouth, that's all I am!" The smile faded. "But mark my words, while the world is focusing on the Middle East, everyone has missed the birth of a far more powerful force: Latin America. That's what I represent. The new order. We can't be ignored any longer."

Roberto Moreno rose and stepped to the window.

Crowning the garden was a poisonwood tree, about forty feet tall. He stayed in this suite often and he liked the tree very much. Indeed, he felt a camaraderie with it. Poisonwoods are formidable, resourceful and starkly beautiful. They are also, as the name suggests, toxic. The pollen or smoke from burning the wood and leaves could slip into the lungs, searing with agony. And yet the tree nourishes the beautiful Bahamian swallowtail butterfly, and white-crowned pigeons live off the fruit.

I am like this tree, Moreno thought. A good image for the article perhaps. I'll mention this too—

The glint again.

In a tiny splinter of a second: A flicker of movement disturbed the tree's sparse leaves, and the tall window in front of him exploded. Glass turned to a million crystals of blowing snow, fire blossomed in his chest.

Moreno found himself lying on the couch, which had been five feet behind him.

But...but what happened here? What is this? I'm fainting, I'm fainting.

I can't breathe.

He stared at the tree, now clearer, so much clearer, without the window glass filtering the view. The branches waved in the sweet wind off the water. Leaves swelling, receding. It was breathing for him. Because he couldn't, not with his chest on fire. Not with the pain.

Shouts, cries for help around him.

Blood, blood everywhere.

Sun setting, sky going darker and darker. But isn't it morning? Moreno had images of his wife, his teenage son and daughter. His thoughts dissolved until he was aware of only one thing: the tree.

Poison and strength, poison and strength.

The fire within him was easing, vanishing. Tearful relief.

Darkness becoming darker.

The poisonwood tree.

Poisonwood...

Poison...

II

THE QUEUE

CHAPTER 2

I S HE ON HIS WAY OR NOT?" Lincoln Rhyme asked, not trying to curb the irritation.

"Something at the hospital," came Thom's voice from the hallway or kitchen or wherever he was. "He'll be delayed. He'll call when he's free."

"'Something.' Well, *that's* specific. 'Something at the hospital.'"

"That's what he told me."

"He's a doctor. He should be precise. And he should be on time."

"He's a doctor," Thom replied, "which means he has emergencies to deal with."

"But he didn't say 'emergency.' He said, 'something.' The operation is scheduled for May twenty-six. I don't want it delayed. That's too far in the future anyway. I don't see why he couldn't do it sooner."

Rhyme motored his red Storm Arrow wheelchair to a computer monitor. He parked next to the rattan chair in which sat Amelia Sachs, in black jeans and sleeveless black shell. A gold pendant of one diamond and one pearl dangled from a thin chain around her neck. The day was early and spring sunlight fired through the east-facing windows, glancing alluringly off her red hair tied in a bun, tucked carefully up with pewter pins. Rhyme turned his attention back to the screen, scanning a crime scene report for a homicide he'd just helped the NYPD close.

"About done," she said.

They sat in the parlor of his town house on Central Park West in Manhattan. What presumably had once been a subdued, quiet chamber for visitors and suitors in Boss Tweed's day was now a functioning crime scene lab. It was filled with evidence examination gear and instrumentation, computers and wires, everywhere wires, which made the transit of Rhyme's wheelchair forever bumpy, a sensation that he experienced only from his shoulders up.

"The doctor's late," Rhyme muttered to Sachs. Unnecessarily since she'd been ten feet away from his exchange with Thom. But he was still irritated and felt better laying on a bit more censure. He carefully moved his right arm forward to the touchpad and scrolled through the last paragraphs of the report. "Good."

"I'll send it?"

He nodded and she hit a key. The encrypted sixty-five pages headed off into the ether to arrive ultimately six miles away at the NYPD's crime scene facility in Queens, where they would become the backbone of the case of *People v. Williams.*

"Done."

Done...except for testifying at the trial of the drug lord, who had sent twelve- and thirteen-year-olds out into the streets of East New York and Harlem to do his killing for him. Rhyme and Sachs had managed to locate and analyze minute bits of trace and impression evidence that led from one of the youngster's shoes to the floor of a storefront in Manhattan to the carpet of a Lexus sedan to a restaurant in Brooklyn and finally to the house of Tye Williams himself.

The gang leader hadn't been present at the murder of the witness, he hadn't touched the gun, there was no record of him ordering the hit and the young shooter was too terrified to testify against him. But those hurdles for the prosecution didn't matter; Rhyme and Sachs had spun a filament of evidence that stretched from the crime scene directly to Williams's crib.

He'd be in jail for the rest of his life.

Sachs now closed her hand on Rhyme's left arm,

strapped to the wheelchair, immobile. He could see from the tendons faintly visible beneath her pale skin that she squeezed. The tall woman rose and stretched. They'd been working to finish the report since early morning. She'd awakened at five. He, a bit later.

Rhyme noticed that she winced as she walked to the table where her coffee cup sat. The arthritis in her hip and knee had been bad lately. Rhyme's spinal cord injury, which rendered him a quadriplegic, was described as devastating. Yet it never gave him a moment's pain.

All of our bodies, whoever we are, fail us to some degree, he reflected. Even those who at present were healthy and more or less content were troubled by clouds on the horizon. He pitied the athletes, the beautiful people, the young who were already anticipating decline with dread.

And yet, ironically, the opposite was true for Lincoln Rhyme. From the ninth circle of injury, he had been improving, thanks to new spinal cord surgical techniques and his own take-no-prisoners attitude about exercise and risky experimental procedures.

Which reminded him again that he was irritated the doctor was late for today's assessment appointment, in anticipation of the upcoming surgery.

The two-tone doorbell chime sounded.

"I'll get that," Thom called.

The town house was disability-modified, of course, and Rhyme could have used a computer to view and converse with whoever was at the door and let them in. Or not. (He didn't like folks to come-a-callin' and tended to send them away— sometimes rudely—if Thom didn't act fast.)

"Who is it? Check first."

This couldn't be Dr. Barrington, since he was going to call once he'd disposed of the "something" that had delayed him. Rhyme wasn't in the mood for other visitors.

But whether his caregiver checked first or not didn't matter apparently. Lon Sellitto appeared in the parlor.

"Linc, you're home."

Safe bet.

The squat detective beelined to a tray with coffee and pastry.

"You want fresh?" Thom asked. The slim aide was dressed in a crisp white shirt, floral blue tie and dark slacks. Cuff links today, ebony or onyx.

"Naw, thanks, Thom. Hey, Amelia."

"Hi, Lon. How's Rachel?"

"Good. She's taken up Pilates. That's a weird word. It's exercise or something." Sellitto was decked out in a typically rumpled suit, brown, and a typically rumpled powder-blue shirt. He sported a striped crimson tie that was atypically smooth as a piece of planed wood. A recent present, Rhyme deduced. From girlfriend Rachel? The month was May—no holidays. Maybe it was a birthday present. Rhyme didn't know the date of Sellitto's. Or, for that matter, most other people's.

Sellitto sipped coffee and pestered a Danish, two bites only. He was perpetually dieting.

Rhyme and the detective had worked together years ago, as partners, and it had largely been Lon Sellitto who'd pushed Rhyme back to work after the accident, not by coddling or cajoling but by forcing him to get off his ass and start solving crimes again. (More accurately, in Rhyme's case, to *stay* on his ass and get back to work.) But despite their history Sellitto never came by just to hang out. The detective first-class was assigned to Major Cases, working out of the Big Building—One Police Plaza—and he was usually the lead detective on the cases for which Rhyme was hired to consult. His presence now was a harbinger.

"So." Rhyme looked him over. "Do you have something good for me, Lon? An engaging crime? *Intriguing?*"

Sellitto sipped and nibbled. "All I know is I got a call from on top asking if you were free. I told 'em you were finishing up Williams. Then I was told to get here ASAP, meet somebody. They're on their way."

"'Somebody'? 'They'?" Rhyme asked acidly. "That's as specific as the 'something' detaining my doctor. Seems infectious. Like the flu."

"Hey, Linc. All I know."

Rhyme cast a wry look toward Sachs. "I notice that no one called *me* about this. Did anybody call you, Sachs?"

"Not a jingle."

Sellitto said, "Oh, that's 'causa the other thing."

"What other thing?"

"Whatever's going on, it's a secret. And it's gotta stay that way."

Which was, Rhyme decided, at least a step toward intriguing.

CHAPTER 3

RHYME WAS LOOKING UP at the two visitors, as different as could be, now stepping into his parlor.

One was a man in his fifties, with a military bearing, wearing an untailored suit—the shoulders were the giveaway—in navy blue, bordering on black. He had a jowly, clean-shaven face, tanned skin and trim hair, marine-style. Has to be brass, Rhyme thought.

The other was a woman hovering around the early thirties. She was approaching stocky, though not overweight, not yet. Her blond, lusterless hair was in an anachronistic flip, stiffly sprayed, and Rhyme noted that her pale complexion derived from a mask of liberally applied flesh-toned makeup. He didn't see any acne or other pocks and assumed the pancake was a fashion choice. There was no shadow or liner around her gun-muzzle black eyes, all the more stark given the cream shade of the face in which they were set. Her thin lips were colorless too and dry. Rhyme assessed that this was not a mouth that broke into a smile very often.

She would pick something to look at—equipment, the window, Rhyme—and turn a sandblast gaze on it until she had stripped it down to understanding or rendered it irrelevant. Her suit was dark gray, also not expensive, and all three plastic buttons were snugly fixed. The dark disks seemed slightly uneven and he wondered if she'd found a perfect-fitting suit with unfortunate accents and replaced them herself. The low black shoes were unevenly worn and had been doctored recently with liquid scuff cover-up.

Got it, Rhyme thought. He believed he knew her employer. And was all the more curious.

Sellitto said of the man, "Linc, this is Bill Myers."

The visitor nodded. "Captain, an honor to meet you." He used Rhyme's last title with the NYPD, from when he'd retired on disability some years ago. This confirmed Myers's job; Rhyme had been right, brass. And pretty senior.

Rhyme motored the electric wheelchair forward and thrust his hand out. The brass noted the jerky motion, hesitated then gripped it. Rhyme noticed something too: Sachs stiffen slightly. She didn't like it when he used the limb and digits like this, unnecessarily, for social niceties. But Lincoln Rhyme couldn't help himself. The past decade had been an effort to rectify what fate had done to him. He was proud of his few victories and exploited them.

Besides, what was the point of a toy if you never played with it?

Myers introduced the other mysterious "somebody." Her name was Nance Laurel.

"Lincoln," he said. Another handshake, seemingly firmer than Myers's, though Rhyme, of course, couldn't tell. Sensation did not accompany movement.

Laurel's sharp gaze took in Rhyme's thick brown hair, his fleshy nose, his keen dark eyes. She said nothing other than "Hello."

"So," he said. "You're an ADA."

Assistant district attorney.

She gave no physical reaction to his deduction, which was partly a guess. A hesitation, then: "Yes, I am." Her voice was crisp, sibilant emphasized.

Sellitto then introduced Myers and Laurel to Sachs. The brass took in the policewoman as if he was very aware of her rep too. Rhyme noticed that Sachs winced a bit as she walked forward to shake hands. She corrected her gait as she returned to the chair. He alone, he believed, saw her subtly pop a couple of Advil into her mouth and swallow dry. However much the pain she never took anything stronger.

Myers too, it turned out, was a captain by rank and ran a branch of the department that Rhyme had not heard of, new apparently. The Special Services Division. His confident demeanor and cagey eyes suggested to Rhyme that he and his outfit were quite powerful within the NYPD. Possibly he was a player with an eye on a future in city government.

Rhyme himself had never had an interest in the gamesmanship of institutions like the NYPD, much less what lay beyond, Albany or Washington. All that interested him at the moment was the man's presence. The appearance of a senior cop with mysterious departmental lineage alongside the focused terrier of an ADA suggested an assignment that would keep at bay the dreaded boredom that, since the accident, had become his worst enemy.

He felt the throbbing of anticipation, his heart, but via his temples, not his insensate chest.

Bill Myers deferred to Nance Laurel, saying, "I'll let her unpack the situation."

Rhyme tried to catch Sellitto's eye with a wry glance but the man deflected it. "Unpack." Rhyme disliked such stilted, coined terms, which bureaucrats and journalists seeded into their dialogue. "Game-changer" was another recent one. "Kabuki" too. They were like bright red streaks in the hair of middle-aged women or tattoos on cheeks.

Another pause and Laurel said, "Captain—"

"Lincoln. I'm decommissioned."

Pause. "Lincoln, yes. I'm prosecuting a case and because of certain unusual issues it was suggested that you might be in a position to run the investigation. You and Detective Sachs. I understand you work together frequently."

"That's right." He wondered if ADA Laurel ever loosened up. Doubted it.

"I'll explain," she continued. "Last Tuesday, May ninth, a U.S. citizen was murdered in a luxury hotel in the Bahamas. The local police there are investigating the crime but I have reason to believe that the shooter's American and is back in this country. Probably the New York area."

She paused before nearly every sentence. Was she picking thoroughbred words? Or assessing liabilities if the wrong one left the gate?

"Now, I'm not going with a murder charge against the perps. It's difficult to make a case in state court for a crime that occurs in a different country. That *could* be done but it would take too long." Now a denser hesitation. "And it's important to move quickly."

Why? Rhyme wondered.

Intriguing...

Laurel continued, "I'm seeking other, independent charges in New York."

"Conspiracy," Rhyme said, his instantaneous deduction. "Good, good. I like that. On the basis that the murder was planned here."

"Exactly," Laurel offered. "The killing was ordered by a New York resident in the city. That's why I have jurisdiction."

Like all cops, or former cops, Rhyme knew the law as well as most lawyers did. He recalled the relevant New York Penal Code provision: Somebody is guilty of conspiracy when—with intent that conduct constituting a crime be performed— he or she agrees with one or more persons to engage in or cause the performance of such conduct. He added, "And you can bring the case here even if the killing took place outside the state because the underlying conduct—murder—is a crime in New York."

"Correct," Laurel confirmed. She might have been pleased he got the analysis right. It was hard to tell.

Sachs said, "Ordered the killing, you said. What was it, an OC hit?"

Many of the worst organized crime bosses were never arrested and convicted for the extortion, murders and kidnappings they perpetrated; they could never be tied to the crime scene. But they often were sent to prison for conspiring to cause those events to happen.

Laurel, however, said, "No. This is something else."

Rhyme's mind danced. "But if we identify and collar the conspirators the Bahamians'll want to extradite them. The shooter, at least."

Laurel regarded him silently for a second. Her pauses were beginning to border on the unnerving. She finally said, "I'll resist extradition. And my chances of success I put at over ninety percent." For a woman in her thirties Laurel seemed young. There was a schoolgirl innocence about her. No, "innocence" was the wrong word, Rhyme decided. Single-mindedness.

Pigheaded was another cliché that fit.

Sellitto asked both Laurel and Myers, "You have any suspects?"

"Yes. I don't have the identity of the shooter yet but I know the two people who ordered the killing."

Rhyme gave a smile. Within him curiosity stirred, along with the sensation a wolf must feel catching a single molecule of a prey's scent. He could tell Nance Laurel felt the same, even if the eagerness wasn't quite visible through the L'Oréal façade. He believed he knew where this was going.

And the destination was far beyond intriguing.

Laurel said, "The murder was a targeted killing, an assassination, if you will, ordered by a U.S. government official—the head of NIOS, the National Intelligence and Operations Service, based here in Manhattan."

This was, more or less, what Rhyme had deduced. He'd thought the CIA or Pentagon, though.

"Jesus," Sellitto whispered. "You wanna bust a fed?" He looked at Myers, who gave no reaction whatsoever, then back to Laurel. "Can you do that?"

Her pause was two breaths' duration. "How do you mean, Detective?" Perplexed.

Sellitto probably hadn't meant anything other than what he'd said. "Just, isn't he immune from prosecution?"

"The NIOS lawyers will try for immunity but it's an area I'm familiar with. I wrote my law review article on immunity of government officials. I've assessed my chance of success at about ninety percent in the state courts, and eighty in the Second Circuit on appeal. We get to the Supreme Court, we're home free."

"What's the law on immunity?" Sachs asked.

"It's a Supremacy Clause issue," Laurel explained. "That's the constitutional provision that says, in effect, when it comes down to a conflict, federal law trumps state. New York can't prosecute a federal employee for state crimes if the employee was acting within the scope of his authority. In *our* situation, I believe the head of NIOS has gone rogue—acting outside what he was authorized to do."

Laurel glanced at Myers, who said, "We pivoted on the issue but there're solid metrics leading us to believe that this man is manipulating the intelligence that formed the basis for the assassination, for his own agenda."

Pivoted ... metrics ...

"And what *is* that agenda?" Rhyme asked.

"We're not sure," the captain continued. "He seems obsessed with protecting the country, eliminating anybody who's a threat—even those who maybe aren't threats, if he considers them unpatriotic. The man he ordered shot in Nassau wasn't a terrorist. He was just—"

"Outspoken," Laurel said.

Sachs asked, "One question: The attorney general's okayed the case?"

Laurel's hesitation this time might have covered up bristling at the reference to her boss and his permission to pursue the investigation. Hard to tell. She answered evenly, "The information about the killing came to our office in Manhattan, the jurisdiction where NIOS is located. The district attorney and I discussed it. I wanted the case because of my experience with immunity issues and because this type of crime bothers me a great deal—I personally feel that any targeted killings are unconstitutional because of due process issues. The DA asked me if I knew it was a land mine. I said yes. He went to the attorney general in Albany, who said I could go forward. So, yes, I have his blessing." A steady gaze at Sachs, who looked back with eyes that were equally unwavering.

Both of those men, the Manhattan DA and the attorney general of the state, Rhyme noted, were in the opposing political party to that of the current administration in Washington. Was this fair to consider? He decided that cynicism isn't cynical if the facts support it.

"Welcome to the hornet's nest," Sellitto said, drawing smiles from everybody but Laurel.

Myers said to Rhyme, "That's why I suggested you, Captain, when Nance came to us. You and Detectives Sellitto and Sachs operate a bit more independently than regular officers. You're not as tethered to the hub as most investigators."

Lincoln Rhyme was now a consultant to the NYPD, FBI and any other organization wishing to pay the substantial fees he charged for his forensic services, provided the case could be fixed somewhere near the true north of challenging.

He now asked, "And who is the main conspirator, this head of NIOS?"

"His name's Shreve Metzger."

"Any thoughts at all about the shooter?" Sachs asked.

"No. He—or she—could be military, which would be a problem. If we're lucky he'll be civilian."

"Lucky?" From Sachs.

Rhyme assumed Laurel meant because the military justice system would complicate matters. But she elaborated, "A soldier's more sympathetic to a jury than a mercenary or civilian contractor."

Sellitto said, "You mentioned two conspirators, along with the shooter. Who else aside from Metzger?"

"Oh," Laurel continued in a faintly dismissive tone, "the president."

"Of what?" Sellitto asked.

Whether or not this required a thoughtful hesitation Laurel paused anyway. "Of the United States, of course. I'm sure that every targeted killing requires the president's okay. But I'm not pursuing him."

"Jesus, I hope not," Lon Sellitto said with a laugh

that sounded like a stifled sneeze. "That's more than a political land mine; it's a fucking nuke."

Laurel frowned, as if she'd had to translate his comment from Icelandic. "Politics aren't the issue, Detective. Even if the president acted outside the scope of his authority in ordering a targeted killing, the criminal procedure in his case would be impeachment. But obviously that's out of my jurisdiction."

CHAPTER 4

H E WAS DISTRACTED MOMENTARILY by the smell of grilling fish, with lime and plantain, he believed. Something else, a spice. He couldn't quite place it.

Sniffing the air again. What *could* it be?

Compact, with crew-cut brown hair, he resumed his casual stroll along the broken sidewalk—and dirt path, where the concrete slabs were missing altogether. He billowed out his dark suit jacket to vent the heat and reflected he was glad he hadn't worn a tie. He paused again beside a weed-filled lot. The street of low shops and pastel houses in need of more pastel paint was deserted now, late morning. No people, though two lazy potcake dogs were lounging in the shade.

Then she emerged.

She was leaving the Deep Fun Dive Shop and walking in the direction of West Bay, a Gabriel Márquez novel in her hand.

Tan and sun-blond, the young woman had a tangle of hair, with a single narrow beaded braid from temple to breast. Her figure was an hourglass but a slim hourglass. She wore a yellow-and-red bikini and a translucent orange wrap around her waist, teasing. It fell to her ankles. She was limber and energetic and her smile could be mischievous.

As it now was.

"Well, look who it is," she said and stopped beside him.

This was a quiet area some distance away from downtown Nassau. Sleepily commercial. The dogs watched lethargically, ears flopped downward like place-marked pages in a book.

"Hey there." Jacob Swann removed his Maui Jims and wiped his face. Put the sunglasses back on. Wished he'd brought sunscreen. This trip to the Bahamas hadn't been planned.

"Hm. Maybe my phone's not working," Annette said wryly.

"Probably is," Swann offered with a grimace. "I know. I said I'd call. Guilty."

But the offense was a misdemeanor at worst; Annette was a woman whose companionship he'd paid for, so her coy remark wasn't as cutting as it might have been under different circumstances.

On the other hand, that night last week *had* been more than john–escort. She'd charged him for only two hours but had given him the entire night. The evening hadn't been *Pretty Woman*, of course, but they'd each enjoyed the time.

The hours of their transaction had fled quickly, the soft humid breeze drifting in and out of the window, the sound of the ocean metrically intruding on the stillness. He'd asked if she'd stay and Annette had agreed. His motel room had a kitchenette and Jacob Swann had cooked a late supper. After arriving in Nassau he'd bought groceries, including goat, onion, coconut milk, oil, rice, hot sauce and local spices. He'd expertly separated meat from bone, sliced it into bite-sized pieces and marinated the flesh in buttermilk. By 11 p.m., the stew had simmered over a low flame for six hours and was ready. They'd eaten the food and drunk a substantial red Rhône wine.

Then they'd returned to bed.

"How's business?" he now asked, nodding back to the shop to make clear which business he was talking about, though the part-time job at Deep Fun was also a feeder for clients who paid her a lot more than for snorkel rental. (The irony of the shop's name was not lost on either of them.)

Annette shrugged her gorgeous shoulders. "Not bad. Economy's taken its toll. But rich people still want to bond with coral and fish."

The overgrown lot was decorated with bald tires

and discarded concrete blocks, a few dented and rusted appliance shells, the guts long scavenged. The day was growing hotter by the second. Everywhere was glare and dust, empty cans, bushes in need of trimming, rampant grass. The smells: grilling fish, lime, plantains and trash fire smoke.

And that spice. What *was* it?

"I didn't remember I'd told you where I work." A nod at the shop.

"Yes, you did." He rubbed his hair. His round skull, dotted with sweat. Lifted his jacket again. The air felt good.

"Aren't you hot?"

"Had a breakfast meeting. Needed to look official. I'm just back for the day. Don't know what your schedule is…"

"Tonight?" Annette suggested. And encouraged.

"Ah, I've got another meeting." Jacob Swann's face was not expressive. He simply looked into her eyes as he said this. No wince of regret, no boyish flirt. "I was hoping now." He imagined they were hungry eyes; that's how he felt.

"What was that wine?"

"That I served with dinner? Châteauneuf-du-Pape. I don't remember which vineyard."

"It was scrumptious."

Not a word Jacob Swann used much—well, ever—but he decided, yes, it was. And so was she.

The ropey straps of the bikini bottoms dangled down, ready to be tugged. Her flip-flops revealed blue nails and she wore gold rings on both her big toes. They matched the hoops in her ears. A complicated assembly of gold bracelets as well.

Annette sized him up too and would be recalling his naked physique, muscular, thin waist, powerful chest and arms. Rippled. He worked hard at that.

She said, "I had plans but..."

The sentence ended in a new smile.

As they walked to his car she took his arm. He escorted her to the passenger side. Once inside she gave him directions to her apartment. He started the engine but before he put the car in gear he stopped. "Oh, I forgot. Maybe I didn't call but I brought you a present."

"No!" She keened with pleasure. "What?"

He extracted a box from the backpack he used as an attaché case, sitting in the backseat. "You like jewelry, don't you?"

"What girl doesn't?" Annette asked.

As she opened it he said, "It's not instead of your fee, you know. It's in addition."

"Oh, please," she said with a dismissing smile. Then concentrated on opening the small narrow box. Swann looked around the street. Empty still. He judged angles, drew back his left hand—open, thumb and index finger wide and stiff—and struck her hard in the throat in a very particular way.

She gasped, eyes wide. Rearing back and gripping her damaged neck.

"Uhn, uhn, uhn. . . ."

The blow was a tricky one to deliver. You had to hit gently enough so you didn't crush the windpipe completely—he needed her to be able to speak—but hard enough to make it impossible to scream.

Her eyes stared at him. Maybe she was trying to say his name—well, the cover name he'd given her last week. Swann had three U.S. passports and two Canadian, and credit cards in five different names. He frankly couldn't recall the last time he'd used "Jacob Swann" with somebody he hadn't known well.

He looked back evenly at her and then turned to pull the duct tape from his backpack.

Swann put on flesh-toned latex gloves and ripped a strip of tape off the roll. He paused. *That* was it. The spice the nearby cook had added to the fish.

Coriander.

How had he missed it?

CHAPTER 5

T HE VICTIM WAS ROBERT MORENO," Laurel told them. "Thirty-eight years old."

"Moreno—sounds familiar," Sachs said.

"Made the news, Detective," Captain Bill Myers offered. "Front page."

Sellitto asked, "Wait, the Anti-American American? What some headline called him, I think."

"Right," the captain said. Then editorialized bitterly: "Prick."

No jargon there.

Rhyme noted that Laurel didn't seem to like this comment. Also, she seemed impatient, as if she had no time for deflective banter. He remembered that she wanted to move quickly—and the reason was now clear: Presumably once NIOS found out about the investigation they'd take steps to stop the case in its tracks—legally and, perhaps, otherwise.

Well, Rhyme was impatient too. He wanted intriguing.

Laurel displayed a picture of a handsome man in a white shirt, sitting before a radio microphone. He had round features, thinning hair. The ADA told them, "A recent picture in his radio studio in Caracas. He held a U.S. passport but was an expatriate, living in Venezuela. On May ninth, he was in the Bahamas on business when the sniper shot him in his hotel room. Two others were killed, as well—Moreno's guard and a reporter interviewing him. The bodyguard was Brazilian, living in Venezuela The reporter was Puerto Rican, living in Argentina."

Rhyme pointed out, "There wasn't much of a splash in the press. If the government'd been caught with their finger on the trigger, so to speak, it would've been bigger news. Who was *supposedly* responsible?"

"Drug cartels," Laurel told him. "Moreno had created an organization called the Local Empowerment Movement to work with indigenous and impoverished people in Latin America. He was critical of drug trafficking. That ruffled some feathers in Bogotá and some Central American countries. But I couldn't find facts to support that any cartel in particular wanted him dead. I'm convinced Metzger and NIOS planted those stories about the cartels to deflect attention from them. Besides, there's something I haven't mentioned. I know for a fact that a NIOS sniper killed him. I have proof."

"Proof?" Sellitto asked.

Laurel's body language, though not her facial features, explained that she was pleased to tell them the details. "We have a whistleblower—within or connected to NIOS. They leaked the order authorizing Moreno to be killed."

"Like WikiLeaks?" Sellitto asked. Then shook his head. "But no, it wouldn't have been."

"Right," Rhyme said. "Or the story would've been all over the news. The DA's Office got it directly. And quietly."

Myers: "That's right. The whistleblower capillaried the kill order."

Rhyme ignored the captain and his bizarre language. He said to Laurel: "Tell us about Moreno."

She did, and from memory. Natives to New Jersey, his family had left the country when the boy was twelve and moved to Central America because of his father's job; he was a geologist with a U.S. oil company. At first, Moreno was enrolled in American schools down there, but after his mother's suicide he changed to local schools, where he did well.

"Suicide?" Sachs asked.

"Apparently she'd had difficulty with the move...and her husband's job kept him traveling to drilling and exploration sites throughout the area. He wasn't home very much."

Laurel continued her portrait of the victim: Even at a young age Moreno had grown to hate the exploitation of the native Central and South Americans by U.S. government and corporate interests. After college, in Mexico City, he became a radio host and activist, writing and broadcasting vicious attacks on America and what he called its twenty-first-century imperialism.

"He settled in Caracas and formed the Local Empowerment Movement as an alternative to workers to develop self-reliance and not have to look to American and European companies for jobs and U.S. aid for help. There are a half dozen branches throughout South and Central America and the Caribbean."

Rhyme was confused. "It's hardly the bio of a terrorist."

Laurel said, "Exactly. But I have to tell you that Moreno spoke favorably about some terrorist groups: al-Qaeda, al-Shabaab, the East Turkestan Islamic Movement in Xinjiang, China. And he formed some alliances with several extremist groups in Latin America: the Colombian ELN— the National Liberation Army—and FARC, as well as the United Self-Defense Forces. He had strong sympathy for the Sendero Luminoso in Peru."

"Shining Path?" Sachs asked.

"Yes."

The enemy of my enemy is my friend, Rhyme reflected. Even if they blow up children. "But still?" he asked. "A targeted killing? For that?"

Laurel explained, "Recently Moreno's blogs and broadcasts were growing more and more virulently anti-American. He called himself 'the Messenger of Truth.' And some of his messages were truly vicious. He really hated this country. Now, there were rumors that people had been inspired by him to shoot American tourists or servicemen or lob bombs at U.S. embassies or businesses overseas. But I couldn't find one incident in which he actually said a single word ordering or even suggesting that a specific attack be carried out. Inspiring isn't the same as plotting."

Though he'd known her only minutes Rhyme suspected that Ms. Nance Laurel had looked very, very hard for any such words.

"But NIOS claimed there was intelligence that Moreno was planning an actual attack: a bombing of an oil company headquarters in Miami. They picked up a phone conversation, in Spanish, and the voiceprint was confirmed to be Moreno's."

She now rifled through her battered briefcase and consulted notes. "This is Moreno: He said, 'I want to go after American Petroleum Drilling and Refining, Florida. On Wednesday.' The other party, unknown: 'The tenth. May tenth?' Moreno: 'Yes, noon, when employees are leaving for lunch.' Then the other party: 'How're you going to, you know, get them there?' Moreno: 'Trucks.' Then there was some garbled conversation. And Moreno again: 'And this's just the start. I have a lot more messages like this one planned.'"

She put the transcript back in her case. "Now, the company—APDR—has two facilities in or near Florida: its southeastern headquarters in Miami and an oil rig off the coast. It couldn't be the rig since Moreno mentioned trucks. So NIOS was sure the headquarters, on Brickell Avenue, was going to be the target.

"At the same time, intelligence analysts found that companies with a connection to Moreno had been shipping diesel fuel, fertilizer and nitromethane to the Bahamas in the last month."

Three popular ingredients in IEDs. Those substances were what had obliterated the federal building in Oklahoma City. Where they also had been delivered by truck.

Laurel continued, "It's clear that Metzger believed if Moreno was killed before the bomb was smuggled into the United States his underlings wouldn't go through with the plan. He was shot the day before the incident in Miami. On May ninth."

So far it sounded like, whether you supported as-sassinations or not, Metzger's solution had saved a number of lives.

Rhyme was about to mention this but Laurel got there first. She said, "It wasn't an *attack* Moreno was talking about, though. It was a peaceful protest. On the tenth of May, at noon, a half dozen trucks showed up in front of the APDR headquar-ters. They weren't delivering bombs; they were delivering people for a demonstration.

"And the bomb ingredients? They were for Moreno's Local Empowerment Movement branch in the Bahamas. The diesel fuel was for a trans-portation company. The fertilizer was for agricul-tural co-ops and the nitromethane was for use in soil fumigants. All legitimate. Those were the only materials cited in the order approving Moreno's killing but there were also tons of seed, rice, truck parts, bottled water and other innocent items in the same shipment. NIOS conveniently forgot to men-tion those."

"Not intelligence failure?" Rhyme offered.

The pause that followed was longer than most and Laurel finally said, "No. I think intelligence *manipulation*. Metzger didn't like Moreno, didn't like his rhetoric. He was on record as calling him a despicable traitor. I think he didn't share with the chain of command all of the information he found. So the higher-ups in Washington approved the mission, thinking a bomb was involved, while Metzger knew otherwise."

Sellitto said, "So NIOS killed an innocent man,"

"Yes," Laurel said with a flick of animation in her voice. "But that's good."

"What?" Sachs blurted, brows furrowed.

A heartbeat pause. Laurel clearly didn't understand Sachs's apparent dismay, echoing the detective's reaction to Laurel's earlier comment that they'd be "lucky" if the shooter was a civilian, not military.

Rhyme explained, "The jurors again, Sachs. They're more likely to convict a defendant who's killed an activist who was simply exercising his First Amendment right to free speech—rather than a hard-core terrorist."

Laurel added, "To me there's no moral difference between the two; you don't execute anybody without due process. *Anybody*. But Lincoln's right, I have to take the jury into account."

"So, Captain," Myers said to Rhyme, "if the case is going to gain traction, we need somebody like you with your feet on the ground."

Poor choice of jargon in this instance, given the criminalist's main means of transportation.

Rhyme's immediate reaction was to say yes. The case was intriguing and challenging in all sorts of ways. But Sachs, he noted, was looking down, rubbing her scalp with a finger, a habit. He wondered what was troubling her.

She said to the prosecutor, "You didn't go after the CIA for al-Awlaki."

Anwar al-Awlaki, a U.S. citizen, was a radical Muslim imam and advocate of jihad, as well as a major player within al-Qaeda's affiliate in Yemen. An expatriate like Moreno, he'd been dubbed the Bin Laden of the Internet and enthusiastically encouraged attacks on Americans through his blog posts. Among those inspired by him were the shooter at Fort Hood, the underwear airplane bomber, both in 2009, and the Times Square bomber in 2010.

Al-Awlaki and another U.S. citizen, his online editor, were killed in a drone strike under the direction of the CIA.

Laurel seemed confused. "How could I bring that case? I'm a New York district attorney. There was no state nexus in al-Awlaki's assassination. But if you're asking if I pick cases I think I can win, Detective Sachs, then the answer's yes. Charging Metzger for assassinating a known and dangerous terrorist is probably unwinnable. So is a case for assassinating a non–U.S.-citizen. But the Moreno shooting I can sell to a jury. When I get a conviction against Metzger and his sniper, then I'll be

able to look at other cases that are more gray."
She paused. "Or maybe the government'll simply reassess its policies and stick to following the
Constitution...and get out of the murder-for-hire
business."

With a glance at Rhyme, Sachs spoke to both
Laurel and Myers. "I'm not sure. Something
doesn't feel right."

"Feel right?" Laurel asked, seemingly perplexed
by the phrase.

Two fingers rubbed together hard as Sachs said,
"I don't know, I'm not sure this's our job."

"You and Lincoln?" Laurel inquired.

"Any of us. It's a political issue, not a criminal
one. You want to stop NIOS from assassinating
people, that's fine. But shouldn't it be a matter for
Congress, not the police?"

Laurel underhanded a glance at Rhyme. Sachs
certainly had a point—one that hadn't even occurred to him. He cared very little about the
broader questions of right and wrong when it came
to the law. It was enough for him that Albany or
Washington or the city council had defined an an-
swerable offense. His job was then simple: tracking down and building a case against the offender.

Just like with chess. Did it matter that the cre-
ators of that arcane board game had decreed that
the queen was all-powerful and that the knight

made right-angle turns? No. But once those rules were established, you played by them.

He ignored Laurel and kept his eyes on Sachs.

Then the assistant DA's posture changed, subtly but clearly. Rhyme thought at first she was defensive but that wasn't it, he realized. She was going into advocate mode. As if she'd stood up from counsel table in court and had walked to the front of the jury—a jury as yet unconvinced of the suspect's guilt.

"Amelia, I think justice is in the details," Laurel began. "In the small things. I don't prosecute a rape case because society becomes less stable when sexual violence is perpetrated against women. I prosecute rape because one human being behaves according to the prohibited acts in New York Penal Code section one thirty point three five. That's what I do, that's what we all do."

After a pause, she said, "Please, Amelia. I know your track record. I'd like you on board."

Ambition or ideology? Rhyme wondered, looking over the compact package of Nance Laurel, with her stiff hair, blunt fingers and nails free of polish, small feet in sensible pumps, on which the liquid cover-up had been applied as carefully as the makeup on her face. He honestly couldn't say which of the two motivated her but one thing he observed: He was actually chilled to see the absence of passion in her black eyes. And it took a great deal to chill Lincoln Rhyme.

In the silence that followed, Sachs's eyes met Rhyme's. She seemed to sense how much he wanted the case. And this was the tipping factor. A nod. "I'm on board," she said.

"I am too." Rhyme was looking, though, not at Myers or Laurel but at Sachs. His expression said, Thanks.

"And even though nobody asked me," Sellitto said with a grumble, "I'm also happy to fuck up my career by busting a senior federal official."

Rhyme then said, "I assume a priority is discretion."

"We have to keep it quiet," Laurel replied. "Otherwise evidence will start disappearing. But I don't think we have to worry at this point. In my office we've done everything we can to keep a lid on the case. I really doubt NIOS knows anything about the investigation."

CHAPTER 6

A S HE DROVE THE BORROWED CAR to a cay on the southwest shore of New Providence Island, near the huge Clifton Heritage Park, Jacob Swann heard his phone buzz with a text. The message was an update about the police investigation in New York into Robert Moreno's death, the conspiracy charges. Swann would be receiving details in the next few hours, including the names of the parties involved.

Moving quickly. Much more quickly than he'd expected.

He heard a thump from the trunk of the car, where Annette Bodel, the unfortunate hooker, was crumpled in a ball. But it was a soft thump and there was no one else around to hear, no clusters of roadside scavengers or hangers-out like you often saw in the Bahamas, sipping Sands or Kalik, joking and gossiping and complaining about women and bosses.

No vehicles either, or boaters in the turquoise water.

The Caribbean was such a contradiction, Swann reflected as he gazed about: a glitzy playground for the tourists, a threadbare platform for the locals' lives. The focus was on the fulcrum where dollars and euros met service and entertainment, and much of the rest of the nation just felt exhausted. Like this hot, weedy, trash-strewn patch of sandy earth, near the beach.

He climbed out and blew into his gloves to cool his sweaty hands. Damn, it was *hot*. He'd been to this spot before, last week. After a particularly challenging but accurate rifle shot had torn apart the heart of the traitorous Mr. Robert Moreno, Swann had driven here and buried some clothes and other evidence. He'd intended to let them stay forever interred. But having received the odd and troubling word that prosecutors in New York were looking into Moreno's death, he'd decided it best to retrieve them and dispose of them more efficiently.

But first, another chore...another *task*.

Swann walked to the trunk, opened it and glanced down at Annette, teary, sweaty, in pain.

Trying to breathe.

He then stepped to the rear seat, opened his suitcase and removed one of his treasures, his favorite chef's knife, a Kai Shun Premier slicing model. It was about nine inches long and had the company's distinctive hammered tsuchime finish, pounded by metalsmiths in the Japanese town of Seki. The blade had a VG-10 steel core with thirty-two layers of Damascus steel. The handle was walnut. This knife cost $250. He had models by the same manufacturer in various shapes and sizes, for different kitchen techniques, but this was his favorite. He loved it like a child. He used it to fillet fish, to slice beef translucent for carpaccio and to motivate human beings.

Swann traveled with this and other knives in a well-worn Messermeister knife roll, along with two battered cookbooks—one by James Beard and one by the French chef Michel Guérard, the *cuisine minceur* guru. Customs officials thought very little about a set of professional knives, however deadly, packed in checked luggage beside a cookbook. Besides, on a job away from home, the knives were useful; Jacob Swann would often cook, rather than hang out in bars or go to movies alone.

Removing the goat meat from the bones last week, for instance, and cubing it for the stew.

My little butcher man, my dear little butcher…

He heard another noise, a thud. Annette was starting to kick.

Swann returned to the trunk and dragged the woman from the car by her hair.

"Uhn, uhn, uhn..."

This was probably her version of "no, no, no."

He found an indentation in the sand, surrounded by reedy plants and decorated with crushed Kalik cans and Red Stripe bottles, used condoms and decaying cigarette butts. He rolled her over onto her back and sat on her chest.

A look around. No one. The screams would be much softer, thanks to the blow to the throat, but they wouldn't be silent.

"Now. I'm going to ask you some questions and you're going to have to form the words. I need answers and I need them quickly. Can you form words?"

"Uhn."

"Say, 'yes.'"

"Ye...ye...yessssss."

"Good." He fished a Kleenex from his pocket, then pinched her nose with his other hand and when she opened her mouth he grabbed her tongue with the tissue, tugged the tip an inch beyond her lips. Her head shook violently until she realized that was more painful than his pinch.

She forced herself to calm.

Jacob Swann eased the Kai Shun forward—admiring the blade and handle. Cooking implements are often among the most stylishly designed of any object. The sunlight reflected off the upper half of the blade, pounded into indentations, as if flickering on waves. He carefully stroked the tip of her tongue with the point, drawing a streak in deeper pink but no blood.

Some sound. "Please" maybe.

Little butcher man...

He recalled scoring a duck breast just a few weeks ago, with this same knife, slicing three shallow slits to help render the fat under the broiler. He leaned forward. "Now, listen carefully," he whispered. Swann's mouth was close to her ear and he felt her hot skin against his cheek.

Just like last week.

Well, *somewhat* like last week.

CHAPTER 7

C APTAIN BILL MYERS HAD TAKEN his grating verbiage and left, now that he'd handed off the baton of the case to Rhyme and crew.

While the Moreno conspiracy investigation was in some ways monumental, it was ultimately just another of the thousands of felony cases active in New York, and other matters surely beckoned the captain and his mysterious Special Services Division.

Rhyme supposed too that he'd want to distance himself. Myers had backed up the DA—a captain had to do that, of course; police and prosecutors were Siamese twins—but now was the moment for Myers to head to an undisclosed location. Rhyme was thinking of the political ambition he'd smelled earlier, and if that was true the brass would step back and see how the case unfolded. He'd then re-turn to the podium in glory, in time for the perp walk. Or vanish completely if the case exploded into a public relations nightmare.

A very likely possibility.

Rhyme didn't mind. In fact, he was pleased Myers was gone. He didn't do well with *any* other cooks in the kitchen.

Lon Sellitto, of course, remained. Technically the lead investigator, he was now sitting in a creaky rattan chair, debating a muffin on the breakfast tray, even though he'd pecked half the Danish away. But he then squeezed his gut twice, as if hoping the message would be that he'd lost enough weight on his latest fad diet to deserve the pastry. Apparently not.

"What do you know about this guy running NIOS?" Sellitto asked Laurel. "Metzger?"

She again recited without the benefit of notes: "Forty-three. Divorced. Ex-wife's a lawyer in private practice, Wall Street. He's Harvard, ROTC. After, went into the army, Iraq. In as a lieutenant, out as a captain. There was talk of him going further but that got derailed. Had some issues I'll tell you about later. Discharged, then Yale, master's in public policy along with a law degree. Went to the State Department, then joined NIOS five years ago as operations director. When the existing NIOS head retired last year, Metzger got his job, even though he was one of the youngest on the management panel. The word is nothing was going to stop him from taking the helm."

"Children?" Sachs asked.

"What?" Laurel replied.

"Does Metzger have children?"

"Oh, you're thinking someone was pressuring him, using the children to force him to take on improper missions?"

"No," Sachs said. "I just wondered if he had children."

A blink from Laurel. Now she consulted notes. "Son and daughter. Middle school. He was disallowed any custody for a year. Now he's got some visitation rights but mostly they're with the mother.

"Now, Metzger's beyond hawkish. He's on record as saying he would've nuked Afghanistan on September twelve, two thousand one. He's very outspoken about our right to preemptively eliminate enemies. His nemesis is American citizens who've gone overseas and are engaged in what he considers un-American activities, like joining insurgencies or vocally supporting terrorist groups. But those're his politics and're irrelevant to me." A pause. "His more significant quality is that he's mentally unstable."

"How so?" Sellitto asked.

Rhyme was beginning to lose patience. He wanted to consider the forensics of the case.

But since both Sachs and Sellitto approached cases "globally," as Captain Myers might have said, he let Laurel continue and he tried to appear attentive.

She said, "He's had emotional issues. Anger primarily. That's largely what's driving him, I think. He left the army with an honorable discharge but he had a half dozen episodes that hurt his career there. Fits of rage, tantrums, whatever you want to call them. Totally lost control. He was actually hospitalized at one point. I've managed to datamine some records and he still sees a psychiatrist and buys meds. He's been detained by the police a few times for violent episodes. Never charged. Frankly, I think he's borderline with a paranoid personality. Not psychotic but has definite issues of delusion and addiction—addicted to anger itself. Well, to be precise, the *response* to anger. From what I've studied up on the subject, the relief you feel in acting out during an episode of anger is addicting. Like a drug. I think ordering a sniper to kill somebody he's come to detest gives him a high."

Studied up indeed. She sounded like a psychiatrist lecturing students.

"How'd he get the job, then?" Sachs asked.

A question that had presented itself to Rhyme.

"Because he's very, very good at killing people.

At least, that's what his service record indicates." Laurel continued, "It'll be hard to get his personality workup to a jury but I'm going to do it somehow. And I can only pray he takes the stand. I'd have a field day. I'd love for a jury to see a tantrum." She glanced from Rhyme to Sachs. "As you pursue the investigation I want you to look for anything that suggests Metzger's instability, anger and violent tendencies."

Now a pause preceded Sachs's response. "That's a little fishy, don't you think?"

The battle of the silences. "I'm not sure what you mean."

"I don't know what kind of forensic evidence we could find showing that this guy has temper tantrums."

"I wasn't thinking forensics. I was thinking general investigation." The ADA was looking up at Sachs—the detective was eight or nine inches taller. "You have good write-ups in your file for psych profiling and witness interrogation. I'm sure you'll be able to find something if you look for it."

Sachs cocked her head slightly, eyes narrowed. Rhyme too was surprised that the ADA had profiled her—and presumably the criminalist himself too.

Studied up...

"So." The word was delivered by Laurel

abruptly. The matter was settled; they'd look for instability. Got it.

Rhyme's caregiver rounded the corner. He was carrying a pot of fresh coffee. The criminalist introduced the man. He noted that Nance Laurel's made-up façade stirred briefly as she looked at Thom. An unmistakable focus was in her eyes, though as good looking and charming as he was, Thom Reston was not a romantic option for the woman—who wore no heart-finger rings. But a moment later Rhyme concluded her reaction arose not from attraction to the aide himself but because he resembled somebody she knew or had known closely.

Finally looking away from the young man, Laurel declined coffee, as if it were some ethics breach to indulge on the job. She was digging in her litigation bag, whose contents were perfectly organized. Folder tabs were color-coded and he noted two computers, whose eyes pulsed orange in their state of hibernation. She extracted a document.

"Now," she said, looking up, "do you want to see the kill order?"

Who could say no to that?

CHAPTER 8

O F COURSE THEY DON'T CALL IT THAT, a kill order," Nance Laurel assured. "That's shorthand. The term is 'STO,' a Special Task Order."

"Almost sounds worse," Lon Sellitto said. "Kind of sanitized, you know. Creepy."

Rhyme agreed.

Laurel handed Sachs three sheets of paper. "If you could tape them up, so we could all see them?"

Sachs hesitated and then did as the prosecutor requested.

Laurel tapped the first. "Here's the email that came to our office last Thursday, the eleventh."

Check the news about Robert Moreno.
This is the order behind it. Level Two
is the present head of NIOS. His idea
to pursue. Moreno was a U.S. citizen.

```
The CD means Collateral Damage. Don
Bruns is a code name for the officer
who killed him.

                    —A person with a conscience.
```

"We'll see about tracing the email," Rhyme said. "Rodney." A glance toward Sachs, who nodded.

She explained to Laurel that they worked with the cybercrimes unit in the NYPD frequently. "I'll send them a request. Do you have the email in digital form?"

Laurel dug a Baggie containing a flash drive from her briefcase. Rhyme was impressed to see that a chain-of-custody evidence card was attached. She handed it to Sachs, saying, "If you could—"

Just as the detective jotted her name on the card.

Sachs plugged the drive into the side of her computer and began to type.

"You're going to let them know that security's a priority."

Without looking up, Sachs said, "It's in my first paragraph." A moment later she sent the request to the CCU.

"Code name sounds familiar," Sellitto pointed out. "Bruns, Bruns..."

"Maybe the sniper likes country-western music,"

Sachs pointed out. "There's a Don Bruns who's a songwriter and performer, folk, country-western. Pretty good."

Laurel cocked her head as if she had never listened to any music, much less something as lively as CW.

"Check with Information Services," Rhyme said. "Datamine 'Bruns.' If it's a NOC, he'll still have a presence in the real world."

Agents operating under non-official covers nonetheless have credit cards and passports that can—possibly— allow their movements to be traced and yield clues to their true identity. Information Services was a new division at the NYPD, a massive datamining operation, one of the best in the country.

As Sachs put the request in, Laurel turned back to the board and tapped a second sheet she'd taped up there. "And here's the order itself."

RET - TOP SECRET - TOP SECRET - TOP SE	
SPECIAL TASK ORDERS	
QUEUE	
8/27	9/27

Task: Robert A.
   Moreno (NIOS ID:
   ram278e4w5)
Born: 4/75, New
   Jersey
Complete by:
   5/8-5/9
Approvals:
   Level Two: Yes
   Level One: Yes
Supporting Documen-
   tation:
   See "A"
Confirmation re-
   quired: Yes
PIN required: Yes
CD: Approved, but
   minimize
Details:
   Specialist as-
   signed: Don Bruns,
   Kill Room. South
   Cove Inn, Bahamas,
   Suite 1200
Status: Closed

Task: Al-Barani
   Rashid (NIOS ID:
   abr942pd5t)
Born: 2/73, Michi-
   gan
Complete by:
   5/19
Approvals:
   Level Two: Yes
   Level One: Yes
Supporting Documen-
   tation:
   N/R
Confirmation re-
   quired: No
PIN required: Yes
CD: Approved, but
   minimize
Details: To come
Status: Pending

The other document on the board was headed "A." This gave the information that Nance Laurel had mentioned earlier, supporting data about the shipments of fertilizer and diesel fuel and chemicals to the Bahamas. The shipments were from Corinto, Nicaragua and Caracas.

Laurel nodded toward the flash drive, still inserted into the computer nearby. "The whistleblower also sent a .wav file, a sound file of a phone call or radio transmission to the sniper, apparently from his commander. This was just before the shooting." She looked expectantly at Sachs, who paused then sat down at the computer again. She typed. A moment later, a brief exchange came from the tinny speakers:

"There seem to be two, no three people in the room."

"Can you positively identify Moreno?"

"It's.. there's some glare. Okay, that's better. Yes. I can identify the task. I can see him."

Then the transmission ended. Rhyme was about to ask Sachs to run a voiceprint but she'd already done so. He said, "It doesn't prove he actually pulled the trigger but it gets him on the scene. Now all we need is a body to go with the voice."

"'Specialists,'" Laurel pointed out. "That's the official job title of assassins, apparently."

"What's with the NIOS ID code?" Sellitto asked.

"Presumably to make sure they get the right R. A. Moreno. Embarrassing to make *that* mistake." Rhyme read. "Interesting that the whistleblower didn't give us the name of the shooter."

"Maybe he doesn't know," Sellitto said.

Sachs: "Looks like he knows everything else. His conscience extends up to a certain point. He'll dime out the head of the organization but he's sympathetic toward the guy who got the assignment to shoot."

Laurel said, "I agree. The whistleblower has to know. I want him too. Not to prosecute, just for information. He's our best lead to the sniper—and without the sniper there's no conspiracy and no case."

Sachs said, "Even if we find him he's not going to tell us willingly. Otherwise he already would have."

Laurel said absently, "You get me the whistleblower...and he'll talk. He'll talk."

Sachs asked, "Any consideration about going after Metzger for the other deaths, the guard and that reporter, de la Rua?"

"No, since only Moreno was named in the kill order and they were collateral damage we didn't want to muddy the waters."

Sachs's sour expression seemed to say: even

though they were just as dead as the target. Can't confuse the precious jury, can we?

Rhyme said, "Give me the details of the killing itself."

"We have very little. The Bahamian police gave us a preliminary report, then everything shut down from them. They're not returning calls. What we know is that Moreno was in his suite when he was shot." She indicated the STO. "Suite twelve hundred. The Kill Room, they're calling it. The sniper was shooting from an outcrop of land about two thousand yards from the hotel."

"Well, that's one hell of a shot," Sachs said, eyebrows rising. She was quite a marksman, competed in shooting matches often and held records in the NYPD and in private competitions, though she favored handguns over rifles. "We call that a million-dollar bullet. The record for a sniper's about twenty-five hundred yards. Whoever it was, that shooter's got some skill."

"Well, that's good news for us," Laurel continued. "Narrows down the field of suspects."

True, Rhyme reflected. "What else do we have?"

"Nothing."

That's *all*? Some emails, a leaked government document, the name of one conspirator.

And notably absent was the one thing Rhyme needed the most: evidence.

Which was sitting somewhere hundreds of miles away, in a different jurisdiction—hell, in a different *country*.

Here he was, a crime scene expert without a crime scene.

CHAPTER 9

S HREVE METZGER SAT AT HIS DESK in lower Manhattan, motionless, as a band of morning light, reflected off a high-rise nearby, fell across his arm and chest.

Staring at the Hudson River, he was recalling the horror yesterday as he'd read the encrypted text from NIOS's surveillance department. The outfit was no more skillful than the CIA's or NSA's, but wasn't quite so visible, which meant it wasn't quite so hobbled by the inconvenience of FISA warrants and the like. And that in turn meant the quality of its information was golden.

Yesterday, early Sunday evening, Metzger had been at his daughter's soccer game, an important one—against the Wolverines, a formidable opponent. He wouldn't have left his seat in the stands, dead center on the field, for anything.

He trod lightly when it came to the children, he'd learned all too well.

But as he pulled on his light-framed glasses—after cleaning the lenses—and read the perplexing then troubling then shattering words, the Smoke formed, fast and unyielding, more a gel than vapor, and it closed around him. Suffocating. He found himself quivering, jaw clenched, hands clenched, heart clenched.

Metzger had recited: I can handle this. This is part of the job. I knew there was a risk of getting found out. He'd reminded himself: The Smoke doesn't define you; it's not part of you. You can make it float away if you want. But you have to *want*. Just let it go.

He'd calmed a bit, unclenched fingers tapping his bony leg in dress slacks (other soccer dads were in jeans but he hadn't been able to change between office and field). Metzger was five ten and three-quarters and clocked in about 150 pounds. Formerly fat, as a boy, he'd melted the weight away and never let it return. His thinning brown hair was a bit long for government service but that's the way he liked it and he wasn't going to change.

Yesterday, as he put the phone away, the twelve-year-old midfielder had turned toward his section in the stands and smiled. Metzger had grinned back. It was fake and maybe Katie knew it. Wished they sold scotch but this was middle school in

Bronxville, New York, so caffeine was the strongest offering on the menu, though the Woodrow Wilson PTO's kick-ass cookies and blondies gave you a high of sorts.

Anyway, liquor was not the way to defeat the Smoke.

Dr. Fischer, I believe you. I think.

He'd returned to the office last night and tried to make sense of the news: Some crusading assistant district attorney in Manhattan was coming after him for Moreno's death. A lawyer himself, Metzger added up the possible counts and knew the biggest, bluntest truncheon would be conspiracy.

And he'd been even more shocked that the DA's Office had learned of Moreno's death because the Special Task Order had been leaked.

A fucking whistleblower!

A traitor. To me, to NIOS, and—worst of all—to the nation. Oh, that had brought the Smoke back. He'd had an image of himself beating the prosecutor, whoever he or she was, to death with a shovel—he never knew the themes his rage would take. And this fantasy, particularly bloody and with a gruesome soundtrack, both mystified and viscerally satisfied with its vivacity and persistence.

When he'd calmed, Metzger had set to work,

making calls and sending texts wrapped in the chrysalis of sublime encryption, to do what he could to make the problem go away.

Now, Monday morning, he turned from the river and stretched. He was more or less functioning, after a grand total of four hours' sleep (very bad; fatigue gives the Smoke strength) and a shower in the NIOS gym. In his twenty-by-twenty office, bare except for safes, cabinets, computers, a few pictures, books and maps, Metzger sipped his latte. He'd bought his personal assistant the same—Ruth's had been assembled with soy milk. He wondered if he should try that. She claimed the substance was a relaxer.

He regarded the framed picture of himself and his children on a vacation in Boone, North Carolina. He recalled the horseback ride at the tourist stable. Afterward an employee had taken this souvenir snap of the three of them. Metzger had noted that the camera the cowboy-clad employee had used was a Nikon, the same company that made the scopes his snipers used in Iraq. Thinking specifically of one of his men firing a Lapua .338 round 1,860 yards into the shoulder of an Iraqi about to detonate an IED. It's not like the movies; a round like that will kill you pretty much anywhere it strikes. Shoulder, leg, anywhere. That insurgent had simply come apart and fallen to the sand, as Shreve Metzger exhaled with warm peace and joy.

Smile, Mr. Metzger. You have wonderful children. Do you want three eight-by-tens and a dozen wallet pictures?

There was no Smoke inside him when he was planning and executing the death of a traitor. None at all. He'd told that to Dr. Fischer. The psychiatrist had seemed uneasy and they didn't explore that theme further.

Metzger glanced at his computer and at his magic phone.

His pale eyes—a hazel color he didn't care for, yellowish green, sickly—looked out his window again at the slice of Hudson River, the view courtesy of a handful of psychotic fools, who, one clear September day, had removed the buildings that interfered with that vista. And who had inadvertently, to their surviving compatriots' loss, driven Metzger into his new profession.

With these thoughts, the Smoke coalesced, as it often did when 9/11 came to mind. The memories of that day used to be debilitating. Now they simply stabbed with searing pain.

Let it go . . .

His phone rang. He regarded caller ID, which reported, in translation, You're fucked.

"Metzger here."

"Shreve!" the caller blurted cheerfully. "How are you? Been a month of Sundays since we chatted."

Metzger had disliked the Wizard of Oz. That is, the wizard himself, as a character (he rather enjoyed the movie). He was furtive and manipulative and arbitrary and had ascended to the throne by false pretense...and yet he commanded all the power in the land.

Much like the caller he was now speaking to.

His own personal Wizard was chiding, "You didn't call me, Shreve."

"I'm still getting facts," he told the man, who happened to be 250 miles away, south, in Washington, DC. "There's a lot we don't know."

Which meant nothing. But he didn't know how much the Wizard knew. Accordingly he would steer the course of ambiguity.

"Imagine it was bum intelligence about Moreno, right, Shreve?"

"Appears to be."

The Wizard: "That happens. That surely happens. What a crazy business we're in. So. All your intel was buttoned up, double- and triple-checked."

Your...

Choice of stark pronoun noted.

"Of course."

The Wizard didn't specifically remind him that Metzger had assured him Moreno's death was necessary to save lives because the expat had been about to blow up American Petroleum's headquarters in Miami. When in fact the worst that had happened was a woman protestor threw a tomato at a policeman and missed.

But with the Wizard, conversations involved mostly subtext and his words—or lack thereof—seemed all the more pointed for it.

Metzger had worked with the man for several years. They didn't meet in person often but on those occasions that they did, the stocky, smiling man always wore blue serge, whatever that exactly was, and impressively patterned socks, along with an American flag pin in his lapel. He never had a problem like Metzger's, the Smoke problem, and when he spoke he did so always with the calmest of voices.

"We had to act fast," Metzger said, resenting that he was on the defensive. "But we know Moreno's a threat. He funds terrorists, he supports arms sales, his businesses launder money, a lot of things."

Metzger corrected himself: Moreno *had been* a threat. He'd been shot to death. He wasn't *is* anything.

The Wizard of Washington continued in that honey voice of his, "Sometimes you just have to move fast, Shreve, that's true. Crazy business."

Metzger took out a fingernail clipper and went to work. He chopped slowly. It kept the Smoke from materializing, a little. Snipping was weird but it was better than gorging on fries and cookies. And screaming at your wife or children.

The Wizard muffled his phone and had another muted conversation.

Who the hell else was in the room with him? Metzger wondered. The attorney general?

Someone from Pennsylvania Avenue?

When the Wizard came back on the line he asked, "And we hear there's some investigation?"

So. Fuck. He did know. How had word gotten out? Leaks are as big a threat to what I'm doing as the terrorists themselves.

Smoke, big time.

"Seems to be."

A pause that clearly asked: And when were you going to mention it to us, Shreve?

The Wizard's stated question, though, was: "Police?"

"NYPD, yes. Not feds. But there's a solid case for immunity." Metzger's law degree had been gathering dust for years but he'd looked up *In re Neagle* and related cases very carefully before taking on the job here. He could recite the conclusion of that case in his sleep: That federal officials could not be prosecuted for state crimes, provided they were acting within the scope of their authority.

"Ah, right, immunity," the Wizard said. "We've looked into that, of course."

Already? But Metzger wasn't really surprised.

A viscous pause. "You're happy that everything *was* within the scope of authority, Shreve?"

"Yes."

Please, Lord, let me keep the Smoke inside now.

"Excellent. Now, it was Bruns who was the specialist, right?"

Either no names or code names over the phone, however well encrypted.

"Yes."

"The police talked to him?"

"No. He's deep cover. There's no way anyone could find him."

"Of course I don't need to say—he knows to be careful."

"He's taking precautions. Everybody is."

A pause. "Well, enough said about that matter. I'll let you take care of it."

"I will."

"Good. Because it turns out some Intelligence Committee budget discussions have come up. Suddenly. Can't understand why. Nothing scheduled but you know those committees. Looking over where the money's going. And I just wanted to tell you that for some reason—it really frosts me, I'll say—NIOS is in their sights."

No Smoke but Metzger was stunned. He couldn't say anything.

The Wizard steamed forward. "Nonsense, isn't it? You *know* we fought hard to get your outfit up and running. Some people were pretty concerned about it." A laugh that seemed utterly devoid of humor. "Our liberal friends didn't like the idea of what you were up to at all. Some of our friends on the other side of the aisle didn't like the fact you were taking business away from Langley and the Pentagon. Rock and a hard place.

"Anyway. Probably nothing'll come of it. Ah, money. Why does it always come down to money? So. How're Katie and Seth?"

"They're fine. Thanks for asking."

"Glad to hear it. Have to go, Shreve."

They disconnected.

Oh, Jesus.

This was bad.

What the cheerful Wizard with his serge wizard suit and brash socks and his dark razor-sharp eyes had actually been saying was: You took out a U.S. citizen on the basis of bad intel and if the case goes to trial in state court it's going to bleed all the way to Oz. A lot of people down in the capital would be keeping a very close eye on New York and the results of the Moreno matter. They were fully prepared to send a shooter of their own after NIOS itself—figurative, of course, in the form of gutted budget. The Service would be out of business in six months.

And the whole affair would have been quiet as a snake's sleep, if not for the whistleblower.

The traitor.

Blinded by the Smoke, Metzger intercommed his assistant and picked up his coffee again.

All your intel was buttoned up, double- and triple-checked...

Well, about that...

Metzger now told himself, Think the situation through: You've made some calls, you've sent some texts. Clean-up was well under way.

"You, ah, all right, Shreve?" Ruth's eyes were on his fingers around the cardboard cup. Metzger realized he was about to crush it and send tepid coffee over his sleeve and several files that only a dozen people in the whole of America were authorized to read.

He released the death grip and managed a smile. "Yes, sure. Long night."

His personal assistant was in her early sixties, a long, attractive face, still dusted with faint freckles, making her appear younger. She'd been, he'd learned, a flower child decades ago. Summer of

Love in San Francisco. Living in the Haight. Now her gray hair was, as often, pulled back in a severe bun and she wore bands of colored rubber on her wrists, bracelets signifying support for various causes. Breast cancer, hope, reconciliation. Who could tell? He wished she wouldn't; messages like that, even if ambiguous, seemed inappropriate in a government agency with a mission like NIOS's.

"Is Spencer here yet?" he asked her.

"About a half hour, he said."

"Have him come to see me as soon as he's in."

"All right. Anything else I can do?"

"No, thank you."

When Ruth had left the office and closed the door, leaving a trail of patchouli oil scent behind her, Metzger sent a few more texts and received some.

One was encouraging.

At least it thinned the Smoke a bit.

CHAPTER 10

RHYME NOTED NANCE LAUREL scrutiniz-
ing her face in the dim mirror of the gas
chromatograph's metal housing. She
gave no reaction to what she was seeing. She
didn't seem like a primping woman.

She turned and asked Sellitto and Rhyme, "How
do you suggest we proceed?"

In Rhyme's mind the case was already laid out
clearly. He answered, "I'll run the crime scene as
best I can. Sachs and Lon'll find out what they can
about NIOS, Metzger and the other conspirator—
the sniper. Sachs, start a chart. Add the cast of characters on there, even if we don't know very much."

She took a marker and walked to an empty
whiteboard, jotted the sparse information.

Sellitto said, "I wanna track down the whistleblower too. That could be tough. He knows he'll
be at risk. He didn't tip off the press that some
company's using shitty wheat in their breakfast ce-

real; he's accusing the government of committing murder. Amelia, you?"

Sachs replied, "I've sent Rodney the information about the email and the STO. I'll coordinate with him and Computer Crimes. If anybody can trace an anonymous upload, he can." She thought for a moment and said, "Let's call Fred too."

Rhyme considered this and said, "Good."

"Who's that?" Laurel asked.

"Fred Dellray. FBI."

"No," Laurel said bluntly. "No feds."

"Why not?" Sellitto's question.

"A chance word'll get to NIOS. I don't think we can risk it."

Sachs countered, "Fred's specialty's undercover work. If we say be discreet, that's how he'll handle it. We need help, and he'll have access to a lot more information than NCIC and state criminal databases."

Laurel debated. Her round, pale face—pretty from some angles, farm girl pretty—registered a very subtle change. Concern? Pique? Defiance? Her expressions were like lettering in Hebrew or Arabic, tiny diacritical marks the only clues to radically different meanings.

Sachs glanced once at the prosecutor, said insistently, "We'll tell him how sensitive it is. He'll go along."

She hit speaker on a phone nearby before Laurel could say any more. Rhyme saw the prosecutor stiffen and wondered if she was actually going to step forward and press her finger down on the cradle button.

The hollow sound of ringing filled the air.

"S'Dellray here," the agent answered. The muted tone suggested he might've been on an undercover set somewhere in Trenton or Harlem and didn't want to draw attention to himself.

"Fred. Amelia."

"Well, well, well how's it goin'? Been a while. Now how imperiled am I, speaking into a telephone that on my end is nice and private but on yours is broadcasting to Madison Square Garden? I do truly hate speakers."

"You're safe, Fred. You're on with me, Lon, Lincoln—"

"Hey, Lincoln. You lost that Heidegger bet, ya know. I'ma peeking in my mailbox everday and as of yesterday, ain't a single check appeared. Pay to the order of Fred Don't-Argue-Philosophy-With Dellray."

"I know, I know," Rhyme grumbled. "I'll pay up."

"Y'owe me fifty."

Rhyme said, "By rights, Lon should pay part of it. He egged me on."

"Fuck no I didn't." Delivered essentially as one word.

Nance Laurel took in the exchange with a bewildered look. Of all the things she wasn't, a banterer would be high on the list.

Or maybe she was just angry that Sachs had overridden her and called the FBI agent.

Sachs continued, "And a prosecutor, ADA Nance Laurel."

"Well, this *is* a special day. Hey there, Counselor Laurel. Good job with that Longshoremen's convic. That was you, right?"

Pause. "Yes, Agent Dellray."

"Never, never, never thought you'd pull that one off. You know the collar, Lincoln? The Joey Barone case, Southern District? *We* got some fed charges on that boy but the jury went for wrist slaps. Counselor Laurel, other hand, ran downfield in state court and bought that boy twenty years min. I heard the U.S. attorney put a pictura you up in his office...on a dartboard."

"I don't know about that" was her stiff response. "I was pleased with the outcome."

"So, *pro*-ceed."

Sachs said, "Fred, we've got a situation. A sensitive one."

"Well, I gotta say the tone of your voice sounds so perplexingly intriguing, don't stop now."

Rhyme saw a brief smile on Sachs's face. Fred Dellray was one of the bureau's best agents, a renowned runner of confidential informants and a family man and father...and amateur philosopher. But his years as an undercover agent on the street had given him a unique speaking style, as bizarre as his fashion choices.

"The perp's your boss, the federal government."

A pause. "Hm."

Sachs glanced at Laurel, who debated a moment and then took over, reiterating the facts they knew so far about the Moreno killing.

Fred Dellray's waiting state was calm and confident but Rhyme detected unusual concern now. "NIOS? They're not really *us* us. They're in their own dimension. And I don't necessarily mean that in a good way."

He didn't elaborate, though Rhyme wasn't sure he needed to.

"I'll check out a few things now. Hold on." The sound of typing flew from the speaker like nutshells on a tabletop.

"Agent Dellray," Laurel began.

"Call me Fred. An' don'tcha fret. I'm as encrypted as can be."

A blink. "Thank you."

"Okay, just looking at our files here, our files..." A lengthy pause. "Robert Moreno, aka Roberto.

Sure, here's some notes on APDR, American Petroleum Drilling and Refining...Looks like our Miami office was scrambled on a potential terrorist incident but it turned out to be a big false a-larm. You want what I got here on Moreno?"

"Please, Fred. Go ahead." Sachs sat at a computer and started a file.

"Hokay, our boy left the country over twenty years ago and only comes back once a year or so. Well, *came* back. Let's see...Watchlisted but never in any active-risk books. He was mostly all talk—so we didn't pri-oritize him. Hobnobbed with al-Qaeda some and Shining Path, folk like that, but never actually shouted out for an attack." The agent was whispering to himself. Then he said, "Note here says that the official word is some cartels might've been behind the shooting. But that couldn't be verified...Ah, here's this."

A pause.

"Fred, you there?" Rhyme asked impatiently.

"Hm."

Rhyme sighed.

Then Dellray said, "This could be helpful. Report from State. Moreno was here. New Yawk City. Arrived April thirty, late. Then left May second."

Lon Sellitto asked, "Anything specific about what he did here, where he went?"

"Nup. That's gotta be your job, friends. Now, I'll keep on it from my end. Make some calls down to my folks in the Caribbean and South America. Oh, I got a picture. Want it?"

"No," Laurel said abruptly. "We need to minimize any communication from your office. I'd prefer phone calls to me or Detectives Sellitto and Sachs or Lincoln Rhyme. Discretion is—"

"The better part of valor," Dellray intoned cryptically. "Not a single problem in the world on that. But broachin' that subject: You *sure* our friends don't know anything yet? At NIOS?"

"No," the ADA said.

"Uh-hum."

Rhyme said, "You don't sound convinced."

He chuckled. "Good luck, one and all."

Sachs clicked the phone off.

"Now, where can I work?" Laurel asked.

"How's that?" Sachs wondered aloud.

The ADA was looking around. "I need a desk. Or table. It doesn't need to be a desk. Just something big."

"Why do you need to be here?"

"I can't work out of my office. How can I?" As if it were obvious. "Leaks. NIOS'll eventually find out we're running the investigation but I need to delay that for as long as possible. Now, that looks good. Over there. Is that all right?"

Laurel pointed to a worktable in the corner.

Rhyme called Thom in and had the aide clear the surface of books and some boxes of old forensics gear.

"I have computers but I'll need my own line and Wi-Fi router too. I'll have to set up a private account on it, encrypted. And I'd prefer not to share the network." A glance toward Rhyme. "If that can be arranged."

Sachs clearly didn't like the idea of this new member of the team. Lincoln Rhyme was by nature a solitary person but at least when a case was ongoing he'd come to tolerate, though hardly relish, the presence of others. He had no particular objection.

Nance Laurel hefted her briefcase and the heavy litigation bag onto the table and began unpacking files, organizing them into separate stacks. She looked as if she were a student moving into a dorm on the first day of freshman year, placing her few possessions on the desk and bedside table for most comfort.

Then Laurel looked up to the others. "Oh, one thing: In working the case I need you to find everything you can to make him look like a saint."

"I'm sorry?" From Sachs.

"Robert Moreno—a saint. He's said a lot of inflammatory things. He's been very critical of the country. So I need you to find what he's done that's good. His Local Empowerment Movement, for instance. Building schools, feeding third-world children, that sort of thing. Being a loving father and husband."

"You *need* us to do that?" Sachs questioned. The emphasis pointed the question in the direction of disbelief...and gave it a nice tidy edge, to boot.

"Correct."

"Why?"

"It's just better." As if obvious.

"Oh." A pause. "That's not really an answer," Sachs said. She wasn't looking at Rhyme and he didn't want her to. The tension between her and the ADA was simmering just fine on its own.

"The jury again." With a glance toward Rhyme who'd apparently fueled her argument earlier. "I need to show he was upright and a good, ethical man. The defense is going to paint Moreno as a danger—like lawyers try to portray a rape victim as somebody who was dressing provocatively and flirting with her attacker."

Sachs said, "There's a big difference between those scenarios."

"Really? I'm not so sure."

"Isn't the point of an investigation to get to the truth?"

A pause for digesting these words. "If you

don't win in court, then what good does having the truth do?"

Then, for her, the subject was settled. Laurel said to everyone, "And we need to work fast. Very fast."

Sellitto said, "Right. NIOS could find out about the case at any time. Evidence could start disappearing."

Laurel said, "That's obvious but it's not what I'm talking about. Look at the board, the kill order."

Everyone did, Rhyme included. Yet he could draw no immediate conclusion. But he suddenly understood. "The queue."

"Exactly," the prosecutor said.

```
RET - TOP SECRET - TOP SECRET - TOP SE


              SPECIAL TASK ORDERS


                    QUEUE


8/27                      9/27
Task: Robert A.          Task: Al-Barani
   Moreno (NIOS ID:         Rashid (NIOS ID:
   ram278e4w5)              abr942pd5t)
Born: 4/75, New          Born: 2/73, Michi-
   Jersey                   gan
```

Complete by:	Complete by:
5/8-5/9	5/19
Approvals:	Approvals:
Level Two: Yes	Level Two: Yes
Level One: Yes	Level One: Yes
Supporting Documen-	Supporting Documen-
tation:	tation:
See "A"	N/R
Confirmation re-	Confirmation re-
quired: Yes	quired: No
PIN required: Yes	PIN required: Yes
CD: Approved, but	CD: Approved, but
minimize	minimize
Details:	Details: To come
Specialist as-	Status: Pending
signed: Don Bruns,	
Kill Room, South	
Cove Inn, Bahamas,	
Suite 1200	
Status: Closed	

She continued, "Now, I can't find out anything about this Rashid or where he is. Maybe *his* kill room's a hut in Yemen, where he's selling nuclear bomb parts. Or given Metzger's zeal, maybe it's a family room in Ridgefield, Connecticut, where

Rashid is blogging against Guantánamo and insulting the president. But we do know that NIOS's going to kill him before Friday. And who'll be the collateral damage then? His wife and children? Some passerby? I want Metzger in custody before that."

Rhyme said, "That won't necessarily stop the assassination."

"No, but it'll send a message to NIOS and Washington that somebody's looking very carefully at what they're up to. They might delay the attack and have somebody independent review the STO and see if it's legitimate or not. That's not going to happen with Metzger in power."

Like counsel in a closing argument Laurel then strode forward and dramatically tapped the kill order. "Oh, and these numbers at the top? Eight/twenty-seven, nine/twenty-seven? They're not dates. They're *tasks* in the queue. That is, victims. Moreno was the eighth person NIOS killed. Rashid'll be the ninth."

"Twenty-seven total," Sellitto said.

"As of a week ago," Laurel said briskly. "Who knows how many it is today?"

CHAPTER 11

A HUMAN FORM, LIKE AN UNFLAPPABLE, patient ghost, appeared in Shreve Metzger's doorway.

"Spencer."

His administrations director—his right-hand man around headquarters—had been enjoying the cool blue skies and quiet lake shore line in Maine when an encrypted text from Metzger had summoned him. Boston had immediately cut short his vacation. If he'd been pissed off, and he probably had been, he'd given no indication of it.

That would be improper.

That would be unseemly.

Spencer Boston's was a faded elegance, a prior generation's. He had a grandfatherly face, creases bracketing his taut lips, and thick, wavy white hair—he was ten years older than Metzger. He radiated an utterly calm and reasonable demeanor. Like the Wizard, Boston wasn't troubled by the

Smoke. He now stepped into the office, shut the door instinctively against prying ears and sat opposite his boss. He said nothing but his eyes dipped to the mobile in his boss's hand. Rarely used, never to leave the building, the device happened to be dark red in color, though that had nothing to do with its top-secret nature. That was the shade that the company had had available for immediate delivery. Metzger thought of it as his "magic phone."

The NIOS director realized his muscles were cramping from the pressure on the unit.

Metzger put the phone away and gave a faint nod to the man he'd worked with for several years, ever since Metzger had replaced the prior head of NIOS, who'd disappeared into the vortex of politics. An unsuccessful vanishing.

"Thanks for coming in," the director said quickly and stiffly, as if he felt he should make some reference to the ruined vacation. The Smoke affected him in many different ways. One of which was to muddle his mind so that, even when he wasn't angry, he'd forget how to behave like a normal person. When an affliction rules your life, you're always on guard.

Daddy, are you... are you okay?

I'm smiling, aren't I?

I guess. It just looks, you know, funny.

The admin director shifted. The chair creaked.

Spencer Boston was not a small man. He sipped iced tea from a tall plastic cup, lifted his bushy brows.

Metzger said, "We've got a whistleblower."

"What? Impossible."

"Confirmed." Metzger explained what had happened.

"No," the older man whispered. "What are you doing about it?"

He deflected that incendiary question and added, "I need you to find him. I don't care what you have to do."

Careful, he reminded himself. That's the Smoke talking.

"Who knows?" Boston asked.

"Well, *he* does." A reverent glance at the magic phone.

No need to be more specific than that.

The Wizard.

Boston grimaced, troubled too. Formerly with another government intelligence agency, he'd been a very successful runner of assets throughout Central America—his region of choice—in such fulcrum countries as Panama. And his specialty? The fine art of regime change. That was Boston's milieu, not politics, but he knew that without support from Washington, you and your assets could be hung out to dry at the worst possible moment.

Several times he'd been held captive by revolutionaries or insurgents or cartel bosses, he'd been interrogated, he'd probably been tortured, though he never talked about that.

And he'd survived. Different threats in DC; same skills at self-preservation.

Boston's hand brushed his enviable hair, gray though it was, and waited.

Metzger said, "He—" Wizard emphasis again. "—knows about the investigation but he didn't say a word about any leaks. I don't think he knows. We have to find the traitor before word trickles down to the Beltway."

Sipping the pale tea, Boston squinted more furrows into his face. Damn, the man could give Donald Sutherland a run for his money in the distinguished older power-broker role. Metzger, though considerably younger, had a much more sparse scalp than Boston and was bony and gaunt. He felt he looked weaselly.

"What do you think, Spencer? How could an STO have gotten leaked?"

A look out the window. Boston had no view of the Hudson from his chair, just more late-morning reflected light. "My gut is it was somebody in Florida. The next choice would be Washington."

"Texas and California?"

Boston said, "I doubt it. They get copies of the

STO but unless one of their specialists is activated, they don't even open them...And, as much as I hate to say it, we can't dismiss the office here completely." The twist of his impressive head indicated NIOS headquarters.

Granted. A co-worker in this office might have sold them out, as painful as it was to think about.

Boston continued, "I'll check with IT security about the servers, copiers and scanners. Polygraph the senior people with download permissions. I'd do a major Facebook autobot search. Well, not just Facebook but blogs and as many other social media sites as I can think of. See if anybody with access to the STO's been posting anything critical of the government and our mission here."

Mission. Killing bad guys.

This made sense. Metzger was impressed. "Good. A lot of work." His eyes strayed to the vista. He saw a window washer on a scaffolding three or four hundred feet up. He thought, as he often did, of the jumpers on 9/11.

The Smoke expanded in his lungs.

Breathe...

Send the Smoke away. But he couldn't. Because *they*, the jumpers on that terrible day, hadn't been able to breathe. Their lungs had been filled with oily smoke rising from the crest of the flames that were going to consume them in seconds, flames roiling into their twelve-by-twelve-foot offices, leaving only one place to go, through windows to the eternal concrete.

His hands began to shake again.

Metzger noted that Boston was regarding him with a close gaze. The NIOS head casually adjusted the photograph of him, Seth and Katie and a snorting horse, taken through a fine set of optics that happened, in that instance, to record a dear memory, but wasn't dissimilar to a scope that could very efficiently direct a bullet through a man's heart.

"They have proof of completion, the police?"

"No, I don't think so. Status is closed, that's all."

Kill orders were just that—instructions to eliminate a task. There was never any documentation that an assassination was actually completed. The standard procedure when asked was to deny, deny, deny.

Boston began to ask, "Are we doing anything...?"

"I've made calls. Don Bruns knows about the case, of course. A few others. We're...handling things."

An ambiguous verb and object. Worthy of the Wizard.

Handling things...

Spencer Boston, of the impressive white mane

and more impressive track record as a spy, sipped more tea. The straw eased farther through the plastic lid and gave a faint vibration like a bow on a viola string. "Don't worry, Shreve. I'll find him. Or her."

"Thanks, Spencer. Anytime. Day or night. Call me, what you find out."

The man rose, buttoned his ill-tailored suit.

When he was gone Metzger heard his magic red phone trill with a text from his surveillance and datamining crowd in the basement.

Identified Nance Laurel as lead prosecutor. IDs of the NYPD investigators to follow soon.

The Smoke diminished considerably at reading this.

At last. A place to start.

CHAPTER 12

JACOB SWANN APPROACHED HIS CAR in the lot of the Marine Air Terminal at LaGuardia airport.

He set his suitcase into the trunk of his Nissan sedan carefully—his knives were inside. No carry-on with them, of course. He dropped heavily into the front seat and stretched, breathing deeply.

Swann was tired. He had left his Brooklyn apartment for the Bahamas nearly twenty-four hours ago and had had only three or so hours' sleep in that time—most while in transit.

His session with Annette had gone more quickly than he'd expected. But, after he'd disposed of the body, finding an abandoned trash fire to burn the evidence of his visit last week had taken some time. Then he'd had to take care of some other housekeeping, including a visit to Annette's apartment and a risky but ultimately successful trip back to the site of Moreno's shooting itself: the South Cove Inn.

He'd then had to get off the island the same way he had last week: from a dock near Millars Sound, where he knew some of the men who clustered daily to work the ships or smoke Camels or ganja and drink Sands, Kalik or, more likely, Triple B malt. They would also handle various odd jobs. Efficiently and discreetly. They'd hurried him via small boat to one of the innumerable islands near Freeport, then there'd been the helicopter ride to a field south of Miami.

That was the thing about the Caribbean. There was Customs and there was custom. And the lower-case version allowed for people like Jacob Swann, with a bankroll of money—his employer had plenty, of course—to get where he needed to be, unnoticed.

After the scoring with the blade, after the blood, he was convinced that Annette had not told anyone about him, about the questions he'd casually asked her a week ago regarding the South Cove Inn, suite 1200, Moreno's bodyguard and Moreno himself. All those facts could be bundled together, resulting in some very compromising conclusions.

He'd only used the Kai Shun a few times, slice, slice…It probably hadn't been necessary, she was so frightened. But Jacob Swann was a very meticulous man. You could ruin a delicate sauce simply by too quickly adding hot liquid to the sizzling flour-and-butter roux. And once you'd done that there was no correction. A matter of a few degrees and few seconds. Besides, you should never miss an opportunity to hone your skills. So to speak.

He now pulled to the airport parking lot's exit kiosk, paid cash then drove a mile on the Grand Central before pulling over and swapping license plates. He then continued on to his house in Brooklyn.

Annette...

Bad luck for the poor prostitute that they'd run into each other when he'd been planning the job at the South Cove. He'd been conducting surveillance when he'd spotted Moreno's guard, Simon Flores, talking and flirting with the woman. Clearly they'd just come out of a room together and he understood from their body language and banter what they'd been doing.

Ah, a working girl. Perfect.

He waited an hour or two and then circled the grounds casually until he found her in the bar, where she was buying herself watered-down drinks and dangling like bait on a hook for another customer.

Swann, armed with a thousand dollars in untraceable cash, had been happy to swim toward her.

After the good sex and over the better stew he'd learned a great deal of solid information for the assignment. But he'd never anticipated that there'd be an investigation, so he hadn't cleaned up as completely as he probably should have. Hence, his trip back to the island.

Successful. And satisfying.

He now returned to his town house in the Heights, off Henry Street, and parked in the garage in the alley. He dropped his bag in the front hall, then shed his clothes and took a shower.

The living room and two bedrooms were modestly furnished, inexpensive antiques mostly, a few Ikea pieces. It looked like the digs of any bachelor in New York City, except for two aspects: the massive green gun safe, in a closet, which held his rifles and pistols, and the kitchen. Which a professional chef might have envied.

It was to this room that he walked after toweling off and pulling on a terry-cloth robe and slippers. Viking, Miele, KitchenAid, Sub-Zero, separate freezer, wine cooler, radiant bulb cookers—his own making. Stainless steel and oak. Pots and implements sat in glass-doored cabinets along one entire wall. (Those ceiling racks are showy, but why have to wash something before you cook in it?)

Swann now made French press coffee. He debated what to make for breakfast, sipping the strong brew, which he drank black.

For the meal he decided on hash. Swann loved challenges in the kitchen and had made recipes that could have been formulated by greats like Heston Blumenthal or Gordon Ramsey. But he knew too that food need not be fancy. When he was in the service he would come back from a mission and in his quarters outside Baghdad whip up meals for his fellow soldiers, using military rations, combined with foods he'd bought at an Arabic market. No one joshed with him about his prissy, sanctimonious approach to cooking. For one thing, the meals were always excellent. For another, they knew Swann had very possibly spent the morning peeling some knuckle skin from a screaming insurgent to find out where a missing shipment of weapons might be.

You made fun of people like that at your peril.

He now lifted a one-pound piece of rib-eye steak from the refrigerator and unwrapped the thick white waxed paper. He himself had been responsible for this perfectly sized and edged piece. Every month or so, Swann would buy a half side of beef, which was kept in a cold-storage meat facility for people like him—amateur butchers. He would reserve a whole glorious day to slice the meat from the bones, shape it into sirloin, short ribs, rump, chuck, flank, brisket.

Some people who bought in bulk enjoyed brains, intestines, stomach and other organ meats. But those cuts didn't appeal to him and he discarded them. There was nothing morally or emotionally troubling about those portions of an animal; for Swann flesh was flesh. It was merely a question of flavor. Who didn't love sweetbreads, crisply sautéed? But most offal tended to be bitter and was more trouble than it was worth. Kidneys, for instance, stank up your kitchen for days and brains were overly rich and tasteless (and jam-packed with cholesterol). No, Swann's time at the two-hundred-pound butcher block, robed in a full apron, wielding saw and knife, was spent excising the classic cuts, working to achieve perfectly shaped specimens while leaving as little on the bone as he possibly could. This was an art, a sport.

This comforted him.

My little butcher man...

Now he set his rib eye on a cutting board—always wood, to save his knives' edges—and ran his fingers over the meat, sensing the tautness of the flesh, examining the grain, the marbling of the fat.

Before slicing, however, he washed and re-edged the Kai Shun on his Dan's Black Hard Arkansas whetstone, which cost nearly as much as the knife itself and was the best sharpening device on the planet. When he'd been sitting atop Annette, he'd moved from tongue to finger, and the blade had an unfortunate encounter with bone. It now needed to be honed back to perfection.

Finally, the knife was ready and he turned back to the steak, slowly slicing the piece into quarter-inch cubes.

He could have made them bigger and he could have worked faster.

But why rush something you enjoy?

When he was done he dusted the cubes in a mixture of sage and flour (his contribution to the classic recipe) and sautéed them in a cast-iron skillet, scooping them aside while still internally pink. He then diced two red potatoes and half a Vidalia onion. These vegetables he cooked in oil in the skillet and returned the meat. He mixed in a bit of veal stock and chopped Italian parsley and set the pan under the broiler to crisp the top.

A minute or two later, the dish was finished. He added salt and pepper to the hash and sat down to eat the meal, along with a rosemary scone, at a very expensive teak table in the bay window of his kitchen. He'd baked the scone several days ago. Better with age, he reflected, as the herbs had bonded well with the hand-milled flour.

Swann ate slowly, as he always did. He had nothing but pity bordering on contempt for people who ate fast, who inhaled their food.

He had just finished when he received an email. It seemed that Shreve Metzger's great national security intelligence machine was grinding away as efficiently as ever.

Received your text. Good to hear success today.

Liabilities you need to minimize/eliminate:

1. Witnesses and allied individuals with knowledge base of the STO operation.
   — Suggest searching Moreno's trip to NY, April 30–May 2.

2. Identified Nance Laurel as lead prosecutor. IDs of the NYPD investigators to follow soon.

3. Individual who leaked STO. Someone is searching for identity now. You may have thoughts on how to learn ID. Proceed at your own discretion.

Swann called the Tech Services people and requested some datamining. Then he pulled on thick
yellow rubber gloves. To clean the skillet, he
scrubbed it with salt and treated the surface with
hot oil; cast-iron should *never* meet soap and water,
of course. He then began to wash the dishes and
utensils in very, very hot water. He enjoyed the
process and found that he did much of his best
thinking standing here, looking out at a dogged
ginkgo in a small garden in front of the building.
The nuts from that plant were curious. They're
used in Asian cuisine—the centerpiece of the de-
licious custard chawanmushi in Japan. They can
also be toxic, when consumed in large quantities.
But dining can be dangerous, of course; when we
sit down to a meal who doesn't occasionally wonder if we've been dealt the salmonella or *E. coli*
card? Jacob Swann had eaten fugu—the infamous
puffer fish with toxic organs—in Japan. He faulted
the dish not for its potential for lethality (training
of chefs makes poisoning virtually impossible) but
for a flavor too mild for his liking.

Scrubbing, scrubbing, removing every trace of
food from metal and glass and porcelain.

And thinking hard.

To eliminate witnesses would cast suspicion on
NIOS and its affiliates, of course, since the kill order was now public. That was unfortunate and un-

der other circumstances he would have tried to arrange accidents or construct some fictional players to take the blame for the murders that were about to happen: the cartels Metzger had claimed were really responsible for Moreno's death, or perps the police and prosecutor had put in jail, out for revenge.

But that wouldn't work here. Jacob Swann would simply have to do what he did best; while Shreve Metzger would deny that kill orders even existed, Swann would make absolutely certain that no evidence of or witnesses to his clean-up operation could possibly tie NIOS or anyone connected with it to the killing.

He could do that. Jacob Swann was a very meticulous man.

Besides, he had no choice but to eliminate these threats. There was no way he'd let anybody jeopardize his organization; its work was too important.

Swann dried the dishes, silver and coffee cup, using thick linen, with the diligence of a surgeon completing the stitches after a successful procedure.

CHAPTER 13

ROBERT MORENO HOMICIDE

— Crime Scene 1.
  — Suite 1200, South Cove Inn, New Providence Island, Bahamas (the "Kill Room").
  — May 9.
  — Victim 1: Robert Moreno.
    — COD: Gunshot wound, details to come.
    — Supplemental information: Moreno, 38, U.S. citizen, expatriate, living in Venezuela. Vehemently anti-American. Nickname: "the Messenger of Truth."
    — Spent three days in NYC, April 30–May 2. Purpose?
  — Victim 2: Eduardo de la Rua.
    — COD: Gunshot wound, details to come.
    — Supplemental information: Journal-

ist, interviewing Moreno. Born
Puerto Rico, living in Argentina.
— Victim 3: Simon Flores.
   — COD: Gunshot wound, details to
     come.
   — Supplemental information: Moreno's
     bodyguard. Brazilian national, living
     in Venezuela.
— Suspect 1: Shreve Metzger.
   — Director, National Intelligence and
     Operations Service.
   — Mentally unstable? Anger issues.
   — Manipulated evidence to illegally au-
     thorize Special Task Order?
   — Divorced. Law degree, Yale.
— Suspect 2: Sniper.
   — Code name: Don Bruns.
   — Information Services datamining
     Bruns.
   — Voiceprint obtained.
— Crime scene report, autopsy report, other
  details to come.
— Rumors of drug cartels behind the killings.
  Considered unlikely.
— Crime Scene 2.
   — Sniper nest of Don Bruns, 2000 yards from
     Kill Room, New Providence Island, Ba-
     hamas.

— May 9.

— Crime scene report to come.

— Supplemental Investigation.

    — Determine identity of Whistleblower.

        — Unknown subject who leaked the
Special Task Order.

        — Sent via anonymous email.

        — Contacted NYPD Computer Crimes
Unit to trace; awaiting results.

Hands on her hips, Amelia Sachs studied the whiteboard.

She noted Rhyme glance without interest at her flowing script. He wouldn't pay much attention to what she'd written until hard facts—evidence, mostly, in his case—began to appear.

It was just the three of them at the moment, Sachs, Laurel and Rhyme. Lon Sellitto had gone downtown to recruit a specially picked canvass-and-surveillance team from Captain Bill Myers's Special Services operation; with secrecy a priority, Laurel didn't want to use regular Patrol Division officers.

Sachs returned to her desk. She didn't do well sitting still and that was largely what she'd been doing for the past two hours. Confined here, the bad habits returned: She'd dig one nail into another, scratch her scalp to bleeding. Fidgety by nature, she felt a compulsion to walk, to be outside, to drive. Her father had coined an expression that was her anthem:

When you move they can't getcha...

The line had meant several things to Herman Sachs. Certainly it could refer to his job, *their* job—he too had been a cop, a portable, walking his beat in the Deuce, Times Square, at a time when the murder rate in the city was at an all-time high. Fast of foot, fast of thought, fast of eye could keep you alive.

Life in general too. Moving...The briefer you were a target for any harm, the better, whether from lovers, bosses, rivals. He'd recited those words a lot, up until he died (some things, your own failing body, for instance, you can't outrun).

But all cases require backgrounding and paperwork and that was particularly true in this one, where facts were hard to come by and the crime scene inaccessible. So Sachs was in desk job prison at the moment, plowing through documents and canvassing—discreetly—via phone. She turned from the board and sat once more as she absently dug a thumbnail into the quick of a finger. Pain spread. She ignored it. A faint swirl of red appeared on a piece of intelligence she was reading and she ignored this too.

Some of the tension was due to the Overseer,

which was how Sachs had come to think of Nance Laurel. She wasn't used to anyone looking over her shoulder, even her superiors—and as a detective third, Amelia Sachs had a lot of those. Laurel had fully moved in now—with two impressive laptops up and running—and had had even more thick files delivered.

Was she going to have a folding cot brought in next?

The unsmiling, focused Laurel, on the other hand, wasn't the least edgy. She hunched over documents, clattered away loudly and irritatingly at the keyboards and jotted notes in extremely small, precise lettering. Page after page was examined, notated and organized. Passages on the computer screen were read carefully and then rejected or given a new incarnation via the laser printer and joined their comrades in the files of *People v. Metzger, et al.*

Sachs rose, walked to the whiteboards again and then returned to the dreaded chair, trying to learn what she could about Moreno's trip to New York on April 30 through May 2. She'd been canvassing hotels and car services. She was getting through to human beings about two-thirds of the time, leaving messages the rest.

She glanced across the room toward Rhyme; he was on the phone, trying to get the Bahamian police to cooperate. His expression explained that he wasn't having any more luck than she was.

Then Sachs's phone buzzed. The call was from Rodney Szarnek, with the NYPD Computer Crimes Unit, an elite group of thirty or so detectives and support staff. Although Rhyme was a traditional forensic scientist, he and Sachs had worked more and more closely with CCU in recent years; computers and cell phones—and the wonderful evidence they retained, seemingly forever—were crucial to running successful investigations nowadays. Szarnek was in his forties, Sachs estimated, but his age was hard to determine for sure. Szarnek projected youth—from his shaggy hair to his uniform of wrinkled jeans and T-shirt to his passionate love of "boxes," as he called computers.

Not to mention his addiction to loud and usually bad rock music.

Which now blared in the background.

"Hey, Rodney," Sachs now said, "could we devolume that a bit. You mind?"

"Sorry."

Szarnek was key to finding the whistleblower who'd leaked the STO. He was tracing the anonymous email with its STO kill order attachment, working backward from the destination, the Manhattan District Attorney's Office, and trying to find where the leaker had been when he sent it.

"It's taking some time," the man reported, over a faint 4/4 rock beat of bass and drum. "The email was routed through proxies halfway around the world. Well, actually *all* the way around the world. So far I've traced it back from the DA's Office to a remailer in Taiwan and from there to Romania. And I'll tell you, the Romanians are *not* in a co-operating mode. But I got some information on the box he was using. He tried to be smart but he tripped up."

"You mean you found the brand of his computer?"

"Possibly. His agent user string...Uhm, do you know what that is?"

Sachs confessed she didn't.

"It's information your computer sends out to routers and servers and other computers when you're online. Anybody can see it and find out exactly what your operating system and browser are. Now, your *whistleblower's* box was running Apple's OS Nine two two and Internet Explorer Five for Mac. That goes back a long time. It really narrows the field. I'm guessing he had an iBook laptop. That was the first portable Mac to have an antenna built in so he could've logged into Wi-Fi for the upload without any separate modem or server."

An iBook? Sachs had never heard of it. "How old, Rodney?"

"Over ten years. Probably one he bought second-hand and paid cash for it, so it couldn't be traced back to him. That's where he tried to be smart. But he didn't figure that we could find out the brand."

"What would it look like?"

"If we're lucky it'll be a clamshell model—they came two-toned, white and some bright colors, like green or tangerine. They're shaped just what they sound like."

"Clams."

"Well, rounded. There's a standard rectangular model too, solid graphite, square. But it'd be big. Twice as thick as today's laptops. That's how you could recognize it."

"Good, Rodney. Thanks."

"I'll stay on the router. The Romanians'll cave. I just need to negotiate."

Up with the music, and the line went dead.

Sachs glanced around and found Nance Laurel looking at her, the expression on the ADA's face both blank and inquisitive. How did she manage that? Sachs told the woman and Rhyme about the cybercrime cop's response. Rhyme nodded, unimpressed, and returned to the phone. He said nothing. Sachs supposed he was on hold.

Laurel nodded approvingly, it seemed. "If you could document that and send it to me."

"What?"

A pause. "What you just told me about the tracing and the type of computer."

Sachs said, "I was just going to write it up on the board." A nod toward the whiteboard.

"I'd actually like everything documented in as close to real time as possible." The ADA's nod was toward her own stacks of files. "If you wouldn't mind."

The prosecutor wielded the words "if you..." like a bludgeon.

Sachs did mind but wasn't inclined to fight this battle. She pounded out the brief memo on her keyboard.

Laurel added, "Thank you. Just send it to me in an email and I'll print it out myself. The secure server, of course."

"Of course." Sachs fired off the document, noting that the prosecutor's micromanagement didn't seem to extend to Lincoln Rhyme.

Her phone buzzed and she lifted a surprised eyebrow, noting caller ID.

At last. A solid lead. The caller was a secretary at Elite Limousines, one of dozens of livery operations Sachs had canvassed earlier, inquiring if Robert Moreno had used their services on May 1. In fact, he had. The woman said the man had hired a car and driver for an as-directed assignment, meaning that Moreno had given the driver

the locations he wished to go to after being picked
up. The company had no record of those stops
but the woman gave Sachs the driver's name and
number.

She then called the driver, identified herself and
asked if she could come interview him in connection with a case.

In a heavily accented voice, hard to understand,
he said he supposed so and he gave her his address.
She disconnected and rose, pulling on her jacket.

"Got Moreno's driver for his visit here on May
first," she said to Rhyme. "I'm going to interview
him."

Laurel said quickly, "Any chance you could
write up your notes on Agent Dellray's news before you go?"

"First thing I'm back."

She noted Laurel stiffen but it seemed that *this*
was a battle the *prosecutor* wasn't willing to fight.

CHAPTER 14

AT THIS POINT IN A STANDARD INVESTIGA-
TION Lincoln Rhyme would have enlisted
the aid of perhaps the best forensics lab
man in the city, NYPD detective Mel Cooper.

But the presence of the slim, unflappable Cooper
was pointless in the absence of physical evidence
and all he'd done was alert the man to be on call—
which to Lincoln Rhyme meant being prepared to
drop everything, short of open-heart surgery, and
get your ass to the lab. Stat.

But that possibility didn't seem very likely at the
moment. Rhyme was now back to the task that had
taken all morning: trying to actually get possession
of some of the physical evidence in the Moreno
shooting.

He was on hold for the fourth time with an official in the Royal Bahamas Police Force in Nassau.
A voice, at last: "Yes, hello. Can I help you?" a
woman asked in a melodious alto.

About time. But he reined in the impatience even though he had to explain all over again. "This is Captain Rhyme. I'm with the New York City Police Department." He'd given up on "consulting with" or "working with." That was too complicated and seemed to arouse suspicion. He'd get Lon Sellitto to informally deputize him if anyone called his bluff. (He wished somebody *would*, in fact; bluff-callers are people who can get things done.)

"New York, yes."

"I'd like to speak to someone in your forensics department."

"Crime Scene, yes."

"That's right." Rhyme pictured the woman he was speaking to as a lazy, not particularly bright civil servant sitting in a dusty un-air-conditioned office, beneath a slowly revolving fan.

Possibly an unfair image.

"I'm sorry, you wanted which department?"

Possibly not.

"Forensics. A supervisor. This is about the Robert Moreno killing."

"Please hold."

"No, please...Wait!"

Click.

Fuck.

Five minutes later he found himself talking to the woman officer he was sure had taken his first call, though she didn't seem to remember him. Or was pretending not to. He repeated his request and this time—after a burst of inspiration—added, "I'm sorry for the urgency. It's just that the reporters keep calling. I'll have to send them directly to your office if I can't give them information myself."

He had no idea what threat this was meant to convey exactly; he was improvising.

"Reporters?" she asked dubiously.

"CNN, ABC, CBS. Fox. All of them."

"I see. Yes, sir."

But the ploy had its effect, because the next hold was for three seconds, tops.

"Poitier speaking." Deep, melodious, with a British accent and a Caribbean inflection; Rhyme knew the lilt not from having been to the islands himself but owing to his role in putting a few people from that part of the world in New York jails. The Jamaican gangs outstripped the Mafia for violence, hands down.

"Hello. This is Lincoln Rhyme with the New York Police Department." He wanted to add, Do *not*, under any fucking circumstances, put me on hold. But refrained.

The Bahamian cop: "Ah, yes." Cautious.

"Who'm I speaking to? Officer Poitier, did I hear?"

"Corporal Mychal Poitier."

"And you're with Crime Scene?"

"No. I'm the lead investigator in the Moreno shooting… Wait, you said you're Lincoln Rhyme. Captain Rhyme. Well."

"You've heard of me?"

"We have one of your forensics books in our library. I've read it."

Maybe this would earn him a modicum of cooperation. On the other hand, the corporal had not said whether he'd liked the book or found it helpful. The latest edition's bio page reported that Rhyme was retired, a fact that Poitier, fortunately, didn't seem to know.

Rhyme now made his pitch. Without naming Metzger or NIOS, he explained that the NYPD believed there was an American connection in the Moreno killing. "I have some questions about the shooting, about the evidence. Do you have some time now? Can we talk?"

A pause worthy of Nance Laurel. "I'm afraid not, sir. The Moreno case has been put on hold for the time being and there are—"

"I'm sorry, on *hold*?" An open case of a homicide that occurred a week ago? This was the time when the investigation should be at its most intense.

"That's correct, Captain."

"But why? You have a suspect in custody?"

"No, sir. First, I don't know what American connection you're speaking of; the killing was committed by members of a drug cartel from Venezuela, most likely. We're waiting to hear from authorities there before we proceed further. And I personally have had to focus on a more urgent case. A part-time student who's just gone missing, an American girl. Ah, these crimes happen some in our nation." Poitier added defensively, "But rarely. Very rarely. You know how it is, sir. A pretty student disappears and the press descends. Like vultures."

The press. Maybe that was why Rhyme finally got put through. His bluff had touched a nerve.

The corporal continued, "We have less rape than Newark, New Jersey, much less. But a missing student in the Islands is magnified like a telephoto lens. And I have to say, with all respect, your news programs are most unfair. The British press too. But now we have lost an American student and not a British one, so it will be CNN and the rest. Vultures. With all respect."

He was rambling now—to deflect, Rhyme sensed. "Corporal—"

"It's most unfair," Poitier repeated. "A student comes here from America. She comes here on holiday or—this girl—to study for a semester. And it's always our fault. They say terrible things about us."

Rhyme had lost all patience but he struggled to remain calm. "Again, Corporal, about the Moreno murder? Now, we're sure the cartels had nothing to do with his death."

Silence now, in stark contrast with the officer's earlier rambling. Then: "Well, my efforts are on finding the student."

"I don't care about the student," Rhyme blurted, bad taste maybe but, in fact, at the moment he didn't. "Robert Moreno. Please. There *is* an American connection and I'm looking into it now. There's some urgency."

Task: Al-Barani Rashid (NIOS ID: abr942pd5t)
Born: 2/73, Michigan

Rhyme couldn't begin to guess who this Rashid was, the next name in the STO queue, and doubted he was an innocent soccer dad in Connecticut. But he agreed with Nance Laurel that the man shouldn't die on the basis of faulty, or faked, information.

Complete by: 5/19...

Rhyme continued, "I'd like a copy of the crime scene report, photos of the scene and the nest the sniper was shooting from, autopsy reports, lab analysis. All the documentation. And any data-mined information about someone named Don Bruns on the island around the time of the shooting. It's a cover. An AKA for the sniper."

"Well, we don't actually have the final report yet. Some notes but it's not complete."

"Not complete?" Rhyme muttered. "The killing was on May ninth."

"I believe that's right."

He *believes*?

Rhyme suddenly felt a stab of concern. "Of course the scene's been searched?"

"Yes, yes, naturally."

Well, this was a relief.

Poitier said, "The day after Mr. Moreno was shot we got right to it."

"Next day?"

"Yes." Poitier hesitated as if he knew this was a misstep. "We had another situation, another case that same day. A prominent lawyer was killed and robbed downtown, in his office. That took priority. Mr. Moreno was not a national. The lawyer was."

Two conditions made crime scenes infinitely less valuable to investigators. The first was contamination from people trudging through the site—including careless police officers themselves. The second was the passage of time between the crime and the search. Evidence key to establishing a suspect's identity and conviction could, literally, evaporate in a matter of hours.

Waiting a day to search a scene could cut the amount of vital evidence in half.

"So the scene is still sealed?"

"Yes, sir."

That was something. In a voice he hoped was suitably grave Rhyme said, "Corporal, the reason we're involved here is that we think whoever killed Moreno will kill again."

"Is that true, do you think?" He sounded genuinely concerned. "Here?"

"We don't know."

Then someone else was speaking to the corporal. A hand went over the mouthpiece of the phone, and Rhyme could hear only mumbles. Poitier came back on the line. "I will take your number, Captain, and if I am able to find anything helpful I will give you a call."

Rhyme's jaw clenched. He gave the number then quickly asked, "Could you search the scene again, please?"

"With all respect, Captain, you have far greater resources in New York than we do here. And, to be honest, this has all been a little overwhelming for me. It's my first homicide case. A foreign activist, a sniper, a luxury resort, and—"

"First homicide case?"

"Well, yes."

"Corporal, with all respect—" Echoing the man's own line. "—could I speak to a supervisor?"

Poitier didn't sound insulted when he said, "One

moment, please." Again the hand went over the receiver. Rhyme could hear muted words. He thought he could make out "Moreno" and "New York."

Poitier came back on a moment later. "I'm sorry, Captain. It seems my supervisor is unavailable. But I have your number. I will be glad to call you when we know something more."

Rhyme believed this might be his only chance. He thought quickly. "Just tell me one thing: Did you recover bullets intact?"

"One, yes, and—" His conversation braked to a halt. "I'm not sure. Excuse me, please. I must go."

Rhyme said, "The bullet? That's key to the case. Just tell me—"

"I believe I may have been mistaken about that. I must hang up now."

"Corporal, what was the department with the police force you transferred from?"

Another pause. "Business Inspections and Licensing Division, sir. And before that, Traffic. I must go."

The line died.

CHAPTER 15

J ACOB SWANN PULLED HIS GRAY Nissan Altima past the house of Robert Moreno's limo driver.

His tech people had come through. They'd learned that Moreno had used an outfit called Elite Limousine when he was in the city on May 1. He discovered too that Moreno had a particular driver he always used. His name was Vlad Nikolov. And, being the activist's regular chauffeur, he probably had information that the investigators would want. Swann had to make sure they didn't get those facts.

He'd made a fast call via his prepaid—"Sorry, wrong number"—and learned the driver was home at the moment. His thickly Russian- or Georgian-accented voice sounded a bit groggy, which meant he'd probably worked the late-night shift. Good. He wasn't going anywhere soon. But Swann knew he'd have to move fast; the police couldn't datamine with the same impunity as his technical services department but traditional canvassing could reveal the driver's identity too.

Swann climbed out of his car and stretched, looking around.

Many livery workers lived in Queens. This was because the parking situation in Manhattan was so horrific and the real estate prices so high. And because limo work often involved shuttles to and from LaGuardia and JFK airports, both of which were located in the borough.

Vlad Nikolov's house was modest but well tended, Swann noted. A spray of flowering plants, thick and brilliant courtesy of the delicate spring temperature and a recent rain, bordered the front of the beige brick bungalow. The grass was trim, the slate slabs leading to the front door had been swept, possibly even scrubbed, in the past day or two. The centerpiece of the yard was two boxwood bushes, diligently shaped.

The utility bill information, including smart electric meter patterns, and food and other purchasing profiles that the tech department had datamined, suggested that the forty-two-year-old Nikolov lived alone. This was unusual for Russian or Georgian immigrants, who tended to be very family-minded. Swann supposed that perhaps he had family back in his native country.

In any event, the man's solitary life worked to Swann's advantage.

He continued past the house, glancing briefly at a window, covered with a gauzy curtain. Lace. Maybe Nikolov had a girlfriend who came to visit sporadically. A Russian man would be unlikely to buy lace. Another person inside would be a problem—not because Jacob Swann minded killing her but because two deaths increased the number of people who might miss a victim and bring the police here all the more quickly. It made a bigger news splash too. He hoped to keep the driver's death quiet for as long as possible.

Swann came to the end of the block, turned and slipped a plain black baseball cap over his head, pulled his jacket off, turned it inside out and slipped it back on. Witnesses see upper garments and headgear mostly. Now, if anyone was looking, it would seem that two different people had walked past the house, rather than one man doing so twice.

Every grain of suspicion counts.

On this second trip he looked the other way— at all the cars on the street in front of and near the house. Obviously no NYPD cruisers but no un-markeds either that he could sense.

He walked up to the door, reaching into his back-pack and withdrawing a six-inch length of capped pipe, filled with lead shot. He wrapped his right hand around this, making a fist. The point of the pipe was to give support to the inside of the fingers so that if he happened to connect with bone or some other solid portion of his victim when he swung, the metacarpals wouldn't snap. He'd learned this the hard way—by missing a blow to the throat and striking a man on the cheek, which had cracked his little finger. He'd regained control of the situation but the pain in his right hand was excruciating. He'd found it was very difficult to flay skin with the knife in one's non-dominant hand.

Swann took a blank, sealed envelope from his bag too.

A glance around. Nobody on the street. He rang the bell with his knuckle, put a cheerful smile on his face.

No response. Was he asleep?

He lifted a paper napkin from his pocket and tried the knob. Locked. This was always the case in New York. Not so in the suburbs of Cleveland or Denver—where he'd killed an information broker last month. All the doors in Highlands Ranch were unlocked, windows too. The man hadn't even locked his BMW.

Swann was about to walk around behind the house and look for a window he might break through.

But then he heard a thud, a click.

He rang the bell again, just to let Mr. Nikolov know that his presence was still requested. This is what any normal visitor would have done.

A grain of suspicion...

A voice, muffled by the thickness of the door. Not impatient. Just tired.

The door opened and Swann was surprised—and pleased—to see that Robert Moreno's preferred driver was only about five feet, six inches and couldn't have weighed more than 160 pounds, 25 fewer than Swann himself.

"Yes?" he asked in a thick Slavic accent, looking at Swann's left hand, the white envelope. The right was not visible.

"Mr. Nikolov?"

"That's right." He was wearing brown pajamas and was in house slippers.

"I've got a TLC refund for you. You gotta sign for it."

"What?"

"Taxi Limousine Commission, the refund."

"Yeah, yeah, TLC. What refund?"

"They overcharged fees."

"You with them?"

"No, I'm the contracting agent. I just deliver the checks."

"Well, they pricks. I don't know about refund

but they pricks, what they charge. Wait, how do I know they not ripping me off? I sign, I sign away my rights? Maybe I should get a lawyer."

Swann lifted the envelope. "You can read this. Everybody's taking the checks but it says you don't have to, you can talk to an arbitrator. I don't care. I deliver checks. You don't want it, don't take it."

Nikolov unlatched the screen door. "Lemme have it."

Swann appreciated that he had no sense of humor but he couldn't help but be struck by the man's unfortunate choice of words.

When the door opened, Swann stepped forward fast and drove his right fist, holding the pipe, into the man's solar plexus, aiming not for the ugly brown cloth of the PJs but for a spot about two inches beyond—inside the man's gut. Which is where blows should always be aimed, never the surface, to deliver the greatest impact.

Nikolov gasped, retched and went down fast.

In an instant Swann stepped past him, grabbed him by the collar and dragged him well inside before the vomiting started. Swann kicked him once, also in the belly, hard, and then looked out a lacy window.

A quiet street, a pleasant street. Not a dog walker, not a passerby. Not a single car.

He pulled on latex gloves, flicked the lock, slipped the pipe away.

"Hellooooo? Helloooo?" Swann called.

Nothing. They were alone.

Gripping the driver by the collar again, he pulled the man along the recently waxed floor, then deposited him in a den, out of view of the windows.

Swann looked down at the gasping man, wincing from the pain.

The beef tenderloin, the psoas major muscle tucked against the short loin and sirloin, lives up to its name—you need only a fork to cut it when prepared right. But the elongated trapezoid of meat, known for Wellington and *tournedos*, starts in a much less agreeable state and takes some prep time. Most of this is knife work. You have to remove any tougher side muscle, of course, but most challenging is the silverskin, a thin layer of connective tissue that encases much of the cut.

The trick is to remove the membrane completely but leave as much flesh intact as you can. Doing this involves moving the knife in a sawing motion, while keeping the blade at a precise angle. You need to practice a great deal to get this right.

Jacob Swann was thinking of the technique now as he withdrew the Kai Shun from its waxed wooden sheath and crouched down.

CHAPTER 16

E N ROUTE TO THE HOUSE of Robert Moreno's limo driver, Amelia Sachs enjoyed
being out from under the Overseer's thumb.
Okay, she thought, not fair.

Nance Laurel was seemingly a good prosecutor.
From what Dellray said, from the woman's preparation for the case.

But that doesn't mean I have to like her.

Find out what church Moreno went to, Amelia,
and how much he donated to good causes and how
many old ladies he helped across the street.

If you would...

I don't think so.

Sachs was at least moving. And moving fast.
She was driving her maroon 1970 Ford Torino Cobra, heir to the Fairlane. The car delivered 405
sleek horsepower and boasted 447 foot-pounds of
torque. Sachs had the optional four-speed transmission, of course. The Hurst shifter was hard and

temperamental but for Sachs this was the only way to run through the gears—for her a more sensuous part of the car than the engine. The only incongruous aspect of the vehicle—aside from its anachronistic appearance on the streets of modern-day New York—was the Chevrolet Camaro SS horn button, a memorial from her first and favorite muscle car, which had been the victim of a run-in with a perp a few years ago.

She now piloted the Cobra over the 59th Street Bridge—the Queensboro. Her father had told her that Paul Simon had written a song about the bridge. She'd meant to look it up on iTunes after he'd told her that. Meant to look it up after he died. Meant to look it up every year or so since.

She never had.

A pop song about a bridge. Interesting. Sachs reminded herself to look it up.

Eastbound traffic was good. The speed nudged a bit higher and she slammed down the clutch and popped the Cobra's gearbox into third.

Pain. And she winced.

Goddamn it. Her knee again. If it wasn't the knee it was the hip.

Goddamn.

The arthritis had plagued her all her adult life. Not rheumatoid—that insidious immune system disorder that works its evil in all your joints. Hers was the more common osteo, whose genesis might have been genes or the consequences of a motorcycle race at age twenty-two—or, more precisely, a spectacular landing *after* the Benelli decided to launch itself off the dirt track only a quarter mile from the finish line. But whatever the cause, oh, how the condition tortured her. She'd learned that aspirin and ibuprofen worked some. She'd learned that chondroitin and glucosamine didn't—at least not for her. Sorry, shark bone lovers. She'd had hyaluronan injections, but they'd sidelined her for several days from inflammation and pain. And, of course, rooster combs could only be a temporary fix. She learned to swallow pills dry and never touch anything that had a *Refill Only 3 Times* label on it.

But the most important thing she'd learned was to smile and pretend the pain wasn't there and that her joints were those of a healthy twenty-year-old.

When you move they can't getcha...

And yet this pain, the joints breaking down, meant she couldn't move nearly as fast as she had. Her metaphor: an emergency brake cable, slack from rusting, that wouldn't quite disengage the shoe.

Dragging, dragging...

And the worst of all: the specter that she'd be sidelined because of the condition. She wondered again: Had Captain Bill Myers's eyes been aimed her way that morning in the lab when a jolt nearly made her stumble? Every time she was around brass she struggled to hide the condition. Had she this morning? She believed so.

She cleared the bridge and downshifted hard into second, matched revs to protect the boisterous engine. She'd done this to prove to herself that the pain wasn't so bad. She was blowing it out of proportion. She could shift whenever she wanted.

Except that lifting her left knee to stomp on the clutch had sent a fierce burst through her.

A reactive tear eased into one eye. She wiped it away furiously.

She drove more moderately toward her destination.

In ten minutes she was easing through a pleasant neighborhood in Queens. Tidy, tiny lawns, shrubs well trimmed, trees rising from perfect circles of mulch

She checked house numbers. Halfway up the block she found Robert Moreno's driver's house. A single-story bungalow, very well maintained. In the driveway, half in the garage, half out, was a Lincoln Town Car, black and polished like a recruit's gun for parade.

Sachs double-parked and tossed the NYPD card onto the dash. Glancing at the house, she saw the flimsy curtain in the living room open slightly then fall back.

So the driver was home. Good. Sometimes when police come a-calling, residents suddenly remember errands they have to run far across town. Or they simply hide in the basement and don't answer the door.

She stepped out, testing her left leg.

Acceptable, though it still hurt. She was between pill times and resisted the urge to take another ibuprofen. That little liver failure thing.

Then she grew impatient with herself for fussing. For God's sake, Rhyme has the use of 5 percent of his body and he never complains. Shut up and get to work. Standing on the front stoop of the driver's house, she pressed the doorbell, heard a Westminster chime inside, an elaborate trilling that seemed ironic, given the minuscule house.

What could the driver tell them? Had Moreno commented that he'd been followed, that he'd received death threats, that someone had broken into his hotel room? Had the driver gotten a description of someone conducting surveillance?

Then footsteps.

She felt, more than saw, someone peering through the gauzy curtain covering the window in the door.

Perfunctorily, she held her badge and shield up.

The lock clicked.

The door swung open.

CHAPTER 17

H ELLO, OFFICER. NO, DETECTIVE. You are a detective? That's what you said when you called."

"Detective, yes."

"And I am Tash. You can call me Tash." He was cautious, as he'd been on the phone when she called earlier, but perhaps because she was a woman and a not unattractive one, he relaxed his guard. His Mideast accent was just as thick as earlier but he was easier to understand face-to-face.

Beaming, he ushered her into the house, dec orated largely with Islamic art. He was a slight man, with a dark complexion, thick black hair, and Semitic features. Iranian, she guessed. He was wearing a white shirt and chino slacks. His full name was Atash Farada and he'd been a driver with Elite Limousines for the past ten years, he explained. Somewhat proudly.

A woman about the same age—Sachs made it mid-forties—greeted her pleasantly and asked if she wanted tea or anything else.

"No, thank you."

"My wife, Faye."

They shook hands.

Sachs said to Farada, "Your company, Elite, said Robert Moreno generally used another driver, right?"

"Yes, Vlad Nikolov."

She asked for the spelling, which he gave. Sachs jotted.

"But he was sick on May first and so they called me instead to drive. Could you tell me what this is about, please?"

"I have to tell you that Mr. Moreno was killed."

"No!" Farada's expression darkened. He was clearly upset. "Please, what happened?"

"That's what we're trying to find out."

"This is such bad news. He was quite the gentleman. Was it robbery?"

Demurring further, she said, "I'd like to know where you drove Mr. Moreno."

"Dead?" He turned to his wife. "Dead, you heard. How terrible."

"Mr. Farada?" Sachs repeated with patient insistence. "Could you tell me where you drove him?"

"Where we drove, where we drove." He looked troubled. But he looked too troubled. Studiously troubled.

Sachs wasn't surprised when he said, "Sadly I am not sure I can remember."

Ah. She got it. "Here's an idea. I could hire you to re-create the route. To start where you picked him up. That might refresh your memory."

His eyes pendulumed away. "Oh. Yes, it might. But I could have a regular assignment for Elite. I—"

"I'll double your fee," Sachs said, thinking about the ethics of paying a potential witness in a homicide investigation. But this case was fat with moral ambiguity from the top down.

Farada said, "I think that might work. I'm so very sad that he died. Let me make a call or two."

He vanished toward a den or study, pulling his mobile from its holster.

Farada's wife asked again, "There is nothing you'd like?"

"No, thank you. Really."

"You are very pretty," the woman said with admiration and envy.

Faye was attractive too, though short and round. Sachs reflected that one always envies whatever one is not. The first thing that she'd noticed about Faye, for instance, was that when she walked forward to shake the detective's hand she did so with-out any hitch in her gait.

Farada returned, wearing a black jacket over the same slacks and shirt. "I am free. I will drive you. I hope I can recall everywhere we went."

She gave him a focused look and he added quickly, "But once we start I think the places will return to me. That's how the memory is, isn't it? Almost a living creature unto itself."

He kissed his wife and said he'd be back before dinner—with a glance toward Sachs so that she could confirm this would be the case.

She said, "A couple of hours, I'd guess."

He and Sachs walked outside and they got into the black Lincoln Town Car.

"You don't want to sit in the back?" he asked, perplexed by her choice of the front passenger seat.

"No."

Amelia Sachs was not a limo girl. She'd been in one only once—at her father's funeral. She had no bad associations with long black sedans based on that experience; she simply didn't do well being driven by others, and sitting in the rear seat expo-nentially increased her discomfort.

They got under way. The man drove expertly through traffic, unwavering but polite and never using the horn, though they encountered several idiots whom Sachs would have blared onto the sidewalk. The first stop was the Helmsley on Central Park South.

"Okay, so I pick him up here about ten thirty a.m."

She climbed out and walked inside to the hotel's check-in desk. The mission, though, was a bust. The clerks were helpful but didn't have any information that bore on the investigation. Moreno had had several room service charges—food for one— but no outgoing or incoming calls. No one remembered if he had had any visitors.

Back into the limo.

"Where next?" she asked.

"A bank. I don't remember the name but I remember where."

"Let's go."

Farada drove her to a branch of American Independent Bank and Trust on 55th Street. She went inside. It was near closing time and some of the staff had left. The receptionist rounded up a manager. Without a warrant, Sachs couldn't get much information. But the woman, one of those template vice presidents, did tell her that Robert Moreno's visit on May first was to close his accounts and move his assets to a bank in the Caribbean. She wouldn't say which one.

"How much? Can you tell me?"

Only: "Mid six figures."

Not like he was laundering huge sums for the cartels. Still, this was suspicious.

"Did he leave any money here?"

"No. And he mentioned he was doing the same for all of his accounts in other banks."

Returning to Tash Farada, Sachs dropped into the passenger seat. "And after this?"

"A beautiful woman," the driver said.

She thought for a moment that Farada was talking about her. She then laughed to herself when he explained that he'd driven Moreno to the East Side and collected a woman who'd accompanied him for the rest of the day. Moreno had given the address—an intersection, Lexington and 52nd—and told the driver to pause in front of the building.

They drove there now and Sachs regarded the structure. A tall, boxy glass office building.

"Who was she?"

He answered, "Dark hair. I am thinking she was about five-eight, in her thirties but youthful, attractive as I was saying. Voluptuous. And her skirt was short."

"Actually I was more interested in her name and business affiliation."

"I caught her first name only. Lydia. And as for business...Well." Farada offered a coy smile.

"Well what?"

"Let me put it this way, I'm sure they hadn't known each other before he picked her up."

"That's not telling me much," Sachs said.

"You see, Detective, we learn things in this job. We learn human nature. Some things our clients do not want us to know, some things *we* do not want to know. We are to be invisible. But we are observant. We drive and we ask no questions except, 'Where do you want to go, sir?' And yet we see."

The esoterica on the Mystic Order of Limo Drivers was wearing and Sachs lifted an impatient eyebrow.

He said in a soft voice, as if someone else were listening, "It was clear to me she was a ... You understand?"

"An escort?"

"Voluptuous, you know."

"One does not necessarily mean the other."

"But then there was the money."

"Money."

"Much of our job is learning not to see things."

Brother. She sighed. "What money?"

"I saw Mr. Moreno give her an envelope. The way they both handled it, I knew it contained money. And he said, 'As we agreed.'"

"And she said?"

"'Thank you.'"

Sachs wondered what prim ADA Nance Laurel

would think of her noble victim picking up a hooker in the middle of the day. "Did there seem to be any connection between this woman and the building? A particular office she worked in?"

"She was in the lobby when we pulled up out front."

Sachs doubted the escort service would have a cover operation here. Maybe this Lydia worked as a temp or had another part-time job. She called Lon Sellitto and explained about the woman, describing her.

"And voluptuous," Tash Farada interjected.

Sachs ignored him and gave the detective the address.

Sellitto said, "I got that canvass team together— from Myers's division. I'll get 'em started on the building. See if anybody's heard of a Lydia."

After they disconnected she asked Farada, "Where did they go from here?"

"Downtown. Wall Street."

"Let's go."

The man eased the Town Car into traffic. Speeding up, the big, spongy Lincoln wove through the congested traffic. If she had to be a prisoner in the passenger seat, at least she could take comfort that the driver wasn't a plodder. She'd rather have a fender-bender than a hesitant ride. And in her opinion faster was safer.

When you move...

As they made their way downtown she asked, "Did you hear what they talked about, Mr. Moreno and Lydia?"

"Yes, yes. But it wasn't what I thought it would be, about her job, so to speak."

Voluptuous...

"He talked much about politics. Lecturing in a way. Lydia, she was polite and asked questions but they were the questions you ask at a wedding or funeral when you're a stranger. Questions you don't care about the answers to. Small talk."

Sachs persisted. "Tell me what he said."

"Well, I remember he was angry with America. This I found troubling, offensive really. Perhaps he thought he could say these things in front of me because of my accent and I am of Middle Eastern descent. As if we had something in common. Now, I cried when the Trade Towers came down. I lost clients that day, who were my friends too. I love this country as a brother. Sometimes you are angry at your brother. Do you have?"

He sped around a bus and two taxis.

"No, I'm an only child." Trying to be patient.

"Well, at times you are angry with your brother but then you make up and all is well. That makes your love real. Because after all you're joined by blood, forever. But Mr. Moreno wasn't willing to forgive the country for what it had done to him."

"Done to him?"

"Yes, do you know that story?"

"No," Sachs said, turning toward him. "Please tell me."

CHAPTER 18

I N ALL ENDEAVORS MISTAKES HAPPEN.
    You can't let them affect you emotionally.
    You try to whip cream without chilling the bowl and beaters and you're going to end up with butter.

You and the tech department datamine the name of a client's regular driver at a limo company and it turns out he was sick the *one* day you need to ask him about. And even removing a few careful strips of flesh couldn't get the man lying in front of you to give up the substitute's name. Which meant that he didn't know.

Silverskin...

Jacob Swann reflected that he should have known this, should have prepared, and that gave him a dose of humble. You can't make assumptions. The first rule to any good meal is prep. Get all the work done ahead of time, all the chopping, all the measuring, all the stock reduction.

Everything.

Only then do you assemble, cook and finish.

He now cleaned up quickly in Vlad Nikolov's house, reflecting that the hour wasn't a complete waste of time—refining your skills never is. Besides, Nikolov might have known something helpful to the police (though as it turned out, he hadn't). Since he had people like that ADA Nance Laurel and the whistleblower to take care of, he wanted to keep Vlad Nikolov's corpse a secret for as long as possible. He wrapped the oozing body in a dozen towels and then in garbage bags, taping them shut. He dragged the corpse to the basement, *thud thud thud* on the stairs, and eased it into a supply room. The odor wouldn't begin to escape for a week or so.

He then used the man's mobile and called Elite Limousines, reporting in hesitant English with a functional Slavic accent that he was Vlad Nikolov's cousin. The driver had learned of a death in the family, back in the old country (he didn't mention Moscow or Kiev or Tbilisi, since he didn't know). Vlad was taking several weeks off. The receptionist protested—only about scheduling, not that the story seemed incredible—but he'd hung up.

Swann surveyed the scene of the interrogation and noted he'd left very little evidence. He'd used trash bags and towels to catch the blood. He now scrubbed the rest, using bleach, and put the towels and phone in a trash bag, which he'd take with him for disposal in a Dumpster on his way home.

As he was about to leave, he received an encrypted email. Well, it seemed that NIOS had learned some very interesting information. The whistleblower was still unknown, though Metzger had people looking into that. However, the tech department had discovered some names of other people involved in the case, in addition to Ms. Nance Laurel, the prosecutor. The lead investigators were two individuals—an NYPD detective named Amelia Sachs and a consultant, someone with the curious name Lincoln Rhyme.

It was time for some more digging and datamining, Swann reflected, pulling out his phone. After all, the strength of the best cookbook in the world, *The Joy of Cooking*, derived from the patient assembly and organization of facts, from *knowledge*, in short—not showy recipes.

CHAPTER 19

D O YOU KNOW ABOUT PANAMA?" Tash Farada asked Sachs, in the passenger seat of the Town Car. He was animated and seemed to enjoy speeding through traffic as they headed toward Wall Street.

She said, "The canal. Some invasion or something down there. A while ago."

The driver laughed and accelerated hard to avoid a slow-moving lane of traffic on the FDR. "Some 'invasion or something.' Yes, yes. I read history a great deal. I enjoy it. In the eighties Panama had a regime change. A revolution. Just like our country."

"Yes, Iran. In 'seventy-nine, wasn't it?"

He glanced at her with a frown.

"Persia, I mean," she corrected.

"No, I'm speaking of seventeen seventy-six. I'm American."

Oh. *Our* country.

"Sorry."

A wrinkle of brow but a forgiving one. "Now, Panama. Noriega used to be an ally of America. Fighting the Communist evil. Helping the CIA and the DEA wage war on the scourge of drugs...Of course, he was also helping the cartel heads wage war on the scourge of the CIA and the DEA. That game caught up with him and in nineteen eighty-nine the U.S. had had enough. We invaded. The problem was that Panama was a dirty little war. You've read George Orwell?"

"No." Sachs might have, long ago, but she never bluffed or tried to impress with knowledge she didn't have command of.

"In *Animal Farm*, Orwell wrote, 'All animals are equal, but some animals are more equal than others.' Well, all wars are bad. But some wars are more bad than others. The head of Panama was corrupt, his underlings were corrupt. They were dangerous men and oppressed the people. But the invasion was very hard too. Very violent. Roberto Moreno was living there, in the capital, with his mother and father."

Sachs recalled her conversation with Fred Dell-ray, who'd told them that Robert Moreno also went by Roberto. She wondered if he'd legally changed it or just used the Latino version as a pseudonym.

"Now, he was a young teenager. That day in the

car he told Lydia, his voluptuous friend, that he didn't have the happiest home life, his father traveling, his mother had sadness problems. She was not much there for him."

Sachs remembered too the father's oil company job, the demanding hours, and the woman's eventual suicide.

"The boy, it seemed, made friends with a family living in Panama City. Roberto and the two brothers became close. Enrico and José, I think were their names. About his age, to hear him tell it."

Tash Farada's voice faded.

Sachs could see where the narrative was headed.

"The brothers were killed in the invasion?"

"One was—Roberto's best friend. He doesn't know who actually fired the shots but he blames the Americans. He said the government changed the rules. They didn't care about people or freedom, like they said. They were happy to support Noriega and tolerate the drugs until he grew unstable and they were worried the canal would close and the oil tankers could not get through. That's when they invaded." A whisper now. "Mr. Moreno found his friend's body. He still had nightmares about it, he told the woman Lydia."

Although the evidence might point to Moreno's being less than a saint, contrary to what Nance Laurel would have liked, Sachs couldn't help but be moved by the sad story. She wondered if Laurel would have been. Doubted it.

The driver added, "And when he was telling this story, telling it to Lydia, his voice grew broken. But then all of a sudden he laughed and gestured around him. He said he was saying goodbye to America and was happy about that. This would be his last trip here. He knew he couldn't return."

"*Couldn't* return?"

"That's right. Couldn't. 'Good riddance,' he said." Tash Farada added darkly, "*I* thought good riddance to *him*. I love this country." A pause then he added, "I'm not happy he's dead, you understand. But he said many bad things about my home. Which I think is the best nation on earth and always has been."

As they approached Wall Street, Sachs nodded toward the site of the September 11 attacks. "Did he want to see ground zero?"

"No," the driver said. "I thought he might. I thought possibly he wanted to gloat, after all he had said. I would have asked him out of the car at that point. But he didn't. He'd grown quiet."

"Where did you take him down here?"

"I just dropped them at this place." He'd pulled over on Fulton Street, near Broadway. "Which I thought was odd. Just on this street corner. They got out and he said they would be several hours. If

I couldn't wait here they would call me. I gave him my card."

"What did you think was odd about that?"

"In this area of the city we limo drivers can get almost anywhere if there's no construction. But it was as if he didn't want me to see where they were going. I assumed to one of the hotels, the Millenium or one of the others. That's the direction they walked in."

For a tryst with his voluptuous friend? But then why not just stay at the hotel uptown?

"Did he call you?" Sachs was hoping to get Moreno's phone number, which might still be in the driver's log.

But the man said, "No. I just waited here. And they returned."

She climbed out of the Lincoln, then walked in the direction that the driver had indicated. She canvassed the three hotels within walking distance but none had a record of a guest under Moreno's name on May 1. If they had checked in, Lydia might have used her name though that lead wasn't going anywhere without more information about her. Sachs also displayed a picture of Moreno but no one recognized him.

Had the activist paid her to have sex with somebody else? she wondered. Had they met with someone in one of the hotels or an office here?

As a bribe or to blackmail him? Sachs walked back outside into the congested street from the last hotel, looking around her at the hundreds of buildings—offices, stores, apartments. A team of NYPD canvassers could have spent a month inquiring about Robert Moreno and his companion and still not scratched the surface.

She wondered too if Lydia might have received her cash for another reason. Was she part of a cell, a terrorist organization that Moreno was working with? Did they meet with a group that wanted to send another violent message in this financial hub of the city?

This conjecture too, while reasonable to Sachs, was surely something that Nance Laurel would not want to hear.

You mean, you can't keep an open mind...

Sachs turned around and walked back to the limo. Dropping into the front seat again, she stretched, winced at a burst of arthritic pain and dug one nail into another. Stop it, she told herself. Dug a bit harder and wiped the blood on her black jeans.

"And after this?"

Farada told her, "I drove them back to the hotel. The woman got out with him but they went different ways. He went inside and she walked east."

"Did they hug?"

"Not really. They brushed cheeks. That was all. He tipped me and he tipped well, even though it's included."

"All right, let's head back to Queens."

He put the car in gear and made his way east through the dense rush-hour traffic. The time was around 7 p.m. As they plodded along she asked Farada, "Did you get any sense that he was being followed or watched? Did he feel uneasy? Did he act suspicious or paranoid?"

"Hm. Ah. I can say he was cautious. He looked around frequently. But there were never any specific concerns. Not like he said, 'That red car is following me.' He seemed like somebody who tried to be aware of his surroundings. I see that much. Businesspeople are that way. I think they must be nowadays."

Sachs was frustrated. She'd learned nothing conclusive about the man's sojourn in New York. Even more questions than answers now floated. And yet she couldn't shake the sense of urgency, thinking of the STO naming Rashid as the next target.

We do know that NIOS's going to kill him before Friday. And who'll be the collateral damage then? His wife and children? Some passerby? . . .

They were on the Williamsburg Bridge when her phone rang.

"Fred, hi."

"Hey, Amelia. Listen, gotta coupla things. Had our people look through SIGINT down in Venezuela. Snagged one of Moreno's voice from 'bout a month ago. Might be relevant. He was saying, 'Yes, May twenty-fourth, that's right...disappearing into thin air. After that, it'll be heaven.'"

The 24th was less than two weeks away. Did he mean he was planning some attack and he'd have to vanish, like Bin Laden?

"Any ideas about that?" Sachs asked.

"No, but we're still checkin'."

She told the agent what Farada had explained about this being Moreno's last trip to New York and his mysterious meeting in the vicinity of ground zero.

"That'd fit," Dellray said. "Yeah, yeah, could be he's got something nasty in mind and is going to ground. Makes sense—'specially when you hear the other thing I'm about to tell you."

"Go on." Her notebook was on her lap, pen poised.

The agent said, "'Nother voice-call trap. Ten days before he died. Moreno was saying, 'Can we find somebody to blow them up?'"

Sachs's gut clenched.

Dellray continued, "The tech geeks think he mentioned the date May thirteen, along with Mexico."

This was two days ago. She didn't remember any incident but Mexico was largely a war zone, with so many drug-related attacks and killings that they often didn't rate a mention on U.S. TV news. "I'm checking t'see if something happened then. Now, lastly—I said *coupla* things; I meant three. We got Moreno's travel records. Ready?"

"Go ahead."

The agent explained. "On May second Moreno flew from New York to Mexico City, maybe to plan for the bombing. Then the next day on to Nicaragua. The day after that to San José, Costa Rica. He stayed there for a few days and then flew to the Bahamas on the seventh, where—coupla days later—he had his run-in with the fine marksmanship of Mr. Don Bruns."

Dellray added, "Some casual surveillance was conducted on him in Mexico City and Costa Rica, where he was spotted outside the U.S. embassies. But there was no evidence that he was lookin' like any kinda threat, so your boy was never detained."

"Thanks, Fred. That's helpful."

"I'll keep at it, Amelia. But gotta tell you, I ain't got oodles of time."

"Why, you have something big going down?"

"Yup. I'm changing my name and moving to Canada. Joining the Mounted Police."

Click.

She didn't laugh. His comment had struck too close to home; this case was like unstable explosives.

A half hour later Tash Farada parked in his driveway and they got out. He struck a certain pose, unmistakable.

"How much do I owe you?" Sachs asked.

"Well, normally we charge from garage to garage, which isn't fair for you. Since the car was here. So it will be from the time we left to the time we arrived." A look at his watch. "We left at four twelve and we've now returned now at seven thirty-eight."

Well, that's some precision.

"For you, I will round downward. Four fifteen to seven thirty. That's three hours and fifteen minutes."

And that's some speedy calculation.

"What's the hourly rate?"

"That would be ninety dollars."

"An hour?" she asked before remembering she'd added the qualifier with her prior question.

A smile. "That's three hundred and eighty-two dollars and fifty cents."

Shit, Sachs thought, she'd assumed it would be about a quarter of that. So, one more reason not to be a limo girl.

He added, "And of course…"

"I agreed to double it."

"That is a grand total of seven hundred and sixty-five dollars."

A sigh. "Will you give me one more ride?" Sachs asked.

"Well, if it won't take too much time." A nod toward the house. "Supper, you know."

"Just to the nearest ATM."

"Ah, yes, yes...And I won't charge you for that trip at all!"

CHAPTER 20

I MAGINATION OR NOT?
No.
Cruising back into Manhattan, in the Torino Cobra, Sachs was sure she was being followed.

Glances into the rearview mirror as she exited the Midtown Tunnel suggested that a car—a light-colored vehicle whose make and model she couldn't nail down—was following. Nondescript. Gray, white, silver. Here and on the streets leaving Farada's house.

But how was this possible? The Overseer had assured them that NIOS, Metzger and the sniper didn't know about the investigation.

And even if they did find out, how could they identify her personal car and locate it?

Yet Sachs had learned from a case she and Rhyme had run a few years ago that anyone with a rudimentary datamining system could track some-one's location pretty easily. Video images of tag numbers, facial recognition, phone calls and credit cards, GPS, E-ZPass transponders, RFID chips— and NIOS was sure to have much more than a basic setup. She'd been careful but perhaps not careful enough.

That was easily remedied.

Smiling, she executed a series of complicated, fast and extremely fun turns, most of which involved smoking tires and cracking sixty mph in second gear.

By the time she performed the last one and stabilized the marvelous Cobra, offering a sweet smile of apology to the Sikh driver she'd skidded around, she was convinced that she'd lost whatever tail might have been after her.

At least until datamining caught up with her again.

And even if this *was* surveillance did the tailer represent a true threat?

NIOS might want information about her and might try to derail or slow down the case but she could hardly see the government physically hurting an NYPD officer.

Unless the threat wasn't from the government itself but an anger-driven psychotic who happened to be *working for* the government, using his position to play out some delusional dream of eliminating those who weren't as patriotic as he liked.

Then too this threat might have nothing to do with Moreno. Amelia Sachs had helped put a lot of people in jail and none of them, presumably, was very pleased about that.

Sachs actually felt a shiver down her spine.

She parked just off Central Park West, on a cross street, and tossed the NYPD placard on the dash. Climbing out, Sachs tapped her Glock grip to orient herself as to its exact position. Every nearby car, it seemed, was light-colored and nondescript and contained a shadowy driver looking her way. Every antenna, water tower and pipe atop every building in this stretch of the Upper West Side was a sniper, training the crosshairs of his telescopic sight on her back.

Sachs walked quickly to the town house and let herself in. Bypassing the parlor, where Nance Laurel was still typing away, exactly as the detective had left her hours ago, she walked into Rhyme's rehab room—one of the bedrooms on the first floor—where he was working out.

With Thom nearby as a spotter, Rhyme was in a sitting position, strapped into an elaborate stationary bicycle, a functional electrical stimulation model. The unit sent electrical impulses into his muscles via wires to mimic brain signals and made his legs operate the pedals. He was presently pumping away like a Tour de France competitor.

She smiled and kissed him.

"I'm sweaty," he announced.

He was.

She kissed him again, longer this time.

Although the FES workout would not cure his quadriplegia it kept the muscles and vascular system in shape and improved the condition of his skin, which was important to avoid sores that were common among those with severe disabilities. As Rhyme often announced, sometimes for pure shock value, "Gimps spend a lot of time on their asses."

The exercise had also enhanced nerve functioning.

This was the aerobic portion of his exercise. The other part involved building up the muscles in his neck and shoulders; it was these elements of his body that would largely control the movement of his left hand and arm, as they now did his right, after his surgery in several weeks, if all went well.

Sachs wished she hadn't thought that last clause.

"Anything?" he called, breathing heavily.

She gave him a rundown of the chauffeur trip, explaining about Moreno's close childhood friend dying at the hands of the American invaders in Panama.

"Grudges can run deep." But he wasn't interested in what he would consider the mumbo-jumbo of the man's psyche; Rhyme never was. More interesting was what she'd learned about Lydia, the closed bank accounts, the mysterious meeting, Moreno's planned self-imposed exile from the United States—his vanishing into "thin air"—and some possible connection with explosions in Mexico City on May 13.

"Fred's going to keep digging. Any luck in the Bahamas?"

"Crap all," he snapped, panting. "I don't know whether it's incompetence or politics—probably both—but I've called back three times and ended up on hold again until I hang up. That's seven times today. I truly resent hold. I was going to call our embassy there or consulate or whatever they have to intervene. But Nance didn't think that was a good idea."

"Why? Word would get back to NIOS?"

"Yeah. I can't disagree, I suppose. She's sure evidence is going to start disappearing the minute they find out. The problem is..." He drew a deep breath and with his functioning right hand turned the speed of the bike up a bit higher. "...there *is* no goddamn evidence."

Thom said, "Slow down a bit there."

"What, my diatribe, or my exercise? That's rather poetic, don't you think?"

"Lincoln."

The criminalist gave it a defiant thirty seconds more and lowered the speed. "Three miles," he announced. "Somewhat uphill."

Sachs took a cloth and wiped a bit of sweat that ran down his temple. "I think somebody might've already found out about the investigation."

He turned those dark, radar eyes her way.

She told him about the car she thought might have been tailing her.

"So our sniper has found out about us already? Any ID?"

"No. Either he was real good, or my imagination was working overtime."

"I don't think we can be too paranoid in this case, Sachs. You should tell our friend in the parlor. And have you told her that Saint Moreno might not be so saintly?"

"Not yet."

She found Rhyme looking at her with a particular expression.

"And that means what?" she asked.

"Why don't you like her?"

"Oil and water."

Rhyme chuckled. "The hydrophobia myth! They *do* mix, Sachs. Simply remove gases from the water and it will blend perfectly well with the oil."

"I should know not to offer a cliché to a scientist."

"Especially when it doesn't answer his question."

It was a thick five seconds before she answered. "I don't know why I don't like her. I'm no good with being micromanaged, for one thing. She leaves *you* alone. Maybe it's a woman thing."

"I have no opinion on the subject."

Digging into her scalp, she sighed. "I'll go tell her now."

She walked to the door and paused, looking back at Rhyme hard at work on the bicycle.

Sachs had mixed feelings about his plans for the forthcoming surgery. The operation was risky. Quads start with a hampered physiological system to begin with; an operation could lead to severe complications that wouldn't be an issue with the non-disabled.

Yes, she certainly wanted her partner to feel good about himself. But didn't he know the truth—that he, like everyone else, was mind and heart first, before he was body? That our physical incarnations always disappoint in one way or another? So he got stared at on the street. He wasn't the only one; when *she* was perused, it was usually by an observer who was a lot creepier than in his case.

She thought now of those days as a fashion model, marginalized because of her good looks and height and flowing red hair. She'd grown angry—even hurt—at being treated like nothing more than a pricey collectible. She'd risked the wrath of her mother to leave the profession and join the NYPD, following in her father's footsteps.

What you believed, what you knew, how you made choices, when you stood your ground… those were the qualities that defined you as a cop. Not what you looked like.

Of course, Lincoln Rhyme was severely disabled. Who in his condition wouldn't want to be better, to grasp with both hands, to walk? But she sometimes wondered if he was undergoing the risky surgery not for himself but for her. This was a topic that had rarely come up and when it did, their words glanced off the subject like bullets on flat rock. But the understood meaning was clear: What the hell are you hanging around with a crip for, Sachs? You can do better than me.

For one thing, "doing better" suggested she was in the market for Mr. Perfect, which was simply not the case and never had been. She'd been in only one other serious relationship—with another cop—and it had ended disastrously (though Nick was finally out of prison). She'd dated some, usually to fill time, until she realized that the boredom of being with someone is exponentially worse than the boredom of solitude.

She was content with her independence and, if

Rhyme weren't in the picture, she'd be comfortable on her own—forever, if no one else came along.

Do what you want, she thought. Have the surgery or not. But do it for yourself. Whatever the decision, I'll be there.

She watched him for a few moments more, a faint smile on her face. Then the smile faded and she walked to the parlor to meet the Overseer and deliver the news.

Saint Moreno might not be so saintly . . .

CHAPTER 21

A S SACHS JOTTED ON THE WHITEBOARDS the information she'd learned on the drive with Tash Farada, Nance Laurel turned her chair toward the detective.

She'd been digesting what Sachs had told her. "An escort?" the prosecutor asked. "You're sure?"

"No. It's a possibility, though. I've called Lon. He's got some of Myers's portables canvassing to see if they can find her."

"A call girl." Laurel sounded perplexed.

Sachs would have thought she'd be more dismayed. Learning that a hooker had accompanied your married victim around New York wasn't going to win the jury's sympathy.

She was even more surprised when the ADA said offhandedly, "Well, men stray. It can be finessed."

Maybe by "finesse" she meant she'd try for a largely male jury, who would presumably be less critical of Moreno's infidelity.

If you're asking if I pick cases I think I can win, Detective Sachs, then the answer's yes...

Sachs continued, "In any case, it's good for us: They might not have spent the entire time in bed. Maybe he took her to meet a friend, maybe she saw somebody from NIOS tailing them. And if she is a pro we'll have leverage to get her to talk. She won't want her life looked into too closely." She added, "And it might be that she's not an escort but is involved in something else, maybe something criminal."

"Because of the money." Laurel nodded at the whiteboard.

"Exactly. I was thinking possibly a terrorist connection."

"Moreno wasn't a terrorist. We've established that."

Sachs thought, *You've* established that. The facts haven't. "But still..." She nodded at the board too. "Never coming back to the U.S., the bank transfers, vanishing into thin air...A reference to 'blowing up' something in Mexico City."

"It could mean a lot of things. Construction work, demolition, for one of his Local Empowerment Movement companies, for instance." Still, the implications of the discoveries seemed to bother her. "Did the driver notice any surveillance?"

Sachs explained what Farada had said about Moreno's looking around, uneasy.

Laurel asked, "Does he know if Moreno saw anything specific?"

"No."

Nance Laurel scooted her chair forward and stared at the evidence board, her pose oddly parallel to Rhyme's when he parked his Storm Arrow in front of the charts.

"And nothing about Moreno's charitable work, anything that cast him in a favorable light?"

"The driver said he was a gentleman. And he tipped well."

This didn't seem to be exactly what Laurel was looking for. "I see." She glanced at her watch. The time was getting close to 11 p.m. She frowned as if she expected the time to be hours earlier. For a moment Sachs actually believed that the woman was considering camping out for the night. But she began to organize all the piles of papers on her table, saying, "I'm going home now." A glance at Sachs. "I know it's late but if you could just write up your notes and what Agent Dellray found, then send them—"

"To you, on the secure server."

"If you could."

WHEELING BACK AND FORTH in front of the sparse whiteboards and listening to the staccato, insistent typing of Amelia Sachs at the keyboard of her computer.

She didn't seem happy.

Lincoln Rhyme certainly wasn't. He scanned the boards again. The goddamn boards...

The case was nothing but hearsay, ambiguous and speculative.

Soft.

Not a single bit of evidence collected, evidence analyzed, evidence rendered into deduction. Rhyme sighed in frustration.

A hundred years ago the French criminalist Edmond Locard said that at every crime scene a transfer occurs between the perpetrator and the scene or the perp and the victim. It might be virtually impossible to see, but it was absolutely there to find...if you knew how to look and if you were patient and diligent.

Nowhere was Locard's Principle more true than in a homicide like Moreno's. A shooting always leaves a wealth of clues: slugs, spent cartridges, friction ridge prints, gunshot residue, footprints, trace materials at the sniper's nest...

He *knew* clues existed—but they remained out of reach. Infuriating. And with every passing day, hell, every *hour*, they grew less valuable as they degraded, were contaminated and possibly were stolen.

Rhyme had been looking forward to analyzing the recovered evidence himself with his own hand, probing, examining…*touching*. An intense pleasure that had been denied him for so many hard years.

But that possibility was looking more and more unlikely, as time passed with no word from the Bahamas.

An officer from Information Services called and reported that while there were many database hits for "Don Bruns" or "Donald Bruns," none was ranked as significant by IS's Obscure Relationship Algorithm system. ORA takes disparate information, like names, addresses, organizations and activities, and uses supercomputers to find connections that traditional investigation might not. Rhyme was only mildly disappointed with the negative results. He hadn't expected much; government agents at that level—especially snipers—surely would swap out their covers frequently, use cash for most purchases and stay off the grid as much as possible.

He now glanced toward Sachs, her eyes fixed on

her notebook as she typed a memo for Laurel. She was fast and accurate. Whatever afflicted her hip and knee had spared her fingers. She never seemed to hit backspace for corrections. He recalled when he started in policing, years ago, women officers never admitted they could type, for fear of being marginalized and treated like administrative assistants. Now that had changed; those who keyboarded faster could get information faster and were therefore more efficient investigators.

Sachs's expression, however, suggested that of a put-upon secretary.

Thom's voice: "Can I get you—?"

"No," Rhyme snapped.

"Well, since the question was directed toward Amelia," the aide fired back, "why don't we let her answer? Can I get you anything to eat, drink?"

"No, thanks, Thom."

Which gave Rhyme a certain sense of petty satisfaction. He declined Thom's offer too. And he returned to brooding.

Sachs took a phone call. Rhyme heard music tinning from her phone and knew who the caller was. She hit speaker.

"What do you have for us, Rodney?" Rhyme called.

"Lincoln, hi. Moving slowly but I've traced the whistleblower's email from Romania to Sweden."

Rhyme looked at the time. The hour was early morning in Stockholm. He supposed the body clock of geeks operated on its own time.

The Computer Crimes Unit cop said, "I actually know the guy operating the proxy service. We had a running argument about *The Girl with the Dragon Tattoo* a year or so ago and we played hack against each other for a while. He's good. Not as good as me, though. Anyway, I charmed him into helping us, as long as he doesn't have to testify."

Despite his sour mood at the moment Rhyme had to laugh. "The good old boy network is alive and well—literally, a *network*."

Szarnek may have laughed too, though it was hard to tell because of the music that filled in the gaps between his words.

"Now, he knows for sure that the email originated in the New York area and that no government servers were involved in any of the routing. They were sent from a commercial Wi-Fi. The whistleblower might've bootlegged somebody's account or used free Wi-Fi at some coffee shop or hotel."

"How many locations?" Sachs asked.

"There are about seven million unprotected accounts in the New York area. Give or take."

"Ouch."

"Oh, but I've managed to eliminate one."

"Only one? Which?"

"Mine." He laughed at his own joke. "But don't worry, we can shrink the number down pretty fast. There's some code we have to break but I'm borrowing supercomputer time at Columbia. I'll let you know ASAP if I find something."

They thanked the cop. He returned to his awful music and beloved boxes, Sachs to her angry keyboarding and Rhyme to the anemic whiteboards.

His own mobile rang and he gripped the unit, noting that the area code was 242.

Well, this is interesting, he thought and answered the call.

CHAPTER 22

H ELLO, IS THAT YOU, CORPORAL?"

"Yes, Captain, yes," replied Royal Bahamas Police Force officer Mychal Poitier. A faint laugh. "You seem surprised to hear me. You didn't think I would call back."

"No, I didn't."

"It's late. I have called at a bad time, maybe?"

"No, I'm glad you did."

Ringing bells sounded in the distance. Where was Poitier? The hour *was* late, yet Rhyme could hear the murmur of crowds, large crowds.

"When we spoke earlier I wasn't alone. Some of my answers may have seemed odd."

"I was wondering about that."

Poitier said, "You may have gathered that there was some disinclination to cooperate." He paused as if wondering whether or not this was actually a word.

"I did gather that."

A blast of music like a calliope, the classic circus theme, swelled.

Poitier continued, "And you were perhaps curious why a young officer like me was put in charge of what would seem to be a very important case when I'd never run a homicide before."

"Are you young?" Rhyme asked.

"I am twenty-six."

Young under some circumstances, not so young under others. But for homicide work, yes, he was a rookie.

Now a loud noise, a clanging, filled the air around Poitier.

The corporal continued, "I'm not in the office."

"I gathered that too." Rhyme laughed. "You're on the street?"

"No, no, I have a job in the evenings. Security at a casino in a resort on Paradise Island. Near the famous Atlantis. You know it?"

Rhyme didn't know. He had never been to a beach resort in his life.

Poitier asked, "Do your police officers have second jobs too?"

"Yes, some of them do. It's hard to make a good living in policing."

"Yes, yes, that is true. I didn't want to come in to work, though. I would rather have stayed on the missing student case but I need the money...Now,

I don't have much time. I bought a phone card, ten minutes. Let me explain about the Moreno case and my involvement. You see, I have been on the waiting list to move to our Central Detective Unit for some time. It's always been my goal to be a detective. Well, last week a supervisor told me that I had been selected for a junior position at CDU. And, far more surprising, that I would be given a case to supervise—the Moreno homicide. I had believed it would be a year or more before I would even be considered for the unit. And to be given a case myself? That was unthinkable. But I was, naturally, delighted.

"Then I was told I'd been selected because the case was merely administrative at that point. A cartel was behind the death—as I told you before. Probably from Señor Moreno's home country of Venezuela. Certainly the sniper had already left the country, returned to Caracas. I was to gather the evidence, take some statements at the inn where Señor Moreno died and send the file to the Venezuelan national police. I would be the liaison if they wished to come to Nassau to investigate further. Then I was to assist some senior detectives running the case of the other murder I mentioned."

The prominent lawyer.

More clanging, shouting. What was it, a slot machine payoff?

There was a pause and then Poitier called to someone nearby. "No, no, they're drunk. Just watch them. I'm busy. I must make this call. Escort them out if they get belligerent. Call Big Samuel."

Back to Rhyme: "You are suspecting conspiracy at the top, dark intrigues, to quash the Moreno investigation. In a way, yes. First, we must ask, why would the cartels want to kill him? Señor Moreno was well liked in Latin America. The cartels are businessmen first. They would not want to alienate the people they need for workers and mules by killing a popular activist. My impression—from some research I have done—is that the cartels and Moreno tolerated each other."

Rhyme told him, "Like I told you, we feel the same."

The corporal paused. "Señor Moreno was very outspoken against America. And his Local Empowerment Movement, with its anti-U.S. bias, was growing in popularity. You know that?"

"Yes, I do."

"And he had connections with organizations that had terrorist leanings. This is no surprise either, I'm sure."

"We're aware of that, as well."

"Now, it occurred to me that perhaps—" His voice lowered. "—your government wished this man dead."

Rhyme realized he'd been selling the corporal short.

"And so you see the situation my superiors—in fact the entire Ministry of National Security and our Parliament—found themselves in." Nearly whispering now. "What if our investigation shows that this was true? The CIA or the Pentagon sent a sniper down here to shoot Señor Moreno? And what if a police investigation finds that man and identifies the organization he works for. The implications could be great. In retaliation for that embarrassing revelation, there might be decisions made in the U.S. to change the immigration policy regarding the Bahamas. Or to change Customs' policy. That would be very hard for us. The economy is not good here. We *need* Americans. We *need* the families who come here so their children can play with the dolphins and grandmother can do aerobics in the pool and husband and wife slip back to the room for their first romance in months. We can't lose our tourists. Absolutely. And that means we can't ruffle the feathers of Washington."

"Do you think there would be that retribution if you conducted a more rigorous investigation?"

"It's a reasonable explanation for the otherwise inexplicable fact that the lead investigator in the Moreno case—that is, myself—was, only two weeks ago, making certain proper fire exits existed in new buildings and that Jet Ski rental companies had paid all their fees on time."

Poitier's voice rose in volume and there was some steel in it. "But I have to tell you, Captain: I may have been assigned to Business Inspections and Licensing but there wasn't a single inspection or license I handled that was not completed in a timely, thorough and honest manner."

"I don't doubt it, Corporal."

"So it is troublesome for me to be given this case and yet not be given this case, if you understand my meaning."

Silence, broken by a slot machine clattering loudly into Rhyme's ear.

When the noise stopped, Mychal Poitier whispered, "The Moreno case is in dry dock here, Captain. But I assume yours is steaming ahead."

"Correct."

"And you are, I assume, pursuing a conspiracy charge."

Selling him short indeed. "That's right."

"I looked for that name, Don Bruns. You said it was a cover."

"Yes."

"There was nothing in any of our records here. Customs, Passport Control, hotel registers. He could easily have slipped onto the island, though, unseen. It's not difficult. But there are two things that might help you. I will say I didn't neglect the case entirely. I interviewed witnesses, as I said. A desk clerk at the South Cove Inn told me that someone called the front desk two days before Robert Moreno arrived to confirm his reservation. A male caller, an American accent. But the clerk thought this was odd because Moreno's guard had called just an hour or so before, also to check on the reservation. Who was the second caller—the one in or from America—and why was he so interested in Moreno's arrival?"

"Did you get the number?"

"I was told it was an American area code. But the full number was not available. Or, to be frank, I was told not to dig further to find the number. Now, the second thing is that the day before the shooting, someone was at the inn, asking questions. This man spoke to a maid about the suite where Señor Moreno was staying, if there were groundskeepers regularly outside, did the suite have curtains, where did his guard stay, about the men's comings and goings. I'm assuming this was the man who called, but I don't know, of course."

"Did you get a description?"

"Male, Caucasian, mid-thirty years of age, short-cut hair, light brown. American accent too. Thin but athletic, the maid said. She said too he seemed military."

"That's our man. First, he called to make sure Moreno was still arriving. Then he showed up the day before the shooting to check out the target zone. Any car? Other details?"

"No, I'm afraid not."

Beep.

Rhyme heard the sound over the line and he thought: Shit, NIOS's tapping us.

But Poitier said, "I only have a few minutes left. That's the tone warning me the time on my card is expiring."

"I'll call you back—"

"I must go anyway. I hope this—"

Rhyme said urgently, "Please, wait. Tell me about the crime scene. I asked you earlier about the bullet."

That's key to the case...

A pause. "The sniper fired three times from a very far distance, more than a mile. Two shots missed and those bullets disintegrated on the concrete wall outside the room. The one that killed Moreno was recovered largely intact."

"One bullet?" Rhyme was confused. "But the other victims?"

"Oh, they were not shot. The round was very powerful. It hit the windows and showered every-

one with glass. The guard and the reporter interviewing Moreno were badly cut and bled to death
before they got to the hospital."

The million-dollar bullet.

"And the brass? The cartridges?"

"I asked a crime scene team to go search where
the sniper had to shoot from. But…" His voice
dimmed. "I was, of course, very junior and they
told me they didn't want to bother."

"They didn't want to bother?"

"The area was rugged, they said, a rocky shore-
line that would be hard to search. I protested but by
then the decision had been made not to pursue the
case."

"You yourself can search it, Corporal. I can tell
you how to find the place he shot from," Rhyme
said.

"Well, the case is suspended, as I said."

Beep.

"There are simple things to look for. Snipers
leave a great deal of trace, however careful they
are. It won't take much time."

Beep, beep…

"I'm not able to, Captain. The missing student
still hasn't been found—"

Rhyme blurted: "All right, Corporal, but
please—at least send me the report, photos, the
autopsy results. And if I could get the victims'

clothing. Shoes particularly. And…the bullet. I really want that bullet. We'll be very diligent about the chain of custody."

A pause. "Ah, Captain, no, I'm sorry. I have to go."

Beep, beep, beep…

The last that Rhyme heard before the line went silent was the urgent hoot of a slot machine and a very drunken tourist saying, "Great, great. You realize it just cost you two hundred bucks to win thirty-nine fucking dollars."

CHAPTER 23

THAT NIGHT RHYME AND SACHS lay in his SunTec bed, fully reclined.

She had assured him that the bed was indescribably comfortable, an assessment for which he would have to take her word, since his only sensation was the smooth pillowcase. Which in fact was quite luxurious.

"Look," she whispered.

Immediately outside the window of Rhyme's second-story bedroom, on the ledge, was a flurry of movement, hard to discern in the dusk.

Then a feather rose and drifted out of sight. Another.

Dinnertime.

Peregrine falcons had lived on this sill, or one of the others outside the town house, ever since Rhyme had been a resident. He was particularly pleased they'd chosen his abode for nesting. As a scientist, he emphatically did not believe in signs or omens or the supernatural, but he saw nothing wrong with the idea of emblems. He viewed the birds metaphorically, thinking in particular of a fact that most people didn't know about them: that when they attack they are essentially immobile. Falling bundles of muscle with legs fixed outward and wings tucked, streamlined. They dive at over two hundred miles per hour and kill prey by impact, not rending or biting.

Immobile, yet predatory.

Another feather floated away as the avian couple bent to their main course. The entrée was what had until recently been a fat, and careless, pigeon. Falcons are generally diurnal and hunt until dusk but in the city they are often nocturnal.

"Yum," said Sachs.

Rhyme laughed.

She moved closer to him and he smelled her hair, the rich scent. A bit of shampoo, floral. Amelia Sachs was not a perfume girl. His right arm rose and he cradled her head closer.

"Are you going to follow up?" she asked. "With Poitier?"

"I'll try. He seemed pretty adamant that he wouldn't help us anymore. But I know he's frustrated he hasn't been allowed to go further."

"What a case this is," she said.

He whispered, "So how does it feel to be repurposed into a granular-level player, Sachs? Are you pivoting to it or not?"

She laughed hard. "And what exactly is that outfit he's working for, Captain Myers: Special Services?"

"*You're* the cop. I thought you'd know."

"Never heard of it."

They fell silent and then, in his shoulder, normal as anyone's, he could feel her stiffen.

"Tell me," he said.

"You know, Rhyme, I'm not feeling any better about this case."

"You're talking about what you said before, to Nance? That you're not sure if Metzger and our sniper are the kinds of perps we want to go after?"

"Exactly."

Rhyme nodded. "I can't disagree, Sachs. I've never questioned an investigation before, in all these years. They haven't been gray. This one's real gray.

"There's one thing, though, to keep in mind, Sachs. About us."

"We're volunteers."

"Yep. We can walk away if we want. Let Myers and Laurel find somebody else."

She was silent and she was motionless, at least according to those places where Rhyme could sense motion.

He continued, "You weren't happy with the case in the first place."

"No, I wasn't. And part of me does want to bail, yeah. There's too much we don't know about the players and what they have in mind, what their motives are."

"My motive queen."

"And when I say players, I mean Nance Laurel and Bill Myers, as much as Metzger and Bruns—or whatever the hell his name is." After a moment: "I have a bad feeling about this one, Rhyme. I know, you don't believe in that. But you were crime scene most of your career. I was street. There *are* hunches."

This sat between them for a minute or two as they both watched the male falcon rise and lift his wings in a minor flourish. They're not large animals but, seen from so close, the preening was regally impressive, as was the bird's momentary but intense gaze into the room. Their eyesight is astonishing; they can spot prey miles away.

Emblems . . .

"You want to keep at it, don't you?" she asked.

He said, "I get what you're saying, Sachs. But for me it's a knot that needs unraveling. I can't let it go. *You* don't need to, though."

There was no delay as she whispered, "No, I'm with you, Rhyme. You and me. It's you and me."

"Good, now I was—"

And his words stopped abruptly because Sachs's mouth covered his and she was kissing him hungrily, almost desperately, flinging blankets back. She rolled on top of him, gripping his head. He felt her fingers on the back of his head, his ears, his cheek, fingers firm one moment, soft the next. Strong again. Stroking his neck, stroking his temple. Rhyme's lips moved from hers to her hair and then a spot behind her ear, then down to her chin and seated on her mouth again. Lingering.

Rhyme had used his newly working arm on the controls of a Bausch + Lomb comparison microscope, with phones, with the computer and with a density gradient device. He had not used it yet for this: drawing Sachs closer, closer, gripping the top of her silk pajama top and smoothly drawing it over her head.

He supposed he could have finessed the buttons, if he'd tried, but urgency dictated otherwise.

III

CHAMELEONS

CHAPTER 24

RHYME WHEELED FROM THE front sitting room of his town house into the marble entryway near the front door.

Dr. Vic Barrington, Rhyme's spinal cord injury specialist, followed him out, and Thom closed the doors to the room and joined them. The idea of physicians' making house calls was from another era, if not a different dimension, but when the essence of the injury makes it far easier to come to the mountain, that's what many of the better doctors did.

But Barrington was untraditional in many ways. His black bag was a Nike backpack and he'd bicycled here from the hospital.

"Appreciate your coming in this early," Rhyme said to the doctor.

The time was six thirty in the morning.

Rhyme liked the man and had decided to give him a pass and resist asking how the "emergency" or the "something" had gone yesterday when he'd had to postpone their appointment. With any other doc he would have grilled.

Barrington had just completed a final set of tests in anticipation of the surgery scheduled for May 26.

"I'll get the blood work in and look over the results but I don't have any indication that anything's changed over the past week. Blood pressure is very good."

This was the nemesis of severely disabled spinal cord patients; an attack of autonomic dysreflexia could spike the pressure in minutes and lead to a stroke and death if a doctor or caregiver didn't react instantly.

"Lung capacity gets better every time I see you and I swear you're stronger than I am."

Barrington was no-bullshit all the way and when Rhyme asked the next question, he knew he'd get an honest response. "What're my odds?"

"Of getting your left arm and hand working again? Close to one hundred percent. Tendon grafts and electrodes're pretty surefire—"

"No, that's not what I mean. I'm talking about surviving the operation or not having some kind of cataclysmic setback."

"Ah, that's a little different. I'll give you ninety percent on that one."

Rhyme considered this. Surgery couldn't do anything about his legs; nothing ever would fix that, at least not for the next five or ten years. But he'd come to believe that with disabilities hands and arms were the key to normal. Nobody pays much attention to people in wheelchairs if they can pick up a knife and fork or shake your hand. When someone has to feed you and wipe your chin, your very presence spreads discomfort like spattered mud.

And those who don't look away give you those fucking sympathetic glances. Poor you, poor you.

Ninety percent...reasonable for getting a major portion of your life back.

"Let's do it," Rhyme said.

"If there's anything that bothers me about the blood work I'll let you know but I don't anticipate that. We'll keep May twenty-sixth on the calendar. You can start rehab a week after that."

Rhyme shook the doctor's hand and then, as he turned toward the front door, the criminalist said, "Oh, one thing. Can I have a drink or two the night before?"

"Lincoln," Thom said. "You want to be in the best shape you can for the surgery."

"I want to be in a good mood too," he muttered.

The doctor appeared thoughtful. "Alcohol isn't recommended forty-eight hours before a procedure like this...But the hard-and-fast rule is nothing in the stomach after midnight the day of the operation. What goes in before that, I'm not too concerned about."

"Thank you, Doctor."

After the man had left, Rhyme wheeled into the lab, where he regarded the whiteboards. Sachs was just finishing writing what Mychal Poitier had told him last night. She was editing, using a thicker marker to present the most recent information.

Rhyme stared at the boards for some time. Then he shouted, "Thom!"

"I'm right here."

"I thought you were in the kitchen."

"Well, I'm not. I'm here. What do you want?"

"I need you to make some phone calls for me."

"I'm happy to," the aide replied. "But I thought you liked making them on your own." He glanced at Rhyme's working arm.

"I like making the calls. I dislike being on hold. And I have a feeling that's what I'd be doing."

Thom added, "And so I'm going to be your surrogate hold-ee."

Rhyme thought for a moment. "That's a good way to put it, though hardly very articulate."

ROBERT MORENO HOMICIDE

Boldface indicates updated information

— Crime Scene 1.
    — Suite 1200, South Cove Inn, New Providence Island, Bahamas (the "Kill Room").
    — May 9.
    — Victim 1: Robert Moreno.
        — COD: **Single gunshot wound to chest.**
        — Supplemental information: Moreno, 38, U.S. citizen, expatriate, living in Venezuela. Vehemently anti-American. Nickname: "the Messenger of Truth." **Planned to "disappear into thin air," May 24. Possibly connected to terrorist incident in Mexico on May 13, reportedly had been searching for someone to "blow them up" on that day.**
        — Spent three days in NYC, April 30–May 2. Purpose?
            — **May 1, used Elite Limousine.**
            — **Driver Tash Farada (regular driver Vlad Nikolov was sick. Trying to locate).**

- **Closed accounts at American
  Independent Bank and Trust,
  prob. other banks too.**
- **Collected woman Lydia, at
  Lexington and 52nd, accom-
  panied him all day.
  Prostitute? Paid her money?
  Canvassing to learn identity.**
- **Reason for anti-U.S. feel-
  ings: best friend killed by
  U.S. troops in Panama inva-
  sion, 1989.**
- **Moreno's last trip to U.S.
  Never would return.**
- **Meeting in Wall Street. Pur-
  pose? Location?**

— Victim 2: Eduardo de la Rua.
  — COD: **Loss of blood. Lacerations
  from flying glass from gunshot.**
  — Supplemental information: Journal-
  ist, interviewing Moreno. Born
  Puerto Rico, living in Argentina.
— Victim 3: Simon Flores.
  — COD: **Loss of blood. Lacerations
  from flying glass from gunshot.**
  — Supplemental information: Moreno's
  bodyguard. Brazilian national, living
  in Venezuela.

— Suspect 1: Shreve Metzger.
  — Director, National Intelligence and Operations Service.
  — Mentally unstable? Anger issues.
  — Manipulated evidence to illegally authorize Special Task Order?
  — Divorced. Law degree, Yale.
— Suspect 2: Sniper.
  — Code name: Don Bruns.
    — Information Services datamining Bruns.
      — **Results negative.**
    — **Possibly individual at South Cove Inn, May 8. Caucasian, male, mid 30s, short cut light brown hair, American accent, thin but athletic. Appears "military." Inquiring re: Moreno.**
    — **Possibly individual with American accent who called South Cove Inn on May 7 to confirm arrival of Moreno. Call was from American area code.**
  — Voiceprint obtained.
  — Crime scene report, autopsy report, other details to come.

- Rumors of drug cartels behind the killings.
  Considered unlikely.
- Crime Scene 2.
    - Sniper nest of Don Bruns, 2000 yards from
      Kill Room, New Providence Island, Ba-
      hamas.
    - May 9.
    - Crime scene report to come.
- Supplemental Investigation.
    - Determine identity of Whistleblower.
        - Unknown subject who leaked the
          Special Task Order.
        - Sent via anonymous email.
        - **Traced through Taiwan to Roma-
          nia to Sweden. Sent from New
          York area on public Wi-Fi, no gov-
          ernment servers used.**
        - **Used an old computer, probably
          from ten years ago, iBook, either
          clamshell model, two tone with
          other bright colors (like green or
          tangerine). Or could be traditional
          model, graphite color, but much
          thicker than today's laptops.**
    - **Individual in light-colored sedan follow-
      ing Det. A. Sachs.**
        - **Make and model not determined.**

CHAPTER 25

S HREVE METZGER RETURNED TO the top floor of the NIOS building from the organization's technical department—the snoops— in the basement.

As he strode through the halls, noting some employees avoid his eyes and make sudden turns into restrooms they undoubtedly didn't need to use, he reflected on what he'd just learned about the investigation from his people, who'd been using some very sophisticated techniques for intelligence gathering—particularly impressive since they were, officially, nonexistent. (NIOS had no jurisdiction within the United States and couldn't tap calls or prowl through email or hack computers. But Metzger had two words for that: back door.)

Observing employees dodge out of harm's way, Metzger found his thoughts wandering. He was hearing voices in his head, no, not that kind of voices, more memories or fragments of them.

Come up with an image of your anger. A symbol. A metaphor.

Sure, Doctor. What do you recommend?

It's not for me to say, Shreve. You pick. Some people pick animals, or bad guys from TV shows or hot coals.

Coals? he'd thought. That did it. He'd hit upon an image for the anger beast within him. He'd recalled an incident when he was an adolescent in upstate New York, before losing the weight. He was standing before an autumn bonfire at his middle school, shyly attentive to the girl beside him. Smoke wafted around them. A beautiful night. He'd moved closer to her on the pretense of avoiding the sting of the smoke. He'd smiled and said hello. She'd said don't get close to the flames; you're so fat you'd catch fire. And she walked away.

A story just made for a shrink. Dr. Fischer had loved it, much more than the tale about the anger going away when he ordered somebody's death.

So "Smoke" it is, uppercase S... Good choice, Shreve.

As he approached his office he noticed Ruth inside, standing over his desk. Normally he would have been upset to see somebody in his private space without permission. But she was allowed here under most circumstances. He'd never had a single temper outburst against her, which wasn't true of most other people he worked with at NIOS.

He'd snapped or even screamed at them and thrown a report or address book occasionally, though most often not directly *at* the object of his fury. But never Ruth. Maybe that was because she worked closely with him. Then he decided that this theory didn't work; Lucinda and Katie and Seth had been close yet he'd lost it with his wife and kids plenty of times and had the divorce decree and the memories of the scared eyes and tears to prove it.

Maybe the reason Ruth had escaped was simply that she had never done anything to make him angry.

But, no, that test didn't work either. Metzger could grow infuriated at people simply by *imagining* they'd offended him, or anticipating that they might. Words still swirled through his mind—a speech he'd prepared if a cop had stopped him en route to the office after Katie's soccer game on Sunday night.

You fucking blue-collar civil servant... Here's my federal government ID. This is a national security matter you're keeping me from. You've just lost your job, my friend...

Ruth nodded at a file, which apparently she'd just put down on his desk. "Some documents from Washington," she reported. "Your eyes only."

Questions about Moreno, of course, and how we

fucked up. Goddamn, those pricks were fast, those fucking bureaucratic sharks. In Washington, how easy it was to sit in a cold dark office and speculate and pontificate.

The Wizard and his cronies had no clue what life was like on the front lines.

A breath.

The anger slowly, slowly went away.

"Thanks." He took the documents, decorated with a stark red stripe. Much like the unaccompanied minor envelope containing the forms he'd had to prepare when he'd put Seth on a plane to go to camp in Massachusetts. "You won't be homesick," Metzger had reassured the ten-year-old, who was looking around with uneasy eyes. But then he noticed that, contrary to *this* worry, the boy seemed somber because he was still in his father's presence. Once released into the company of the flight attendant the kid grew animated, happy.

Anything to be away from his time bomb of a parent.

Metzger ripped open the envelope, lifted his glasses from his breast pocket.

He laughed. He'd been wrong. The information was simply intelligence assessments for some potential STO tasks in the future. That's another thing the Smoke did. You made assumptions.

He scanned the pages, pleased that the intelligence was about the al-Barani Rashid mission, next prioritized in the queue after Moreno.

God, he wanted Rashid. Wanted him so badly.

He set the reports down and glanced at Ruth. He asked, "You have the appointment this afternoon, right?"

"That's right."

"I'm sure it'll go fine."

"I'm sure it will too."

Ruth sat at her desk, which was decorated with pictures of her family—her two teen daughters and her second husband. Her first spouse died in the initial Gulf War. Her present one had been a soldier too, wounded and confined to a less-than-pleasant VA hospital for months.

The sacrifice people make for this country and how little they're appreciated for it...

The Wizard should talk to her, learn what she'd given up for this country—the life of one husband, the health of another.

Metzger sat and read the assessment but found he wasn't able to concentrate. The Moreno matter roiled.

I've made calls. Don Bruns knows about the case, of course. A few others. We're...handling things...

The efforts were completely illegal, of course, but they were also proceeding well. The Smoke dissipated a bit more. He asked Ruth to summon Spencer Boston. He then read encrypted texts regarding the efforts to derail the investigation.

Boston arrived a few minutes later. He was wearing a suit and tie, as he always did. It was as if the old-school intelligence community had a dress code. The distinguished man instinctively swung the door shut. Metzger saw Ruth's eyes gazing into the office for a moment before the heavy oak panel closed with a snap.

"What do you have?" Metzger asked.

Spencer Boston sat, removed a fleck of lint from his slacks that turned out to be a pill of cloth. He stopped pulling before a run appeared. Boston didn't seem to have had much sleep, which, for someone in his sixties, made him seem haggard. And what the hell do *I* look like? Metzger wondered, brushing his chin to see if he'd remembered to shave. He had.

Despite Metzger's reputation, Boston never hesitated to give him bad news. Running assets in Central America gives you a fortitude that won't be scuffed by a younger bureaucrat, however ill-tempered. He said evenly, "Nothing, Shreve. Nothing. I've checked every log-in for the kill order files. And all the outgoing email and FTP and upload servers, had our IT security people see if they could find anything. And the security folks at Homestead. Nobody downloaded it except those on the list. That means somebody probably snagged it off a desk here, Washington or in Florida, smuggled it out and copied it or scanned it at home or a Kinko's."

At NIOS and its affiliated organizations, all photocopying and logging on were automatically recorded.

"Kinko's. Jesus."

The administrations director continued, "And I went back and looked over the vetting assessments here. Not a hint that anybody'd have a problem with STO missions. Hell, most of our people knew what we were up to before they joined."

NIOS was created after 9/11 largely for the purpose of targeted remedies, along with other extreme operational activities, like kidnappings, bribery and other dirty tricks. Most of the office's specialists had a history of military service and had taken lives in the course of their careers before joining NIOS. It seemed inconceivable that any of them would have a change of heart and try to bring down his operation. As for the other staff, Boston was right, most applicants knew what the organization was up to before they signed on.

Unless, of course, that was why they joined in the first place. Moles. Despicable.

Metzger: "We'll have to keep looking. And for

God's sake, there can't be any *more* leaks. *He* already knows too much."

Wizardly.

Boston's white eyebrows furrowed. He whispered, "They're not... This isn't going to knock us out, is it?"

Metzger was painfully aware that he didn't have a clue what Washington was thinking, since he hadn't heard a word from the man after the initial phone call.

It turns out some Intelligence Committee budget discussions have come up. Suddenly. Can't understand why ...

"Jesus, Shreve. They *can't*. We're the best ones suited for this kind of work."

True. But apparently not the best suited for keeping this kind of work secret.

Which Metzger didn't say.

Boston asked, "What more do you know about the investigation, the police?"

Now Metzger grew cautious. He said, "Not much. Still circling the wagons. Just to be safe." And glanced at his magic phone, the red one, which happened to contain an acid capsule that would melt the drive in a matter of seconds. The screen reported no messages.

He exhaled. "Fact is, I don't think it's moving very quickly. I got the names of the investigators and've checked them out. The cops're using a skeleton crew to stay under the radar, not standard NYPD. Keeping it quiet. It's really just Nance Laurel, the prosecutor, and two others and some support staff. The main cop's a detective named Amelia Sachs and, get this, the other guy is a consultant, Lincoln Rhyme. Retired from the force a while ago. They're operating out of his apartment on the Upper West Side. A private residence, not police headquarters."

"Rhyme, wait. I've heard of him," Boston said, frowning. "He's famous. I saw a show on him. He's the best forensic scientist in the country."

Metzger knew this, of course. Rhyme was the "other" investigator gunning for him, the intel memo had reported yesterday. "I know. But he's a quadriplegic."

"What does that matter?"

"Spencer, where's the crime scene?"

"Oh, sure. The Bahamas."

"What's he going to do, roll around in the sand looking for shell casings and tire prints?"

CHAPTER 26

S O, THIS IS THE CARIBBEAN."

His hand on the joystick of his candy-apple-red wheelchair, Lincoln Rhyme steered out a door at Lynden Pindling Airport in Nassau into an atmosphere hotter and more dank than he could recall experiencing in years.

"Takes your breath away," he called. "But I like it."

"Slow down, Lincoln," Thom said.

But Rhyme would have none of that. He was a child on Christmas morning. Here he was in a foreign country for the first time in many years. He was excited at the prospect of the trip itself. But also at what it might yield: hard, physical evidence in the Moreno case. He'd decided to come down here because of something he was nearly ashamed to admit: intuition, that fishy crap that Amelia Sachs was always going on and on about. He had a feeling that the only way he was going to get that million-dollar bullet and the rest of the evidence was to wheel right up to Corporal Mychal Poitier and ask him for it. In person.

Rhyme knew the officer was genuinely troubled by the death of Robert Moreno and troubled too that he was a pawn being used by his superiors to marginalize the case.

There wasn't a single inspection or license I handled that was not completed in a timely, thorough and honest manner . . .

He didn't think it would take much to convince the corporal to help them.

And so Thom had thrown himself upon the sword of airline and hotel reservation telephone hold, listening to bad music—the aide announced several times—to arrange the flight and motel, an assignment made complicated by Rhyme's condition.

But not as complicated as they'd thought.

Certainly some issues had to be contended with when traveling as a quad—special wheelchairs to the seat, particular pillows, concerns about the Storm Arrow in storage, the practical matters of the piss and shit details that might have to be attended to on the flight.

In the end, though, the journey wasn't bad. We're all disabled in the eyes of the Transportation

Security Administration, all immobile, all objects, all baggage to be shuffled about at whim. Lincoln actually felt that he was better off than most of his fellow travelers, who were used to being mobile and independent.

Outside the baggage claim area, on the ground floor of the airport, Rhyme motored to the edge of the sidewalk filled with tourists and locals bustling for cars and taxis and mini vans. He looked at a small garden of plants, some of whose varieties he'd never seen. He had no interest in horticulture for aesthetics but he found flora extremely helpful in crime scene work.

He'd also heard the rum was particularly good in the Bahamas.

Returning to where Thom was standing, making a phone call, Rhyme phoned Sachs and left a message. "Made it okay. I..." He turned, hearing a caterwauling screech behind him. "Christ, scared the hell out of me. There's a parrot here. He's talking!"

The cage had been placed there by a local tourist commission. Inside was an Abaco Bahamian parrot, according to the sign. The noisy bird, gray with a flourish of green on the tail, was saying, "Hello! Hi! *¡Hola!*" Rhyme recorded some of the greeting for Sachs.

Another breath of the dank, salty air, tinged with

a sour aroma, what he realized was smoke. What was burning? No one else seemed alarmed.

"Got the bags," came a voice from behind them.

NYPD patrolman Ron Pulaski—young, blond, thin—was wheeling the suitcases on a cart. The trio didn't expect to be here long but the nature of Rhyme's condition was such that he required accessories. A lot of them. Medicines, catheters, tubes, disinfectants, air pillows to prevent the sores that could lead to infections.

"What's that?" Rhyme asked as Thom retrieved a small backpack from one bag and slung it on the back of the wheelchair.

"It's a portable respirator," Pulaski answered.

Thom added, "Battery-powered. Double oxygen tank. It'll last for a couple of hours."

"What the hell did you bring that for?"

"Flying with cabin pressure at seven thousand feet," the aide replied as if the answer were obvious. "Stress. There're a dozen reasons it can't hurt to have one with us."

"Do I look stressed?" Rhyme asked petulantly. He had weaned himself off the ventilator years ago, to breathe on his own, one of the proudest achievements possible for a quad. But Thom had apparently forgotten—or disregarded—that accomplishment. "I don't need it."

"Let's hope you don't. But what can it hurt?"

Rhyme had no answer to that. He glanced at Pulaski. "And it's not a respirator, by the way. Respiration is the exchange of oxygen and carbon dioxide. Ventilation is the introduction of gas into the lungs. Hence, it's a *ventilator*."

Pulaski sighed. "Got it, Lincoln."

At least the rookie had stopped his irritating habit of calling Rhyme "sir" or "captain."

The young officer then asked, "Does it matter?"

"Of course, it matters," he snapped. "Precision is the key to everything. Where's the van?"

Another of Thom's tasks was getting a disabled-accessible vehicle in the Bahamas.

Still on the phone, he glanced at Rhyme, grimacing. "I'm on hold again."

The aide finally made contact with somebody and several minutes later the van was pulling up to the curb near the resort mini bus waiting area. The white Ford was battered and stank of old cigarette smoke. The windows greasy. Pulaski loaded the luggage into the back while Thom signed forms and handed them to the lean, dark-skinned man who'd delivered the vehicle. Credit cards and a certain amount of cash were exchanged and the driver disappeared on foot. Rhyme wondered if the van had been stolen. Then decided that this was unfair.

You're in a different world, not Manhattan anymore. Keep an open mind.

With Thom at the wheel, they drove along the main highway toward Nassau, a two-lane road in good repair. Traffic from the airport was heavy, mostly older American cars and imports from Japan, beat-up trucks, mini vans. Hardly any SUVs, not surprising in a land of expensive gas and no ice, snow or mountains. Curiously, though the driving here was left-sided—the Bahamas was a former British colony—most of the cars had left-hand drive, American-style.

As they poked along east, Rhyme noted along the roadside small businesses without signage to indicate what their products or services were, many unkempt plots of land, vendors selling fruits and vegetables out of the backs of their cars; they seemed uninterested in making sales. The van passed some large, rambling homes behind gates, mostly older construction. A number of smaller houses and shacks seemed abandoned, victims of hurricanes, he guessed. Nearly all the locals had very dark skin. Most of the men were dressed in T-shirts or short-sleeved shirts, untucked, and jeans or slacks or shorts. Women wore similar outfits too but many were in plain dresses of floral patterns or bright solid colors.

"Well," Thom exclaimed breathlessly, braking hard and managing to avoid the goat while not capsizing their belongings.

"Look at that," Pulaski said. And captured the animal on his cell phone camera.

Thom obeyed the GPS god and before they came to downtown Nassau itself they turned off the main road, away from dense traffic. They drove past the limestone walls of an old fort. In five minutes the aide pulled the van, rocking on a bad suspension, into the parking lot of a modest but well-kept-up motel. He and Pulaski handed off the luggage to a bellman and the aide went to the front desk to check in and examine the accessible aspects of the motel. He returned to report they were acceptable.

"Part of Fort Charlotte," Pulaski said, reading a sign beside a path that led from the motel to the fort.

"What?" Rhyme asked.

"Fort Charlotte. After it was built, nobody ever attacked the Bahamas. Well, never attacked New Providence Island. That's where we are."

"Ah," Rhyme offered, without interest.

"Look at this," Pulaski said, pointing to a lizard standing motionless on the wall next to the front door of the place.

Rhyme said, "A green anolc, an American chameleon. She's gravid."

"She's what?"

"Pregnant. Obviously."

"That's what 'gravid' means?" the young officer asked.

"The technical definition is 'distended with eggs.' *Ergo*, pregnant."

Pulaski laughed. "You're joking."

Rhyme growled, "Joking? What would be funny about an expectant lizard?"

"No. I mean, how'd you know that?"

"Because I was coming to an area I'm not familiar with, and what's in chapter one of my forensics book, rookie?"

"The rule that you have to know the geography when you run a crime scene."

"I needed to learn the basic information about geology and flora and fauna that might help me here. The fact that nobody invaded after Fort Charlotte was built is pointless to me, so I didn't bother to learn that. Lizards and parrots and Kalik beer and mangroves *might* be relevant. So I read up on them on the flight. What were *you* reading?"

"Uhm, *People*."

Rhyme scoffed.

The lizard blinked and twisted its head but otherwise remained motionless.

Rhyme removed his mobile phone from his shirt pocket. The prior surgery, on his right arm and hand, had been quite successful. The movements were slightly off, compared with those of a non-disabled limb, but they were smooth enough so that an onlooker might not notice they weren't quite natural. His cell was an iPhone and he'd spent hours practicing the esoteric skills of swiping the screen and calling up apps. He'd had his fill of voice-recognition, because of his condition, so he'd put Siri to sleep. He now used the recent calls feature to dial a number with one touch. A richly accented woman's voice said, "Police, do you have an emergency?"

"No, no emergency. Could I speak to Corporal Poitier, please?"

"One moment, sir."

A blessedly short period of hold. "Poitier speaking."

"Corporal?"

"That's right. Who is this, please?"

"Lincoln Rhyme."

Silence for a lengthy moment. "Yes." The single word contained an abundance of uncertainty and ill ease. Casinos were far safer places for conversations than the man's office.

Rhyme continued, "I would have given you my own credit card. Or called you back on my line."

"I couldn't speak any longer. And I'm quite busy now."

"The missing student?"

"Indeed," said the richly inflected baritone.

"Do you have any leads?"

There was a pause. "Not so far. It's been over twenty-four hours. No word at her school or part-time job. She most recently had been seeing a man from Belgium. He appears to be very distraught but..." He let the lingering words fade to smoke. Then he said, "I'm afraid I'm unable to help you in regard to your case."

"Corporal, I'd like to meet with you."

The fattest silence yet. "Meet?"

"Yes."

"Well, how can that be?"

"I'm in Nassau. I'd suggest someplace other than police headquarters. We can meet wherever you like."

"But...I...You're *here*?"

"Away from the office might be better," Rhyme repeated.

"No. That's impossible. I can't meet you."

"I really must talk to you," Rhyme said.

"No. I have to go, Captain." There was a desperation in his voice.

Rhyme said briskly, "Then we'll come to your office."

Poitier repeated, "You're really here?"

"That's right. The case's important. We're taking it seriously."

Rhyme knew this reminder—that the Royal Bahamas Police seemed not to be—was blunt. But he was still convinced that Poitier would help him if he pushed hard enough.

"I'm very busy, as I say."

"Will you see us?"

"No, I can't."

There was a click as the corporal hung up.

Rhyme glanced at the lizard, then turned to Thom and laughed. "Here we are in the Caribbean, surrounded by such beautiful water—let's go make some waves."

CHAPTER 27

ODD. JUST PLAIN ODD.
Dressed in black jeans, navy-blue silk tank top and boots, Amelia Sachs walked into the lab and was struck again at how different this case was.

Any other week-old homicide investigation would find the lab in chaos. Mel Cooper, Pulaski, Rhyme and Sachs would be parsing the evidence, jotting facts and conclusions and speculations on the whiteboards, erasing and writing some more.

Now the sense of urgency was no less—the leaked kill order taped up in front of her reminded that Mr. Rashid, and scores of others, were soon to die—but the room was quiet as a mausoleum.

Bad figure of speech, she decided.

But it was apt. Nance Laurel was not here yet and Rhyme was taking his first trip out of the country since his accident. She smiled. Not many criminalists would go to that kind of trouble to search a crime scene, and she was happy he'd decided to, for all kinds of reasons.

But not having him here was disorienting.

Odd…

She hated this sensation, the chill emptiness.

I have a bad feeling about this one, Rhyme…

She passed one of the long evidence examination tables, on which sat racks of surgical instruments and tools, many of them in sterile wrappers, for analyzing the evidence they didn't have.

At her improvised workstation Sachs sat down and got to work. She called Robert Moreno's regular driver for Elite Limousines, Vladimir Nikolov. She hoped he might know who the mysterious Lydia, possible escort, possible terrorist, might be. But, according to the company, the driver was out of town on a family emergency. She'd left a message at Elite and one on his personal voice mail too.

She'd follow up later if she didn't hear back.

She ran a search for suspected terrorist or criminal activities in the vicinity of where Tash Farada had dropped Moreno and Lydia off on May 1, via the consolidated law enforcement database of state and federal investigations. She discovered a few warrants for premises and surveillance in the area but they related, not surprisingly given the locale, to insider trading and investor fraud at banks and brokerage houses. They were all old cases and she could see no connection whatsoever to Robert A. Moreno.

Then, finally, a break.

Her phone rang and, noting the incoming number, she answered fast. "Rodney?" The cyber-crimes expert, trying to trace the whistleblower.

Chunka, chunka, chunka, chunka...

Rock in the background. Did he *always* listen to music? And why couldn't it be jazz or show tunes?

The volume diminished. Slightly.

Szarnek said, "Amelia, remember: Supercomputers are our friends."

"I'll keep it in mind. What do you have?" Her eyes were on the empty parlor, in which dust motes ambled through a shaft of morning sun like hot-air balloons seen from miles away. Again, she was painfully aware of Rhyme's absence.

"I've got the location where he sent the email from. I won't bore you with nodes and networks but suffice it to say that your whistleblower sent the email and the STO attachment from Java Hut near Mott and Hester. Think about it: A Portland, Oregon, coffee chain setting up shop in the heart of Little Italy. What would the Godfather say?"

She glanced at the header on the copy of the

whistleblower's messages taped to the board. "Is the date on the email accurate? Could he have faked it?"

"No, that's when it was sent. He could write whatever date he wanted in the email itself but routers don't lie."

So their man was in the coffee shop at 1:02 p.m., May 11.

The cybercrimes detective continued, "I've checked. You can log onto Wi-Fi there without any identifying information. All you have to do is agree to the three-page terms of service. Which everybody does and not a single soul in the history of the world has ever read."

Sachs thanked the tech cop and disconnected. She called the coffee shop and got the manager, explaining that she was trying to identify someone who had sent important documents via the Wi-Fi on May 11 and she wanted to come in and talk to him about that. She added, "You have a security camera?"

"We do, yeah. They're in all the Java franchises. In case we get stuck up, you know."

Without expecting much, she asked, "How often docs the video loop?" She was sure new footage would overwrite the old every few hours.

"Oh, we've got a five-terabyte drive. It's got about three weeks of video on it. The quality's pretty crappy and it's black and white. But you can make out a face if you need to."

A ping of excitement. "I'll be there in a half hour."

Sachs pulled on a black linen jacket and rubber-banded her hair back in a ponytail. She took her holstered Glock from the cabinet, checked it as she always did, a matter of routine, and clipped it to her jeans belt. The double-mag holster went on her left hip. She was slinging her large purse over her shoulder when her mobile buzzed. She wondered if the caller was Rhyme. She knew he'd landed safely in the Bahamas but she was concerned that the trip might have taken a toll on his health.

But, no, the caller was Lon Sellitto.

"Hey."

"Amelia. The Special Services canvass team is about halfway through the building where Moreno and the driver picked up Lydia. Nothing yet. They're running into a lot of Lydias—who'da thought? —but none of 'em are the one. You know, how hard is it to name your kid Tiara or Estanzia? They'd be a fuck of a lot easier to track down."

She told him about the lead to the coffee shop and that she was on her way there now.

"Good. A security cam, excellent. Hey, Linc's really down in the Caribbean?"

"Yep, landed safe. I don't know how he's going to be treated. Interloper, you know."

"Bet he can handle it."

There was silence.

Something's up. Lon Sellitto brooded some but it was usually noisy brooding.

"What?" she asked.

"Okay, you didn't hear this."

"Go on."

The senior detective said, "Bill came by my office."

"Bill Myers, the captain?"

So how does it feel to be repurposed into a granular-level player...

"Yeah."

"And?"

Sellitto said, "He asked about you. Wanted to know if you were okay. Physically."

Shit.

"Because I was limping?"

"Maybe, I don't know. Anyway, s'what he said. Listen, a fat old fart like me, you can get away with some bad days, hobbling around. But you're a kid, Amelia. And skinny. He checked your reports and the ten-seventeens. Saw you volunteered for a lot of tactical work, first through the door on the lead teams sometimes. He just asked if you'd had any problems in the field or if anybody'd said they weren't comfortable with you on take-downs or rescues. I told him no, absolutely not. You were prime."

"Thanks, Lon," she whispered. "Is he thinking of ordering a physical?"

"The subject didn't come up. But that doesn't mean no."

To become an NYPD officer an applicant has to take a medical exam but once on the force—unlike firefighters or emergency medical techs—he or she never has to again, unless a supervisor orders one in specific cases or the officers want to earn promotion credit. Aside from that first checkup, years ago, Sachs had never had a department physical. The only record of her arthritis was on file with her private orthopedists. Myers wouldn't have access to that but if he ordered a physical, the extent of her condition would be revealed.

And that would be a disaster.

"Thanks, Lon."

They disconnected and she stood motionless for a moment, reflecting: Why was it that only part of this case seemed to involve worrying about the perps? Just as critical, you had to guard against your allies too, it seemed.

Sachs checked her weapon once more and walked toward the door, defiantly refusing to give in to the nearly overwhelming urge to limp.

CHAPTER 28

AMELIA SACHS HAD A 3G MOBILE PHONE, Jacob Swann had discovered.

And this was good news. Cracking the encryption and listening to her conversations were harder than with phones running GPRS—general packet radio service, or 2G—but, at least, it was feasible because 3G featured good old-fashioned A5/1 voice encryption.

Not that his tech department was allowed to do such a thing, of course.

Yet there must have been a screwup somewhere, because just ten minutes after discussing the matter casually—and, of course, purely theoretically— with the director of Technical Services and Support, Swann found himself enraptured by Sachs's low, and rather sexy, voice, coming to him over the airwaves.

He already had a lot of interesting facts. Some specific to the Moreno investigation. Some more general, though equally helpful: for instance, that this Detective Amelia Sachs had some physical problems. He'd filed that away for future reference.

He'd also learned some troubling information: that the other investigator on the case, Lincoln Rhyme, was in the Bahamas. Now, this was potentially a real problem. Upon learning it, Swann had immediately called contacts down there—a few of the Sands and Kalik drinkers on the dock—and made arrangements.

But he couldn't concentrate on that at the moment. He was occupied. Crouching in an unpleasantly aromatic alleyway, picking the lock of the service door to a Starbucks wannabe. A place called Java Hut. He was wearing thin latex gloves—flesh-colored so that at fast glance his hands would appear unclad.

The morning was warm and the gloves and concealing windbreaker made him warmer yet. He was sweating. Not as bad as with Annette in the Bahamas. But still...

And that god-awful stench. New York City alleys. Couldn't somebody blast them with bleach from time to time?

Finally the lock clicked. Swann cracked the door a bit and looked inside. From here he could see an office, which was empty, a kitchen in which a skinny Latino labored away with dishes and, beyond that, part of the restaurant itself. The place wasn't very crowded and he guessed that since this was a tourist area—what was left of Little Italy— most of the business would be on weekends.

He now slipped inside, eased the door mostly closed and stepped into the office, pulling aside his jacket and making sure his knife was easily accessible.

Ah, there was the computer monitor, showing what the security camera was seeing on the restaurant floor at the moment. The camera scanned slowly back and forth, in hypnotic black and white. He'd have a good image of the leaker, the whistleblower, when he scrolled back to May 11, the date the prick had uploaded the STO kill order to the District Attorney's Office.

He then noticed a switch on the side of the monitor: *1–2–3–4.*

He clicked the last and the screen divided into quadrants.

Oh, hell...

The store had *four* cameras. And one was presently recording Swann himself, crouching down in front of the machine. Only his back was being shot but this in itself was still very troubling.

He quickly studied the computer and was even more troubled to see that dismantling it and stealing the hard drive, as he'd planned, was impossible. The large computer was fixed to the floor with straps of metal and large bolts.

Right, as if somebody would steal a five-year old piece of crap, with Windows XP as the operating system. He equated a machine like this to a plastic Sears hand mixer, versus what he had: a six-hundred-dollar KitchenAid, with a bread kneading hook and fresh pasta maker.

Then Swann froze. He heard voices, a giddy young woman's and then a Latino man's. He reached for the Kai Shun.

Their words faded, though, and the hallway remained empty. He turned back to his task. He tested the bolts and straps. They weren't giving way. And he didn't have the right tools to undo them. Of course he could hardly blame himself for that. He had a basic tool set with him but this would require an electric hacksaw.

A sigh.

The next best thing, he decided, was to make sure that the police didn't get the drive either.

Too bad, it wasn't his first choice, but he had no other options.

Now voices from the front of the restaurant again. He believed a woman was saying, "I'm looking for Jerry, please?"

Could it be? Yes. The tone was familiar.

Good old-fashioned A5/1 voice encryption…

"I'm Jerry. Are you the detective who called?"

"That's right. I'm Amelia Sachs."

She'd gotten here faster than Swann had expected.

Hunching forward to hide what he was doing from the camera, he reached into his backpack and removed an improvised explosive device, an antipersonnel model that would not only destroy the computer but send a hundred bits of jagged shrapnel throughout the back half of the coffee shop. He debated a moment. He could have set the timer for a minute. But Swann decided it would be best to set the detonator for a bit longer. That would give Ms. Sachs enough time to come into the office and start scrolling through the tapes before it blew.

Hitting the arm button and then the trigger, Swann slipped the box behind the computer itself.

He then rose slowly and backed out of the office, careful not to display his face to the camera.

CHAPTER 29

THE AIR IN JAVA HUT WAS RICH with a dozen different scents-- vanilla, chocolate, cinnamon, berry, chamomile, nutmeg... and even coffee.

Jerry, the manager, was a lanky young man with more extensive tats on his arms than a manager for a national franchise coffee shop probably should have. Even one headquartered in Portland He shook her hand firmly, snuck a glance toward her hips. Men often did this—not checking out the body; he wanted a glimpse of her gun.

The dozen people here were all busy—typing on or examining some electronic device or another. A few were reading from paper. Only one, an elderly woman, was sitting quietly, looking out the window and doing nothing but leisurely enjoying a cup of coffee.

Jerry asked, "Would you like something? On the house?"

She declined. She wanted to get to the one lead in the case that had the potential to pay off.

"Just like to check out the security videos."

"Sure," he said, trying for another look at her weapon. She was glad she'd kept the jacket buttoned. She knew he'd want to ask her if she'd used it recently. And talk calibers.

Men. Sex or guns.

"Now, we've got one camera there." He pointed above the cash register. "Everybody who comes in'll get photographed at least once, pretty up close. What did this guy upload? Like insider information?"

"Like that, yes."

"Bankers. Man, don't you just hate 'em? And two other cameras." Pointing.

One was mounted on a side wall and it scanned back and forth slowly like a lawn sprinkler. The tables were arranged perpendicularly to the camera, which meant that while patrons might not be visible head-on, it was likely she would get a clear profile shot of the whistleblower.

Good.

The other camera scanned a small alcove to the left of the main door, with only four tables inside. This too would get good side images of the patrons and was closer to those tables than the first camera was to those in the main room.

"Let's see the video," she said.

"It's in the office. After you." He extended his arm, covered with a multicolored tattoo of some Chinese writing, hundreds of characters long.

Sachs couldn't help but think, What could it possibly say that was worth the pain?

Not to mention how he's going to explain it to his grandkids.

CHAPTER 30

MAN, THE ALLEY ON A WARM AFTER-NOON.

Gross.

New York City alleys had a kind of charm, you looked at it one way: They were sort of like history moved into the present day, like in a museum. The fronts of the apartments and—here in Little Italy—the shops changed every generation but the alleys were pretty much what they would've been a century ago. Decorated with faded metal and wooden signs giving delivery directions and warnings. *Use Chocks for Your WAGON!* The walls, brick and stone, were unpainted, unwashed, shabby. Uneven, improvised doors, loading docks, pipes that led nowhere and wires that you didn't dare touch.

And the air stank.

On hot days like this the kitchen helper hated

taking the trash down to the Dumpster, shared with a couple of other restaurants, because the sushi place next door had dumped their garbage last night. No need to guess what this afternoon's atmosphere was like.

Fish.

Still, one thing he liked about the alley: the building above Java Hut. It had apparently been the home of somebody famous. The waiter Sanchez had told him it was some American writer. Mark Twin, he thought. The helper could read English okay and had told Sanchez he was going to find something that this Twin had written but he never got around to it.

He now made the drop, holding his breath, of course, and then turned back toward his deli. He noticed a car parked in the alley here, close to Java Hut, in fact. A reddish Ford Torino Cobra.

Sweet.

But gonna get towed.

The kitchen helper realized he was holding his breath still. He exhaled and then inhaled, wrinkling his nose. The smell actually stung.

Old fish. Warm fish.

He wondered if he was going to puke. But he headed to the car to check it out. He liked cars. His brother-in-law had been arrested for stealing a very nice BMW M3, one of the new ones. That took some doing. Anybody could steal an Accord. But only a man with balls could boost an M3. Not necessarily brains, however. Ramon was arrested exactly two hours and twenty minutes later. But you had to give him credit.

Oh, hey, check it out! This one had an NYPD placard on the dash. What kinda cop'd drive a car like this? Maybe—

At that moment a ball of flame and smoke erupted from the back door of Java Hut and the helper found himself flying backward. He tumbled into a stack of cardboard cartons outside the back of the Hair Cuttery. The helper rolled off the boxes and lay stunned on the oily, wet cobbles.

Jesus...

Smoke and fire flowed from the coffee shop.

The helper unholstered his mobile and forcibly pinched tears away.

He squinted to make out the keypad. But then he realized what would happen if he called, even anonymously.

Sir, what's your name, address, phone number and by the way do you have a driver's license or passport?

Or maybe a birth certificate? A green card?

Sir, we have your mobile number here...

He put the phone away.

Didn't matter anyway, he decided. Other people

would have called by now. Besides, the explosion was so strong, there was no doubt there'd be no survivors inside and Mr. Mark Twin's town house would be a pile of smoldering rubble in a matter of minutes.

CHAPTER 31

THE VAN DROVE ALONG BAY STREET, then through downtown Nassau, past wood-clad stores and residences painted soft pink, yellow and green, the shades of the mint candy disks Lincoln Rhyme remembered from the Christmases of his youth.

The city was mostly flat; what dominated the skyline were the ocean liners, docked or easing through the water to their left. Rhyme had never seen one up close. They were massive, soaring hundreds of feet into the air. Downtown was clean and ordered, much more so than the areas around the airport. Unlike in New York City, trees were everywhere, blossoming heavily, roots buckling sidewalks and streets. This area was a mix of serious business—lawyers and accountants and insurance agents—and stores that sold any object whatsoever that might conceivably separate cruise ship tourists from their money.

Pirate gear was a popular way to do this. Every other child on the sidewalk carried a plastic saber and wore a black skull-and-crossbones hat.

They drove past some houses of government. Parliament Square, Rhyme noted. In front was a statue of seated and sceptered Queen Victoria, gazing off into the distance as if her mind was on more important, or perhaps more troublesome, colonies.

The accessible van fit right in here; much of the transportation was via similar vehicles and mini buses, different only in the absence of a motorized ramp. As earlier, the pace of traffic here was leisurely, irritating. Rhyme decided that this was not lazy driving. There were simply too many wheels on too few streets and roads.

Scooters too. They were everywhere.

"Is this the best route?" he muttered.

"Yes," his aide replied, turning right onto East Street.

"It's taking a longer time than I would have thought."

Thom didn't reply. The area grew scruffier as they headed south. More hurricane damage, more shacks, more goats and chickens.

They passed a sign:

Protect Ya Things!
Use a Rubber EVERYTIME

Rhyme had had to make several calls to find exactly where Mychal Poitier was located—naturally without calling the corporal himself. Nassau had a separate Central Detective Unit, not attached to headquarters. Poitier had implied he was working with the CDU but the receptionist there said that while she believed he was assigned to the unit he wasn't based there. She wasn't sure where his office was.

Finally he'd called the main number and learned Poitier was at the RBPF headquarters on East Street.

When they arrived Rhyme looked around the facility through the spattered glass of the van's windows. Headquarters was a complex of mismatched structures—with the main building modern and light-colored, in the shape of a cross laid flat. Ancillary buildings were scattered randomly around the grounds. One seemed to be a lockup (a nearby side street was named Prison Lane). The grounds were a mix of grass—some patches trim, some shaggy—and parking lots dusted with pebbles and sand.

Functional law enforcement.

They got out of the van. Again, the piquant smell of smoke was in the air. Ah, yes. With a glance at a nearby private residence's backyard, Rhyme realized the source: trash fires. They must be everywhere.

"Look, Lincoln, we need one of those," Pulaski said. He was pointing toward the front of the main building.

"What?" Rhyme snapped. "A building, a radio antenna, a doorknob, a jail?"

"A crest."

The RBPF did have a rather impressive logo, promising the citizens of the islands courage, integrity and loyalty. Where on earth could you find all three of these in one tidy package?

"I'll buy you a T-shirt for a souvenir, rookie." Rhyme motored his way up the sidewalk and brashly into the lobby, an unimpressive place, scuffed and dinged. Ants crawled and flies strafed. There seemed to be no plainclothes cops; everyone was in uniform. Most commonly these were white jackets and black trousers with subdued red stripes on the side; the few women officers wore such jackets and striped skirts. Much of the personnel—who were all black—had headgear, traditional police hats or white sun helmets.

Colonial…

A dozen locals and tourists waited on benches or in line to speak to officers, presumably to report a crime. Mostly they seemed put out, rather than traumatized. Rhyme assumed the bulk of cases here would be pickpocketing, missing passports, groping, stolen cameras and cars.

He was aware of the attention he and his small entourage were drawing. A middle-aged couple, American or Canadian, was in line ahead of him. "No, sir, please, you go first." The wife was speaking as if to a five-year-old. "We insist."

Rhyme resented their condescension and Thom, sensing this, stiffened, probably expecting a tirade, but the criminalist smiled and thanked them. The waves he intended to make would be reserved for the RBPF itself.

A tall man presently at the head of the queue in front of Rhyme had gleaming black skin and wore jeans and an untucked shirt. He was complaining to an attractive and attentive desk officer about a stolen goat.

"It might have walked off," the woman said.

"No, no, the rope was cut. I took a picture. Do you want to see? It was cut with a knife. I have pictures! My neighbor. I know my neighbor did this."

Tool mark evidence could link the cut pattern on the rope to the neighbor's blade. Hemp fibers are particularly adhesive; there would have been some evidentiary transfer. There'd been a recent rain. Footprints surely still existed.

Easy case, Rhyme reflected, smiling to himself. He wished Sachs were here so he could share the story with her.

Goats . . .

The man was persuaded to search a bit longer.

Then Rhyme moved forward. The desk officer rose slightly and peered down at him. He asked for Mychal Poitier.

"Yes, I'll call him You are, please?"

"Lincoln Rhyme."

She placed the call. "Corporal, it's Constable Bethel, at the desk. A Lincoln Rhyme and some other people are here to see you." She stared down at her beige, old-fashioned phone, growing tenser as she listened. "Well, yes, Corporal. He's here, as I was saying... Well, he's right in front of me."

Had Poitier told her to pretend he was out?

Rhyme said, "If he's busy, tell him I'm happy to wait. For as long as necessary."

Her eyes flicked uncertainly to Rhyme's. She said into the phone, "He said..." But apparently Poitier had heard. "Yes, Corporal." She set the receiver down. "He'll be here in a minute."

"Thank you."

They turned away and moved to an unoccupied portion of the waiting room.

"God bless you," said the woman who had given up her space in line for the pathetic figure.

Rhyme felt Thom's hand on his shoulder but, once again, he merely smiled.

Thom and Pulaski sat on a bench beside Rhyme, under dozens of painted and photo portraits of senior commissioners and commanders of the Royal Bahamas Police Force, going back many years. He scanned the gallery. This was like walls of service everywhere: faces unrevealing and, like Queen Victoria's, looking off into the distance, not directly at the painter or camera. Unemotional, yet oh what those eyes would have seen in the collective hundreds of years of duty as law enforcers.

Rhyme was debating how long Poitier was going to stall when a young officer appeared from a hallway and approached the desk. He was in those ubiquitous black slacks, red-striped, and an open-collar, short-sleeved blue shirt. A chain from the top button disappeared into his left breast pocket. A whistle? Rhyme wondered. The dark-skinned man, who was armed with a semiautomatic pistol, was bareheaded and had thick but short-trimmed hair. His round face was not happy.

Constable Bethel pointed Rhyme out to the officer. The young man turned and blinked in stark surprise. Though he tried to stop himself he stared immediately down at the wheelchair and at Rhyme's legs. He blinked again and seemed to swell with discomfort.

Rhyme knew that it was more than his presence upsetting the officer.

Forget murder, forget geopolitics. I have to deal with a *cripple*?

Poitier delayed a moment more, perhaps wondering if he'd been spotted. Could he still escape? Then, composing himself, he broke away reluctantly from the desk and approached them.

"Captain Rhyme, well." He said this with a casual, almost cheerful tone. Identical to the woman tourist's a moment ago. Poitier's hand was half extended as if he didn't want to shake but thought it would be a moral lapse not to make the effort. Rhyme lifted his hand and the officer quickly, very quickly, gripped and let go.

Quadriplegia is not contagious, Rhyme thought sourly.

"Corporal, this is Officer Pulaski with the NYPD. And my caregiver, Thom Reston."

Hands were shaken, this time with less uncertainty. But Poitier looked Thom up and down. Perhaps the concept of "caregiver" was new to him.

The corporal gazed about him and found several fellow officers frozen in different attitudes, like children playing the game of statue, as they stared.

Mychal Poitier's attention returned at once to the wheelchair and Rhyme's insensate legs. The slow movements of the right arm seemed to rivet him the most, though. Finally, Poitier, using all his willpower, forced himself to stare into Rhyme's eyes.

The criminalist found himself at first irritated at this reaction but then he felt a sensation he hadn't experienced for some time: He was ashamed. Actually ashamed of his condition. He'd hoped the sense would morph into anger but it didn't. He felt diminished, weakened.

Poitier's dismayed look had burned him.

Ashamed...

He tried to push aside the prickly feeling and said evenly, "I need to discuss the case with you, Corporal."

Poitier looked around again. "I'm afraid I've told you all I can."

"I want to see the evidence reports. I want to see the crime scene itself."

"That's not practical. The scene is sealed."

"You seal crime scenes from the public, not from forensics officers."

"But you're..." A hesitation; Poitier managed not to look at his legs. "You're not an officer here, Captain Rhyme. Here you are a civilian. I'm sorry."

Pulaski said, "Let us help you with the case."

"My time is very occupied." He was happy to glance toward Pulaski, someone who was on his feet. Someone who was normal. "Occupied," Poitier repeated, turning now to a bulletin board on which was pinned a flyer: The headline was

MISSING. Beneath that stark word was a picture of a smiling blonde, downloaded from Facebook, it seemed.

Rhyme said, "The student you were mentioning."

"Yes. The one you..."

The corporal had been going to add: the one you don't care about. Rhyme was sure of this.

But he'd refrained.

Because, of course, Rhyme wasn't fair game. He was weak. A snide word might shatter him beyond repair.

His face flushed.

Pulaski said, "Corporal, could we just see copies of the evidence report, the autopsies? We could look at them right here. We won't take them off the premises."

Good approach, Rhyme thought.

"I'm afraid that will not be possible, Officer Pulaski." He endured another look at Rhyme.

"Then let us have a fast look at the scene."

Poitier coughed or cleared his throat. "I have to leave it intact, depending on what we hear from the Venezuelan authorities."

Rhyme played along. "And I will make sure the scene remains uncontaminated for them."

"Still, I'm sorry."

"Our case for Moreno's death is different from

yours—you pointed that out the other day. But we still need certain forensics from here."

Otherwise the risk you took in calling me from the casino that night will be wasted. This was the implicit message.

Rhyme was careful not to mention any U.S. security agencies or snipers. If the Bahamians wanted Venezuelan drug runners he wasn't going to interfere with that. But he needed the goddamn evidence.

He glanced at the poster of the missing student.

She was quite attractive, her smile innocent and wide.

The reward for information was only five hundred dollars.

He whispered to Poitier, "You have a firearms tracing unit. I saw the reference on your website. At the very least, can I see their report on the bullet?"

"The unit has yet to get to the matter."

"They're waiting for the Venezuelan authorities."

"That's right."

Rhyme inhaled deeply, trying to remain calm. "Please—"

"Corporal Poitier." A voice cut through the lobby.

A man in a khaki uniform stood in an open doorway, a dim corridor beyond. His dark face—both in complexion and expression—was staring toward the four men beside the wall of service.

"Corporal Poitier," he repeated in a stern voice.

The officer turned. He blinked. "Yes, sir."

A pause. "When you have finished your business there, I need your presence in my office."

Rhyme deduced: The stern man would be the RBPF's version of Captain Bill Myers.

"Yes, sir."

The young officer turned back, shaken. "That's Assistant Commissioner McPherson. He is in charge of all of New Providence. Come, you must leave now. I will see you to your car."

As he escorted them out, Poitier paused awkwardly to open the door for Rhyme and, once again, avoided looking at the disturbing sight of a man immobile.

Rhyme motored outside. Thom and Pulaski were in the rear. They headed back to the van.

Poitier whispered, "Captain, I went to a great risk to give you the information I did—about the phone call, about the man at the South Cove Inn. I had hoped you'd follow up on it in the United States. Not here."

"And I appreciate what you told me. But it wasn't enough. We need the evidence."

"That's not possible. I asked you not to come.

I'm sorry. I can't help." The slim young officer looked away, back toward the front lobby door, as if his boss was still observing. Poitier was furious, Rhyme could see. He wanted to rage. But the officer's only reaction was a figurative pat on the head.

God bless you...

"There is nothing for you here, sir. Enjoy a day or two, some restaurants. I don't imagine you get out..." He braked his words to a halt. Then changed tack. "You are probably so busy at your job you don't get a chance to enjoy yourself. There are some good restaurants down by the docks. For the tourists."

Where the facilities are disabled-accessible because of the elderly passengers from the cruise ships.

Rhyme persisted, "I offered to meet you elsewhere. But you declined."

"I didn't think you would actually come."

Rhyme stopped. He said to Thom and Pulaski. "I'd like a word with the corporal in private."

The two men wandered back toward the van.

Poitier's eyes swept the criminalist's legs and body once more. He began, "I wish—"

"Corporal," Rhyme spat out, "don't play these fucking games with me." The shame had finally solidified into the ice of anger.

The officer blinked in shock.

"You gave me a couple of leads that don't mean shit without the forensics to back them up. They're useless. You might as well've saved your god-damn phone card money."

"I was trying to help you," he said evenly.

"You were trying to purge your guilt."

"My—?"

"You didn't call me up to help the case. You called me so you could feel better about doing a lousy job as a cop. Hand off some useless tidbits to me and you go back to quote waiting for the Venezuelan authorities like you'd been told."

"You don't understand," Poitier fired back, his own anger freed as well. Sweat covered his face and his eyes were focused and fierce. "You make your salary in America—ten times what we make here—and if that doesn't work you go take another job and make just as much money or more. We don't have those options, Captain. I've already risked too much. I tell you in confidence certain things and then..." He was sputtering. "And then here you are. And now my commissioner knows! I have a wife and two children I am supporting. I love them very much. What right do you have to put my job at stake?"

Rhyme spat out, "Your job? Your job is to find out what happened on May ninth at the South Cove

Inn, who fired that bullet, who took a human life in your jurisdiction. *That's* your job, not hiding behind your superior's fairy tales."

"You do not understand! I—"

"I understand that if you claim you want to be a cop, then be one. If not, go back to Inspections and Licensing, Corporal."

Rhyme spun around and aimed toward the van, where Pulaski and Thom were staring his way with troubled, confused faces. He noticed too a man in one of the nearby windows, peering their way. Rhyme was sure it was the assistant commissioner.

CHAPTER 32

AFTER LEAVING THE RBPF HEADQUAR-
TERS, Thom steered the van north and west
through the narrow, poorly paved streets
of Nassau.

"Okay, rookie, you've got a job. I need you to do
some canvassing at the South Cove Inn."

"We're not leaving?"

"Of course we're not leaving. Do you want your
assignment or do you want to keep interrupting?"
Without waiting for an answer, Rhyme reminded
the young officer about the information that Corporal Poitier had provided via phone the other
night in New York: the call from an American inquiring about Moreno's reservation, and the man at
the hotel the day before the shooting asking a maid
about Moreno—Don Bruns, their talented sniper.

"Thirties, American, athletic, small build, short
brown hair." Pulaski had remembered this from
the chart.

"Good. Now, I can't go myself," the criminalist said. "I'd make too much of a stir. We'll park in the lot and wait for you. Walk up to the main desk, flash your badge and find out what the number was of the person who called from America and anything else about the guy asking about Moreno. *Don't* explain too much. Just say you're a police officer looking into the incident."

"I'll say I just came from RBPF headquarters."

"Hm. I like that. Suitably authoritarian and yet vague at the same time. If you get the number—*when* you get the number—we'll call Rodney Szarnek and have him talk to the cell or landline provider. You clear on all of that?"

"You bet, Lincoln."

"What does that mean, 'You bet'?"

"I'll do it," he said.

"Mouth filler, expressions like that." He was still hurt and angry about what he considered Poitier's betrayal—which was only partly his refusal to help.

As they bobbed along the streets of Nassau an idea occurred to Rhyme. "And when you're at the inn, see if Eduardo de la Rua, the reporter who died, left anything there. Luggage, notebook, computer. And do what you can to get your hands on it."

"How?"

"I don't know. I don't care. I want any notes or recordings that de la Rua made. The police haven't been very diligent about collecting evidence. Maybe there's still something at the inn."

"Maybe he recorded Moreno talking about somebody surveilling him."

"That," Rhyme said acerbically, "or somebody *conducting* surveillance, since what you said may be correct but is a shameless example of verbing a perfectly fine noun." And he couldn't resist a smile at his own irony.

Pulaski sighed. Thom smiled.

The young officer thought for a moment. "De la Rua was a reporter. What about his camera? Maybe he took some pictures in the room or on the grounds before the shooting."

"Didn't think of that. Good. Yes. Maybe he got some pictures of a surveiller." Then he grew angry again. "The Venezuelan authorities. Bullshit."

Rhyme's mobile buzzed. He looked at the caller ID.

Well, what's this?

He hit answer. "Corporal?"

Had Poitier been fired? Had he called to apologize for losing his temper, while reiterating that there was nothing he could do to help?

The officer's voice was a low, angry whisper: "I eat a late lunch every day."

"Excuse me?"

"Because of my shift," Poitier continued harshly. "I eat lunch at three p.m. And do you wish to know *where* I eat lunch?"

"Do I...?"

"It's a simple question, Captain Rhyme!" the corporal snapped. "Do you wish to know where I eat my lunch every day?"

"I do, yes," was all that Rhyme could muster, thoroughly confused.

"I have lunch at Hurricane's on Baillou Hill Road. Near West Street. *That* is where I have lunch!"

The line went silent. There was no sound other than a soft click but Rhyme imagined the corporal had angrily slammed his thumb onto the disconnect button.

"Well." He told the others about the exchange. "Sounds like he might be willing to help us out after all."

Pulaski said, "Or he's going to arrest us."

Rhyme started to protest but decided the young officer had a point. He said, "In case you're right, rookie, change of plans. Thom and I are going to have lunch and/or get arrested. Possibly both. *You're* going to canvass at the South Cove Inn. We'll rent you a car. Thom, didn't we pass a rental place somewhere?"

"Avis. Do you want me to go there?"

"Obviously. I wasn't asking for curiosity's sake."

"Don't you get tired of being in a good mood all the time, Lincoln?"

"Rental car. Please. Now."

Rhyme noticed that he'd had a call from Lon Sellitto. He'd missed it in the "discussion" he'd had with Poitier. There was no message. Rhyme called him back but voice mail replied. He left a phone-tag message and slipped the mobile away.

Thom found the Avis office via GPS and steered in that direction. Just a few minutes later, though, he said uncertainly, "Lincoln."

"What?"

"Somebody's following us. I'm sure of it."

"Don't look back, rookie!" Rhyme didn't spend much time in the field any longer, for obvious reasons, but when he'd been active he had frequently worked "hot" crime scenes—those where the perp might still be lingering, for the purposes of learning which cops were on the case and what leads they were finding, or sometimes even trying to kill the officers right then. The instincts he'd honed over the years of working scenes like that were still active. And rule one was don't let anybody know you're on to them.

Thom continued, "A car was oncoming but as

soon as we passed, it made a U. I didn't think much of it at first but we've been taking a pretty winding path and it's still there."

"Describe it."

"Gold Mercury, black vinyl top. Ten years or older, I'd guess."

The age of many cars here.

The aide glanced in the mirror. "Two, no, three people inside. Black males. Late twenties or thirties. T-shirts, one gray, one green, short-sleeved. One sleeveless yellow. Can't make out their faces."

"You sound just like a patrol officer, Thom." Rhyme shrugged. "Just police keeping an eye on us. That commissioner—McPherson—isn't very happy we strangers've come to town."

Thom squinted into the rearview mirror. "I don't think they're cops, Lincoln."

"Why not?"

"The driver's got earrings and the guy next to him's in dreads."

"Undercover."

"And they're passing a joint back and forth."

"Okay. Probably not."

CHAPTER 33

FEW THINGS ARE MORE REPULSIVE than the chemical smoke aftermath of an IED plastic explosive detonation.

Amelia Sachs could smell it, taste it. She shivered from the cloying assault.

And then there was the ringing in her ears.

Sachs was standing in front of what remained of Java Hut, waiting—impatiently—for the Bomb Squad officers to make their rounds. She would run the crime scene search herself but the explosives experts from the Sixth Precinct in Greenwich Village always did the first post-blast sweep to check for secondary, delayed devices, intended to take out rescue workers. This was a common technique, at least in countries where bombs were just another means of making a political statement. Maybe Don Bruns had learned his skills abroad.

Sachs snapped her fingers next to each ear and was pleased to find that over the tinnitus ring she could hear pretty well.

What had saved her life and those of the coffee drinkers had at first made her laugh.

She and Jerry, the inked manager of Java Hut, had gone into the small, dimly lit office, where the store's computer was located. They'd pulled up chairs and he'd bent forward, entering a passcode on the old Windows system.

"Here's the program for the security video." Jerry had loaded it and then showed her the commands for reviewing the .mpg files, how to rewind and fast-forward, how to capture stills and write clips to separate files for uploading or copying to a flash drive.

"Got it, thanks."

She'd scooted forward and looked closely at the screen, which was divided into quadrants, one scene for each camera: two were of the floor of the shop, one of the cash register, one of the office.

She had just started scrolling back in time from today to May 11—the date the whistleblower had leaked the STO from here—when she noticed a scene of a man in the office where they now sat, walking forward.

Wait. Something was odd. She'd paused the video.

What was off about this?

Oh, sure, that was it. She'd laughed. In all the other scenes, because she was scrolling in reverse, people were moving backward. But on the office video, the man was moving forward, which meant that in real time he had been *backing* out of the office.

Why would anyone do that?

She'd pointed it out to the manager, who hadn't, however, shared her smile. "Look at the time stamp. That was just ten minutes ago. And I don't know who he is. He doesn't work here."

The man was trim, with short hair, it seemed, under a baseball cap. He wore a windbreaker-style jacket and carried a small backpack.

Jerry had risen and walked to the back door. He'd tried it. "It's open. Hell, we've been broken into!"

Sachs scrolled back farther, then played the video forward. They saw the man come into the office, try to log on to the computer several times and then struggle to pick it up, only to be stymied by the steel bars securing it to the floor. Then he'd glanced at the monitor and must have noticed that he was being filmed. Rather than turn and face the security camera, he'd backed out of the office.

She knew it had to be the sniper.

Somehow he too had learned about the whistle-blower and had come here to see if he could find the man's identity. He must've heard her and Jerry approach. Sachs had run the tape again, noting this time that before he left he seemed to place a small object behind the computer. What—?

Oh, hell, no!

He'd left an IED—*that's* what he'd planted behind the computer. He couldn't steal it; so he'd destroy the Dell. Try to disarm or not? No, he'd have set it to detonate at any minute. "Out, everybody out!" she'd cried. "Bomb. There's a bomb! Clear the place. Everybody out!"

"But that's—"

Sachs had grabbed Jerry by his ideogramed arm and dragged him into the restaurant, calling for the baristas, dishwasher and customers to flee. She'd held up her badge. "NYPD, evacuate now! There's a gas leak!"

Too complicated to explain about bombs.

The device had blown just as she'd shoved the last customer out the door, a contrary young student whining that he hadn't gotten his refill yet.

Sachs had still been inside when she'd felt the detonation in her chest and ears and, through the floor, her feet. Two plate-glass windows had shattered and much of the interior flew into pieces. Instantly the place had been enveloped by that vile, greasy smoke. She'd leapt through the door but stayed upright, sure that if she'd dived to the concrete—à la that clichéd scene in thriller movies—her knee would never forgive her.

Now the Bomb Squad officers made their way through the front door. "It's clear," she heard, though it sounded like the lieutenant was speaking through cotton. The bomb had really been quite loud. Plastic explosives detonate at around twenty-five thousand feet per second.

"What was it?" she said and when he smiled she knew she'd been shouting.

"Can't tell for sure until we send off details to the bureau and ATF. But my guess? Military—we found some camouflaged shrapnel. It's primarily anti-personnel. But it works real good for blowing up anything nearby."

"Like computers."

"What?" the officer asked.

Thanks to her haywire hearing, she'd spoken too softly this time. "And computers."

"Works *real* good against computers," the Bomb Squad officer said. "Hard drive's in a million pieces and most of them're melted. Humpty Dumpty's fucked."

She thanked him. A crime scene team from Queens arrived in the RRV, a van filled with evidence collection equipment. She knew the two officers, an Asian American woman and a round young man from Georgia. He waved a greeting. They'd back her up but she'd walk the grid alone, per Lincoln Rhyme's rule.

Sachs surveyed the smoky remains of Java Hut, hands on her hips.

Brother . . .

Not only is there nothing so distinctive as the smell of an IED but nothing contaminates a scene like one.

She donned the Tyvek coveralls—the deluxe version from Evident, which protect the wearer from dangerous materials as much as they protect the crime scene itself from the searchers. And because of the fumes she wore sealed goggles and a filtering mask.

Her first thought was: How is Lincoln going to hear me through the mask?

But then she remembered that she wasn't going to be online with him, as she usually was, via radio or video hookup. She was alone.

That same chill, hollow sense from earlier wafted through her.

Forget it, she told herself angrily. Get to work.

And with evidence collection bags and equipment in one hand, she began to walk the grid.

Moving through the shambles of the place, Sachs concentrated on collecting what she could of the bomb itself, which, as the officer had warned, wasn't very much. She was particularly dismayed that the suspect hadn't used simply a demolition charge but one meant to kill.

Sachs concentrated on the entrance/exit route, the back doorway, where Bruns would have paused before he broke in and where the blast damage was minimal. She took dozens of samplars: trace from the alleyway and doorjamb, enough to draw a profile of substances common to this area of the city. Anything that was unique might represent evidence the perp had left and lead to his home or office.

How helpful this would be, she wasn't sure. Here, as in any New York City alleyway, there were so many instances of trace evidence that it would be hard to isolate the relevant ones. Too much evidence is often as much of a problem as too little.

After she finished walking the grid she stripped off the overalls quickly—not because she was worried about contamination but because she was by nature claustrophobic and the confining plastic made her edgy.

Breathing deeply, closing her eyes momentarily, she let the feeling settle, then fade.

The whistleblower...How the hell to find him now that the security video was gone?

It seemed hopeless. Anybody who used a complicated email proxy system to hide his tracks would have been smart about the mechanics of finding a place to upload the documents. He wouldn't be a regular here and wouldn't have used a credit card. But an idea occurred: what about other customers? She could track down at least some of those who'd been here around 1 p.m. on May 11. They might have noticed the whistleblower's unusual computer, the iBook. Or maybe tourists had taken some cell phone shots of each other and possibly captured an image of the whistleblower accidentally.

She walked up to Jerry, the now very shaken manager of the late store, and asked him about credit card records. When he tore himself away from his mournful gaze at his shop he called Java Hut central operations. In ten minutes she had the names of a dozen customers who were here at the time in question. She thanked him and had the file uploaded to Lon Sellitto. Then she followed up with a call to the detective.

She asked if he could get some of Bill Myers's Special Services officers to contact them and see if anyone had taken pictures in Java Hut on the day in question or remembered anybody with an odd-looking, older computer.

Sellitto replied, "Yeah, sure, Amelia. I'll order it." He grunted. "This takes the case to a whole new level. An IED? You think it was Bruns, or whatever his real name is?"

"Had to be him, I'd think. It was hard to see in

the video but he roughly fit the description from the maid at the South Cove Inn. So he's cleaning up after the assignment—probably on Metzger's orders." She gave a sour laugh. "And Java Hut's about as clean as it can be."

"Jesus— Metzger and Bruns've gone off the deep end. It's that important to them, to keep this kill order program going that they're taking out innocents."

"Listen, Lon. I want to keep this quiet."

He gave a gruff laugh. "Oh, sure. A fucking IED in Manhattan?"

"Can we play up the story it was a gas leak, still being investigated. Just keep the lid on for a few days?"

"I'll do what I can. But you know the fucking media."

"That's all I'm asking, a day or two."

He muttered, "I'll give it a shot."

"Thanks."

"Anyway, listen, I'm glad you called. Myers's canvassing boys tracked down the woman that Moreno drove around the city with on May 1, Lydia. They'll have her address and phone number in a few minutes."

"The hooker."

He chuckled. "When you speak to her? I don't think I'd say that."

CHAPTER 34

HIS RIGHT HAND ROSE SLOWLY to his mouth and Lincoln Rhyme fed himself a conch fritter—crisp outside and tender within—dabbed with homemade hot sauce. He then picked up and sipped from a can of Kalik beer.

Hurricane's restaurant—curious name, given the local weather—was austere, located on a weedy side street in downtown Nassau. Bright blue and red walls, a warped wooden floor, a few flyblown photographs of the local beaches—or maybe Goa or the Jersey Shore. You couldn't tell. Several overhead fans revolved slowly and did nothing to ease the heat. Their only effect was to piss off the flies.

The place, though, boasted some of the best food Rhyme had ever had.

Though he decided that any meal you can spear with a fork yourself, and not have to be fed, is by definition very, very good.

"Conch," Rhyme mused. "Never had any univalve tissue evidence in a case. Oyster shells once. Very flavorful. Could you cook it at home?"

Thom, sitting across from Rhyme, rose and asked the chef for the recipe. The formidible woman in a red bandanna, looking like a Marxist revolutionary, wrote it down for him, cautioning to get fresh conch. "Never canned. Ever."

The time was nearly three and Rhyme was beginning to wonder if the corporal had given him the tantalizing invitation just to keep him occupied while, as Pulaski suggested, he was preparing an arrest team.

That *is where I have lunch!*...

Rhyme decided not to worry about it and had more conch and beer.

At their feet a black-and-gray dog begged for scraps. Rhyme ignored the small, muscular animal but Thom fed it some bits of conch crust and bread. He was about two feet high and had floppy ears and a long face.

"He'll never leave you alone now," Rhyme muttered. "You know that."

"He's cute."

The server, a slimmer, younger version of the chef, daughter probably, said, "He's a potcake dog. You only see them in the Islands here. The name comes from what we feed stray dogs—rice and green peas, potcake."

"And they hang out in restaurants?" Rhyme asked sardonically.

"Oh, yes. Customers love them."

Rhyme grunted and stared at the door, through which he expected momentarily to see either My-chal Poitier or a couple of armed, uniformed RBPF officers with an arrest warrant.

His phone buzzed and he lifted it. "Rookie, what do you have?"

"I'm at the South Cove Inn. I got it. The number of the man who called about Moreno's reservation. It's a mobile exchange from Manhattan."

"Excellent. Now, it'll be a prepaid, untraceable. But Rodney can narrow down the call to a fairly small area. Maybe an office or gym or a Star-bucks where our sniper enjoys his lattes. It won't take—"

"But—"

"No, it's easy. He can work backward from the cell base stations and then interpolate the signal data from adjacent towers. The sniper will've thrown the phone out by now but the records should be able to—"

"Lincoln."

"*What?*"

"It's not prepaid and it's still active."

Rhyme was speechless for a moment. This was unbelievably good luck.

"And are you ready for this?"

Words returned. "Rookie! Get to the point!"

"It's registered in the name of Don Bruns."

"Our sniper."

"Exactly. He used a Social Security number on the phone account and gave an address."

"Where?"

"PO box in Brooklyn. Set up by a shell corporation in Delaware. And the social's fake."

"But we've got the phone. Start Rodney scanning for usage and location. We can't get a Title Three at this point, but see if Lon or somebody can charm a magistrate into approving a five-second listen-in for a voiceprint."

This would allow them to compare the vocal pattern with the .wav file the whistleblower had sent and confirm that it was, in fact, the sniper, who was presently using the phone.

"And have Fred Dellray look into who's behind the company."

"I will. Now, a couple other things."

Couple *of* other things. But Rhyme refrained. He'd beaten the kid up enough for one day.

"The reporter, de la Rua? He didn't leave anything here at the inn. He came to the interview with a bag or briefcase but they're sure the police took it with them, along with the bodies."

He wondered if Poitier—if he actually showed

up and was in a cooperative mood—would give them access to those items.

"I'm still waiting to talk to the maid about the American who was here the day before the shooting. She gets in in a half hour."

"A competent job, Pulaski. Now, are you being cautious? Any sign of that Mercury with our dope-smoking surveillers?"

"No, and I've been looking. How about with you?...Oh, wait. If you asked *me*, that means you gave 'em the slip."

Rhyme smiled. The kid was learning.

CHAPTER 35

"S O LYDIA'S NOT A PROSTITUTE," Amelia Sachs said.

"Nope," Lon Sellitto replied, "she's an interpreter."

"Translating wasn't a cover for being a call girl? You're sure?"

"Positive. She's legit. Been a commercial interpreter for ten years, works for big companies and law firms. And, I still checked: no rap sheet—city, state or FBI, NCIC. Looks like Moreno had used her before."

Sachs gave a brief, cynical laugh. "I was making assumptions. Escort service, terrorist. Brother. If she's legitimate, Moreno wouldn't have used her at any illegal meetings but odds are she'll know something helpful. Probably she'd have a lot of information about him."

"She'd have to," Sellitto agreed.

And what exactly *did* Lydia know? Jacob Swann

wondered, sitting forward in the front seat of his Nissan, parked in Midtown, listening to this conversation in real time, having tapped once again into Amelia Sachs's 3G, easily tappable phone. He was now pleased she hadn't been blown to nothingness by the IED in Java Hut. This lead was golden.

"What languages?" Sachs was asking. Swann had the other caller's mobile identification number. Lon Sellitto, another NYPD cop, the Tech Services people had told him.

"Russian, German, Arabic, Spanish and Portuguese."

Interesting. Now, more than ever, Swann wanted her surname and address. If you please.

"I'll go interview her now."

Well, that would be particularly convenient: Detective Sachs and a witness, together in a private apartment. Along with Jacob Swann and the Kai Shun knife.

"Got a pen?"

"I'm ready."

So am I, thought Jacob Swann.

Sellitto said, "Her full name's Lydia—"

"Wait!" Sachs shouted.

Swann winced at the volume and held his mobile away from his ear.

"What?"

"Something's wrong, Lon. It just occurred to me: How did our perp know about Java Hut?"

"Whatta you mean?"

"He didn't follow me there. He got there *first*. How did he find out about the place?"

"Fuck. You think he's got a tap on your phone?"

"Could be."

Oh, hell. Swann sighed.

Sachs continued, "I'll find a different phone, a landline, and give you a call through the main number at headquarters."

"Sure."

"I'm dumping my mobile. You do the same."

The line disconnected, leaving Jacob Swann listening to pure silence.

CHAPTER 36

A T FIRST, AMELIA SACHS WAS CONTENT to pull the battery out of her phone.

But then paranoia seeped in like water in the badly grouted basement of her Brooklyn town house and she pitched the unit into a sewer grate outside the smoking cave of Java Hut.

She found a Patrol officer and swapped her smallest bill, a ten, for four bucks' worth of change and called Police Plaza from a nearby pay phone, then was transferred.

"Sellitto."

"Lon."

"You think he was really listening?" he asked.

"I'm not taking any chances."

"Okay, fine with me. But it pisses me off. That was a new Android. Fucker. *Now* are you ready?"

She had pen in hand and a notepad balanced on the stained shelf under the phone. "Go ahead."

"The interpreter's name is Lydia Foster." He

gave Sachs her address on Third Avenue. Her phone number too.

"How'd the canvassers find her?"

"Legwork," Sellitto explained. "Started at the top floor of that office building where Moreno picked her up and worked their way down twenty-nine stories. Naturally, they didn't get a hit till floor three, took 'em forever. She was working freelance, translating for a bank."

"I'm going to call her now." She added, "How the hell did he tap our lines, Lon? It isn't just anybody who can do that."

The older detective muttered, "This guy is too fucking connected."

"And he knows your number too now," she pointed out. "Watch your back."

He gave a gruff laugh. "That's a cliché Linc definitely wouldn't approve of."

His words made her miss Rhyme all the more.

"I'll let you know what I find," she said.

A few minutes later Sachs was speaking with Lydia Foster, explaining the purpose for the call.

"Ah, Mr. Moreno. Yes, I was very sad to hear that. I interpreted for him three times over the last year."

"Each time in New York?"

"That's right. The people he met with spoke pretty good English but he wanted to speak through me in their native languages. He thought he could get a better feel for them. I was supposed to tell him what I thought their attitudes were, in addition to the words."

"I talked to the driver who took you two around the city on May first. He said you had some general conversations with Mr. Moreno too."

"That's right. He was very social."

Sachs found her heart pounding a bit faster. The woman could be a well of information.

"You and he met how many people on the latest trip?"

"Four, I think. Some nonprofit organizations, run by Russians and some people out of Dubai, and at the Brazilian consulate. He also met somebody by himself. That man he was meeting spoke English and Spanish. He didn't need me so I waited at Starbucks downstairs in the office building."

Or maybe he didn't want you to hear the substance of that meeting.

"I'd like to come over and talk to you."

"Yes, anything I can do to help. I'm home for the day. I'll find all my transcripts for the job and organize them."

"You keep copies of everything?"

"Every word. You'd be surprised how many times clients lose what I send them or don't back them up."

Even better.

Just then her phone hummed with an incoming text, marked urgent. "Hold on a second, please," she told Lydia Foster. And read the message

```
Druns's phone in use. Voiceprint
checks—it's him. Tracking in real
time. He's in Manhattan at moment.
Call Rodney Szarnek.


                              —Ron
```

She said, "Ms. Foster, I've got to follow up on something but I'll be there soon."

CHAPTER 37

RHYME HAD JUST FINISHED HIS KALIK BEER at Hurricane's restaurant when he heard a voice behind him.

"Hello."

Mychal Poitier.

The corporal's blue shirt was Rorschached with sweat and his dark slacks, with the regal red stripe, sandy and dotted with mud. He carried a backpack. He waved to the server and she smiled, surprised when he took a seat with the disabled man from America. She put in an order without asking him what he wanted and brought him a coconut soft drink.

"I am late because, I'm sorry to say, we have found the student. She died in a swimming accident. Excuse me for a moment. I will upload my report." He took an iPad in a battered leather case from the bag and booted it up. He typed some words and then hit the send button.

"This will buy me a little time with you. I'll tell them I'm following up on several other issues regarding the loss." He nodded at the iPad. "Unfortunate situation," he said and his face was grave. It occurred to Rhyme that Traffic, his first assignment, and then Business Inspections and Licensing had probably not provided much opportunity to experience firsthand the tragedies that fundamentally change law enforcement officers—that either temper or weaken them. "She drowned in an area of water that generally isn't dangerous but she'd been drinking, it seems. We found rum and Coke in her car. Ah, students. They believe they are immortal."

"May I see?" Rhyme asked.

Poitier turned the device and Rhyme studied the pictures that slowly slideshowed past. The body of the victim was starkly white from loss of blood, and water-wrinkled. Fish or other creatures had eaten away much of her face and neck. Hard to guess her age. Rhyme couldn't recall from the poster. He asked.

"Twenty-three."

"What was she studying?"

"Latin American literature for the semester at Nassau College. And working part time—and, of course, partying." He sighed. "Apparently to excess. Now, I've called her family in America. They're coming to claim the body." His voice faded. "I have never made a call like that before. It was very difficult."

She had a trim figure, athletic, a modest tat on her shoulder—a starburst—and she favored gold jewelry, though a silver necklace of small leaves surrounded her neck, now stripped of skin.

"A shark attack?"

"No, barracuda probably. We rarely get shark attacks here. And the barracuda were just feeding, after she died. They'll occasionally bite a swimmer but the injuries are minor. She probably got caught in the riptide and drowned. Then the fish went to work."

Rhyme noted the worst damage was around the neck. Stubby tubes of the carotid were visible through tatters of flesh. Much of the skull was exposed. With his fork Rhyme speared and then ate some more conch.

Then he slid the iPad back to the officer. "I assume, Corporal, that you are not here to arrest us."

He laughed. "It did occur to me. I was quite angry. But, no, I've come here to help you again."

"Thank you, Corporal. And now in fairness I'll share with you everything that *I* know." And he explained about NIOS, about Metzger, about the sniper.

"Kill Room. What a cold way to put it."

Now that he knew Poitier was, more or less, on

his side, Rhyme told him that Pulaski was waiting to speak to the maid at the South Cove Inn to learn more about the sniper's reconnaissance mission the day before he shot Moreno.

Poitier grimaced. "An officer from New York is forced to do my job for me. What a state of things, thanks to politics."

The server brought the food—a hot stew of vegetables and shreds of dark meat, chicken or goat, Rhyme guessed. Some fried bread too. Poitier tore a piece off the bread and fed it to the potcake dog. He then pulled his plate toward him, tucked his napkin into his shirt, just where the chain that led to his breast pocket was affixed to a collar button. He keyboarded on the iPad then looked up. "I will eat now and while I eat I can tell Thom about the Bahamas, the history, the culture. If he'd like."

"I would, yes."

Poitier pushed the iPad close to Rhyme. "And you, Captain, might wish to look at some pictures in the photo gallery of our beautiful scenery here."

As the corporal turned to Thom and they struck up a conversation Rhyme began scrolling through the gallery.

A picture of the Poitier family, presumably, at the beach. A lovely wife and laughing children. Then they were at a barbecue with a dozen other people.

A picture of the sunset.

A picture of a grade school music recital.

A picture of the first page of the Robert Moreno homicide report.

Like a spy, Poitier had photographed it with the camera in the iPad.

Rhyme looked up at the corporal but the cop ignored him, continuing to share with Thom the history of the colony, and with the potcake dog more lunch.

First, there was an itinerary of Moreno's last days on earth, as the corporal could piece it together.

The man and his guard, Simon Flores, had arrived in Nassau late Sunday, May 7. They had spent Monday out of the inn, presumably at meetings; Moreno did not seem like the sort to swim with the dolphins or go Jet Skiing. The next day beginning at nine he had several other visitors. Shortly after they left, about ten thirty, the reporter Eduardo de la Rua arrived. The shooting was around eleven fifteen.

Poitier had identified and interviewed Moreno's other visitors. They were local businessmen involved in agriculture and transport companies. Moreno planned to form a joint venture with them when he opened the Bahamian branch of his Local Empowerment Movement. They were legitimate and had been respected members of the Nassau business community for years.

No witnesses reported that Moreno had been under surveillance or that anyone had shown any unusual interest in him—other than the phone call before he arrived and the brown-haired American.

Then Rhyme turned to the pages of the scene itself. He was disappointed. The RBPF crime scene team had found forty-seven fingerprints—other than the victims'—but had analyzed only half of them. Of those identified, all were attributed to the hotel staff. A note reported that the remaining lifted prints were missing.

Little effort had been made to collect trace from the victims themselves. Generally, in a sniper killing, such information about the spot where the victim is shot wouldn't be that helpful, of course, since the shooter was a distance away. In this case, though, the sniper had been in the hotel, albeit a day earlier, and might even have snuck into the Kill Room to see about vista and shooting angles. He could easily have left some trace, even if he didn't leave any prints. But virtually no trace had been collected from the room, only some candy wrappers and a few cigarette butts beside an ashtray near the guard's body.

However, the next pages on the iPad, photos of the Kill Room itself, were illuminating. Moreno had been shot in the living room of the suite. Everything and everyone in the room was covered with shards of glass. Moreno lay sprawled on a couch, head back, mouth open, a bloodstain on his shirt, in the center of which was a large black dot, the entrance wound. The upholstery behind him was covered in dark blood and gore, from what would have been a massive exit wound caused by the sniper's bullet.

The other victims lay on their backs near the couch, one a large Latino, identified in the photo as Simon Flores, Moreno's guard, the other a dapper bearded balding man in his fifties, de la Rua, the reporter. They were covered with broken glass and blood, their skin torn and slashed in dozens of places.

The bullet itself was photographed lying on the floor next to a small sandwich board evidence location card bearing the number 14. It was lodged in the carpet a few feet behind the couch.

Rhyme flipped the page, expecting to see more.

But the next image was of the corporal with his wife again, sitting in beach chairs.

Without looking his way, Poitier said, "That's all there is."

"Not the autopsy?"

"One has been done. We don't have the results."

Rhyme asked, "The victims' clothing?"

Now he regarded the criminalist. "At the morgue."

"I asked my associate at the South Cove to track down de la Rua's camera, tape recorder and any thing else he had with him. He said they went to the morgue. I'd love to see them."

Poitier gave a skeptical laugh. "I would have too."

"Would *have*?"

"Yes, you caught that, Captain. By the time I inquired about them they were missing, along with the victims' more valuable personal effects."

Rhyme had noticed in the picture of the bodies that the guard wore a Rolex watch, and a pair of Oakley sunglasses protruded from his pocket. Near the reporter lay a gold pen.

Poitier added, "Apparently you must be fast here securing evidence when you run a scene. I'm learning that. The lawyer I was mentioning?"

"The *prominent* lawyer."

"Yes," Poitier said. "After he was killed and before our detectives got there, half the office was looted."

Rhyme said, "You have the bullet, though."

"Yes. In our evidence locker. But that meeting with Assistant Commissioner McPherson after you left headquarters? It was to order me to deliver to him all the evidence in the Moreno case. He has taken custody and sealed the locker. No one else can have access. Oh, he also ordered me to have no contact whatsoever with you."

Rhyme sighed. "They really don't want this case to go forward, do they?"

With a bitterness Rhyme had not heard before, he said, "Ah, but the case has gone forward. Indeed, it is concluded. The cartels have murdered the victim out of retribution for one thing or another. Who can tell, with those inscrutable cartels?" The man grimaced. Then his voice lowered. "Now, Captain Rhyme, I couldn't get you your physical evidence, as I'd hoped. But I can play tour guide."

"Tour guide?"

"Indeed. We have a wonderful tourist attraction on the southwest coast of New Providence Island. A spit of land a half mile long, ravaged by hurricanes, composed mostly of rock and beaches with tainted sand. The highlights are a trash tip, a metal fabrication plant cited frequently for polluting and a company that shreds tires for recycling."

"Sounds charming," Thom said.

"It's quite popular. At least it was for one American tourist. He visited it on the ninth of May. At around eleven fifteen in the morning. One of the more attractive sights he enjoyed was of the South Cove Inn. An unobstructed view, exactly two thousand one hundred and ten yards away. I thought that you, as a tourist to our country, might enjoy the sights as well. Am I right?"

"You are indeed, Corporal."

"Then we should go. I will not have a career as a tour guide for much longer."

CHAPTER 38

A S SHE SPED DOWNTOWN, Amelia Sachs disconnected the call from Rodney Szarnek, with the Computer Crimes Unit. She'd used a prepaid mobile—paid for out of her own pocket, with cash, of course—and was confident that the conversation hadn't been intercepted by the man they were now in the process of tracking down.

Szarnek had told her that the NIOS sniper was presently having a conversation near the Wall Street area of the city while on foot.

The cybercrimes cop had given Sachs the general location of the man and she was speeding there now. When she arrived she'd call back and Rodney'd try to pinpoint the exact coordinates.

She slammed the clutch of her Torino Cobra to the floor and downshifted hard, rev-matched and then sped up, leaving a twin-stripe signature in rubber on the concrete.

She wove through traffic until a jam loomed. "Come on, come on." She detoured onto a crosstown street east, skidding into what would have been a U-turn, except to avoid a sudden jaywalker she had to make it a Q. She tried again and was soon bolting through side streets, making her way east and south, toward downtown.

"Hell," Sachs muttered, faced with another jam, and decided to conscript the closest cross street, which was more or less clear, though it happened to be one-way, against her. The maneuver threw drivers into panic and raised a symphony of off-pitch horns. Some single fingers too. Then she zipped past a yellow cab just before the driver sought the sidewalk and she was on Broadway, heading south. She paused for most of the red lights.

There's a lot of controversy about cell phone companies' giving law officers details about phone use and location. Generally in an emergency, the providers will cooperate without a warrant. Otherwise, most will require a court order. Rodney Szarnek didn't want to take any chances and so after learning the sniper's number from Pulaski in the Bahamas he'd contacted a magistrate and gotten paper issued—both for a five-second listen-in, to snag the voiceprint, and to track the location.

Szarnek had learned that the phone was in use

around the corner of Broadway and Warren Street, using basic triangulation for that information, which gave rough estimates. He was presently working on interpolating signal data from the nearby network antennas. Searching in urban areas was much easier because many more towers were erected there than in rural areas. The downside, of course, was that there were many more users in any given area of a city, so it was harder to isolate your particular suspect than, say, in farmland.

Szarnek was hoping to nail down GPS data, which was the gold standard of tracking and would give the location of the sniper to within a few feet.

Finally Sachs arrived in the general vicinity, took a turn at forty, missing both a bus and a hot dog stand by inches, and skidded to a stop on a side street off Broadway. The aroma of baking tires rose, a smell nostalgic and comforting.

She looked around at the hundreds of passersby, about 10 percent of them on their phones. Was the shooter one of the people she was peering at right now? The lean young man with the crew cut, wearing khaki slacks and a work shirt? He looked military. Or the sullen, dark-complected man who was in a badly fitting suit and looking around suspiciously from behind darkly tinted sunglasses? He looked like a hit man but might have been an accountant.

How long would Bruns stay on the line? she wondered. If he disconnected they could still follow him, unless he pulled the battery out. But it was easier to spot someone actually using a phone.

She reminded herself too: This could be a trap. She recalled all too clearly the explosion at Java Hut. The sniper knew about the investigation. He clearly knew about her; Sachs's phone was the one he'd tapped to learn about the coffee shop. A trickle of electric fear down her spine once more.

Her own mobile trilled.

"Sachs."

"Got him on GPS," Rodney Szarnek called excitedly, like a teenager (he'd once said being a cop was nearly as much fun as playing Grand Theft Auto). "We're in real time, on the provider's server. He's walking on the west side of the street, Broadway. Just at Vesey now."

"I'm on the move." Sachs started in the direction he'd indicated, feeling the pain in her left hip; the knee alone wasn't torment enough apparently. She dug into her back pocket—felt past the switchblade and pulled out a blister pack of Advil. Ripped it open with her teeth, swallowed the pills fast and littered the wrapper away.

She closed in on her target as quickly as she could.

Szarnek: "He's stopped. Maybe for a light."

Dodging through pedestrian traffic the same way she'd woven through vehicular moments ago, Sachs got closer to the intersection where a red light stopped southbound traffic and pedestrians.

"Still there," Szarnek said. There was no rock music pumping into his office at the moment.

She could see, about forty feet away, the red light yield to green. Those waiting at the curb surged across the street.

"He's moving." One block later, Szarnek said unemotionally, "He's disconnected."

Shit.

Sachs sped up to see if she could spot anybody holstering a phone. No one. And she couldn't help but think that maybe the most recent call was the last he'd make with the tainted phone. Their sniper was, after all, a pro. He must know there was some liability in mobiles. Maybe he'd even spotted her and was about to send his cell into the same sewer system graveyard she just had.

At Dey Street the light changed to red. She had to stop. Surrounded by a crowd of perhaps twenty people—businessmen and -women, construction workers, students, tourists. Quite the ethnic mix, of course, Anglo, Asian, Latino, black and all combinations.

"Amelia?" Rodney Szarnek was on the line.

"Go ahead," she said.

"He's getting an incoming call. Should be ringing now."

Just as the phone in the pocket of the man inches to Sachs's right began to buzz.

They were literally shoulder-to-shoulder.

He fit the rough description of the man in the South Cove Inn, according to Corporal Mychal Poitier, the Bahamian cop: white male, athletic figure, compact. He wore slacks, shirt and a windbreaker. A baseball cap too. She couldn't tell if he had brown hair; it seemed more dark blond, but a witness could easily have described that as brown. The cut was short, like their sniper's. His laced shoes were polished to a shine.

Military.

She said cheerfully into her phone, "Sure. That's interesting."

Szarnek asked, "You're next to him?"

"That's exactly right." Don't overdo the playacting, she told herself.

The light changed and she let him step away first.

Sachs wondered if there was anything she could do to get the man's identity. She and Rhyme had worked a case a few years ago in which they'd sought the help of a young woman illusionist and sleight-of-hand artist, whose skills included pickpocketing—for theatrical entertainment only, she'd laughingly assured them—Sachs could have used her now. Was there any way she herself might slip her fingers into the man's jacket pocket to boost a wallet or receipt?

Impossible, she decided. Even if she'd had this skill, the man seemed far too vigilant, looking around frequently.

They crossed the street and continued down Broadway, leaving Liberty behind. Then the sniper turned right suddenly and cut through Zuccotti Park, presently unoccupied, just as Szarnek said, "He's heading west through Zuccotti."

"You're right about that." Keeping up the act even though her target probably couldn't hear her.

She followed him diagonally through the park. On the west end he headed south on Trinity.

Szarnek asked, "How're you going to handle it, Amelia? Want me to call in backup?"

She debated. They couldn't collar him; there wasn't enough evidence for that. "I'll stay with him as long as I can, try to get a picture," she said, risking speaking for real to Szarnek; the sniper was well out of hearing range now. "If I'm lucky he's going to his car and I'll pick up the tag. If not, maybe I'll be taking a subway ride to Far Rockaway. I'll call you back."

Pretending to continue the call, Sachs sped up and walked past the sniper, then paused at the next red light. She turned, as if lost in her conversation, aiming the lens of her phone toward him, and pressed the shutter a half dozen times. When the light changed, she let the sniper cross the street before her. He was lost in his own conversation and didn't seem to notice Sachs.

She resumed the tail and called Szarnek back. The tech cop said, "Okay, he's disconnected now."

Sachs watched the man slip his phone into his pocket. He was making for a ten- or twelve-story building on the gloomy canyon of Rector Street. Rather than entering through the front door of the structure, though, he walked around the side into an alleyway. Halfway down that narrow avenue, he turned and, slipping an ID card lanyard over his neck, walked through a gate into what seemed to be a parking lot, bejeweled with serious razor wire.

Staying to the shadows, Sachs had Szarnek transfer her to Sellitto. She told the detective that she'd found the shooter and needed a surveillance team to keep on him.

"Good, Amelia. I'll get somebody from Special Services on it right away."

"I'll upload some pictures of him. Have them contact Rodney. He can keep tracing the phone and let them know when he's on the move again. I'll stay here with him until they show up. Then I'll go interview Lydia Foster."

"Where are you exactly?" Sellitto asked.

"Eighty-Five Rector. He went through a gate at the side of the building, a parking lot. Or maybe a courtyard. I didn't want to get too close."

"Sure. What's the building?"

Sachs gave a laugh. She'd just noticed a subtle sign.

National Intelligence and Operations Service.

She told Sellitto, "It's his office."

CHAPTER 39

TERRIBLE NEWS: THAT NICE Mr. Moreno was dead.

In her apartment on Third Avenue, Lydia Foster now made a cup of Keurig coffee, picking hazelnut flavored from the hundreds of capsules, and returned to the living room, wondering when that policewoman was going to be here.

Lydia had liked him quite a bit. Smart, courteous. And quite the gentleman. She knew she was pretty well built and had been described as attractive, but unlike some men using her services as an interpreter, Mr. Moreno hadn't flirted once. On the first translating job for him, several months ago, he'd shown her pictures of his children—adorable! Which men do sometimes as a prelude to trying to pick you up, which Lydia found incredibly tacky, even for the single dads. But Mr. Moreno had followed the pictures of the bambinos with a picture of his wife and announced that he was looking forward to their wedding anniversary.

What a nice man. Polite—holding the car door for her, even though they had a chauffeur. Moreno had been charming. And talkative. They had some engaging conversations. They were, for instance, both fascinated with language. He was a writer for blogs and magazines and a radio host, while she made her living interpreting other people's words. They'd spoken about similarities between languages and even technical aspects: nominative and dative and possessive cases, as well as verb conjugations. He told her he disliked English intensely, though it was his mother tongue, which she found curious. One may not like the tonal quality of a tongue for being too harsh—German or Xhosa, for instance—or be dismayed at the difficulty of achieving fluency, like Japanese, but to dislike a language in general was something Lydia had never heard of.

He characterized it as random and lazy (all the irregular constructions), confusing and inelegant. It turned out that his real objection was a bit different. "And it's rammed down the throats of people throughout the world, like it or not. Just another way to make other nations dependent on the U.S."

But Mr. Moreno had been opinionated about a lot of things. Once he'd started lecturing about politics, you couldn't dislodge him. She found herself steering away from those subjects.

She'd have to tell the detective that Mr. Moreno had seemed concerned for his safety. He'd looked around quite a bit as they'd driven through the city and walked to their meetings. Once, they'd left one meeting and were on their way to another when Mr. Moreno had stopped suddenly.

"That man? Haven't we seen him before, outside the other office? Is he following us?" The person he noted was a young, somber-faced white guy, looking through a magazine. That alone struck Lydia as odd, something out of an old-time detective film, where a PI pretends to read a newspaper on the street while spying on a suspect. Nobody lounges on the streets of New York, browsing through reading material; they check iPhones or BlackBerrys.

Lydia would be sure to tell the police officer about the incident; maybe that man had something to do with Mr. Moreno's death.

Digging through Redweld folders, she assembled her notes from the assignments she'd had with Mr. Moreno over the past few months. She'd saved everything. As an interpreter, she worked with the police and court system from time to time. She had gotten into the habit of being very conscientious about retaining all her files in such cases because a mistaken phrasing of a detective's question or a suspect's answer could easily result in an innocent man being convicted or a guilty one going free. This diligence carried over into her commercial interpreting assignments too.

The police would get nearly a thousand pages of translated material by and about the late Mr. Moreno.

The intercom buzzer rang and she answered. "Yes?"

"Ms. Foster, I'm with the NYPD," a male voice said. "Detective Sachs spoke to you earlier? She's been delayed and asked me to come by and ask you a few questions about Robert Moreno."

"Sure, come on up. Twelve B."

"Thank you."

A few minutes later a knock on the door. She looked out through the peephole, to see a pleasant-looking man in his thirties, wearing a suit. He was holding up a leather wallet containing a gold badge.

"Come on in," she said, unbolting and unchaining.

He nodded a greeting and stepped inside.

As soon as she closed the door she noted that there was something wrong with his hands. They were wrinkled. No, he was wearing flesh-colored gloves.

She frowned. "Wait—"

Before she could scream he struck her hard in the throat with an open hand.

Gurgling, crying, she dropped to the floor.

CHAPTER 40

H E SOMETIMES WONDERED ABOUT PEOPLE, Jacob Swann did.

Either you were conscientious or you weren't. Either you scrubbed every bit of scorch off your copper-bottomed, stainless-steel sauté pan or you didn't. Either you went the distance with the soufflé, and saw it rise five inches over the top of the ramekin, or you said to hell with it and for dessert served Häagen-Dazs, spelled in faux Scandinavian but made in the U.S. of A.

Standing over a crumpled, gasping Lydia Foster, he was thinking of Amelia Sachs.

She'd been smart enough to destroy her cell phone (and it *was* destroyed, not simply castrated, his tech people had learned). But then she'd made the mistake of calling Detective Sellitto back from a pay phone only about twenty-five feet from Java Hut. By the time she called, those same tech gurus at headquarters had rammed a tap on this phone—and several others nearby.

(While of course officially claiming they didn't know how to do it and, even if they had known, never would.)

Sometimes your Miele oven conks out—just before you're ready to slip the lamb roast in, natch—and you have to improvise.

Sure enough, Sachs had delivered to Lon Sellitto—and inadvertently to Jacob Swann—the vitals about Lydia Foster.

He now moved through the apartment quietly, verifying that they were alone. He probably didn't have a lot of time. Sachs had said she'd be delayed but presumably she'd call or arrive soon. Should he wait for her? He'd have to consider that. She might not show up alone, of course. There was that and while he did have a pistol, shooting, as opposed to cutting, was the sloppiest (and least enjoyable) way of solving problems.

But if Sachs *was* alone? Several options presented themselves.

Slipping the knife away, he now returned to the interpreter, grabbed her by the hair and collar of her blouse and dumped her in a heavy dining room chair. He tied her to this with lamp wire, cut with a cheap utility knife he carried—*not* the Kai Shun, of course. He never even used the blade to slice string for tying beef roulade, one of his favorite recipes.

Tears streamed down her face and, gasping from the throat-punch, Lydia Foster shivered and kicked.

Jacob Swann reached into his breast pocket and removed his Kai Shun from the wooden scabbard. Her reaction, the terror, didn't deepen. We are dismayed only by the unexpected. She would have seen this coming.

My little butcher man...

He crouched beside her as she sat making ungodly sounds and shaking madly.

"Be still," he whispered into her ear.

He thought of the Bahamas, yesterday, of Annette *uhn-uhn-uhn*ing in a clearing near the beach, surrounded by silver palm and buttonwood trees strangling to death from orange love vines.

The interpreter didn't comply exactly but she calmed enough.

"I have a few questions. I'm going to need all the material about your assignments for Robert Moreno. What you talked about. And who you met. But first of all, how many officers have you talked to about Robert Moreno?" He was concerned that somebody had called her after Amelia Sachs.

She shook her head.

Jacob Swann rested his left hand on the back of hers, tied tightly down. "That's not a number. How many officers?"

She made more bizarre sounds and then, when he brushed the knife against her fingers, she whispered, "No one."

She glanced toward the door. It meant she believed she could save herself if she stalled, to give the police time to arrive.

Jacob Swann curled the fingers of his left hand and rested the side of the Kai Shun blade, pounded with indentations, against his knuckles. The razor edge lowered to her middle and ring fingers. This was the way all serious chefs wielded their knives when they sliced food, fingertips of the guide hand curved below and away from the dangerous blade. You had to be very careful when you cut. He'd sliced through his own fingertips on several occasions. The pain was indescribable; fingers contain more nerve endings than any other part of the body.

He whispered, "Now, I'm going to ask you once more."

CHAPTER 41

THE DRIVE TO THE SNIPER'S NEST on the outcropping of land near the South Cove Inn took considerably longer than it otherwise might have.

Mychal Poitier gave Thom a complicated route to get to the main highway that led them to their destination—SW Road. The point of this evasion was to see if the gold Mercury was following them. Poitier assured him that the car did not contain officers of the Royal Bahamas Police Force conducting surveillance. The tail might have to do with Moreno or something else entirely. A well-dressed and vulnerable American in a wheelchair might simply have aroused the interest of thieves.

Rhyme called Pulaski, who was still at the inn, and told him where they'd be. The young officer continued to wait for the maid who might have more information about the sniper's intelligence gathering at the inn the day before the shooting.

Once past the airport the traffic thinned and Thom sped up, piloting the van along SW Road and its gentle arc around the island, past manicured gated communities, past shacks decorated with laundry on lines and goats in pens, past swamps and then an endless mass of forest and greenery— Clifton Heritage Park.

"Here, turn here," Poitier said.

They had arrived at a dirt road, which veered right and led through a wide, rusting gate, which was open. The road followed a narrow outcropping of land that extended a half mile into Clifton Bay. The spit was a few feet above sea level, dotted with trees and brush and scruffy bare spots, lined with a shore that was rocky in some places, sandy in others. The road was bordered with *Do Not Swim* signs. No explanation was given but the water was noxious, sickly green and singularly unappealing.

Thom followed the road, which skirted the north edge of the spit, past the several commercial facilities Poitier had alluded to in the restaurant earlier. The first they passed, at the intersection of the unnamed drive and SW Road, was the public trash yard where several fires burned and a dozen people wandered about, picking for anything of value. Next was the tire recycling operation and finally the metal fabricating plant composed of several low shacks so unsubstantial that it looked as if a gentle breeze, forget a hurricane, could have blown them down. The businesses were identified by hand-painted signs. Fences were topped with barbed wire and tense dogs prowled the grounds, squat and broad-chested—very different from the potcake they'd shared lunch with.

Clouds of smoke, yellow and gray, lingered defiantly, as if too heavy to be moved by the breezes.

As Thom picked his way along the pitted road, the view to the right suddenly opened up and they were looking at the bay of azure water beneath a stunning blue sky and white clouds dense as wads of cotton. About a mile away was the low beige line of land and buildings that was the South Cove Inn and surrounding grounds. Somewhere along this north edge of the spit from here to the end, about a hundred yards away, the sniper would have set up his nest.

"Anywhere here," Rhyme said. Thom drove a short distance to a pull-off and parked. He shut the engine off and two sounds filled the van—some harsh rhythmic pounding from the metal factory and the faint crash of waves on the rocks that lined the shore.

"One thing first," Poitier said. He reached into his backpack and extracted something then offered it to Rhyme. "Do you want this?"

It was a pistol. A Glock. Very much like Amelia

Sachs's. Poitier verified it was loaded and pulled the slide to chamber a round. With a Glock there is no safety catch, you simply have to pull the trigger to fire it.

Rhyme stared at the pistol, glanced at Thom and then took the weapon in his right hand. He had never cared for firearms. The opportunity to use them—in his specialty of forensics, at least—was next to never, and he was always worried that he'd have to draw and use his gun. The reluctance stemmed not from fear of killing an attacker but from what even a single shot could do to contaminate a crime scene. Smoke, blast pressure, gunshot residue, vapors...

That was no less true here but curiously he was now struck by the sense of power the weapon gave him.

In contrast with the utter helplessness that had enwrapped his life since the accident.

"Yes," he said.

Though he couldn't feel it in his fingers, the Glock seemed to burn its way into his skin, to become a part of his new arm. He aimed it carefully out the window at the water, recalling his firearms training. Assume every weapon is loaded and ready to fire, never point a weapon at anything you aren't prepared to send a bullet into, never shoot unless you see exactly what is behind your target, never put your finger on the trigger until you're prepared to shoot.

A scientist, Rhyme was actually a pretty good shot, using physics in calculating how to get the bullet to its desired destination.

"Yes," he said again and slipped the gun into the inside pocket of his jacket.

They got out of the van and surveyed the area: pipes and gutters directing runoff into the ocean, dozens of piles of sludge rising like huge ant hills and cinder blocks and car parts and appliances and rusted industrial machinery littering the ground.

No Swimming...

No kidding.

Thom said, "The haze is bad and the inn's so far away. How could he see well enough to get a clear target?"

Poitier said, "A special scope, I decided. Adaptive optics, lasers."

Rhyme was amused. Apparently the corporal had done more research about the case than he'd let on—or than Assistant Commissioner McPherson would have been happy with.

"Could have been a clearer day too."

"Never very clear here," Poitier said, waving his arm at a low chimney rising above the tire plant. It spewed bile-green and beige smoke.

Then, surrounded by the nauseating smell of rotten eggs and hot rubber from the pollution, they made their way closer to the shore. Rhyme studied the ground for the best place to set up a sniper's nest—good cover and an indentation that would allow support on which to rest the rifle. A half dozen sites would have worked.

No one interfered with the search; they were largely alone. A pickup eased up and parked just across the road. The driver, in a sweat-stained gray shirt, speaking into his cell phone, walked to the back of his truck and began tossing trash bags into a ditch beside the road. The concept of littering as a crime seemed not to exist in the Bahamas. Rhyme could also hear some laughing and shouts from the other side of the fence surrounding the metal fabrication plant but otherwise they had the place to themselves.

Looking for the nest, Thom, Poitier and Rhyme walked, and wheeled, through the weeds and patches of dirt and sand, the Storm Arrow doing a fair job of finding purchase in the uneven terrain. Poitier and Thom could get closer to the edge and he told them what to look for: cut-back brush, indentations, foot or boot prints leading to a flat area. "And look at the patches of sand." Even a spent cartridge leaves a distinctive mark.

"He's got to be a pro," Rhyme explained. "He'd've had a tripod or sandbags to rest the gun on but he might've used rocks too and left them set up. Look for stones out of place, maybe one balanced on another. At that distance, the rifle would have to be absolutely steady."

Rhyme squinted—the pollution and the wind stung his eyes. "I would love some brass," he said. But he doubted the sniper would have left any empty cartridges behind; pros always collected them because they contained a wealth of information about the weapon and the shooter. He peered into the water, though, wondering if a spent shell had been ejected there. The sea was black and he assumed very deep.

"A diver'd be good."

"Our official divers wouldn't be available, Captain," Poitier said regretfully. "Since this, of course, isn't even an investigation."

"Just an island tour."

"Yes, exactly."

Rhyme wheeled close to the edge and looked down.

"Careful there," Thom called.

"But," Poitier said, "I dive. I could come back and see if there is anything down there. Borrow some of the underwater lights from our waterside station."

"You would do that, Corporal?"

He too peered into the water. "Yes. Tomorrow, I—"

What happened next happened fast.

Finger-snap fast.

At the sound of clattering suspension and a hissing, badly firing engine, Rhyme, Thom and Poitier turned to look at the dirt road they'd just driven down. They saw the gold Mercury bounding directly toward them, now with only two occupants in it.

And Rhyme understood. He glanced back, seeing the man in the gray T-shirt, the litterer from the pickup truck, race across the narrow road and tackle Poitier as he was drawing his gun. The weapon went flying. The assailant rose fast and kicked the gasping corporal in the side and head, hard.

"No!" Rhyme cried.

The Mercury squealed to a stop and two of the men they'd seen following earlier leapt out—the one with the dreads in the sleeveless yellow shirt and his partner, shorter, wearing the green T. The man in green ripped Thom's phone from his hand and doubled him over with a blow to the belly.

"Don't!" Rhyme shouted—a cry as involuntary as it was pointless.

The man in the gray T-shirt said to his partners, "Okay, you see anyone else?"

"No."

Of course, that's why he was on the phone. He

hadn't come here to pitch out trash at all. He'd followed them and used the phone to let the others know their victims had arrived at the killing site.

Poitier gasped for breath, clutching his side.

Rhyme said firmly, "We're police officers from the United States. We work with the FBI. Don't make this worse on yourself. Just leave now."

It was as if he hadn't spoken.

The man in gray walked toward Poitier's pistol, lying in the dust ten feet away.

"Stop," Rhyme commanded.

The man did. He blinked at the criminalist. The other attackers froze. They were looking at the Glock in Rhyme's hand. The pistol was unsteady, for sure, but from this distance he could easily send a bullet into the torso of the assailant.

The man lifted his hands slightly, rising. Eyes on the pistol. Back to Rhyme. "Okay, okay, mister. Don't do with that."

"All of you, step back and lie down on the ground, facedown."

The two who'd been in the car turned their eyes on the man in gray.

Nobody moved.

"I'm not going to tell you again." Rhyme wondered what the recoil would do to his hand. He supposed there might be some damage to the tendons. But all he needed after the shot was to keep the weapon in his grip. The others would flee after he'd killed their leader.

Thinking of the Special Task Order. No due process, no trial. Self-defense. Taking a life before your enemy did.

"You gonna shoot me, sir?" The man was studying him, suddenly defiant.

Rhyme rarely had a chance to meet adversaries face-to-face. They were usually long gone from the crime scene by the time he saw them, which was usually in court where he was an expert witness for the prosecution. Still, he had no trouble staring down the man in gray.

His partner, the one in yellow, the one with the impressive muscles, stepped forward but stopped fast when Rhyme spun the gun toward him.

"Hokay, easy, mon, easy." Hands raised.

Rhyme aimed again at the leader, whose eyes were fixed on the weapon, his hands up. He smiled. "Are you? Are you going to shoot me, sir? I'm not so sure you are." He stepped forward a few feet. Paused. And then walked directly toward Rhyme.

There was nothing more to say.

Rhyme tensed, hoping the recoil wouldn't damage the results of the delicate surgery, hoping he could keep the weapon in his hand. He sent the command to close his index finger.

But nothing happened.

Glocks—dependable, Austrian-made pistols—have a trigger pull of only a few pounds pressure.

Yet Rhyme couldn't muster that, couldn't deliver enough strength to save the life of his aide and the police officer who'd risked his job to help him.

The man in gray continued forward, perhaps assuming Rhyme lacked the fortitude to shoot, even as he tried desperately to pull the trigger. Even more insulting, the man didn't approach from the side, he kept on a steady path toward the muzzle that hovered in his direction.

The man closed his muscular hand around the gun and easily yanked it from Rhyme's.

"You know, you a freak, mon." He braced himself, put his foot in the middle of Rhyme's chest and pushed hard.

The Storm Arrow rolled back two feet and went off the rocky edge. With a huge splash, Rhyme and the chair tumbled into the water. He took a deep breath and went under.

The water was not as deep as he'd thought, the darkness was due to the pollution, the chemicals and waste. The chair dropped ten feet or so and came to rest on the bottom.

Head throbbing, lungs in agony as his breath depleted, Rhyme twisted his head as far as he could and with his mouth gripped the strap of the canvas bag hanging from the back of the chair. He tugged this forward and it floated to just within his reach. He managed to wrap his arm around it for stability and undid the zipper with his teeth, then lowered his head and fished for the portable ventilator's mouthpiece. He gripped it hard and worked it between his lips.

His eyes were on fire, stinging from the pollutants in the water, and he squinted but kept them open as he searched for the switch to the ventilator.

Finally, there. That's it.

He clicked it on.

Lights glowed. The machine hummed and he inhaled a bit of wonderful, sweet oxygen.

Another.

But there was no third. Apparently the water had worked its way through the housing and short-circuited the unit.

The ventilator went dark. The air stopped.

At that moment he heard another sound, muffled through the water, but distinct: Two sounds, actually.

Gunshots.

Spelling the deaths of his friends: one he'd known seemingly forever and one he'd grown close to in just the past few hours.

Rhyme's next breath was of water.

He thought of Amelia Sachs and his body relaxed.

CHAPTER 42

No.

OH, NO.

At close to 5 p.m. she parked in front of Lydia Foster's apartment building on Third Avenue.

Sachs couldn't get too close; police cars and ambulances blocked the street.

Logic told her that the reason for the vehicles *couldn't* be the death of the interpreter. Sachs had been following the sniper for the past hour and a half. He was still in his office downtown. She hadn't left until Myers's Special Services surveillance team showed up. Besides, how could the sniper have learned the interpreter's name and address? She'd been careful to call from landlines and prepaid mobiles.

That's what logic reported.

Yet instinct told her something very different, that Lydia was dead and Sachs was to blame. Because she'd never considered what she realized was the truth: They had two perps. One was the man she'd been following through the streets of downtown New York—the sniper, she knew, because of the voiceprint match—and the other, Lydia Foster's killer, an unsub, unidentified subject. He was somebody else altogether, maybe the shooter's partner, a spotter, as many snipers used. Or a separate contractor, a specialist, hired by Shreve Metzger to clean up after the assassination.

She parked fast, tossed the NYPD placard on the dash and stepped out of the car, hurrying toward the nondescript apartment building, the pale façade marred by off-white water stains as if the air-conditioning units had been crying.

Ducking under the police tape, she hurried up to a detective, who was prepping a canvass team. The slim African American recognized her, though she didn't know him, and he nodded a greeting. "Detective."

"Was it Lydia Foster?" Wondering why she bothered to ask.

"Right. This involves a case you're running?"

"Yeah. Lon Sellitto's the lead, Bill Myers's overseeing it. I'm doing the legwork."

"It's all yours, then."

"What happened?"

She noticed the man was shaken up, eyes twitching away from hers as he fiddled with a pen.

He swallowed and said, "Scene was pretty bad, I gotta tell you. She was tortured. Then he stabbed her. Never seen anything like that."

"Torture?" she asked in a whisper.

"Sliced the skin off her fingers. Slow."

Jesus...

"How did he get in?"

"Some reason, she let him in. No signs of break-in."

Dismayed, Sachs now understood. The unsub *had* tapped a line—probably the landline she'd used near Java Hut—and learned about the interpreter. He'd fronted he was a cop, flashing a fake badge, saying he worked with Sachs; he'd know her name by now.

That conversation between Sachs and Sellitto was Lydia Foster's own personal Special Task Order.

She felt a burst of breathtaking anger toward the killer. What he'd done to Lydia—the pain he'd inflicted—had been unnecessary. To get information from a civilian you needed only to threaten. Physical torture was always pointless.

Unless you enjoyed it.

Unless you got pleasure in wielding a knife, slicing precisely, skillfully.

"Why'd you get the call?" she asked.

"Fucker cut her so much, she bled through the ceiling. Neighbors downstairs saw blood on the wall. Called nine one one." The detective continued, "The place was ransacked. I don't know what he was looking for but he went through everything she had. There wasn't a single drawer untouched. No computer or cell phone either. He took it all."

The files on the Moreno interpreting assignment, probably already shredded or burned.

"CS on the way?"

"I called a team from Queens. They'll be here any minute."

Sachs had a set of basic crime scene gear in the trunk of the Torino. She returned to the vehicle and began to pull on the powder-blue overalls and booties and shower cap. She'd get started now. Every minute that passed degraded evidence.

And every minute that passed let the monster who'd done this get farther and farther away.

———————

WALKING THE GRID.

Garbed like a surgeon, Amelia Sachs was moving through Lydia Foster's apartment in the classic crime scene search pattern, the grid: one pace at a time from wall to wall, turn, step aside slightly and return. And when that was done you covered the same ground in the same way, only perpendicular to your earlier search.

This was the most time-consuming method of searching a scene but also the most thorough. This was how Rhyme had searched his scenes and it was the way he insisted those working for him did too.

The search is perhaps the most important part of a crime scene investigation. Photos and videos and sketches are important. Entrance and exit routes, locations of shell casings, fingerprints, smears of semen, blood spatter. But finding crucial trace is what crime scene work is all about. *Merci, M. Locard.* When you walk the grid you need to open up your whole body to the place, smelling, listening, touching and, of course, looking. Scanning relentlessly.

This is what Amelia Sachs now did.

She didn't think she was a natural at forensic analysis. She was no scientist. Her mind didn't make those breathtaking deductions that came so quickly to Rhyme. But one thing that did work to her advantage was her empathy.

When they'd first started working together, Rhyme had apparently spotted within her a skill he himself did not have: the ability to get into the mind of the perpetrator. When she walked the grid she found she was actually able to mentally *become* the killer or rapist or kidnapper or thief. This could be a harrowing, exhausting endeavor. But when it worked, the process meant she would think of places in the scene to examine that a typical searcher might not, hiding places, improbable entrance and escape routes, vantage points.

It was there that she would discover evidence that would otherwise have remained hidden forever.

The techs from Crime Scene in Queens arrived. But, as before, she was handling the preliminary work alone. You'd think more people made for a better search but that was true only in an expansive area like those involving mass shootings. In a typical scene a single searcher is less distracted—and is also aware that there's no one else to catch what he misses, so he concentrates that much harder.

And one truth about crime scene work: You've only got one chance to find the critical clue; you can't go back and try again.

As she walked through the apartment where Lydia Foster's corpse sat, head back and bloody, tied to a chair, Sachs felt an urge to speak to Rhyme to tell him what she was seeing and smelling and thinking. And once again, as when walking the grid at Java Hut, the emptiness at being unable to hear his voice chilled her heart. Rhyme was only a thousand miles away but she felt as if he'd ceased to exist.

Involuntarily she thought again of the surgery scheduled for later in the month. Didn't want to consider it, but couldn't help herself.

What if he didn't survive?

Both Sachs and Rhyme lived on the edge—her lifestyle of speed and danger, his physical condition. Possibly, *probably*, this element of risk made life together more intense, their connection closer. And she accepted this most of the time. But now, with him away and her searching a particularly difficult scene involving a perp all too aware of her, she couldn't help but think that they were always just a gunshot or heartbeat away from being alone forever.

Forget this, Sachs thought harshly. Possibly said it aloud. She didn't know. Get to work.

She found, though, that her empathy wasn't kicking in, not on this scene. As she moved through the rooms, she felt blocked. Maybe like a writer or artist who couldn't quite channel a muse. The ideas wouldn't come. For one thing, she didn't know who the hell the killer was. The latest information was confusing. The man who'd done this wasn't the sniper, but, most likely, another of Metzger's specialists. Yet who?

The other reason she wasn't connecting was that

she didn't understand the unsub's motive. If he wanted to eliminate witnesses and hamper the investigation, then why the horrific torture, the precise knife cuts? The slashes where he flayed off skin, leisurely, it seemed? Sachs found herself distracted as she stared at the strips of flesh on the floor below the chair where Lydia was tied. The blood.

What did he want?

Maybe if Rhyme had been speaking into her ear, working the scene with her via radio or video, it might be different, insights might leap out.

But he wasn't, and the killer's psyche eluded her.

The search itself didn't take long. Whatever his motive, Lydia Foster's killer had been careful—wearing rubber gloves. She could tell this from the wrinkles in some of the blood smears, where he'd touched her body while slicing her skin. He'd been careful to avoid stepping in the blood and so there were no obvious shoe prints, and an electrostatic wand sweep of the non-carpeted floor revealed no latents. She collected trace, a few receipts and Post-it notes, stuffed into the pockets of jeans hung on the bathroom door. But this was all the documentary evidence Sachs could track down. She processed the body, noting again the appalling wounds, small but precise, as the unsub had flayed the skin from the woman's fingers. The single, fatal stab wound through the chest. There seemed to be bruises around the site of the incision, as if he had firmly palpated her flesh to find an entrance to her heart free of bones.

Why was that?

Sachs then radioed down to her colleagues to let them know they could come upstairs for the videos and stills.

At the door she paused, glancing back for one last look at Lydia Foster's body.

I'm sorry, Lydia. I didn't think!

I should have considered that he'd tap the land-lines near Java Hut. I should have thought there might be two perps.

Sachs had another thought too: She regretted being too late to get the information that the woman would have provided. The details the interpreter had known and the records she had were clearly crucial. Otherwise, why interrogate her?

And she apologized to Lydia Foster a second time, for having this selfish thought.

Outside, she stripped off the overalls and deposited them in a burn bag; they were streaked with Lydia's blood. She used cleanser on her hands. Checked her Glock. Scanned the area for any threats. All she saw were a hundred black windows, dim cul-de-sacs, paused cars. Each a perfect vantage point for the unsub to be standing to target her.

Sachs was about to hook her phone holster into place too but she paused. Thinking: I really want to talk to Rhyme.

She hit speed dial on her most recent prepaid mobile; it was his number. But the call went right to voice mail. Sachs thought about leaving a message but hung up. She found she wasn't sure what she wanted to say.

Maybe just that she missed him.

CHAPTER 43

LINCOLN RHYME BLINKED. His eyes stung like hell and in his mouth were conflicting tastes; the sweetness of oil and the sourness of chemicals.

He'd just come back to consciousness and was, to his surprise, not coughing as much as he thought he ought to be. An oxygen mask was over his mouth and nose and he was breathing deeply. His throat hurt, though, and he guessed he had been coughing plenty earlier, when he'd been dead to the world.

He looked around, noting that he was in the back of an ambulance, excessively hot, parked on the spit of land where the attack had taken place; he could see the South Cove Inn in the distance, over the choppy blue-and-green bay. A stocky medic with a round black face was leaning forward, manning a flashlight, examining his eyes. He removed the oxygen mask to study Rhyme's mouth and nose.

The man's own face, very dark, gave away nothing. Finally he said in an American inflection, not British: "That water. Very bad. Runoff. Chemicals. All kinds of things. But it doesn't look too bad. Irritation. It hurts?"

"Stings. Bad. Yes."

As if the medic's staccato syntax were contagious.

Rhyme inhaled deeply. "But please, you have to tell me! The two men who were with me? What—?"

"How're his lungs?"

The question was from Thom Reston, who was approaching the back of the ambulance. The aide coughed once then twice, hard.

Rhyme squelched his own cough and muttered in astonishment, "You're...you're all right?"

Thom pointed to his eyes, which were bright red. "Nothing serious. Just a lot of crap in that water."

Very bad. Runoff...

His clothes were soaking, Rhyme noted, and that answered several questions. First, that the aide had been the one who'd rescued him.

And, second, that the two shots he'd heard had been meant for Mychal Poitier.

I have a wife and two children I am supporting. I love them very much...

Rhyme was heartsick at the man's death. After

the corporal had been killed Thom must have dived into the water to save Rhyme as the attackers fled.

The medic listened to his chest again. "Surprising. They're good, your lungs. I see the scar, the ventilator, but it's an old scar. You've done well. You work out. And your right arm, the prosthetic system. I've read about that. Very impressive."

Except not impressive enough to save Mychal Poitier.

The paramedic rose and said, "I would rinse them, your eyes and mouth. Water. Nothing else. Bottled. Three, four times a day. And see your own doctor. When you get home. I'll be back in a moment." He turned and stepped away, his feet crunching on the sand and gravel.

Rhyme said, "Thank you, Thom. Thank you. Saved my life yet again and not with clonidine." The medicine to bring down blood pressure after an attack of autonomic dysreflexia. "I tried the ventilator."

"I know. It was tangled around your neck. I had to pull it off. Wish I'd had Amelia's switchblade."

Rhyme sighed. "But Mychal. It's terrible…"

Thom lifted a sphygmomanometer from a rack in the ambulance. He took Rhyme's blood pressure himself. As he did this, he shrugged. "It's not that serious."

"The blood pressure?"

"No, I mean Poitier. Quiet. I need to hear the pulse."

Rhyme was sure he'd misheard; his ears were still clogged with water. "But—"

"Shhh." The aide was holding a purloined stethoscope to Rhyme's arm.

"You said—"

"Quiet!" A moment later he nodded. "Pressure's fine." A glance in the direction in which the medic had disappeared. "Not that I didn't trust him but I wanted to see for—"

"What do you mean it isn't that serious, about Mychal?"

"Well, you saw: He got kicked and hit. But nothing too bad."

"He was shot!"

"Shot? No, he wasn't."

"I heard two gunshots."

"Oh, that."

Rhyme snapped, "What do you mean, 'Oh, that'?"

Thom explained, "The guy who kicked you into the water, in the gray shirt? He was shooting at Ron."

"Pulaski? Jesus, he all right?"

"He's fine too."

"What the fuck happened?" Rhyme blurted.

Thom laughed. "Glad you're feeling better."

"What. Happened?"

"Ron finished up at the South Cove and came over here. You told him that's where we'd be. He drove up in the rental just after you went for your swim. He saw what was going on and drove right toward the one with the gun, really floored it. The guy shot at the car twice but must've figured Ron was the first of the reinforcements and since there was only one way out they jumped in the Mercury and the pickup and beat it."

"Mychal's all right?"

"That's what I said."

The relief was immeasurable. Rhyme said nothing for a moment as his eyes took in the choppy water nearby, an arc of spray in the sunlight, low to the west. "The wheelchair?"

Thom shook his head. "That's *not* so all right."

"Pricks," Rhyme muttered. He had no sentimental feelings about hardware, either professional or personal. But he'd grown quite attached to the Storm Arrow as a practical matter because it was such a fine piece of machinery and he'd worked hard to master it. Operating a wheelchair is a true skill. He was furious at the thugs.

The aide continued, "I'm borrowing one of theirs." A glance at the medical team. "Non-motorized. Well, motorized by yours truly."

Another figure appeared.

"Well, the rookie saves the day."

"You don't look too bad," Pulaski said. "Damp. I don't think I've ever seen you damp, Lincoln."

"What'd you find at the inn?"

"Not much else. The maid confirmed pretty much what Corporal Poitier told us. A tough-looking American was asking about Moreno and suite twelve hundred. He said he was a friend and was thinking of throwing a party for him. Wanted to know who was with him, what his schedule was, who was his friend—I assume that was his guard."

"Party," Rhyme grunted and looked around the ambulance. The medic returned with burly assistants, one of whom was pushing a battered wheelchair. Rhyme asked, "You have any brandy or anything?"

"Brandy?"

"Medicinal brandy."

"Medicinal brandy?" The man's large face drew into a frown. "Let me think. I suppose doctors down here do administer that some—being a third-world island, of course. I'm afraid I missed that course when I got my emergency health services degree at the University of Maryland."

Touché.

But the doctor was clearly amused, not offended, and gestured to the assistants, who got Rhyme into the battered chair. He couldn't remember the last time he'd been in one that didn't have a battery and motor, and he didn't like the sensation of helplessness. It took him back to the days just after the accident.

"I want to see Mychal," he said. Instinctively he reached for the chair's controller before recalling it wasn't there. He didn't bother to go for the handgrip on the wheel to propel himself forward. If he couldn't pull the fucking trigger of a gun he wasn't going to be able to move his own deadweight over broken asphalt and sand with one hand.

Thom wheeled him the thirty feet to where Poitier sat on a creosote-soaked eight-by-eight beam, beside the two RBPF officers who'd responded to the emergency call.

Poitier rose. "Ah, Captain. I heard you were safe. Good, good. You look none the worse for wear."

"Damp," Pulaski repeated. Drawing a smile from Thom and scowl from Rhyme.

"And you?"

"Fine. Little groggy. They gave me some pain medicine. My first fight in five years on the force and I didn't do very well. Blindsided. I was blindsided."

"Did anyone see tag numbers?" Rhyme asked.

"There were none, no number plates. And it won't do any good to look up gold-and-black Mercurys or white pickup trucks. I'm sure they were stolen. I will look at mug shots back in the station but that will be useless too. Still we have to go through the motions."

Suddenly a plume of dust rose from the direction of the SW Road. A car, no, two cars were moving in fast.

The RBPF officers who were standing nearby stiffened uneasily.

Not because these cars represented a physical threat. Rhyme could see that the unmarked Ford sported red grille lights, which flashed dramatically. He wasn't surprised that the man in the backseat was Assistant Commissioner McPherson. A second car, a marked RBPF cruiser, was behind.

They both skidded to a stop near the ambulance and McPherson climbed angrily from the car, slammed the door.

Storming toward Poitier, he said, "What has happened here?"

Rhyme explained, shouldering the blame.

The assistant commissioner glared at him then turned and raged in a low growl at his corporal, "I will not have this insubordination. You should have told me."

Rhyme expected the young man would roll over. But he stared into his boss's eyes.

"Sir, with all respect. I was given the Moreno homicide to handle."

"It was your case to handle according to proper procedures. And that doesn't include bringing an interloper into the field with you."

"This was a lead. The sniper was here. I should have searched last week."

"We have to see what the—"

Poitier interjected, "Venezuelan authorities have to say."

"Do not interrupt me again, Corporal. And do not take that attitude with me."

"Yes, sir. Sorry, sir."

Rhyme said, "This is an important case, Commissioner, with implications for both our countries."

"And you, Captain Rhyme, you. Do you understand you nearly got a policeman on my force killed?"

The criminalist fell silent.

His voice flinty he added, "And yourself too. We don't need any more dead Americans in the Bahamas. We've had our share." A cool glance to his side. "You're suspended, Corporal. There will be an inquiry that may result in your termination. At the very least, you'll be reassigned back to Traffic."

Dismay flooded Poitier's face. "But—"

"And you, Captain Rhyme, you are leaving the Bahamas immediately. My officers here will escort you to the airport, along with your associates. Your belongings will be collected from your motel and given to you there. We have already called the airline. You have seats on a flight that leaves in two hours. You'll be in custody until then. And you, Corporal, you will surrender your weapon and your identification at headquarters."

"Yes, sir."

But suddenly Ron Pulaski strode forward and confronted the assistant commissioner, who was easily twice his weight and several inches taller. "No," the young patrolman said.

"I beg your pardon?"

The young officer said firmly, "We're going to spend the night at our motel. Leave in the morning."

"What?" McPherson blinked.

"We are not leaving tonight."

"That's not acceptable, Officer Pulaski."

"Lincoln nearly died. He's not getting on an airplane until he's had some rest."

"You've committed crimes—"

Pulaski unholstered his phone. "Should we call the embassy and discuss the matter with them? Of course, I'd have to mention what we're doing down here, the specific crime we're investigating."

Silence, except for the clang of the mysterious machinery in the factory behind them and the lapping of the shimmering waves.

The brass glowered. "All right," McPherson muttered. "But you take the first flight in the morning. You'll be escorted to your motel and confined to your room until then."

Rhyme said, "Thank you, Commissioner. I appreciate it. I apologize for any difficulties I've caused your force. Good luck with this case. And with the murder investigation of the American student." He looked at Poitier. "And again, I'm sorry to you too, Corporal."

Five minutes later Rhyme, Thom and Pulaski were in the Ford van, leaving the spit, with a police escort behind them to make sure they arrived—and stayed put—at their motel. The two large officers in the squad car were unsmiling and wary. Rhyme in fact didn't mind their presence; after all, the trio from the gold Mercury was still at large.

"Goddamn good job, rookie."

"Better than competent?"

"You exceeded competence."

The young officer laughed. "I had a hunch you needed to buy some time."

"That's exactly right. I liked the embassy part, by the way."

"Improvising. So what do we do next?"

"We let the bread bake," Rhyme said cryptically. "And see if we can't rustle up some of this Bahamian rum I've been hearing about."

CHAPTER 44

INTO THE PARLOR OF THE TOWN HOUSE, the laboratory, Amelia Sachs carted a milk crate containing the evidence from the Lydia Foster crime scene.

"Did Lincoln call?" she asked Mel Cooper, who eyed the crate with interest.

"Nope, not a word."

Cooper, the expert lab man, was now officially on board, thanks to a call by Lon Sellitto and Captain Myers, to arrange for his reassignment to the Rhyme Precinct. Cooper, an NYPD detective, was balding and diminutive and wore thick Harry Potter glasses that never seemed to remain exactly perched where they should be. You would think his off-hours life would be filled with math puzzles and *Scientific American* but his leisure time was largely taken with ballroom dancing competitions, with his stunningly gorgeous Scandinavian girlfriend, a mathematics professor at Columbia University.

Nance Laurel was at her desk. The woman glanced blankly at the physical evidence, then back to the policewoman, and Sachs didn't know if this was a greeting or a symptom of one of the pauses before she spoke.

Sachs offered grimly, "I got it wrong. There're two perps." She explained about her erroneous assumption. "I was following the sniper. The man who killed Lydia Foster's somebody else."

"Who do you think?" Cooper asked.

"Bruns's backup."

"Or a specialist hired by Metzger to clean up," Laurel said. It seemed to Sachs that her voice brightened at this. Good news for the case, good news for the jury—that their primary suspect would order one of his officers to do something so heartless. Not a word of sympathy for the victim, not a frown of concern.

Sachs truly hated the woman at this moment.

She continued, pointedly speaking only to Mel Cooper, "Lon's agreed to keep it a motive-unknown case for the time being—like the IED at the Java Hut's still officially a gas main explosion. I thought it was better not to let Metzger know how the investigation's going."

Laurel was nodding. "Good."

Sachs stared at the whiteboards then began to revise them in light of what they'd learned. "Let's give Lydia Foster's killer the title Unsub Five Sixteen. After today's date."

Laurel asked, "Anything more about the ID of the shooter, the man you followed to NIOS?"

"No. Lon's got a surveillance team on him. They'll call as soon as they make an ID."

Another pause. Laurel said, "I'm just curious: Did you think about getting his fingerprints?"

"His—"

"When you were following the sniper downtown? The reason I'm asking is I was working a case once and an undercover detective dropped a glossy magazine. The subject picked it up for her. We got his prints."

"Well," Sachs said evenly, "I didn't."

Because if I had done that we'd have his fucking ID by now. Which we don't.

An impenetrably cryptic nod from Laurel.

Just curious . . .

That was as irritating as "if you don't mind."

Sachs turned away from her, wincing slightly, and handed off the evidence from the Lydia Foster crime scene to Mel Cooper, who regarded the slim pickings with the same dismay that Sachs felt.

"That's it?"

"Afraid so. Unsub Five Sixteen knows what he's

doing." Sachs was looking at the photos of Lydia Foster's bloody corpse, which she was downloading from the crime scene team in Queens and printing out.

Lips tight, she stepped to one of the whiteboards and taped the pictures up.

"He tortured her," Laurel said softly but with no other reaction.

"And took everything Lydia had about the assignment for Moreno."

"What could she have known?" the ADA wondered. "If he had a commercial interpreter with him on the business trip, he obviously wasn't taking her to meet criminals. She'd be a good witness to testify that Moreno wasn't a terrorist." She added, "That is, *would* have been a good witness."

Sachs felt a burst of anger that the woman's reaction was less about Lydia Foster's death than that she'd lost a brick in the prosecution against Shreve Metzger. Then recalled her own dismay at seeing the body, part of which stemmed from her being too late to get solid information from the interpreter.

The policewoman said, "I had a brief conversation with her earlier. I know she had meetings with Russian and Emirates charities and the Brazilian consulate. That's all."

I never got the chance to find out more, she reflected. Still furious with herself. If Rhyme had been here, he would have speculated that there might be two perps. Shit.

Forget it, she sternly thought. Get on with the case.

She looked at Cooper. "Let's see if we can make some connections. I want to know whether it was Bruns or the unsub who set the IED. You found anything from the Java Hut scene, Mel?"

Cooper explained that there'd been very few clues but he had in fact made some discoveries. The Bomb Squad had delivered the information that the IED was an off-the-shelf anti-personnel device, loaded with Semtex, the Czech plastic explosive. "They're available on the arms market, pretty easily if you have the right connections," Cooper explained. "Most purchasers are military users, both government and mercenaries."

Cooper had run the latent prints Sachs had been able to lift at the coffeehouse and had sent them to IAFIS. They'd come back negative.

The tech said, "You got me a lot of good samplars from the Java Hut but there wasn't a lot of trace that could reasonably be attributed to the perp. Two things were unique, though, which means they might've come from our bomber. The first was eroded limestone, coral and very small bits of shell—sand, in other words, and it's sand from a tropical location. I also found organic crustacean waste."

"What's that?" Laurel asked.

"Crab shit," Sachs answered.

"Exactly," Cooper confirmed. "Though, to be accurate, it could be from lobsters, crayfish, shrimp, krill and barnacles too. There are over sixty-five thousand crustacean species. What I can tell you, though, is that it's typical of beaches in the Caribbean. And the trace includes residue consistent with evaporated seawater."

Sachs frowned. "So he might've been the man in the South Cove Inn just before Moreno was shot. Would sand still cling after a week?"

"These were fine grains. Yes, it's possible. They can be very adhesive."

"What else did you catch, Mel?"

"Something I've never found at a crime scene— 1,5-dicaffeoylquinic acid."

"Which is?"

"Cynarine," Cooper said, reading from a computer database of chemical substances. "Most commonly it's the biologically active component of artichokes. It gives them the sweet flavor."

"And our perp left traces of that?"

"Can't say for sure but I found some on the doorstep of Java Hut, on the knob and on a fragment of the IED."

Sachs nodded. Artichokes. Curious but that's how crime scene work went. Many pieces to the puzzle.

"Nothing else."

"That's *it* for the Java Hut?"

"Yep."

"So we still don't know who planted the bomb."

Then she and Cooper turned to the Lydia Foster scene.

"First," the tech said, nodding at the photos of her body, "the knife wounds. They look unusual, very narrow. But there's no database to let us know."

The United States, home of the National Rifle Association, was the gunshot capital of the world. Death by knife was common in the United Kingdom and other countries with strict gun control laws but in America, with the ubiquity of guns, knives were relatively rare weapons in homicides. So no law enforcement agency had compiled a knife wound computer image database, at least none that Sachs and Rhyme knew about.

Even though she was sure he'd worn gloves, Sachs had still lifted prints from around—and on—Lydia Foster's corpse. You never knew if a perp might have taken his gloves off at some point. But as with Java Hut, these came back from the automated database negative.

"Didn't expect anything different," she muttered. "But I found a hair that didn't match the samplars. There, in the envelope." Sachs handed it to the tech. "Brown and short. Might be the perp's. Remember Corporal Poitier said the man checking out Moreno's suite the day before the killing had short brown hair. Oh, the follicle's attached."

"Good. I'll get it to CODIS."

The nationwide DNA database was expanding at an exponential rate. Whoever the hair belonged to might be in the system; if so, they'd have his identity and, possibly, his present whereabouts soon.

Sachs began looking through the rest of the evidence. Though the killer had taken every single document, computer and media storage device that might have mentioned Robert Moreno, she had found something that might be relevant. A Starbucks receipt. The date and time printed at the top indicated the afternoon of May 1. Sachs recalled that this was probably when Moreno had his private meeting, the one Lydia had not attended. It might be possible to identify the office where the activist went.

Tomorrow she'd go to the location—a building on Chambers Street.

Sachs and Cooper went through the rest of the trace from Lydia's apartment but weren't able to isolate very much. Cooper ran a sample through the gas chromatograph and looked up toward the women. "Got something here. A plant. It's *Glycyrrhiza glabra*—a legume, sort of like a bean or pea. Basically, it's licorice."

Sachs said, "Anise or fennel?"

"No, no relation, though the tastes are similar."

Nance Laurel looked mystified. "You didn't look anything up. Cynarine, *Glycyrrhiza*...I'm sorry, but how do you *know* all this?"

Cooper shoved his black glasses higher on his nose and said, as if it were obvious, "I work for Lincoln Rhyme."

CHAPTER 45

FINALLY A BREAK: They caught the shooter's real name.

Captain Myers's Special Services surveillance team had followed the sniper from NIOS headquarters to his home. He'd gotten off in Carroll Gardens and walked to a house that was owned by Barry and Margaret Shales. A motor vehicle search had returned a picture of Shales. It was clearly the same man whom Sachs had been following that afternoon and taken a picture of with her mobile phone's camera.

Barry Shales was thirty-nine. Former military—retiring as a captain in the air force and decorated several times. The man was now working civilian as an "intelligence specialist" with NIOS. He and his wife—a teacher—had two children, boys in elementary school. Shales was active in his Presbyterian church and volunteered at the boys' schools, a reading tutor.

Learning this bio, Sachs was troubled. Most of the perps she and Rhyme pursued were hardened criminals, serial offenders, organized crime bosses, psychotics, terrorists. But this case was different. Shales was probably a devoted civil servant, probably a decent husband and father. Just doing his duty, even if it happened to involve shooting terrorists in cold blood. Upon his arrest and conviction, a family would be destroyed. Metzger might have been using NIOS for his own delusional approach in safeguarding the country and using a specialist for clean-up. But Shales? He might have been just following orders.

Still, even if he hadn't been the one who'd tortured and killed Lydia Foster, he was part of the organization that possibly had.

Sachs called Lon Sellitto and told him of their discovery. Then she placed a call to Information Services, requesting every fact they could dig up on Barry Shales—most important where he'd been and what he was doing on May 9, the day of the shooting.

The lab phone rang and Sachs, noting the caller ID, hit speaker. "Fred."

She wasn't worried that Unsub 516 was tapping this particular phone line; Rodney Szarnek had sent over a device he called a "tap-trap," which could detect anyone's listening in. The monitor showed that the conversation was private.

"Amelia. Is it true what I'm hearing? Your friend and mine is sunning himself in the Caribbean."

His astonishment was so exaggerated that Sachs had to smile. Cooper did too. Nance Laurel did not.

"He sure is, Fred."

"Why oh why do *my* assignments take me to the prime vacation spots of the South Bronx and Newark? While Mr. Lincoln Rhyme's on a beach, courtesy of the city of New York? Where's the fairness in that? Is he enjoying those sissy drinks with umbrellas and plastic sea horses?"

"I think he's paying for it himself, Fred. And how do you know they serve drinks down there with plastic sea horses?"

"Busted," the agent admitted. "The coconut ones, they're my personal favorites. Now, how's the case goin'? That homicide on Third Avenue, that was related? Lydia Foster. Saw it on the wire."

"Afraid it was. We think it's a clean-up op, probably that Metzger ordered."

"Fuck," Dellray spat out. "Man's gone rogue big time."

"He sure has." Sachs told him too that they'd

found there were two perps. "We still don't know which of them set the bomb at the coffee shop."

"Well, I gotcha a few things you might be interested in."

"Go ahead. Anything."

"First off, the mobile your sniper was using—the one registered to Mr. Code Name Don Bruns, with that fake Social Security number and a Delaware corporation? The company's buried way deep but I traced it to some shell outfits that NIOS's used in the past. Probably why the phone's still active. Lotta time the government thinks they're too smart to get found out. Or too big. But you didn't hear that from me."

"Good. Thanks, Fred."

"And turns out your friend the late and great Mr. Moreno was *not* planning to detonate a big bang of mass destruction and move into a cave."

He explained he was referring to Robert Moreno's mysterious message about "vanishing into thin air, May twenty-fourth."

"What was it about?" Sachs asked.

The FBI agent continued, "Was a play on words, seems. What it is: Some of our folk down in Venezuela found out that Moreno and his family were moving into a new house on the twenty-fourth."

He gave them the details: Robert Moreno had

bought a four-bedroom home in the Venezuelan city of San Cristóbal, one of the more upscale locales in the country. It was on a mountaintop.

Thin air...

Laurel nodded at his words, obviously pleased. So Moreno might not be the Western Hemisphere's answer to Bin Laden.

Gotta keep the jury happy, Sachs thought cynically.

The agent continued, "Oh, and the IED attack in Mexico City on May thirteen? Now, this one's almost funny. The only thing with a Moreno connection on that date in Mexico City was a big fund-raiser for a charity he was involved with. Classrooms for the Americas. Called Balloon Day. Everbody bought a balloon for ten dollars then you popped it and got a prize inside. They had over a thousand balloons. I gotta say, *my* lungs aren't up to a task like that."

Sachs slumped, closing her eyes. Jesus.

Can we find somebody to blow them up?...

"Thanks, Fred." She disconnected.

Upon hearing these revelations, Laurel said, "Interesting how first impressions can be so completely wrong. Isn't it?" She didn't seem to be gloating but Sachs couldn't tell.

If you don't mind...

I'm just curious...

Sachs fished out her phone and called Lincoln Rhyme.

His answering words: "I'm thinking we should get a chameleon."

Not "Hello" or "Sachs."

"A...lizard?"

"They're quite interesting. I haven't seen one change color yet. Do you know how they do it, Sachs? Metachrosis is what it's called, you know. They use hormonal cell signaling to trigger changes in the chromatophore cells in their skin. I find it truly fascinating. So how's the case going up *there*?"

She ran through the developments.

Rhyme considered this. "I suppose that makes sense, two different perps. Metzger isn't going to use his star sniper in New York to clean up. I should have thought of that."

I should have too, she reflected sadly. Picturing Lydia Foster's body.

"Upload a picture of Shales, DMV or military."

"Sure. I'll do it when we hang up." Then in a somber voice she told him in detail about the death of Moreno's interpreter, Lydia.

"Torture?"

She described the knife work.

"Distinctive technique," he assessed. "That might be helpful."

He'd be referring to the fact that perps who use knives or other mechanical weapons, like clubs, tended to leave wounds that were consistent from one victim to another, which can often identify them. She noted too that this detached, clinical comment was his only reaction to the horrific attack.

But this was just Lincoln Rhyme. She knew it; she accepted it. And wondered in passing why the same attitude in Nance Laurel set her so on edge.

She asked, "How's it going down in the balmy Caribbean?"

"Not making much headway, Sachs. We're under house arrest."

"*What?*"

"One way or the other, it'll be resolved tomorrow." He clearly wasn't going to say any more, maybe concerned that *his* line was tapped. "I should go. Thom's making something for dinner. I think it's ready. And you really should try dark rum sometime. It's quite good. Made from sugar, you know."

"I may pass on the rum. There are some unpleasant memories. Though I guess they're not memories if you can't remember them."

"What do you think of the case now, Sachs? You still in the policy and politics camp? Leaving it all to Congress?"

"Nope. Not anymore. One look at the crime scene at Lydia Foster's convinced me. There're some real bad sons of bitches involved in this. And they're going down. Oh, and Rhyme, by the way: If you hear something about an IED blast up here, don't worry, I'm fine." She explained about the explosion that took out the computer at the coffee shop, without going into the details of the near miss.

He then said, "It's rather pleasant down here, Sachs. I'm thinking we might want to come back some time—unofficially."

"A vacation. Yeah, Rhyme, let's do it."

"You couldn't drive very fast. Traffic's terrible."

She said, "I've always wanted to try a Jet Ski. And you could go to a beach."

"I've already been in the water," he told her.

"Seriously?"

"Yes, indeed. I'll tell you about it later."

She said, "Miss you." She disconnected before he had a chance to say the same.

Or not.

Nance Laurel received a call on her own mobile. Sachs was aware of her reacting stiffly as she glanced at caller ID. When she answered, the tone in the ADA's voice told Sachs immediately that this was a private matter, unrelated to the case. "Well, hi... How are you?"

The woman turned away from Sachs and Cooper, turned as far as she could. But Sachs could still hear. "You need them? I didn't think you did. I packed them up."

Odd. Sachs had not thought of the prosecutor as having a personal life. She wore no wedding or engagement ring—very little jewelry at all. Sachs could imagine her vacationing with her mother or sister; Nance Laurel as a wife or lover was hard to picture.

Still coddling her conversation, Laurel said into the phone, "No, no. I know where they are."

What was that tone?

Sachs realized: She's vulnerable, defenseless. Whoever she was talking to had some kind of personal power over her. A breakup that isn't completely broken yet? Probably.

Laurel disconnected, sat for a moment, as if collecting her thoughts. And then she rose, picked up her purse. "There's something I have to take care of."

Odd to see her so shaken.

Sachs found herself asking, "Anything I can do?"

"No. I'll see you in the morning. I . . . I'll be back in the morning."

Clutching her briefcase, the prosecutor walked from the parlor and out the front door of the town house. Sachs noted that her workstation remained cluttered, documents shuffled and scattered about—completely the opposite of how she'd left things last night.

As Sachs gazed toward the table, one piece of paper stood out. She walked over and picked it up. She read:

From: Assistant District Attorney Nance Laurel
To: District Attorney Franklin Levine (Man-
  hattan County)
Re: People v. Metzger, et al. Update, Tuesday
  May 16

In researching leads to the case, I identified the chauffeur with Elite Limousines who drove Robert Moreno throughout the city on May 1. The driver's name is Atash Farada. There are several things to consider from my research, relevant to this case.

  1. Robert Moreno was accompanied by a woman in her thirties, possibly an escort or prostitute. He might have paid her a "significant" sum of cash. Her given name was "Lydia."

  2. He and this individual left the driver in his limo at a downtown location for a pe-

riod of several hours. Farada's impression was that Moreno did not want him to know where he was going.

3. *The driver offered a motive for Moreno's anti-American sentiments. A good friend was killed by U.S. troops in the Panama invasion, December 1989.*

Sachs was taken aback. The memo was nearly identical to the email she had sent to Laurel earlier, as instructed by the Overseer. Except for a few variations.

From: Detective Amelia Sachs, NYPD
To: Assistant District Attorney Nance Laurel
Re: Moreno Homicide, Update, Tuesday
  May 16

In researching leads to the case I identified the driver (Atash Farada) with Elite Limo, who drove Robert Moreno throughout the city on May 1. My discussions with him revealed several things of importance to the investigation:

1. *Moreno was accompanied by a woman in her thirties possibly an escort or prostitute. I considered too whether or not she was a*

terrorist or other operative. He might have paid her a "significant" sum of cash. Her first name was Lydia.

2. *He and the woman left the driver in a downtown location for a period of time. Driver's impression was that Moreno did not want him to know where he and Lydia were going.*

3. *Driver suggested motive for anti-American activity. Good friend was killed in Panama invasion.*

Laurel stole my work.

And not only that but she had to fucking edit it too.

Sachs went through the half dozen other memos that she'd dutifully written and sent to the ADA.

If you don't mind...

Well, Sachs *did* mind—because they were all doctored to make it sound like Laurel had done the research. In fact, Sachs's name didn't appear on a single piece of paper. Rhyme's was prominently featured but Sachs was virtually cut out of the investigation altogether.

Goddamn it. What was this about?

Looking for answers, she dug through the stacks.

Many of the documents were copies of court opin-
ions and legal briefs.'

But one at the bottom was different.

And it explained a great deal.

Sachs glanced at Mel Cooper, who was hunched
over a microscope. He hadn't seen her pilfering
Laurel's paperwork. Sachs took the document
she'd just uncovered and photocopied it, slipping
the sheet into her purse. She returned the original
to Laurel's workstation and was very careful to put
it back exactly where she'd found it. Even though
the space seemed cluttered, Sachs wouldn't have
been surprised if the prosecutor had memorized the
position of every paper—and paper clip—before
leaving.

Sachs wanted to be sure the woman had no idea
she'd been busted.

IV

SLICE

CHAPTER 46

C APTAIN RHYME, YOU ARE FEELING BET-
TER?"

After a suitable pause: "I am," he told
Royal Bahamas Police Force assistant commissioner McPherson. "Thank you for asking. We're
packed and will be en route to the airport shortly."
Rhyme's mobile was on speaker.

The time was 8 a.m. and Rhyme was in the living
room of the hot and oh-so-humid motel suite. Thom
and Pulaski were sitting on the veranda, sipping
coffee, in the company of two more chameleons.

A pause. "May I ask a question, Captain
Rhyme?"

"I suppose." He sounded put out. Tired. Pris-
onerish.

"I am perplexed by one thing you said."

"What was that?"

"You said you wished us luck in the *murder* investigation of the American student."

"Yes?"

"But the young woman died in an accident. Drinking and swimming."

Rhyme let several seconds of silence build, as if he were confused. "Oh, I'd be very surprised if that were the case."

"How do you mean, Captain?"

"I don't really have time to discuss it, Commissioner. We have to be at the airport soon. I'll leave it to you to—"

"Please... You really think the student was murdered?"

"I'm sure of it, yes."

The conclusion that the student's death was a murder had occurred to him while enjoying conch fritters in the Hurricane Café and looking over the gruesome crime scene photos. He had, however, decided to refrain from offering his thoughts to Corporal Poitier just then.

The assistant commissioner said, "Go on, please."

"Go on?" Rhyme asked, sounding perplexed.

"Yes, tell me about your thoughts. They're intriguing."

We let the bread bake...

"Be that as it may, I have to get to the airport. Good luck again, Assistant Commissioner."

"Wait! Please! Captain Rhyme, perhaps I was

somewhat hasty yesterday. It was an unfortunate incident that happened at Clifton Bay. And Corporal Poitier was, after all, acting insubordinately."

"Frankly, Assistant Commissioner, my experience has been that in our line of work the best results are often achieved by the most insubordinate."

"Yes, perhaps that's true. But could you just give me some thoughts about—"

Rhyme said quickly, "I might be able to help..." His voice faded.

"Yes?"

"But in exchange I would like Corporal Poitier reinstated."

"He hasn't been precisely de-stated. The paperwork is sitting on my desk as we speak. But I haven't signed anything yet."

"Good. And I would need access to the Robert Moreno crime scene at the South Cove Inn, as well as the autopsy reports and the three victims' clothing. And any relevant evidence collected there—the bullet in particular. I must see that bullet."

A faint tap from the speakerphone. The assistant commissioner was clearly not used to negotiating.

Rhyme looked over the others, on whom the sun was beginning to fall in its searing glory. Pulaski gave him an encouraging grin.

After a pause—a gravid pause, Rhyme thought

wryly—the assistant commissioner said, "Very good, Captain. You perhaps can come to my office now to discuss this matter?"

"Provided my associate is there too?"

"Your associate?"

"Corporal Poitier."

"Of course. I'll arrange it now."

CHAPTER 47

THE ASSISTANT COMMISSIONER'S OFFICE at the Royal Bahamas Police Force was opulently shabby, more residential than official.

The chamber exuded colonial ambience, which made Rhyme feel right at home. His own working space, the laboratory *née* parlor, dated back to the era of Victoria. Here, though the RBPF building was newer, McPherson's office too was cast in an earlier time—with a chintz sofa, a washbasin and pitcher, a large oak armoire, yellow-shaded lamps and, on the wall, pictures of men who had to be governors-general or similar officials. Several formal uniforms—one spotless white, one navy blue—hung stiffly on racks.

Some touches of modern times were present, of course: battered gray file cabinets, three mobile phones sitting on the functional beige desk and two impressive computers. Dominating one wall was a detailed map of New Providence Island.

The climate in here was warm—the air-conditioning was struggling—and the humidity intense. Rhyme deduced that McPherson kept the windows open most of the time and had artificially cooled the room in honor of his visitors this morning. The deduction was supported by another attendee—a chameleon sitting on the sill inside.

The large man, in a pressed khaki uniform, rose and shook Rhyme's hand carefully. "You're well, Captain Rhyme?"

"Yes. Some rest was just what I needed."

"Excellent."

He shook the hands of Pulaski and Thom as well. A moment later Mychal Poitier walked uncertainly into the room. Greetings all 'round.

The assistant commissioner sat and suddenly he was all business, regarding Rhyme with narrow, focused eyes. "Now, the student. Please, sir. You said murder."

Rhyme said, "She was definitely killed intentionally, yes. It was planned out beforehand. And she was beaten before she died, I think."

"Beaten?" Poitier tilted his head.

The criminalist said, "The clue is her jewelry. In the crime scene photos I noted that her bracelets, watch, finger and toe rings were gold. But her necklace was silver leaves. That seemed out of place, mixing the two."

"What does—?" the assistant commissioner started. Then fell silent. Rhyme had frowned at the interruption.

"I think her assailant beat her badly and wanted to hide that fact. When he was finished, he drowned her and put the necklace on. He knew that scavenger fish'd be attracted to the shiny metal—I read about that on the flight here. I assume it's in all the guidebooks: warnings not to wear anything flashy. Silver is particularly attractive because it resembles fish scales, more so than gold. The fish took care of the evidence of the beating by removing most of the facial skin.

"We know her killer planned this all out ahead of time because he brought the silver necklace with him."

Poitier asked, "Why would he do that? There was no evidence of sexual assault."

"Revenge maybe. But I have some thoughts that might lead us a bit farther. We'll need to talk to the medical examiner. I'd like to know about the student's postmortem blood workup." When the assistant commissioner remained staring at Rhyme, the criminalist said to him, "It would be helpful to know that now."

"Yes. Of course." McPherson lifted the receiver

from his desk phone and made a call. He spoke for a moment to a clerk or assistant, it seemed, then he said into the mouthpiece, "I don't care if he's in an autopsy. The body will be just as dead when he returns. Fetch him."

After a brief pause McPherson resumed his conversation. He looked at Rhyme, holding the phone away from his ear. "The results are in. The coroner has the report in front of him."

The criminalist asked, "Blood alcohol?"

The question was posed. Then: "Point zero seven."

Pulaski said, "Not legally drunk but close."

Rhyme asked quickly, "What was she drinking?"

Poitier said, "We found Bacardi rum, eighty proof, and Coca-Cola in the car. Both open."

"Diet or regular? The soft drink."

"Regular."

Rhyme then said to McPherson, "Ask the coroner her postmortem glucose level. And I don't want the vascular system results. Those aren't reliable; glycolysis continues after death. I want the *vitreous* concentration." He explained, "No glycolytic enzymes there."

McPherson stared. In fact, everyone in the room did.

Rhyme continued impatiently, "I want the glucose level from the vitreous fluid in her eye. It's standard procedure. I'm sure they ran it."

The man posed the question. The answer was 4.2 milligrams per deciliter.

"Low normal." The criminalist smiled. "I knew it. She wasn't drinking recreationally. If she'd mixed Coke and rum the level would be higher. Her killer forced her to swallow some rum straight and then just left the soft drink bottle open to make it look like she'd been mixing them." Rhyme turned back to the assistant commissioner again. "Drug screen?"

Again the question was posed.

"Negative for everything."

"Good," Rhyme said enthusiastically. "We're getting somewhere. Now we need to look into her job."

Poitier said, "She was a part-time salesclerk in Nassau."

"No, not *that* job. Her job as a prostitute, I mean."

"What? How do you know?"

"The pictures." He glanced at Poitier. "The pictures that you showed me on your iPad. She had multiple injection marks on her arm. Her blood was negative for narcotics or other drugs, we just learned, so why the tracks? Can't be insulin; diabetics don't inject intravenously there. No, it was probably—probably, mind you, not for certain—that she had regular blood tests for sexually transmitted disease."

"A prostitute." The assistant commissioner seemed pleased by this. The American who'd died under his watch wasn't an innocent student after all.

"You can hang up now." Rhyme's eyes dipped to the phone, hanging like a motionless pendulum.

McPherson did, after an abrupt goodbye to the medical examiner.

"So, our next step?" Poitier asked.

"To find out where the woman worked," Pulaski said, "and picked up her johns."

Rhyme nodded. "Yes. That's probably where she met her killer. The gold jewelry was expensive and tasteful. She was in very good shape, healthy. Her face pretty. She wouldn't've been a streetwalker. Check her purse for credit card receipts. We'll see where she bought her cocktails."

The assistant commissioner nodded to Mychal Poitier, who made a call, apparently to the evidence room or someone in the Detective Unit.

The young officer had an extended conversation and eventually hung up. "Well, this is interesting," Poitier said. "Two receipts for the bar in the—"

Something in his tone deposited a fast thought in Rhyme's mind. "The South Cove Inn!"

"Yes, that's right, Captain. How did you know?"

Rhyme didn't answer, he gazed out the window for a full minute. The thoughts were coming quickly. "What's her name?" he asked.

"Annette. Annette Bodel."

"Well, I have good news for both of us, Commissioner McPherson. For you: Ms. Bodel's killer was not Bahamian but American—that's a public relations coup for your country. And for me, I think we've found a connection to the Moreno case. I was wrong about one thing—she was tortured, yes. But I think he used a knife, not his fists, cutting her cheek or nose or tongue."

"How do you know this?" McPherson asked.

"I don't know it, not yet. But I think it's likely. My associate in New York told me that a man who's eliminating witnesses in the case specializes in using knives. He's not the sniper. My guess is that he's the sniper's backup or spotter and was the American who was at the inn on May eighth, learning what he could about suite twelve hundred and Moreno and his guard. He probably picked Annette up in the bar, used her to get information and then left the Bahamas with the sniper after the shooting. But when he heard about the investigation he came back two days ago, Monday, tortured her to find out if she'd told anyone about him and then killed her."

Pulaski said, "We should take a look at the beach where she was found, search it again—this time as a crime scene."

The assistant commissioner looked at Poitier but the corporal shook his head. "This man was smart, sir. He killed her at low tide. The site is under three feet of water."

"Smart indeed." Rhyme's eyes held the assistant commissioner's steadily. He said, "The evidence we're looking at doesn't leave a lot of doubt that Robert Moreno was killed by a U.S. government sniper and that his partner or at least somebody in his organization is cleaning up afterward, including murdering Ms. Bodel in Nassau. That information is going to be public pretty soon. You can stick to the story that the Venezuelan cartel is behind the shooting and ignore the American connection. But then it'll look like you were part of the cover-up. Or you can help us find the shooter and his backup man."

Pulaski broke in: "You ought to know, Commissioner, that it looks like the man who ordered the killing probably acted outside the scope of his authority. If you help us find the perps, it's not going to upset Washington as much as you might think."

Excellent call, Rhyme reflected.

"I'll order the forensics unit to the spit of land to look for the sniper's nest." McPherson turned his broad face to Mychal Poitier. "Corporal, you will escort Captain Rhyme and his associates to the South Cove Inn for a second search of the Moreno crime scene. Assist him in any other way you can. Is that understood?"

"It is, sir."

Speaking now to Rhyme: "And I'll arrange to have the full crime scene report and autopsy information released. Oh, and the evidence too. I assume you'll want that, won't you, Captain?"

"Evidence, yes. I would very much like that." And, with some difficulty, refrained from adding that it was about goddamn time.

CHAPTER 48

BACK ON SW ROAD.

With Thom driving, Poitier, Pulaski and Rhyme were in the accessible van, taking the same route to South Cove Inn they'd been on yesterday for the illicit, and nearly fatal, visit to the outcropping of land in Clifton Bay.

The sun was behind them, high even at this early hour, and the vegetation glowed green and red and rich yellow. A few white flowers, which Rhyme knew Sachs would love to see.

Miss you . . .

She'd disconnected just as he'd drawn a breath to say the same. He smiled at the timing.

They'd stopped briefly to pick up basic evidence collection equipment at the Royal Bahamas Police Force crime scene facility. The gear was high quality and Rhyme was confident that Pulaski and Poitier could find something in the Kill Room that would help them indisputably link Barry Shales to the shooting and, possibly, find clues to Unsub 516's identity.

Soon they were at the inn and pulled up to the front of the impressive but subdued place, in an architectural style that Rhyme supposed was nouveau colonial. Thom steered Rhyme, in the manual wheelchair, down the sidewalk at the entryway, surrounded by beautifully tended gardens.

They entered the lobby and Mychal Poitier greeted the pleasant desk clerk. She was more curious at the presence of a man in a wheelchair than the police officer; the hotel had surely had its share of those recently. The inn seemed accessible, being on one level, but Rhyme supposed the resort— primarily a beach club and golf course—didn't get many disabled guests.

The manager was busy at the moment but the clerk didn't hesitate to prepare a key card for suite 1200.

Pulaski, who'd met her yesterday, nodded a greeting and displayed the picture of Barry Shales that Sachs had emailed. Neither she nor anyone else had ever seen Shales.

Which just about confirmed what Rhyme believed: that it was Unsub 516 who was at the inn on May 8 as Shales's backup man.

With Pulaski and Poitier carrying the collection

equipment, the entourage headed down the corridor the clerk had indicated.

After a walk of several minutes—the inn was quite large—Thom nodded at a sign.

SUITES 1200–1208 →

"Almost there."

They turned the corner. And stopped abruptly.

"Wait," Poitier muttered. "What's this?"

Rhyme was looking at the double doors to suite 1200, the Kill Room—the crime scene that had presumably been marked with police tape and strident warnings not to trespass, duly sealed.

But was no longer.

The doors were wide open and a workman in stained white overalls stood in the middle of the room, with a paint roller, putting what seemed to be the final coat on the wall above the fireplace. The floors of the room were bare wood. The carpet had been removed. And everything else—the bloody sofa, the shards of glass—was gone.

CHAPTER 49

JACOB SWANN WAS EATING a very well-crafted omelet at a diner on the Upper West Side, near Central Park West.

He was in jeans, a windbreaker (black, today), running shoes and white T-shirt. His backpack was at his side. This was a neighborhood in which many people worked jobs where suits and ties weren't required and regular hours weren't the norm—performing arts, museums, galleries. Food service too, of course. Swann blended right in.

The coffee he was sipping was hot and not bitter. The toast thick and buttered before meeting the heating element—the only way to do it. And the omelet? Better than well crafted, he decided. Damn good.

Eggs are the trickiest of ingredients and can make a dish sublime or turn it into a complete rout if you're careless or conditions betray: toughening or curdling or collapsing. A bit of yolk in the whites you're trying to meringue and your baked

390 / JEFFERY DEAVER

Alaska is fucked. And there's always the chance of unpleasant bacteria reproducing eagerly in God's perfect oval (gestating *is* what shells are made for, after all).

But these eggs had been whisked just right—casually and without a whisper of liquid—and then cooked over high heat, the fresh-chopped tarragon, chive and dill sprinkled in at just the right moment, not too soon. The completed mezzaluna-shaped dish was yellow, brown and white, crisp outside, gently curded within.

Despite the food, though, Swann was growing a bit impatient with Amelia Sachs.

She had been inside Lincoln Rhyme's town house now for hours. She'd finessed the phone call issue, switching prepaid mobiles every few hours, it seemed—everybody on the team was using them now—and she had a wiretap alert on the landline into the town house, which there was no way to defeat without physically breaking into the central switch.

But with her being the lead investigator she'd have to emerge sooner or later.

He reflected on her partner, Rhyme. Now, *that* was a setback. It had cost his organization nearly two thousand dollars to eliminate the man, his male nurse and another cop. But his contacts down there from the dock crowd had blown the attempt.

They'd asked if Swann wanted them to try again but he'd told them to get the hell off the island. It would be very difficult to trace them back to Swann and his boss but it could be done.

He was sure there'd be another opportunity to take care of Rhyme. The man certainly couldn't move very fast to get away from the Kai Shun. Swann had looked up Rhyme's condition, quadriplegia, and discovered that the criminalist had no feeling whatsoever in most of his body. Swann was intrigued with the idea of the man's just sitting still and watching someone flay his skin off—and slowly bleed to death—while feeling no pain.

What an interesting idea: butchering a creature while it was alive.

Curious. He'd have to—

Ah, but here is our beautiful Amelia.

She wasn't coming from the direction he'd expected her—the L-shaped cul-de-sac for deliveries behind the town house, near where her Ford Torino was parked. She'd apparently left via the front door, which faced Central Park West. She was now walking west along the crosstown street's sidewalk, across from the diner.

He'd hoped to get her in the cul-de-sac; there were too many pedestrians, stragglers on their way to work, here at the moment. But finding her alone would be only a matter of time.

Swann casually wiped the utensils and coffee mug, smearing prints. He paid by slipping a ten and a five under the plate, rather than taking the check to the cashier. He'd gotten these bills in change from a hotel concierge across town; cash from an ATM is frighteningly traceable, so he'd engaged in a little micro money laundering, leaving a generous but not overly so tip.

Now he was out the door, climbing into his Nissan.

He observed Sachs through the windshield. Vigilant, she looked around carefully, though not toward him—only at those places where an attacker might come from. Interesting too: She looked up, scanning.

Don't worry, Swann thought to her. That's not where the bullet's going to come from.

As she fished for car keys her jacket slipped away from her hip and he noted she wore a Glock.

He started his car at the same time she did hers, to cover the sound of his ignition.

As Sachs's Torino sped away from the curb, Swann followed.

His only regret was that her fate would be that bullet he'd just been thinking of; using the Kai Shun on her silken flesh wasn't an option in the present recipe.

CHAPTER 50

MYCHAL POITIER WAS SPEAKING to the manager of the South Cove.

"But, Officer, I thought you knew," said the tall, curly-haired man in a very nice beige suit. He was presently frowning creases deep into his rosily tanned forehead. His accent was mildly British.

"Knew what?" Poitier muttered.

"You told us we could reopen the room and clean it, repair the damage."

"I? I never said any such thing."

"No, no, not you. But someone from your department. They called me and said to release the scene. I don't remember his name."

Rhyme asked, "He *called*? No one came here in person?"

"No, it was a phone call."

Rhyme sighed. He asked, "When was this?"

"Monday."

Poitier turned and looked at Rhyme with a dismayed gaze. "I gave very strict orders that the scene should have remained sealed. I can't imagine who in the department—"

"It wasn't anybody in your department," Rhyme said. "Our unsub made the call."

And the accomplice, of course, was the manager's fervent desire to eliminate any sign that a murder had been committed here. Crime scene placards in hallways do not make for good public relations.

"I'm sorry, Corporal," the manager said defensively.

Rhyme asked, "Where's the carpet, sofa, the shattered window glass? The other furniture?"

"A rubbish tip somewhere, I should suppose. I have no idea. We used a contractor. Because of the blood, they said they would burn the carpet and couch."

All the trash fires...

Pulaski said, "Right after he killed Annette, our unsub makes one call and, bang, there goes the crime scene. Pretty smart, you think about it. Simple."

It was. Rhyme looked into the immaculate room. The only evidence of the crime was the missing window, over which plastic had been taped.

"If there's anything I can do," the manager said.

When no one said a word, he retreated.

Thom wheeled Rhyme into the suite and, since the Kill Room wasn't wheelchair-accessible, he was helped down two low stairs by Poitier and Pulaski.

The room was pale blue and green—the paint still wet on several walls—and measured about twenty by thirty feet, with two doors leading to what appeared to be bedrooms to the right. These too were empty and were primed for painting. To the left upon entering was a full kitchen.

Rhyme looked out one of the remaining windows. There was a trim garden outside the room, dominated by a smooth-trunked tree that rose about forty feet into the air. He noted that the lower branches had all been trimmed back; the leaves didn't start until about twenty or more feet off the ground. Looking straight over the garden, under the canopy of leaves, he could clearly see the infamous spit of land where Barry Shales had fired from, and where the men in the room now had nearly died.

He squinted up at the tree.

Well, we may just have a crime scene after all.

"Rookie!" Rhyme called.

"Sure, Lincoln."

Pulaski joined him. Mychal Poitier did too.

"Notice anything odd about this scene?"

"One hell of a shot. That's an awfully long way away. And look at that pollution he had to fire through."

"It's the same shooting scenario we saw yesterday from the *other* side of the water," he grumbled. "Nothing's changed about it. Obviously I'm not talking about that. I'm saying: Don't you see something strange about the horticulture?"

The young officer examined the scene for a moment. "The shooter had help. The branches."

"That's right." Rhyme explained to Poitier, "Somebody cut those lower branches so the sniper would have a clear shot. We should search the garden."

But the corporal shook his head. "It is a good theory, Captain. But no. That tree? It's a poisonwood. Are you familiar with it?"

"No."

"It's just like the name suggests, like poison oak or sumac. If you burn it, for instance, the smoke will be like tear gas. If you touch the leaves you can end up in the hospital from the irritation. They are flowering trees and very pretty so the resorts here don't cut them down but they do trim all but the highest branches so people don't touch them."

"Ah, well, nice try," Rhyme muttered. He absolutely hated it when a solid theory crashed. And, with it, any hope of a proper crime scene to search.

He told Pulaski, "Get some pictures, take samples of the carpet right outside the door, soil samples from the beds around the front sidewalk, dust the knobs here for prints. Probably useless but as long as we're here…"

Rhyme watched the young man collect the evidence and slip it into plastic bags, documenting where it had been found. Pulaski then took perhaps a hundred pictures of the scene. He lifted three latent prints. He finished and deposited what he'd collected in a large paper bag. "Anything else, Lincoln?"

"No," the criminalist grumbled.

The search of the Kill Room and the inn was perhaps the fastest in the history of forensic analysis.

Someone appeared in the doorway, another uniformed officer, skin very dark, face circular. He glanced at Rhyme with what seemed like admiration. Perhaps Mychal Poitier's copy of Rhyme's crime scene manual had recently made the rounds of the Royal Bahamas Police. Or maybe he was simply impressed to be in the same room as the odd cop from America who had in a series of simple deductions transformed the case of the missing student into a murder investigation.

"Corporal," said the young officer to Poitier, with a deferential nod. He carried a thick folder and a large shopping bag. "From Assistant Commissioner McPherson: a full copy of the crime scene report and autopsy photos. And the autopsy reports themselves."

Poitier took the folder from the man and thanked him. He nodded at the bag. "The victims' clothing?"

"Yes, and shoes. Evidence that was collected here just after the shooting too. But I have to tell you, much has gone missing, the morgue administrator told me. He doesn't know how."

"Doesn't know how," Poitier scoffed.

Rhyme recalled that the watches and other valuables had vanished between here and the morgue, as had Eduardo de la Rua's camera and tape recorder.

"I'm sorry, Corporal."

Poitier added, "Any word on the shell casings?" He cast a glance through the window at the spit of land across the bay. The divers and officers with metal detectors had been at work for the past hour or so.

"I'm afraid not. It seems the sniper took the brass with him and we still can't find where the nest was."

A shrug from Poitier. "And any hits on the name Barry Shales?"

As they'd driven here Poitier had had his intelligence operation see if Customs or Passport Control had a record of the sniper entering the country. Credit card information too.

"Nothing, sir. No."

"All right. Thank you, Constable."

The man saluted then gave a tentative nod to Rhyme, turned and, with impressive posture, marched from the room.

Rhyme asked Thom to push him closer to Poitier and he peered into the shopping bag, noting three plastic-wrapped bundles, all tightly sealed, attached to which were chain-of-custody cards, properly filled out. He clumsily reached in and extracted a small envelope on top. Inside was the bullet. Rhyme estimated it as a bit bigger than the most common sniper round, the .338 Lapua. This was probably a .416, a caliber growing in popularity. Rhyme studied the bit of deformed copper and lead. Like all rounds, even this large caliber, it seemed astonishingly small to have caused such horrific damage and stolen a human life in a fraction of a second.

He replaced it. "Rookie, you're in charge of these. Fill out the cards now."

"Will do." Pulaski jotted his name on the chain-of-custody cards.

Rhyme said, "We'll take good care of them, Corporal."

"Ah, well, I doubt the evidence will be useful to

us. If you arrest this Shales and his partner, your unsub, I don't think your courts will send them back here for trial."

"Still, it's evidence. We'll make sure it's returned to you uncontaminated."

Poitier looked around the pristine room. "I'm sorry we don't have a crime scene for you, Captain."

Rhyme frowned. "Oh, but we *do*. And I suggest we get to it as quickly as we can before something happens to that one too. Propel me, Thom. Let's go."

CHAPTER 51

H E RESEMBLED A TOAD.
Henry Cross was squat and dark-complexioned and he had several visible warts that Amelia Sachs thought could be easily removed. His black hair was thick and crowned a large head. Lips, broad. Hands, wide with ragged nails. As he talked he would occasionally lift a fat cigar and stick it in his mouth to chew the unlit stogie enthusiastically. This was gross.

Cross said, with a shake of his head, "It sucks, Roberto dying. Sucks big time." His voice had a faint accent, Spanish, she supposed; she recalled Lydia Foster said he spoke that language and English perfectly—like Moreno.

He was the director of the Classrooms for the Americas Foundation, which worked with churches to build schools and hire teachers in impoverished areas of Latin America. Sachs recalled that Moreno had been involved in this.

Blowing up the balloons...

"Roberto and his Local Empowerment Movement were one of our biggest supporters," Cross said. He stabbed a blunt finger at the gallery of pictures on a scuffed wall. They showed the CAF offices in Caracas, Rio and Managua, Nicaragua. Moreno was standing with his arm around a smiling, swarthy man at a construction site. They were both wearing hard hats. A small group of locals seemed to be applauding.

"And he was a friend of mine," Cross muttered.

"Had you known him long?"

"Five years maybe."

"I'm sorry for your loss." A phrase that instructors actually teach you at the police academy. When Amelia Sachs uttered these words, though, she meant them.

"Thank you." He sighed.

The small dark office was in a building on Chambers Street in lower Manhattan. The foundation was the one stop on Moreno's trip to New York that Sachs had been able to track down—thanks to the receipt from Starbucks she'd found at Lydia Foster's apartment. Sachs had checked the office sign-in sheet in the building that housed the coffee shop and found that on May 1 Moreno was visiting CAF.

"Roberto liked it that we're not a charity. We call ourselves a distributor of resources. My organization doesn't just give money away to the indigent.

We fund schools, which teach people skills so they can work their way out of poverty. I don't have any patience for anyone with their hands out. It really irks me when..."

Cross stopped speaking, raised a hand and laughed. "Like Roberto, I tend to lecture. Sorry. But I'm speaking from experience, speaking from getting my hands dirty on the job, speaking from knowing what it's like to live in the trenches. I used to work in the shipping industry and one thing I noticed was that most people *want* to work hard. They want to improve themselves. But they can't do it without a good education, and schools down there were basically shit, excuse me. I wanted to change it. That's how I met Roberto. We were setting up an office in Mexico and he was in town speaking at some empowerment group for farmers. We kind of connected." The big lips formed a wan smile. "Power to the people...It's not a bad sentiment, I have to say. Roberto did his thing through microbusinesses; I do mine through education."

Though he still seemed more like the owner of a button factory in the Fashion District or a personal injury lawyer than a foundation director.

"So you're here about those drug assholes who killed him?" Cross barked. Chewed on his cigar ferociously for a moment then set it down on a glass ashtray in the shape of a maple leaf.

"We're just getting information at this point," Sachs said noncommittally. "We're looking into his whereabouts on the recent trip to New York—when he met with you. Can you tell me where else he went in the city?"

"Some other nonprofits, he said, three or four of them. I know he needed an interpreter for some of them, if that helps."

"Did he mention which ones?"

"No, he just came by to drop off a check and find out about some new projects we were putting together. He wanted something named after him. A classroom. Not a whole school. See, that was Roberto. He was realistic. He donated X amount of money, not a zillion dollars, so he knew he wouldn't have a whole school named after him. He was happy with a classroom. Modest guy, you know what I'm saying? But he wanted some recognition."

"Did he seem worried about his safety?"

"Sure. He always was. He was, you know, real outspoken." A sad smile. "He hated this politician or that CEO and, man, he wasn't afraid to say it on the air or in his blogs. He called himself the Messenger, the voice of conscience. He made a lot of enemies. Those fucking drug assholes. Pardon my French. I hope they get the chair or lethal injection or whatever."

"He mentioned cartels or gangs as a threat?"

Cross leaned back and thought for a moment. "You know, not by name. But he said he was being followed."

"Tell me."

Cross ran a finger over a cluster of moles on his neck. "He said there was this guy who was there but not there, you know what I'm saying? Following him on the street."

"Any description?"

"White, a guy. Looked tough. That's it."

She thought immediately of Barry Shales and Unsub 516.

"But there was something else. The airplane. That freaked him out the most."

"Airplane?"

"Roberto traveled a lot. He said he'd noticed this private jet three or four times in different cities he'd been in—placcs with small airports, where a private jet was more, you know, noticeable. Bermuda, the Bahamas, Caracas, where he lived. Some towns in Mexico. He said it was strange—because the plane always seemed to be there *before* he arrived. Like somebody knew his travel schedule."

By tapping his phone, for instance? A favorite sport of Metzger, Shales and Unsub 516.

The cigar got chomped. "The reason he recognized it: He said most private jets're white. But this one was blue."

"Markings, designations, numbers?"

A shrug. "No, he never said. But I was thinking, somebody in a *jet's* following you? What's that all about? Who the hell could it be? Those things cost money."

"Anything else you can remember?"

"Sorry."

Sachs rose and shook his hand, reflecting that the convoluted trail here—starting with the limo driver—had paid off with a solid clue. If a cryptic one.

The blue jet ...

Cross sighed, looking at another picture of himself and Moreno, this one snapped in a jungle. They were surrounded by cheerful workers. More shovels, more hard hats, more mud.

"You know, Detective, we were good friends but I've gotta say I never quite figured him out.. He was always down on America, just hated the place. Wouldn't shut up about it. I told him one time, 'Come on, Roberto. Why're you dissing the one country on earth where you *can* say those things and not get shot in an alley by a truth squad or hauled off to a secret prison in the middle of the night? Ease up.'"

A bitter laugh escaped the fat, damp mouth. "But he just wouldn't listen."

CHAPTER 52

JACOB SWANN BRAKED HIS CAR to a stop a half
block from Amelia Sachs's, near Lincoln
Rhyme's town house.

He'd followed her downtown, where she'd had a
meeting on Chambers Street, and he'd looked for a
chance to shoot. But there had been too many people down there. Always a problem in Manhattan.
Now she was back, aggressively parallel parking
in an illegal spot near the cul-de-sac once again.

He looked up and down the shadowy avenue.
Deserted at last. Yes, this would be the place and
the time. In his latex-gloved hand Swann gripped
the SIG Sauer, adjusted it to be able to draw
quickly.

He wasn't going to kill her. He'd decided that
would create too much of a stir—too many police,
too intense a manhunt, too much press. Instead
he'd shoot into her back or legs.

Once she stepped out, he'd double-park, climb

out, shoot her and then drive off, pausing a few blocks away to swap plates again.

Sachs got out of the Torino, looking around carefully again, hand near her hip. This keen gaze kept Swann in the front seat of his Nissan, head down. When she started up the street he opened the door of the car but paused. Sachs didn't head for the cul-de-sac leading to Rhyme's town house or toward Central Park West but rather walked across the street—to a Chinese restaurant.

He saw her step inside, laughing as she spoke with the woman at the register. Sachs examined the menu. She was getting an order to go. A glance up and then she was waving at one of the busboys. He smiled back.

Swann pulled the Nissan forward, noted a space a few car lengths away. He parked and shut the engine off. His hand slipped inside his jacket and made sure once again he knew just where the pistol was. The receiver was more cumbersome than a Glock's, with safeties and slide catches, but the gun itself was heavy, which guaranteed the subsequent shots after the first would be particularly accurate; light weapons need more recentering on target than heavy ones do.

He studied Sachs through the streaked glass.

Such an attractive woman.

Long, red hair.

Tall.

Slim too. So slim. Did she not like to eat? She didn't seem the cooking type. This made Swann dislike her. And takeout from a place like this, salt and overused grease? Shame on you, Amelia. You'll be right at home for the next few months, eating Jell-O and pudding while you recuperate.

In ten minutes she was out the door, take-out food in one hand, and playing the cooperative target: walking straight into the cul-de-sac.

She paused at the entrance, looking into the bag, apparently making sure the restaurant had included the extra rice or fortune cookies or chopsticks. Still fiddling with the bag, she continued toward Rhyme's town house.

Swann eased his car back into the street but had to brake fast, as a bicyclist sped in front of him and stopped, debating for some reason whether to turn around or continue on to Central Park. Swann was angry but didn't want to draw attention by honking. He waited, face flushed.

The biker headed on—opting for the beautiful green of a spring park—and Swann punched the accelerator to get to the cul-de-sac fast. But the delay had cost him. Walking quickly, Sachs had reached the end of the L-shaped passage and disappeared to the left, toward the back of the town house.

Not a problem. Better actually. He'd park, follow her in and shoot her as she approached the door. The geometry of the cul-de-sac there would mute the gunshots and send the sounds in a hundred different directions. Whoever heard would have no idea where they came from.

He looked around. No cops. Little traffic. A few oblivious passersby, lost in their own worlds.

Swann pulled the car into the mouth of the cul-de-sac, put the transmission in park and stepped out. With the gun drawn, but hidden under his windbreaker, he started over the cobblestones.

He recited to himself: two shots, low in her back, one toward the knee. Although he vastly preferred his knife he was a good marksman. He'd have to—

A voice behind him, a woman's: "Excuse me. Could you help me?" British accent.

It belonged to a slim, attractive jogger in her early thirties. She stood about eight feet away, between him and the open driver's door of his car.

"I'm from out of town. I'm trying to find the reservoir. There's a running path..."

And then she saw it.

His windbreaker had eased away from his body. She saw the gun.

"Oh, God. Look, don't hurt me. I didn't see anything! I swear."

She started to turn but Swann moved fast; he was

in front of her in an instant. She took a breath to scream but he struck her in the throat, his open-handed blow. She dropped hard to the concrete, out of sight of a couple across the street, arguing about something.

Swann glanced back up the dim canyon between the nearby buildings. Would Sachs be inside by now?

Maybe not. He didn't know how far the L of the cul-de-sac extended behind Rhyme's.

But he had only a matter of seconds to decide. He glanced down at the woman, gasping for breath, just the way Annette had in the Bahamas and Lydia Foster had here.

Uhn, uhn, uhn. Hands to her neck, eyes wide, mouth open.

Yes or no? He debated.

Choose now.

He decided: Yes.

CHAPTER 53

AMELIA SACHS STOOD IN THE CUL-DE-SAC behind the town house, Glock drawn, aimed toward where the dim canyon made a right turn and eventually joined the crosstown street.

The Chinese takeout she'd ordered was sitting on the cobblestones and she was in a combat shooting stance: feet planted parallel, toes pointed at your enemy, leaning forward slightly with gun hand gripping hard, other hand cradling the trigger guard for stability. Your dominant arm stiff; if the muscles aren't taut the recoil might not eject the spent shell and chamber another. A jam can mean death. You and your gun have to be partners.

Come on, Sachs thought to her adversary. Come on, present! This was, of course, Unsub 516. She knew it wasn't Barry Shales, the sniper; he was still under surveillance by Lon Sellitto's team.

Several times today she'd noticed a light-colored sedan—first, near Henry Cross's office building on Chambers Street. Then on the drive here and again fifteen minutes ago. She hadn't seen the car clearly but it was likely the same one that had been following her from Tash Farada's house in Queens.

Noting the car pull into a space at the end of the block, she'd debated how to handle it. To call Central Dispatch or to approach him by herself on the street might have precipitated a firefight, a bad idea in this densely populated area.

So she'd decided to take him in the cul-de-sac. She'd bought the Chinese takeout to give him a chance to spot her. Before leaving, she'd slipped her weapon into the bag. Then she'd started across the street, careful not to present a target, and into the cul-de-sac, apparently focusing on her order but actually sensing from her periphery when the man would make his move.

She'd hurried to the bend in the cul-de-sac, aware that the car was approaching then stopping. At that point she'd turned, dropped the food and gripped her weapon.

Now she was waiting for the target to present.

Would he drive farther in? Probably not. Too easy to get blocked in, if a delivery or moving truck showed up.

Was he out of the car and moving fast toward her?

Palms dry, both eyes open—you never squint when you shoot. And you focus on two things only: your target and the front sight of your weapon. Forget the blade sight at the back of the receiver. You can't bring everything into definition.

Come on!

Breathing steadily.

Where was he? Prowling forward, about to leap around the corner and drop into his own shooting stance?

Or what if he'd anticipated she was on to him? He might have grabbed a passerby to shove into the cul-de-sac as a distraction. Or use him or her as a shield, hoping that Sachs would react and shoot the innocent.

Inhale, exhale, inhale...

Did she hear a voice? A soft cry?

What was that? Easing forward, Sachs crept toward the other leg of the L. Paused, flattened against the brick.

Where the hell was he? Was *his* weapon up too, pointed at exactly the spot where she'd appear if she stepped forward?

Okay, go. Just go low and get ready to shoot. Watch your backdrop.

One...two...

Now!

Sachs leapt into the main part of the cul-de-sac, gun up, and dropped into a crouch.

Which is when her left knee gave out completely.

Before she got a clear look at where the unsub might be waiting for her, she tumbled sideways onto the cobblestones, managing to lift her finger off the trigger before she pulled off a random round or two. Amelia Sachs rolled once and lay stunned, a perfect target.

Even her vision had deserted her. Tears from the pain.

But she forced herself to ignore the agony and scrabbled into a prone position, gun muzzle aimed down the cul-de-sac, where Unsub 516 would be coming for her. Aiming at her. Sending hollow-point bullets into her.

Except that he wasn't.

She blinked the moisture from her eyes, then wiped them fiercely with her sleeve.

Empty. The cul-de-sac was empty. Five sixteen was gone.

Struggling to her feet, she holstered her weapon and massaged her knee. She limped to the street and conducted a canvass of those on the sidewalk. But no one had paid any attention to light-colored cars, no one had seen a compact man with brown hair and military bearing acting strangely, no one had seen any weapons.

Standing with hands on hips, looking west then east. All was peaceful, all was normal. A typical day on the Upper West Side.

Sachs returned to the cul-de-sac, fighting the limp. Man, that hurt. She collected the Chinese and tossed it into a Dumpster.

In New York City alleyways the five-second rule about dropped food does not apply.

CHAPTER 54

"YOU WERE RIGHT, CAPTAIN," Mychal Poitier called from the second-story porch outside Annette Bodel's apartment in Nassau. "The side window has been jimmied. Barry Shales or your unsub broke in here, either before or after he killed her."

Rhyme gazed up, squinting into the brilliant sky. He couldn't see the corporal, just the silhouette of a palm waving lethargically near the roof of the building in which prostitute-student Annette had lived.

This was the other crime scene he'd referred to. He'd known that Annette's killer had to come here to find any information she might have had about him and his visit to South Cove last week. Poitier and his men had been here before—after she was reported missing—but merely to see if she, or her body, was present. The door locks had not been disturbed and the officers hadn't investigated further.

"Probably afterward," Rhyme called. Part of the questions during Annette's torture would have been about address books and computer files that might have referenced him. Diaries too, of course. All of that would be gone but, he hoped, some trace of the unsub remained.

A small cluster of locals, faces tanned and faces black, were nearby, checking out the entourage. Rhyme supposed their words ought to be delivered more discreetly but twenty-five vertical feet separated him from Poitier and so there was no choice but to shout.

"Don't go inside, Corporal. Ron will handle it." He turned. "Rookie, how we doing?"

"Almost ready, Lincoln." He was suiting up in RBPF crime scene coveralls and assembling the basic collection equipment.

Rhyme didn't even consider running this scene himself, though he'd earlier been tempted. There was no elevator in the building and it would be nearly impossible to carry the heavy wheelchair up the narrow rickety stairs. Besides, Pulaski was good. Nearly as good as Amelia Sachs.

The officer now paused in front of Rhyme as if expecting a briefing. But the criminalist offered simply, "It's your scene. You know what to do."

A nod from the young man and up the stairs he trotted.

———————

IT TOOK ABOUT AN HOUR for him to walk the grid.

When Pulaski emerged, with a half dozen collection bags, he asked Rhyme and Poitier if they wanted to review the evidence now. Rhyme debated but in the end he decided to take everything back to New York and do the analysis there.

Part of this was the familiarity of working with Mel Cooper.

Part was that he missed Sachs, a fact he wouldn't share with another human being...except her.

"What are our travel options?" he asked Thom.

· He checked his phone. "If we can get to the airport in a half hour, we can make the next flight."

Rhyme glanced at the corporal.

"We're twenty minutes at the most," Poitier said.

"Even in the infamous Bahamian traffic?" Rhyme asked wryly.

"I have red lights."

Pulaski headed toward the van, still in coveralls, booties and shower cap.

"Get into street clothes, rookie. I think you'd upset the passengers, dressed like that."

"Oh, right."

The flashing lights did help and soon they were at the terminal. They exited the van and, while Pulaski saw to the luggage and Thom arranged for the vehicle to be collected, Rhyme remained next to Poitier. The area was bustling with tourists and locals, and the air filled with dust and the endless bangs and catcalls of construction. And that constant perfume, trash fire smoke.

Rhyme began to speak, then found words had abandoned him. He forced them into line. "I'm sorry about what happened at the sniper nest, Corporal. The assistant commissioner was right. I nearly got you killed."

Poitier laughed. "We aren't in a business like librarians or dental workers, Captain. Not all of us go home every night."

"Still, I wasn't as competent as I should have been." These words seared him. "I should have anticipated the attack."

"I have not been a real police officer for very long, Captain, but I think it's safe to say that it would be impossible to anticipate everything that could happen in this profession. It's really quite mad, what we do. Little pay, danger, politics at the top, chaos on the streets."

"You'll do well as a detective, Corporal."

"I hope so. I certainly feel more at home here than in Business Inspections and Licensing."

A flashing light caught Rhyme's eye and he could hear a siren as well. A police car was speeding into the airport, weaving through traffic.

"Ah, the last of the evidence," Poitier said. "I was worried it wouldn't arrive in time."

What evidence could it be? Rhyme wondered. They had everything that existed from the Moreno sniper shooting, as well as from Annette Bodel's apartment. The divers had given up searching for Barry Shales's spent cartridges.

The corporal waved the car over.

The young constable who'd met them at the South Cove Inn was behind the wheel. Holding an evidence bag, he got out and saluted, the gesture aimed halfway between the two men he faced.

Rhyme resisted a ridiculous urge to salute back.

Poitier took the bag and thanked the officer. Another tap of stiff fingers to his forehead and the constable returned to the car, speeding away and clicking on the siren and lights once more, though his mission had been accomplished.

"What's that?"

"Can't you tell?" Poitier asked. "I remember in your book you instruct officers to always smell the air when they're running the crime scene."

Frowning, Rhyme leaned down and inhaled.

The fragrant aroma of fried conch rose from the bag.

CHAPTER 55

*S*USSS, *SUSSS*...

In his kitchen Jacob Swann sipped a Vermentino, a light pleasant Italian wine, in this case from Liguria. He returned to honing his knife, a Kai Shun, though not the slicer. This was an eight-and-a-half-inch Deba model for chopping and for removing large pieces of meat intact.

Susss, susss, susss...

He stroked from side to side, on the Arkansas whetstone, his personal style for sharpening. Never in a circle.

The hour was around 8 p.m. Jazz played on his turntable. Larry Coryell, the guitarist. He excelled at standards, his own compositions and even classical. "Pavane for a Dead Princess" was an unmatched interpretation.

Aproned, Swann stood at the butcher-block island. Not long ago he'd received a text from headquarters complimenting him on his work today, confirming that he'd made the right decision to delay the attack on Sachs. Shreve Metzger had provided yet more info but there was nothing more to do at the moment. He could stand down for the evening. And he was taking advantage of that.

The lights were low, the shades and curtains drawn.

There was, in a way, a sense of romance in the air. Swann looked at the woman sitting nearby. Her hair was down, she wore one of his T-shirts, black, and plaid boxers, also his. He believed he could smell a floral scent, laced with spice. Smell and flavor are inextricably linked. Swann never cooked anything of importance when he had a cold or a sinus infection. Why waste the effort? Eating at a time like that meant the food was simply fuel.

A sin.

The woman, whose name was Carol Fiori—odd moniker for a Brit—looked back. She was crying softly.

Occasionally she'd make the *uhn uhn uhn* sound, like earlier. Carol was the jogger who had approached him in the alleyway earlier and ruined his chance to disable Amelia Sachs. A throat-punch and into the trunk she'd gone. He'd driven off quickly, returning home. He'd get the detective later.

Once back in Brooklyn, he'd dragged Carol into the house. While she initially said she was traveling with "friends," she was actually single and touring the United States on her own for a month, thinking of writing an article about her adventures.

Alone...

He'd been debating what to do with his trophy.

Now he knew.

Yes, no?

Yes.

She'd given up staring at him pleadingly and whispering pleadingly and now turned her damp eyes to the Deba as he sharpened *susss, susss.* She shook her head occasionally. Swann had bound her wrists and legs to a very nice and comfortable Mission-style chair, à la Lydia Foster.

"Please," she mouthed, her eyes on the blade. So the pleading wasn't quite abandoned.

He examined the knife himself, tested the edge carefully with his thumb. It gave just the right resistance; perfect sharpness. He sipped more wine and then began to remove ingredients from the refrigerator.

When Jacob Swann was a boy, long before college, long before the military, long before his career *after* the military, he came to appreciate the value of meals. The only moments when he could count on spending time with his mother and father involved preparing and eating supper.

Bulky Andrew Swann was not stern or abusive, simply distant and forever lost in his schemes, obligations and distractions, which derived mostly from his job in the gambling world of Atlantic City. Young Jacob never knew exactly what his father did—given his own present career, Andrew might have been on the enforcement side of things. That genetic stuff. But the one thing that Jacob and his mother knew about the man was that he liked to eat and that you could get his attention and hold it through food.

Marianne was not a natural cook, probably had hated it. She'd begun to work on her skills only after she and Andrew started dating. Jacob had overheard her tell a woman friend about one of the first meals she'd served.

"Whatsis?" Andrew had demanded.

"Hamburger Helper and lima beans and—"

"You told me you could cook."

"But I did." She'd waved at the frying pan.

Andrew had tossed down his napkin and left the table, casino bound.

So she'd bought a Betty Crocker cookbook the next day and started to work.

In the afternoons in their tract house, young Jacob would watch her feverishly fricasseeing a chicken or pan-sautéing cod. She fought the food, she wrestled. She didn't learn first principles and rules (it's all about chemistry and physics, after all). Instead she attacked each recipe as if she'd never seen a steak or a piece of flounder or pile of cool flour. Her sauces were lumpy and bizarrely seasoned and always oversalted—though not to Andrew, so perhaps they weren't over, at all.

Unlike her son, Marianne stressed mightily before and during the preparation of each meal and invariably had more than one glass of wine. A bit of whiskey too. Or whatever was in the cabinet.

But she worked hard and managed to produce meals functional enough to hold Andrew's presence for an hour or so. Inevitably, though, with a clink of dessert fork on china, a last gulp of coffee—Andrew didn't sip—he would rise and vanish. To the basement to work on his secret business projects, to a local bar, back to the casino. To fuck a neighbor, Jacob speculated, when he learned about fucking.

After school or weekends, if he wasn't slamming his wrestling match opponents into the mat or competing on the rifle team at school, Jacob would hang out in the kitchen, flipping through cookbooks, sitting near his mother as she laid waste the kitchen, with dribbles of milk and tomato sauce everywhere, shrapnel of poppy seeds, the detritus of herbs, flour, cornstarch, viscera. The spatter of blood too.

Sometimes she'd get overwhelmed and ask him to help by removing gristle and boning meat and slicing scaloppine. Marianne seemed to think that a boy would be more inclined to use a knife than an egg beater.

"Look at that, honey. Good job. You're my little butcher man!"

He found himself taking over more and more and instinctively repairing the stew, chopping more finely, offing the heat at the right moment before a disastrous boil. His mother patted his cheek and poured more wine.

Now Swann looked at the woman strapped to his chair.

He continued to be angry that she'd ruined his plans that afternoon.

She continued to cry.

He returned to preparing his three-course dinner for tonight. The starter would be asparagus steamed in a water-vermouth mixture, infused with a fresh bay leaf and a pinch of sage. The spears would rest on a bed of mâche and be dotted with homemade hollandaise sauce—that verb being key, "dotted," since anytime yolk meets butter, you can easily overdo. The trick about asparagus, of course, is timing. The Romans had a cliché—

doing something in the duration it took to cook asparagus meant doing it quickly.

Swann sipped the wine and prepared the steamer liquid. He then trimmed the herbs from his window box.

When his mother left them—wine plus eighty-two mph without a seat belt—sixteen-year-old Jacob took over the cooking.

Just the two of them, dad and son.

The teenager did the same as his mother, corralling Andrew with meals, the only differences being that the boy enjoyed the act of cooking and was far better than his mother. He took to serving serial courses—like a chef's tasting menu—to stretch out the time the men could be together. One other difference emerged eventually: He found he liked the cooking better than the hour or so spent consuming the meal; he realized he didn't really like his father very much. The man didn't want to talk about the things that Jacob did: video games, kickboxing, wrestling, hunting, guns in general and bare-knuckle boxing. Andrew didn't want to talk about much at all except Andrew.

Once, when Jacob was eighteen, his father returned home with a beautiful, a really beautiful blonde. He had told the woman what a good cook "my kid is." Like he was showing off a tacky pinkie ring. He'd said to Jacob, "Make Cindi here something nice, okay? Make something nice for the pretty lady."

Jacob was well aware of *E. coli* by then. Yet as much as he wanted to see twenty-four-year-old Cindi retch to death, or at least retch, he couldn't bring himself to intentionally ruin a dish. He received raves from the woman for his chicken Cordon Bleu, which he made not by pounding the poultry breast flat but by slicing the meat into thin sheets to enwrap the Gruyère cheese and—in his recipe—prosciutto ham from Parma.

Butcher man...

Not long after that, terrorism struck the nation. When Jacob enlisted in the army, the question of aptitude and interests came up but he didn't let on he could cook, for fear he'd be assigned to mess hall kitchens for the next four years. He knew there'd be no pleasure in cooking steam-table food for a thousand soldiers at a time. Mostly he wanted to kill people. Or make them scream. Or both. He didn't see a big distinction between humans and animals for slaughter. In fact, think about it, beef cattle and lambs were innocent and we sliced them up without a second thought; people, on the other hand, were all guilty of some transgression or another, yet we're oh so reluctant to apply the bullet or knife.

Some of us.

He regarded Carol once more. She was very muscular but pale. Maybe she worked out in gyms mostly or wore sunscreen when she ran. He offered her some wine. She shook her head. He gave her water and she drank half the bottle as he held it.

His second course for this evening would be a variation on potatoes Anna. Sliced and peeled russets, layered in a spiral and then cooked in butter and olive oil, with plenty of sea salt and pepper. In the middle would be a dollop of crème fraîche, which he whipped up with, of all things, a little— very little—fresh maple syrup. To finish, black truffle slivers. This dish he made in a small cast-iron skillet. He would start the potatoes on the stove then crisp the top under the Miele's broiler.

Potatoes and maple and truffles. Who would have thought?

Okay, he was getting hungry.

When Jacob was in his early twenties, his father died of what could be called gastric problems, though not ulcers or tumors. Four 9mm rounds to the belly.

The young soldier had vowed revenge but nothing ever came of that. A lot of people might have killed the man—Andrew, it turned out, had been up to all kinds of double crosses he should have known were not a good idea in Atlantic City. Finding the killers would have taken ages. Besides, truth be told, Jacob wasn't all that upset. In fact, when he hosted a reception after the funeral, the murderer might very well have been among the business associates who'd attended. There was, however, some subtle vengeance played out at the event. The main course was penne alla puttanesca, the spicy tomato-based dish whose name in Italian means "in the style of a whore." He'd made it in honor of his father's present girlfriend, who wasn't Cindi but could easily have been.

Tonight, Jacob Swann's third course, the main course, would be special. The Moreno assignment had been difficult and he wanted to pamper himself.

The entrée would be Veronique-style, which he prepared with grapes sliced into disks and shallots, equally thin, in a beurre blanc sauce—made with slightly less wine (he never used vinegar) because of the presence of the grapes.

He would slice the very special meat into nearly translucent ovals, dredge them in type 45 French pastry flour then quickly sauté them in a blend of olive oil and butter (always the two, of course; butter alone burns faster than an overturned tanker).

He offered Carol more water. She wasn't interested. She'd given up.

"Relax," he whispered.

The liquid was boiling in the asparagus steamer,

the potatoes browning nicely under the broiler, the oil and butter slowly heating, off-gassing their lovely perfume.

Swann wiped down the cutting board he'd use to slice the meat for the main course.

But before getting to work, the wine. He opened and poured a New Zealand Sauvignon Blanc, a Cloudy Bay, one of the best on the planet. He'd debated about the vineyard's fine sparkling wine, the Pelorus, but he didn't think he could finish a whole bottle alone, and bubbles, of course, don't keep.

V

THE MILLION-DOLLAR BULLET

CHAPTER 56

"YOU'VE GOT A TAN," SELLITTO SAID.

"I don't have a tan."

"You do. You oughta wear sunscreen, Linc."

"I don't have a goddamn tan," he muttered.

"I think you do," Thom added.

It was nearly 8 a.m. Thom, Pulaski and Rhyme had arrived from LaGuardia airport late, nearly eleven last night, and the aide had insisted that Rhyme get some sleep immediately. The case could wait till this morning.

There'd been no argument; the criminalist had been exhausted. The dunk in the water had taken its toll. The whole trip had, for that matter. But that didn't stop Rhyme from summoning Thom the moment he'd awakened at six thirty with the push-button call switch beside the bed. (The aide had called the device very *Downton Abbey*, a reference Rhyme did not get.)

The parlor was humming now, with Sellitto, Cooper and Sachs present. And Ron Pulaski—who *did* seem to have a tan—was just walking through the door. Nance Laurel had a court appearance on one of her other cases and would arrive later.

Rhyme was in a new wheelchair, a Merits Vision Select. Gray with red fenders. It had been delivered and assembled yesterday, before Rhyme's return from the Bahamas. Thom had called their insurance company from Nassau and negotiated a speedy purchase. ("They didn't know what to say," the aide reported, "when I gave the reason for the loss as 'immersion in ten feet of water.'")

Rhyme had picked this particular model because it was known for off-road navigation. His old reticence to be in public had disappeared—largely because of his trip to the Bahamas. He wanted more travel and he wanted to work scenes himself again. That required a chair that would get him to as many places as possible.

The Merits had been pimped out a bit to make allowances for Rhyme's particular condition—such as the strap for his immobile left arm, a touchpad under his working left ring finger and, of course, a cup holder, big enough for both whiskey tumbler and coffee mug. He was now enjoying the latter beverage through a thick straw. He looked over Scllitto, Sachs and Pulaski, then studied the whiteboard, which contained Sachs's notations of the investigation in his absence.

"Time's a-wasting." He nodded at the STO order. "Mr. Rashid is going to meet his maker in a day or two if we don't do something about it. Let's see what we have." He now wheeled back and forth in front of the whiteboards containing the analysis of the evidence Sachs had collected at the IED scene at Java Hut and Lydia Foster's apartment.

"A blue airplane?" he asked, regarding that notation.

Sachs explained about what Henry Cross had told her. The private jet that seemed to be dogging Moreno around the United States and Central and South America.

"I've got one of Captain Myers's Special Services officers searching but they aren't having much luck. There's no database of aircraft by color. If it was sold recently, though, brokers might have sales literature with pictures. He's still checking."

"All right. Now, let's look at what we found in the Bahamas. Number one, the Kill Room."

Rhyme explained to Sachs and Cooper how unsub 516 or Barry Shales had ruined the scene at the inn, but he had some things, including the preliminary report that the local police had done, along with the photos, which Sachs now taped up on a separate whiteboard, along with the paltry crime scene report that the RBPF had originally prepared.

For the next half hour, Sachs and Cooper carefully unpacked and analyzed the shoes and clothing of the three victims who'd been in suite 1200 on the morning of May 9. Each plastic bag was opened over a large sheet of sterile newsprint, and each item of clothing and the shoes were picked over and scraped for trace.

The shoes of Moreno, his guard and de la Rua produced fibers identical to those in the hotel carpet and dirt that matched samples taken from the sidewalk and grounds in front of the inn. Their clothing contained similar trace as well as elements of recent meals, presumably breakfast; they died before lunch. Cooper found pastry flakes, jam and bits of bacon in the case of Moreno and his guard, and allspice and some indeterminate type of pepper sauce on the reporter's jacket. Moreno and his guard also had traces of crude oil on their shoes, cuffs and sleeves, probably from their meeting on Monday out of the hotel; there weren't many refineries in New Providence so maybe they had eaten dinner by the docks. The guard had some trace of cigarette ash on his shirt.

This information went up on the board and

Rhyme noted but didn't dwell on any of it; after all, their killer had been a mile away when he'd fired the bullet. Unsub 516 had been in the hotel but even if he'd snuck into the Kill Room itself, none of that trace remained.

He said, "Now. The autopsy report."

No surprises here either. Moreno had been killed by a massive gunshot trauma to the chest, and the others by blood loss due to multiple lacerations from the flying glass, of varying sizes, mostly three or four millimeters wide, two to three centimeters long.

Cooper looked over the cigarette butts and the candy wrapper that Poitier's original crime scene searchers had found in the Kill Room but these yielded nothing helpful. The butts were the same brand as the pack of Marlboros found on the guard's body, the candy had come from a gift basket for Moreno when he arrived. The fingerprints that Pulaski had lifted, not surprisingly, were negative for hits in any database.

"Let's move on to the prostitute's apartment. Annette Bodel."

Pulaski'd done a good job, collecting plenty of trace from near where the killer had searched, along with samplars to eliminate any that was probably not from him. Cooper examined the items and, occasionally, ran samples through the gas chromatograph/mass spectrometer. He finally announced, "First, we've got two-stroke fuel."

These were smaller engines, two-strokes, like those in snowmobiles and chain saws, in which the lubricating oil is mixed directly with gasoline.

"Jet Ski maybe," Rhyme said. "She worked in a dive shop part-time. Might not be from our perp but we'll keep it in mind."

"And sand," the tech announced. "Along with seawater residue." He compared the chemical breakdown of these items with what was on the board for two of the prior scenes. "Yep, it's virtually the same as what Amelia found at Java Hut."

Rhyme lifted an eyebrow at this. "Ah, a definitive link between Unsub Five Sixteen and the Bahamas. We know he was in Annette's apartment and I'm ninety-nine percent sure he was the one in the South Cove on May eighth. Now, anything linking him to Lydia Foster?"

Pulaski pointed out, "The brown hair, which is what Corporal Poitier said the man in the South Cove Inn had, the one who was there just before Moreno was killed."

"It *suggests*; it doesn't prove. Keep going, Mel."

The tech was staring into the eyepiece of a microscope. "Something odd here. Some membrane, orange. I'll run part of it through the GC/MS."

Some minutes later he had the results from the gas chromatograph/mass spectrometer.

Cooper read, "DHA, C22:6n-3—docosahexaenoic acid."

"Fish oil," Rhyme said, looking at the screen on which the microscopic image was being projected. "And with that membrane, see in the upper right corner? I'd say fish eggs: Roe. Or caviar."

"Also some $C_8H_8O_3$," Cooper said.

"You've got me," Rhyme muttered.

The lookup took thirty seconds. "Vanillin."

"As in vanilla extract?"

"That's right."

"Thom! Thom, get in here. Where the hell are you?"

The aide's voice drifted into the room. "What do you need?"

"You. Present. Here. In the room."

Rolling down his sleeves, the aide joined them. "How could I resist such a polite summons?"

Sachs laughed.

Rhyme frowned. "Look over those charts, Thom. Put your culinary skills to work. Tell me what you think about those entries, knowing that the docosahexaenoic acid and the $C_8H_8O_3$ are, respectively, caviar and vanilla."

The aide stood for a moment, looking over the charts. His face shifted into a smile. "Familiar…

Hold on a minute." He went to a nearby computer and pulled up the *New York Times*. He did some browsing. Rhyme couldn't see exactly what he was looking at. "Well, that's interesting."

"Ah, could you *share* the interesting part?"

"The other two scenes—Lydia Foster and the Java Hut—have traces of artichoke and licorice, right?"

"Right," Cooper confirmed.

He spun the computer for them to look at. "Well, combine those ingredients with caviar and vanilla and you have a real expensive dish that's served at the Patchwork Goose. There was just an article about it in the Food section recently."

"Patchwork...the fuck is that?" Sellitto muttered.

Sachs said, "It's one of the fanciest restaurants in town. They serve seven or eight courses over four hours and pair the wine. They do weird things like cook with liquid nitrogen and butane torches. Not that I've ever been, of course."

"That's right," Thom said, nodding at the screen. It appeared to be a recipe. "And that's one of the dishes: trout served with artichoke cooked in licorice broth and garnished with roe and vanilla mayonnaise. Your perp left traces of those ingredients?"

"That's right," Sachs said.

Sellitto asked, "So he works in the restaurant?"

Thom shook his head. "Oh, I doubt it. You're committed to working six days a week, twelve-hour days at a place like that. He wouldn't have time to be a professional hit man. And I doubt it's a customer. I don't think the ingredients would transfer or last more than a few hours on his clothes. More likely he made the dish at home. From the recipe here."

"Good, good," Rhyme whispered. "*Now* we know Unsub Five Sixteen went to the Bahamas on May fifteenth to kill Annette Bodel, set the IED at Java Hut and killed Lydia Foster. He was probably the one at the South Cove Inn just before Moreno was shot. He was helping Barry Shales prep for the killing."

Sachs said, "And we know he likes to cook. Maybe he's a former pro. That could be helpful."

Cooper lifted his phone and took a call; Rhyme hadn't heard it ring and wondered if the tech had the unit on vibrate or if he himself was suffering from water on the ear from his swim. Lord knew his eyes still stung.

The crime scene tech thanked the caller and announced, "We ran the bulb of the brown hair that Amelia recovered from Lydia Foster's. That was the results of the CODIS analysis. Nothing. Whoever the unsub is, he's not in any criminal DNA databases."

As Sachs wrote their latest findings on the white-board Rhyme said, "Now we're making some progress. But the key to nailing Metzger is the sniper rifle and the key to the rifle is the bullet. Let's take a look at it."

CHAPTER 57

ALTHOUGH PEOPLE HAVE BEEN ELIMINATING each other with firearms for more than a thousand years, the forensic analysis of guns and bullets is a relatively new science.

In probably the first instance of applying the discipline, investigators in England in the middle of the nineteenth century got a confession from a killer based on matching a bullet with the mold that made it. In 1902 an expert witness (Oliver Wendell Holmes, no less) helped prosecutors convict a suspect by matching a bullet test-fired by the suspect's gun to the murder slug.

However, it wasn't until Calvin Goddard, a medical doctor and forensic scientist, published "Forensic Ballistics" in 1925 that the discipline truly took off. Goddard is still known as the father of ballistic science.

Rhyme had three goals in applying the rules Goddard had laid down ninety years ago. First, to identify the bullet. Second, from that information to identify the types of guns that could have fired it. Third, to link this particular bullet to a specific gun of that sort, which could be traced to the shooter, in this case Barry Shales.

The team now turned to the first of these questions. The bullet itself.

Gloved and masked, Sachs opened the plastic bag containing the bullet, a misshapen oblong of copper and lead. She looked it over. "It's a curious round. Unusual. First, it's big—three-hundred grain."

The weight of the projectile fired from the gun—called a slug—is measured in grains. A three-hundred-grain bullet is about three-quarters of an ounce. Most hunting, combat and even sniper rifles fire a bullet that's much smaller, around 180 grains.

She measured it with a caliber gauge, a flat metal disk with holes of various sizes punched into it. "And a rare caliber. A big one. Four twenty."

Rhyme frowned. "Not four sixteen?" His first thought upon seeing it in the Kill Room. The .416 was a recent innovation in rifle bullets, designed by the famous Barrett Arms. The cartridge was a variation on the .50 round used by snipers around the world. While some countries and states in the U.S. banned the .50 for civilian use, the .416 was still legal most places.

"No, definitely bigger." Sachs then examined the round with a microscope, low power. "And it's a sophisticated design. It's a hollow-point with a plastic tip—a modified spitzer."

Arms manufacturers began to incorporate aerodynamics into the design of their projectiles around the time, not surprisingly, that airplanes were developed. The spitzer round—from the German word for "pointed bullet"—was developed for long-distance rifle shooting. Being so streamlined, it was very accurate; the downside was that it remained intact on striking the target and caused much less damage than a blunt-tipped, hollow-point round, which would mushroom inside the flesh.

Some bullet manufacturers came up with the idea of grafting a sharp plastic tip onto a hollow-point slug. The tip produced the streamlined quality of a spitzer round but broke away upon hitting the target, allowing the projectile to expand.

This was the type of bullet that Barry Shales had used to kill Robert Moreno.

Completing the streamlined design, she added, the slug was a boattail—it narrowed in the rear, just like a racing yacht, to further cut drag as it sped through the air.

She summarized, "It's big, heavy, accurate as hell." Nodded at the crime scene photo of Moreno sprawled on the couch in the Kill Room, blood and tissue radiating out behind him. "And devastating."

She scraped the slug and analyzed some of the ejecta residue—the gas and particles that result when the powder ignites. "The best of the best," she said. "The primers were Federal 210 match quality, the powder was Hodgdon Extreme Extruded—made to the highest tolerances. This's your Ferrari of bullets."

"Who makes it?" This was the important question.

But an Internet search returned very few hits. None of the big manufacturers like Winchester, Remington or Federal offered it and none of the retail ammo sellers stocked the bullet. Sachs, however, found some references to the mysterious round's existence in some obscure shooting forums and learned that an arms company in New Jersey, Walker Defense Systems, might be the maker. Its website revealed that, though Walker didn't make rifles, it manufactured a plastic-tipped spitzer .420 boattail.

Sachs looked at Rhyme. "They only sell to the army, police... *and* the federal government."

The first goal was satisfied, the ID of the bullet. Now the team turned to finding the type of weapon that had fired it.

"First of all," Rhyme asked, "what kind of action was it? Bolt, semiauto, three-shot burst, full auto? Sachs, what do you think?"

"Snipers never use full auto or bursts—too hard to compensate for repeated recoil over distance. If it was bolt-action, he wouldn't have fired three rounds. If the first one missed, he'd've alerted the target, who'd go to cover. Semiauto, I'd vote."

Sellitto said, "Can't be that hard to find. There's gotta be only one or two kinds of guns in the world that'll fire a slug like that. It's pretty unique."

"*Pretty* unique," Rhyme blurted, with a frosting of sarcasm. "Just like being *sort of* pregnant."

"Linc," Sellitto replied cheerfully, "you ever think about teaching grade school? I'm sure the kids'd love ya."

Sellitto was right substantively, though, Rhyme knew. The rarer the bullet, the fewer the types of guns that will fire it. This would make it easier to identify the rifle and therefore easier to trace it to Barry Shales.

The two characteristics of a bullet that link it to the weapon that fired it are caliber, which they now knew, and rifling marks.

All modern firearms barrels have spiral troughs cut into them to make the bullet rotate and thus move more accurately to the target. This is known as rifling (even though it applies to pistols too).

Gun manufacturers make these troughs—called lands (the raised part) and grooves—in various configurations, depending on the type of gun, the bullet it's intended to shoot and its purpose. The twist, as it's called, might spin the bullet clockwise or counter, and will spin it faster or slower depending on how many times the slug revolves in the barrel.

A look at the slug revealed that Barry Shales's gun spun the slug counterclockwise, once every ten inches.

This was unusual, Rhyme knew; spirals are generally tighter, with the ratio of 1:7 or 1:8.

"Means it's a long barrel, right?" Rhyme asked Cooper.

"Yep. Very long. Odd."

Given the rare caliber and rifling, it would normally be easy to isolate brands of semiautomatic rifles that produced characteristics like that. Ballistics databases correlate all this information and a simple computer search returns the results in seconds.

But nothing was normal about this case.

Sachs looked up from her computer and reported, "Not a single hit. No record of any commercial arms manufacturer making a rifle like that."

"Is there anything else we can tell about the

gun?" Rhyme asked. "Look over the crime scene photos, Moreno's body. See if that tells us anything."

The crime scene specialist shoved his glasses up high and rocked back and forth as he regarded the grim pictures. If anybody had insights it would be Mel Cooper. The detective was active in the International Association for Identification, which was nearly a hundred years old, and he had the highest levels of certification you could attain from the IAI, in all areas of specialty: Forensic Art, Footwear and Tire Track Analysis, Forensic Photography/Imaging, Tenprint Fingerprint, and Latent Print—as well as Bloodstain Pattern Analysis, a personal interest of both Cooper and Rhyme.

He could read crime scene photos the way a doctor could an X-ray. He now said, "Ah, take a look at that, the spread." He touched a photo, indicating the blood and bits of flesh and bone on the couch and floor behind it. "He fired from two thousand yards, right?"

"About that," Rhyme said.

"Amelia, what would the typical velocity of a round that big be?"

She shrugged. "Out of the muzzle at twenty-seven hundred feet per second, tops. Speed at impact? I'd say eighteen hundred."

Cooper shook his head. "That slug was traveling

at over three thousand feet a second when it hit Moreno."

Sachs said, "Really?"

"Positive."

"Fast. Real fast. Confirms the rifle had a particularly long barrel and means the shell'd be loaded with a lot of powder. Normally a slug that size would have forty or forty-two grains of propellant. For that speed, I'd guess *twice* as much, and that means a reinforced receiver."

This was the part of the rifle that held the cartridge for firing. The receiver was thicker than the barrel to withstand the initial pressure of the expanding gases, so that the gun didn't blow up when the shooter pulled the trigger.

"Any conclusions?"

"Yeah," Sachs said. "That Barry Shales, or somebody at NIOS, made the gun himself."

Rhyme grimaced. "So there's no way to trace a sale of a serial-numbered rifle to NIOS or Shales. Hell."

His third goal, linking the bullet to Shales through his weapon, had just grown considerably more difficult.

Sachs said, "We're still waiting on Information Services to get back to us on the datamining. Maybe they'll find a record of Shales buying gun parts or tools."

Rhyme shrugged. "Well, let's see what else the slug tells us. Mel, friction ridge?"

Fingerprints actually can survive a bullet's transit through the air, through a body and sometimes even through a wall.

Provided Darry Shales had touched the bullets with his bare fingers. Which wasn't the case. Sachs, goggled, was blasting the slug with an alternative light source wand. "None."

"What about trace?"

Cooper was going over the slug now. "Bits of glass dust from the window." He then used tweezers to remove some minuscule bits of material. He examined the specimens closely under the microscope. "Vegetation," Rhyme postulated, looking at the monitor.

"Yes, that's right," the tech said. He ran a chemical analysis. "It's urushiol. A skin irritating allergen." He looked up. "Poison ivy, sumac?"

"Ah, the poisonwood tree. Outside the window of the Kill Room. The bullet must've passed through a leaf before it hit Moreno."

The tech also found a fiber, identical to those making up Moreno's shirt, and traces of blood, which matched the activist's blood in type.

Cooper said, "Aside from that and the ejecta, there's nothing else on the bullet."

Rhyme turned his new chair to face the evidence

boards. "Ron, if you could update our opus with your fine Catholic school handwriting? I need to optic the big picture," he added, unable to resist a bit of jargon worthy of their leader in absentia, Captain Bill Myers.

CHAPTER 58

ROBERT MORENO HOMICIDE

Boldface indicates updated information

— Crime Scene 1.
- — Suite 1200, South Cove Inn, New Providence Island, Bahamas (the "Kill Room").
- — May 9.
- — Victim 1: Robert Moreno.
    - — COD: Single gunshot wound to chest.
    - — Supplemental information: Moreno, 38, U.S. citizen, expatriate, living in Venezuela. Vehemently anti-American. Nickname: "the Messenger of Truth." **Determined that "disappear into thin air" and "blowing them up" NOT terrorism references.**
- — **Shoes contained fibers associated**

with carpet in hotel corridor, dirt
from hotel entryway, also crude
oil.
— **Clothing contained traces of
breakfast: pastry flakes, jam and
bacon, also crude oil.**
— Spent three days in NYC, April 30–
May 2. Purpose?
  — May 1, used Elite Limousine.
  — Driver Tash Farada (regular
    driver Vlad Nikolov was sick.
    Trying to locate).
  — Closed accounts at American
    Independent Bank and Trust,
    prob. other banks too.
— **Drove around city with inter-
  preter Lydia Foster (killed
  by Unsub 516).**
— Reason for anti-U.S. feelings:
  best friend killed by U.S.
  troops in Panama invasion,
  1989.
— Moreno's last trip to U.S.
  Never would return.
— Meeting in Wall Street. Pur-
  pose? Location?
    — **No record of terrorist
      investigations in area.**

- **Met with unknown individuals at Russian, UAE (Dubai) charities and Brazilian consulate.**
- **Met with Henry Cross, head of Classrooms for the Americas. Reported that Moreno met with other charities, but doesn't know which. Man following Moreno, white and "tough looking." Private jet tailing Moreno? Blue color. Checking for identification.**

— Victim 2: Eduardo de la Rua.
  - COD: Loss of blood. Lacerations from flying glass from gunshot, **measuring 3–4mm wide, 2–3cm long.**
  - Supplemental information: Journalist, interviewing Moreno. Born Puerto Rico, living in Argentina.
  - **Camera, tape recorder, gold pen, notebooks missing.**
  - **Shoes contained fibers associated with carpet in hotel corridor, dirt from hotel entryway.**
  - **Clothing contained traces of breakfast: allspice and pepper sauce.**

— Victim 3: Simon Flores.
  — COD: Loss of blood. Lacerations
    from flying glass from gunshot, **mea-
    suring 3–4mm wide, 2–3cm long.**
  — Supplemental information: Moreno's
    bodyguard. Brazilian national, living
    in Venezuela.
  — **Rolex watch, Oakley sunglasses
    missing.**
  — **Shoes contained fibers associated
    with carpet in hotel corridor, dirt
    from hotel entryway, also crude
    oil.**
  — **Clothing contained traces of
    breakfast: pastry flakes, jam and
    bacon, also crude oil and cigarette
    ash.**
— **Chronology of Moreno in Bahamas.**
  — **May 7. Arrived Nassau with Flores
    (guard).**
  — **May 8. Meeting out of hotel all
    day.**
  — **May 9. 9 a.m. Meeting two men
    about forming Local Empower-
    ment Movement in Bahamas.
    10:30 a.m. de la Rua arrives. At
    11:15 a.m. Moreno shot.**
— Suspect 1: Shreve Metzger.

- — Director, National Intelligence and
  Operations Service.
- — Mentally unstable? Anger issues.
- — Manipulated evidence to illegally au-
  thorize Special Task Order?
- — Divorced. Law degree, Yale.
- Suspect 2: Unsub 516.
  - — **Determined not to be sniper.**
  - — Possibly individual at South Cove Inn,
    May 8. Caucasian, male, mid 30s,
    short cut light brown hair, American
    accent, thin but athletic. Appears
    "military." Inquiring re: Moreno.
  - — .**Could be sniper's partner or hired
    by Metzger independently for
    clean-up and to stop investigation.**
  - — **Determined to be perpetrator of Ly-
    dia Foster and Annette Bodel homi-
    cides, and IED attack at Java Hut.**
  - — **Amateur or professional chef or
    cook of some skill.**
- Suspect 3: Barry Shales.
  - — **Confirmed to be sniper, code name
    Don Bruns.**
  - — **39, former Air Force, decorated.**
  - — **Intelligence specialist at NIOS.
    Wife is teacher. Have two sons.**
  - — Individual who placed a call to the

South Cove Inn on May 7 to confirm arrival of Moreno. **Call was from phone registered to Don Bruns, through NIOS cover company.**
- **Information Services datamining Shales.**
- Voiceprint obtained.

— Crime scene report, autopsy report, other details.

- **Crime scene cleaned and contaminated by Unsub 516 and largely useless.**
- **General details: Bullet fired through and shattered floor-to-ceiling window, garden outside, poisonwood tree leaves cut back to 25 feet height. View to sniper's nest obscured by haze and pollution.**
- **47 fingerprints found; half analyzed, negative results. Others missing.**
- **Candy wrappers recovered.**
- **Cigarette ash recovered.**
- **Bullet lodged behind couch where Moreno's body was found.**
  - **Fatal round.**
  - **.420 caliber, made by Walker Defense Systems, NJ.**

- **Spitzer boattail round.**
- **Extremely high quality.**
- **Extremely high velocity and high power.**
- **Rare.**
- **Weapon: custom made.**
- **Trace on bullet: glass dust, fiber from Moreno's shirt and poisonwood tree leaf.**

— Crime Scene 2.
  — Sniper nest of Barry Shales, 2000 yards from Kill Room, New Providence Island, Bahamas.
  — May 9.
  — **Unable to find spent cartridges or other evidence of location of sniper's nest.**
— **Crime Scene 2A.**
  — **Apartment 3C, 182 Augusta Street, Nassau, Bahamas.**
  — **May 15.**
  — **Victim: Annette Bodel.**
  — **COD: TBD, probably strangulation, asphyxiation.**
  — **Suspect: Determined to be Unsub 516.**
  — **Victim was probably tortured.**
  — **Trace:**
    — **Sand associated with sand found at Java Hut.**

- Docosahexaenoic acid—fish oil. Likely caviar or roe. Ingredient in dish from NY restaurant.
- Two-stroke engine fuel.
- $C_8H_8O_3$, vanillin. Ingredient in dish from NY restaurant.
- Crime Scene 3.
  - Java Hut, Mott and Hester Streets.
  - May 16.
  - IED explosion, to destroy evidence of whistleblower.
  - Victims: No fatalities, minor injuries.
  - Suspect: Determined to be Unsub 516.
  - Military-style device, anti-personnel, shrapnel. Semtex explosive. Available on arms market.
  - Located customers in shop when whistleblower was present, canvassing for info, pictures.
  - Trace:
    - Sand from tropical region.
- Crime Scene 4.
  - Apartment 230, 1187 Third Avenue.
  - May 16.
  - Victim: Lydia Foster.
  - COD: Blood loss, shock from knife wounds.
  - Suspect: Determined to be Unsub 516.

— **Hair, brown and short (from Unsub 516), sent to CODIS for analysis.**
— **Trace:**
  — **Glycyrrhiza glabra—licorice. Ingredient in dish from NY restaurant.**
  — **Cynarine, chemical component of artichokes. Ingredient in dish from NY restaurant.**
— **Evidence of torture.**
— **All records of interpreting assignment for Robert Moreno on May 1 stolen.**
— **No cell phone or computer.**
— **Receipt for Starbucks where Lydia waited during Moreno's private meeting on May 1.**
— Rumors of drug cartels behind the killings. Considered unlikely.
— Supplemental Investigation.
  — Determine identity of Whistleblower.
    — Unknown subject who leaked the Special Task Order.
    — Sent via anonymous email.
    — Traced through Taiwan to Romania to Sweden. Sent from New York area on public Wi-Fi, no government servers used.
    — Used an old computer, probably from ten years ago, iBook, either clamshell

model, two tone with other bright
colors (like green or tangerine). Or
could be traditional model, graphite
color, but much thicker than today's
laptops.
— Individual in light-colored sedan following
Det. A. Sachs.
— Make and model not determined.

"Some mysteries here," Rhyme said, musing, as he stared at the whiteboards, losing himself in the facts. Half whispering: "Do we like mysteries, rookie?"

"I'd say we do, Lincoln."

"Ah, right you are. And why?"

"Because they keep us from being, you know, complacent. They make us wonder and when we wonder we discover."

A smile.

"Now, what do we have, what do we have? First, Unsub Five Sixteen. We've got plenty of evidence against him—for the murder of Annette in the Bahamas, the bomb in Java Hut and the murder of Lydia Foster. If—excuse me *when*—we get his ID we can make a solid case against him for explosives and murder.

"Now, the conspiracy case against Shales and Metzger. We can link them—they both work together at NIOS—and we've got Shales's code name, Don Bruns, on the kill order. All we need now is the last piece of the puzzle: proof that Barry Shales was in the Bahamas on May 9. Once we do we've got both of them for conspiracy."

Whispering to himself as he stared at the boards. "Nothing in the physical evidence placing him there. We can prove the unsub was in the South Cove the day before the shooting but not Shales." He looked toward Sachs. "How's the datamining coming—is there anything about Shales's travel history?"

"I'll call Information Services." She picked up her mobile.

We don't need much, Rhyme reflected. A connection could be inferred by the jury—that's what circumstantial evidence was all about. But there had to be *some* basis for a valid inference. A jury can find a man guilty of DUI hit-and-run, even if he's found sober and denying the next morning, if a bartender testifies that he downed a dozen beers an hour before the accident and the jury takes that testimony as credible.

Vehicle E-ZPass transponders, credit cards, RFID chips in employee badges, subway Metro-Cards, TSA records, Customs documents, traffic cameras and security cameras in stores...dozens of sources of information could be used to place suspects at scenes.

He noted that Sachs was jotting quick notes. Good. They'd struck gold, he had a feeling.

Something would pin Barry Shales to the Bahamas on May 9.

Sellitto was looking at the chart and he echoed Rhyme's thought. "There's gotta be something. We know Shales's the shooter."

Amelia Sachs disconnected the call and with an uncharacteristically bewildered expression said, "Actually, Lon, no, he's not."

CHAPTER 59

A HALF HOUR LATER NANCE LAUREL, was in Rhyme's town house.

"Impossible," she whispered.

Sachs said, "He's not the sniper. Look for yourself."

And she tossed a number of documents on the table in front of Laurel with a bit more force than Rhyme supposed was necessary under the circumstances. On the other hand, clearly these two women were never destined to be friends. He'd been expecting a knock-down-drag-out between them the way a storm chaser eyes a pea-green overcast and thinks: Tornado's brewing.

What the Information Services operation of the NYPD had discovered was that Barry Shales had *not* been in the Bahamas on the day Moreno was shot. He was in New York City all day—in fact, he hadn't been out of the country in months.

"They ran a dozen searches, cross-referenced

everything. I asked them to double-check. They *triple*-checked. Radio frequency ID chip scans of him going into the NIOS office at nine and leaving for lunch, I'd guess—about two. During that time he went to Bennigan's, paid with a credit card. Handwriting scan is his, and then went to an ATM—the scan by the cash machine camera is positive. Sixty-point facial recognition. Returned to the office at three. Left at six thirty."

"May nine. You're sure?"

"Positive."

An odd sound, a snake's hiss. The breath easing from Nance Laurel's mouth.

"Where's that leave us?" Sachs asked.

"With Unsub Five Sixteen," Pulaski said.

Sellitto added, "We have nothing to suggest he's the sniper—he seems more like backup, or clean-up. But we have charges against him."

Rhyme said, "Here's an alternative case. We forget the Moreno homicide altogether. We prove Metzger had Unsub Five Sixteen kill Lydia Foster and set the IED. At the least there's your conspiracy charge. It's probably likely to get Metzger murder two."

But Laurel looked doubtful. "That's not the case I want."

"You want?" Sachs asked, as if she'd decided the ADA sounded like a spoiled little girl.

"Right. My case is against Metzger and his sniper for conspiring to commit an illegal targeted assassination." Her voice rose, the first edge Rhyme had heard in it. "The kill order was the whole basis for that." She stared at the copy on the whiteboard as if it had betrayed her.

"We can still nail Metzger," Sachs countered petulantly. "Does it matter how?"

Ignoring her, the ADA turned and walked to the window in the front of the parlor. She was staring out at Central Park.

Amelia Sachs gazed after her. Rhyme knew exactly what she was thinking.

I *want*...

My *case*...

Rhyme's eyes swiveled to Laurel. The tree she was looking at was a swamp white oak, *Quercus bicolor*, a thick and not particularly tall tree that did well in Manhattan. Rhyme knew about it not because of a personal interest in arboriculture but because he'd discovered a minuscule fragment of a swamp white oak leaf in the car of one Reggie "Sump" Kelleher, a particularly unpleasant Hell's Kitchen thug. The sliver, along with a bit of limy soil, had placed Kelleher at a clearing in Prospect Park, where the body of a Jamaican drug kingpin had been found, though the head had not.

Rhyme was focusing on the tree when the idea occurred to him.

He turned quickly to the evidence charts and stared for a long moment. He was vaguely aware that people were saying things to him. He paid no attention, muttering to himself.

Then he called over his shoulder, "Sachs, Sachs! Fast! I need you to take a drive."

CHAPTER 60

THE BUSINESS OF WAR WAS winding down around the world and some of the buildings in the New Jersey headquarters of Walker Defense Systems were shuttered.

But Sachs observed that there must be *some* market left for weapons of mass—and personal— destruction; dozens of high-end Mercedeses and Audis and BMWs dotted the parking lot.

And an Aston Martin.

Man, Sachs thought. I would love to take that Vanquish for a spin—and she fantasized about letting the horses loose on the company's private drive.

Inside the fifties-style building, she checked with reception and was led to a waiting area.

"Sterile" was the word that came to mind and that was true in two senses: The decor was minimal and austere, a few gray and black paintings, some ads for products whose purpose she couldn't quite figure out. And sterile in another sense: She felt she was a virus that researchers didn't quite trust and were keeping isolated until they knew more.

Rather than a *People* or a *Wall Street Journal* with last week's news, for waiting-room reading she chose a glossy company brochure, detailing its divisions, including missile guidance, gyroscopic navigation, armor, ammunition...all sorts of items.

Yes, maybe the company was downsizing but the literature showed impressive facilities in Florida, Texas and California, in addition to the headquarters. Overseas, they had operations in Abu Dhabi, São Paulo, Singapore, Munich and Mumbai. She walked to the window and studied the expansive grounds.

Soon a thirtyish man in a suit stepped into the lobby and greeted her. He was clearly surprised to see that an NYPD detective came in such a package and couldn't quite restrain the flirt as he led her through the labyrinthine and equally sterile halls to the CEO's office. He charmingly asked her about her job—what it was like to be a cop in New York, what were her most interesting cases, did she watch *CSI* or *The Mentalist*, what kind of gun did she have?

Which reminded her of the inked manager of Java Hut.

Men…

When it was clear that this theme of conversation wasn't working, he took to telling her about the company's achievements. She nodded politely and immediately forgot all of the factoids. With a frown he glanced at her leg; she realized she'd been limping and instantly forced herself into a normal gait.

After a trek they came to a corner office in the one-story building, Mr. Walker's. A spray-haired brunette at an impressive desk looked up, defensive, probably because her boss was being visited by the NYPD. Sachs noticed that many of the shelves here were occupied by a collection of plastic and lead soldiers. Whole armies. Sachs's first thought: Dusting would be a bitch.

The flirter who'd escorted her seemed to try to think of some way to ask her out on a date but nothing occurred to him. He turned and left.

"He'll see you now," the PA said.

As Sachs stepped into Harry Walker's office, she couldn't help but smile.

A weapons manufacturer had to be narrow of face, unsmiling and suspicious, if not sadistic, right? Plotting ways to sell ammunition to Russia while simultaneously shipping to Chechnyan separatists. The head of Walker Defense, however, was a pudgy and cherubic sixty-five-year-old, who happened to be sitting cross-legged on the floor, putting together a pink tricycle.

Walker wore a white shirt, which bulged at the belly over tan dress slacks. His tie was striped, red and blue. He offered a casual smile and rose— with some difficulty; a screwdriver was clutched in one hand and a set of assembly instructions in the other. "Detective Sachs. Amanda?"

"Amelia."

"I'm Harry."

She nodded.

"My granddaughter." He glanced at the bike. "I have a degree from MIT. I have two hundred patents for advanced weapons systems. But can I put together a Hello Kitty trike? Apparently only with great difficulty."

Every part was carefully laid out on the floor, labeled by Post-it Notes.

Sachs said, "I work on cars. I always end up with an extra bolt or nut or strut. But things seem to run fine without them."

He set the tool and instructions on his desk and sat behind it. Sachs took the chair he gestured at.

"So, now, what can I do for you?" He was smiling still —just like the middle manager who'd escorted her from the lobby but in Walker's case the expression wasn't a flirt. His grin hid both curiosity and caution.

"You're one of the oldest manufacturers of bullets and weapons systems in the country."

"Well, thanks to Wikipedia, why deny it?"

Sachs settled back into the comfortable chair, also leather, beige. She glanced at the pictures on the wall, some men at a rifle range, probably around the time of the First World War.

He told her, "We were founded by my great-granddad. Quite an amazing man. I say that like I knew him. But he died before I was born. He invented the recoil system of automatic weapons loading. Of course, there were a half dozen other inventors who did the same and he didn't get to the patent office first. But he made the best, the most efficient models."

Sachs hadn't known about Walker Senior's contribution but was impressed. There were several ways to get a weapon to fire repeatedly but the recoil system had won out as the most popular. A talented shooter can get off a bullet every few seconds with a bolt-action rifle. A modern automatic weapon can spit nine hundred rounds a minute, some esoteric types even more.

"You're familiar with firearms?" he asked.

"I shoot as a hobby."

He eyed her carefully. "How do you feel about the Second Amendment?" A provocative question wearing a gown of mere curiosity.

She didn't hesitate. "Open to interpretation—the militia versus personal rights."

The brief Second Amendment of the Constitution guaranteed the right of *militias* to keep and bear arms. It didn't specifically say that all citizens had that right.

Sachs continued, "I've read George Mason's notes, and personally I think his intent was that he was referring exclusively to militias." She held up a hand as Walker was about to interrupt. "But then he added, 'Who are the militia? They consist now of the whole people, except a few public officers.' That means the right applies to everybody—back then every citizen was potentially militia."

"I'm with you!" Walker beamed. "That's nearly a direct quote, by the way. So, don't trammel our rights." He nodded.

"Not quite so fast," Sachs added coyly. "It's not the end of the argument."

"No?"

"The Constitution gives us a lot of rights but it also lets Congress regulate us in a thousand different ways. You need a license to drive a car or fly a plane or sell liquor. You can't vote until you're eighteen. Why shouldn't you have a license to own or shoot a gun? I have no problem with that. And it doesn't conflict with the Second Amendment at all."

Walker responded happily, enjoying their argument, "Ah, but of course if we get licenses, then Washington knows where the guns are and they'll come in the middle of the night and take them away. Don't we need our weapons to stop them from doing that?"

Sachs riposted, "Washington has nukes. If they want our guns they'll take our guns."

Walker nodded. "True, there is that. Now, we've been digressing. How can I help you?"

"We recovered a bullet at a crime scene."

"One of ours, I assume."

"You're the only company making a four twenty spitzer boattail, aren't you?"

"Oh, our new sniper round. And a very fine cartridge it is. Better than the four sixteen, if you ask me. Fast. Oh, fast as a demon." Then he frowned in apparent confusion. "And the round was involved in a crime?"

"That's right."

"We don't sell to the public. Only government, the army and police SWAT teams. I don't know how a criminal could have gotten his hands on one—unless he, or she, fell into those categories. Where exactly was the scene?"

"I can't say at this point."

"I see. And what do you want to know?"

"Just some information. We're trying to find the

rifle this slug was fired from but not having any luck. We're assuming they're custom-made."

"That's right. The loads are too big to fire in re-tooled commercial rifles. Most of the shooters find somebody to make their weapons for them. A few do it themselves."

"Do you know anyone who does that work?"

He smiled coyly. "I can't say at this point."

She laughed. "And that goes for information about customers you've sold these bullets to?"

Walker grew serious now. "If somebody had broken into one of our own warehouses—" A nod out the window toward nearby buildings. "—and the rounds were used in a crime, then I'd be happy to help you out. But I can't give you customer information. We have gag clauses in all our contracts, and in most cases there're additional national security requirements. To give you information like that would be a crime." His face grew troubled. "Can you tell me *anything* about what happened, though? Was it a homicide?"

Sachs debated. "Yes."

Walker's face was still. "I'm sorry about that. I truly am. It doesn't do us any good when somebody misuses our products and something tragic happens."

But that didn't mean he was going to help. Walker rose and extended his hand.

She stood too. "Thanks for your time."

Walker picked up the instructions and screw-driver and walked back to the trike.

Then he smiled and picked up a bolt. "You buy a Harley-Davidson, you know, it comes already as-sembled."

"Good luck with that, Mr. Walker. Call me if you can think of anything, please." She handed him one of her cards—which, she suspected, he'd pitch out before she was halfway to the lobby.

Didn't matter.

Sachs had everything she needed.

CHAPTER 61

I N RHYME'S DARK PARLOR, redolent of trace materials burned into incriminating evidence by the gas chromatograph, Sachs pulled her jacket off and held up the brochure from Walker Defense.

Ron Pulaski taped it up on a whiteboard. The glitzy piece sat next to the kill order.

"So," Rhyme said, "what did it look like?"

"Pretty short and hidden between two buildings but I caught a glimpse from Walker's office. There was a windsock at one end and what looked like a small hangar at the other."

Sachs's mission had nothing to do with getting customer information or the names of people fabricating long-range rifles, which Rhyme knew Walker wouldn't divulge anyway. Her job was to find out as much about the company's products as she could—more than its preening and ambiguous website offered. And—most important—to find out if it had a length of asphalt or concrete that could be used as an airstrip; Google Earth had not been helpful in that regard.

"Excellent," Rhyme said.

As for the other products, they too were just what he'd hoped: instruments and devices for guidance, navigation and control systems, in addition to ammunition. "Gyroscopes, GPS sighting systems, synthetic aperture radar, things like that," Sachs explained.

The criminalist read through the brochure.

He said slowly, "Okay, we have our answer. The case is back on. Barry Shales *did* kill Robert Moreno. He was just a little farther away from the target than two thousand feet. In fact, he was here in New York when he pulled the trigger."

Sellitto shook his head. "We should've thought better. Shales wasn't infantry or special forces. He was air force."

Rhyme's theory, now supported by Sachs's legwork, was that Barry Shales was a drone pilot.

"We know his code name is Don Bruns and Bruns was the one who killed Moreno. The data show he was in the NIOS office downtown on the day the man died. He'd have been piloting a drone from some control facility there." He paused, frowned. "Oh, hell, that's the 'Kill Room' the STO refers to. It's not the hotel suite where Moreno was shot; it's the drone cockpit or whatever you call it, where the pilot sits."

Sachs nodded at the brochure. "Walker makes those bullets, they make gun sights and stabilization and radar and navigation systems. They've built or armed a specialized drone that uses a rifle as a weapon."

Rhyme spat out, "Look at the STO—there's a period after 'Kill Room,' not a comma! 'Suite twelve hundred' doesn't modify it. They're separate places." He continued, "Okay, this is all making sense now. What's the one problem with drone strikes?"

"Collateral damage," Sachs said.

"Exactly. A missile takes out terrorists but it also kills innocent people. Very bad for America's image. NIOS contracted with Walker Defense to come up with a drone that minimizes collateral. Using a precision rifle with a very big bullet."

Sellitto said, "But they fucked up. There *was* collateral."

"The Moreno assassination was a fluke," Rhyme said. "Who could've anticipated broken glass would be lethal?"

Sellitto gave a laugh. "You know, Amelia, you were right. This *was* a million-dollar bullet. Literally. Hell, given what drones cost, it's probably a ten-million-dollar bullet."

"How'd you guess?" Nance Laurel asked.

"Guess?" Sachs offered acerbically.

But Rhyme didn't need any defense. He was delighted with his deduction and was happy to explain:

"Trees. I was thinking of trees. There was poisonwood leaf trace on the bullet. I saw the tree outside the window of the suite. All the branches up to about twenty-five feet or so were cut back—because the hotel didn't want anyone touching the leaves. That meant the bullet struck Moreno at a very steep downward angle—probably forty-five degrees. That was too acute even for a shooter on the spit to aim high to correct for gravity. It meant the bullet came from the air.

"If Shales fired through the trees, that means he was using some kind of infrared or radar sighting system to quote see Moreno through the leaves. I was also curious why there was no pollution on the slug—from the fumes and crap in the air over the spit. A hot bullet would have picked up plenty of trace. But it didn't."

Pulaski said, "By the way, Lincoln, they're UAVs, unmanned aerial vehicles. Not drones."

"Thank you for the correction. Accuracy is everything. You're a wealth of knowledge."

"Discovery Channel."

Rhyme laughed and continued, "It also reconciles why Mychal Poitier's divers didn't find any spent brass. It's out to sea. Or maybe the drone retains the spent shells. Good, good. We're moving ahead."

Cooper said, "And he was a lot closer than two thousand yards. That's why the high velocity of the bullet."

Rhyme said, "I'd guess the UAV couldn't've been any more than two or three hundred yards out, to make an accurate shot like that. It'd be easy for people on the ground to miss it. There would have been camouflage—just like with our chameleons. And the engine would've been small—two-stroke, remember. With a muffler you'd never hear it."

"It launched from Walker's airstrip in New Jersey?" Pulaski asked.

Rhyme shook his head. "The airstrip's just for testing the drones, I'm sure. NIOS would launch from a military base and as close to the Bahamas as possible."

Laurel dug through her notes. "There's a NIOS office near Miami." She looked up. "Next to Homestead Air Reserve Base."

Sachs tapped the brochure. "Walker has an office near there. Probably for service and support."

Laurel's crisp voice then added, "And you recall what Lincoln said earlier?" She was speaking to them all.

"Yep," Sellitto said, compulsively stirring his coffee, as if that would make it sweeter; he'd added only half a packet of sugar. "We don't need conspiracy anymore. Barry Shales was in New York City when he pulled the trigger. That means the crime's now murder two. And Metzger's an accessory."

"Very good, Detective, that's correct," Laurel said as if she were a fifth-grade teacher praising a student in class.

CHAPTER 62

S HREVE METZGER TILTED HIS HEAD back so the lower lens of his glasses brought the words on his magic phone better into focus.

```
Budgetary meetings proceeding apace.
Much back-and-forth. Resolution tomor-
row. Can't tell which way the wind is
blowing.
```

He thought to the Wizard, And what the hell am I supposed to do with this bit of fucking non-information? Get my résumé in order or not? Tell everybody here that they're about to be punished for being patriots and saying no to the evil that wants to destroy the greatest country on earth? Or not?

Sometimes the Smoke could be light, irritating. Sometimes it could be that inky mass of cloud, the sort you see rising from plane crashes and chemical plant explosions.

He digitally shredded the message and stalked downstairs to the coffee shop, bought a latte for himself and a soy-laced mochaccino for Ruth. He returned and set hers on her desk, between pictures of soldier husband one and soldier husband two.

"Thank you," the woman said and turned her stunning blue eyes on him. The corners crinkled with a smile. Even in her advanced decade Ruth was attractive in the broadest sense of the word. Metzger did not believe in souls or spirits but, if he did, that would be the part of Ruth that so appealed.

Maybe you could just say she had a good heart.

And here she is working for someone like me...

He brushed aside the Smokey cynicism.

"The appointment went okay," she told him.

Metzger replied, "I was confident. I knew it would. Could you have Spencer come in, please?"

Stepping into his office, he dropped into his chair, sipped the coffee, angry at what he felt was the excessive heat radiating through the cardboard. This reminded him of another incident: A street vendor selling him coffee had been rude. He still fantasized about finding the man's stand and ramming it with his car. The incident was three years ago.

Can't tell which way the wind is blowing.

He blew on the coffee—Smoke exhaling, he imagined.

Let it go.

He began checking emails, extracted from the rabbit hole of encryption. One was troubling: Some disturbing news about the Moreno investigation, a setback. Curiously this just exhausted him, didn't infuriate.

A knock on the jamb. Spencer Boston entered and sat.

"What've you got on our whistleblower?" Metzger asked without a greeting.

"Looks like the first round of polygraphs is negative. That was people actually signing off on or reviewing the STO. There are still hundreds who might've slipped into an office somewhere and gotten their hands on a copy."

"So all the senior people in the command are clear?"

"Right. Here and at the centers."

NIOS had three UAV command centers: Pendleton in California, Fort Hood in Texas and Homestead in Florida. They all would have received a copy of the Moreno STO, even though the UAV launched from Homestead.

"Oh," Boston said. "I passed too, by the way."

Metzger gave a smile. "Didn't occur to me." It truthfully hadn't.

"What's good for the asset is good for the agent."

Metzger asked, "And Washington?"

At least a dozen people down in the nation's capital knew about the STO. Including, of course, key members of the White House staff.

"That's harder. They're resisting." Boston asked, "Where are they now in the investigation, the cops?"

Metzger felt the Smoke arising. "Apparently that Rhyme managed to get down to the Bahamas after all." He nodded at his phone where certain emails used to reside. "The fucking sand didn't deter him as much as we'd hoped."

"What?" Boston's eyes, normally shaded by sagging lids, grew wide.

Metzger said judiciously, "There was an accident, it seems. But it didn't stop him."

"An accident?" Boston asked, looking at him closely.

"That's right, Spencer, an accident. And he's back here, going gangbusters. That woman too."

"The prosecutor?"

"Well, yes, her. But I meant that Detective Sachs. She's unstoppable."

"Jesus."

Though his present plans would, in fact, stop her quite efficiently.

Laurel too.

Well, yes, her...

Boston's concern was evident and the display

angered Metzger. He said dismissingly, "I can't imagine Rhyme found anything. The crime scene was a week old, and how competent could the police down there be?"

The memory of the coffee vendor came back, immediate and stark. Instead of ramming the stand, Metzger had thought about pouring hot coffee on himself and calling the police, saying the vendor did it and having him arrested.

The Smoke made you unreasonable.

Boston intruded on the memory. "Do you think you ought to give anybody else a heads-up?"

Heads-up. Metzger hated that expression. When you analyze it, the phrase could only mean that you should glance up in time to say a prayer before something large crushed you to death. A better expression would be "eyes-forward."

"Not at this time."

He looked up and he noted Ruth standing in the doorway.

Why the hell hadn't he closed the door? "Yes?"

"Shreve. It's Operations."

A flashing red LED light on Metzger's phone console.

He hadn't noticed it.

What now?

He held up an index finger to Spencer Boston and answered. "Metzger here."

"Sir, we have Rashid." The OD was younger even than Metzger and his voice revealed that.

Suddenly the Smoke vanished. And so did Nance Laurel, Lincoln Rhyme and virtually every other blot on his life. Rashid was the next man in the Special Task Order queue, after Moreno. Metzger had been after him for a very long time. "Where?"

"He's in Mexico."

"So *that's* his plan. The prick got closer than we thought."

"Slippery, sir. Yes. He's in a temporary location, a safe house the Matamoros Cartel has in Reynosa. We have a short window. Should I forward details to the GCS and Texas Center?"

"Yes."

The operations director asked, "Sir, are you aware that the STO has been modified in Washington?"

"In what regard?" he asked, troubled.

"The original order provided for minimizing collateral damage but it didn't prohibit CD. This one does. Approval is rescinded if anyone else present is a casualty, even wounded."

Rescinded . . .

Which means that if anybody is killed with Rashid, even al-Qaeda's second-in-command about to push a nuclear launch button, I've acted outside the scope of my authority.

And I'm fucked.

It didn't matter that a pure asshole died and a thousand innocent people were saved.

Maybe this was part of the "budgetary" meetings.

"Sir?"

"Understood."

He disconnected and told Boston the news. "Rashid? I thought that son of a bitch was going to hide out in San Salvador till the attack. He paid off members of the Mara Salvatrucha gang—aka the MS-13s—for protection. Had some place in District Six, near Soyapango. If you want to get lost to the world, that's the place to do it."

Nobody knew Central America like Spencer Boston.

A flag arose on his computer. Metzger opened his encrypted emails and read the new STO there, the death warrant for al-Barani Rashid, suitably modified. He read it again and added his electronic signature and PIN number, approving the kill.

The man was, like Moreno, a U.S.-born expatriate, who'd been living in northern Africa and the Gulf states until a few months ago.

He'd been on a watch list for several years but only under informal surveillance, not in any of the active-risk books. He'd never done anything overt that could be proven. But he was as vehemently anti-American as Moreno. And he too had been seen in the company of groups that were actively engaged in terrorist actions.

Metzger scrolled through the intelligence analysis accompanying the revised STO, explaining to Boston the details. Rashid was in the undistinguished town of Reynosa, Mexico, on the Texas border. The U.S. intelligence assets NIOS was using down there believed Rashid was in town to meet with a senior man in northeastern Mexico's biggest cartel. Terrorists had taken to working closely with the cartels for two reasons: to encourage drug flow into America, which supported their ideology of eroding Western society and institutions, and because the cartels were incredibly well equipped.

"We'll have him handle it?"

"Of course." Him. Bruns, that is, Barry Shales. He was the best in the stable. Metzger texted him now and ordered him to report to the Kill Room.

Metzger spun the computer and together he and Boston studied the images, both on-the-ground surveillance and satellite. The safe house in Reynosa was a dusty one-story ranch structure, good-sized, with weathered tan paint and bright green trim. It squatted in the middle of a sandy one-acre lot. All the windows were shaded and barred. The car, if there was one, would be tucked away in the garage.

Metzger assessed the situation. "We'll have to go with a missile. No visuals to use LRR."

The Long-Range Rifle program, in which a specially built sniper gun was mounted into a drone, had been Metzger's brainchild. LRR was the centerpiece of NIOS. The arrangement served two purposes. It drastically minimized the risk of innocent deaths, which nearly always happened with missiles. And it gave Metzger the chance to kill a lot more enemies; you had to be judicious about launching missiles and there was never much doubt after the fact where the Hellfire had come from: the U.S. military, CIA or other intelligence service. But a single rifle shot? The shooter could be anybody. Plant a few references to a gunman working for an opposing political party, a terrorist group, or—say—a South American cartel, and the local authorities and the press would tend not to look elsewhere. The victim could even have been shot by a jealous spouse.

But he'd known from the beginning that LRR drones wouldn't always work. For Rashid, with no visible target the only option was a missile, with its twenty-pound high-explosive warhead.

Boston's long face was aimed out the window. He brushed his white hair absently with his fingers and played with a stray thread escaping from a cuff button. Metzger wondered why he always wore a jacket in the office.

"What, Spencer?"

"Is this a good time for another STO? With the Moreno fallout?"

"*This* intel's solid. Rashid is guilty as sin. We have assessments from Langley and the Mossad and the SIS."

"I just meant we don't know how much of the queue got leaked. Maybe it was just Moreno's order; maybe it was more, Rashid's included. His was next on the list, remember? His death'll make the news. Maybe that damn prosecutor'll come after us for this one too. We're on thin ice here."

These were all obvious considerations but Metzger had the *need* inside his gut and, accordingly, was free of the Smoke.

He absolutely didn't want this relief, this sense of comfort, of freedom, to go away.

"And if we don't take him out, you know what Rashid's got planned for Texas or Oklahoma."

"We could call Langley and arrange a rendition."

"Kidnap him? And do what? We don't need information from him, Spencer. All we need from Rashid is no more Rashid."

Boston yielded. "All right. But what about the collateral damage risk? Firing a Hellfire into a residence with no visual reference?"

Metzger scrolled down the intel assessment until he found the surveillance report. Current as of ten minutes ago. "Safe house is empty, except for

Rashid. The place's been under DEA and Mexican Federales surveillance for a week for suspected mules. Nobody's gone inside until Rashid this morning. According to the intel, he'll be meeting the cartel man anytime now. Once that guy leaves, we'll blow the place to hell."

CHAPTER 63

Al-Barani Rashid looked over his shoulder a great deal.

Figuratively and literally.

The tall, balding forty-year-old, with a precise goatee, knew he was in danger—from the Mossad, the CIA and that New York–based security outfit, NIOS. Probably some people in China too.

Not to mention more than a few fellow Muslims He was on record as condemning the fundamentalists of his religion for their intellectual failings by blindly adhering to a medieval philosophy unsustainable in the twenty-first century. (He had also publicly excoriated moderates of the faith for their cowardice in protesting that they were misunderstood, that Islam was basically Presbyterianism with a different holy book. But *they* simply blogged insults; they weren't going to fatwa him.)

Rashid wanted a new order, a complete reimagining of faith and society. If he had any model, it wasn't Zawahiri or Bin Laden. It would be a hybrid of Karl Marx and Ted Kaczynski, the Unabomber, who happened to have attended his own school—the University of Michigan.

But as unpopular as he was, Rashid believed in his heart he was right. Remove the cancer and the world will right itself.

The metastasizing cells were, of course, the United States of America. From the subprime crisis, to Iraq, to the insulting carrot of foreign aid, to the racist diatribes of Christian preachers and politicians, to the deification of consumer goods, the country was a sea anchor on the progress of civilization. He'd left the country after a graduate degree in political science, never to return.

Yes, enemies were eager as wolves to get to him because of his views. Even those countries that didn't like America *needed* America.

But he felt more or less safe at the moment, presently in a sprawling ranch-style house in Reynosa, Mexico, as he awaited the arrival of an ally.

He couldn't say "friend," of course. His relationship with the slick individuals of the Matamoros Cartel was symbiotic but their motives diverged considerably. Rashid's was ideological, the war against American capitalism and society (and support for Israel, but that went without saying). The cartel's purpose was, in a way, the opposite, making vast sums of money from that very society. But its goals were basically the same. Get as many drugs as you can into the country. And kill those who want to stop you from doing that.

Sipping strong tea, he looked at his watch. One of the cartel bosses was sending his chief bomb maker to see Rashid within the hour. He would provide what Rashid needed to build a particularly smart device, which would, in two days, kill a DEA regional director in Brownsville, Texas, together with her family and however many others happened to be nearby at the picnic.

Rashid was presently sitting at a coffee table, bent over a pad of yellow paper, and clutching a mechanical pencil as he drew engineering diagrams for the IED.

Although Reynosa was a thoroughly unpleasant town, dusty, dun-colored and filled with small, sagging factories, this house was large and quite pleasant. The cartel had put some good money into maintaining it. It had decent air-conditioning, plenty of food and tea and bottled water, comfortable furniture and thick shades on all the windows. Yes, not a bad house at all.

Though occasionally noisy.

He walked to the back bedroom door and knocked, then opened it. One of the enforcers with the cartel, a heavyset unsmiling man named Norzagaray, nodded a greeting.

Rashid looked over the cartel's hostages: The husband and wife, both native Mexican and stocky, their teenage son and little girl sat on the floor, in front of a TV. The father's and wife's hands were bound with bell wire, loose enough so they could drink water and eat. Not so loose they could attack their kidnappers.

In Rashid's opinion, they should have bound the wife's more tightly. *She* was the danger; *she* had the rage. It was obvious as she comforted her daughter, a slim child whose head was crowned with dark, curly hair. The husband and boy were more frightened.

Rashid had been told by his contacts here that he could use the house but he would have to share it with these hostages, who'd been here for eight or nine days. The man's small business had been spending that time struggling to raise the two million dollars in ransom the drug lords had demanded—because of the man's defiance of the cartel.

Rashid said to Norzagaray, "Could you turn the volume down please?" A nod at the TV, on which a cartoon was playing.

Their guard did so.

"Thank you." He looked the family over carefully now, taking no pleasure in their terror. This was crime for profit; he didn't approve. He regarded the teenager and then a soccer ball in the corner. The colors were those of Club América, the pro team in Mexico City.

"You like football?"

"Yes."

"What do you play?"

"Midfield."

"I did too when I was your age." Rashid didn't smile. He never did but his voice was soft. He looked at them a moment more. Though they did not know it yet, Rashid had been told the negotiations were nearly complete and the family would be released tomorrow. Rashid was pleased at this. These people were not the enemy. The father wasn't working for an American company that was exploitative and amoral. He was just a small businessman who'd fallen on the wrong side of the cartel. Rashid wanted to reassure them that they would survive the ordeal. But this wasn't his concern.

He closed the door and returned to the diagrams he was working on. He reviewed them for long moments. And finally concluded: First, no one could possibly survive being in the proximity of the device they described. And second—he allowed himself the immodest thought—the drawings were as elegant as the finest zellige terra-cotta tiles, a cornerstone of Moroccan art.

CHAPTER 64

LINCOLN RHYME WAS SAYING, "And the same evidence we thought exculpated Shales by placing him in New York at the time of the shooting now helps *implicate* him: the phone calls from his mobile to the South Cove Inn to verify when Moreno was checking in, the metadata that placed him at NIOS headquarters in New York at the time of the death. We'll need more, though. We need to place him at the joystick of the drone. *UAV*, excuse me, rookie. How can we do that?"

"Air traffic control in Florida and the Bahamas," Sachs said.

"Good."

Sachs called their federal liaison, Fred Dellray, with the request and had a lengthy conversation with him. Finally Sachs disconnected. "Fred's calling the FAA here and the Civil Aviation Department in Nassau. But he gave me another idea." She was typing on her computer.

Rhyme couldn't see clearly. It appeared that she was examining a map. "Well," she whispered.

"What?" Rhyme wondered.

"Fred suggested we ought to try to get a look at the Kill Room itself."

"What?" Sellitto barked. "How?"

Google apparently.

Sachs smiled. She'd called up a satellite image of the block in which NIOS headquarters was located in downtown Manhattan. Behind the building itself was a parking lot, separated from the street with an impressive-looking security fence and overseen by a guard station. In the corner was a large rectangular structure, like a shipping container—the sort you see bolted to decks and cruising down highways behind tractor-trailer semis. Next to it a ten-foot antenna pointed skyward.

"That's the Ground Control Station, Fred told me. GCS. He said most of the UAVs are controlled from portable facilities like that."

"The Kill Room," Mel Cooper said.

"Perfect," Laurel said briskly to Sachs. "Print that out, if you would."

Rhyme could see Sachs bristle, hesitate and then with a thumb and finger—with a dot of dried blood behind the nail—tap hard on the keyboard. A printer began to exhale.

When the document was disgorged, Laurel slipped it from the tray and added it to her files.

Sachs's phone buzzed. "It's Fred again," she announced. She hit speaker.

Rhyme called, "Fred. Don't insult anybody."

"I can hear. Well, well, you all have yourself quite a case here. Good luck on this one. Hey, see any funny-lookin' airplanes hovering outside your windows? Might wanta think about closing the blinds."

This was not as funny as Dellray intended, Rhyme decided, given Barry Shales's skill at firing million-dollar bullets.

"Hokay, the radar situation. Sentcha screenshots. What we put together is the morning of May nine a small aircraft, no transponder, was tracked heading east over the Atlantic, south of Miami."

"Where Homestead air base is," Sellitto pointed out.

"Right you are. Now, the craft was on visual flight rules, no flight plan. Speed was very slow—about a hundred ten miles an hour. Which is typical drone speed. We all together on that?"

"With you, Fred. Keep going."

"Well, it's about a hundred eighty miles to Nassau from Miami. Exactly one hour and fifty-two minutes later, ATC in Nassau tracked a small aircraft, no transponder, ascend into radar range, about six hundred feet." Dellray paused. "And then it stopped."

"Stopped?"

"They thought it stalled. But it didn't drop off the screen."

"It was hovering," Rhyme said.

"My guess. They figured that with no transponder the plane was an ultralight—one of those homemade gizmos that sometimes just sit like birds in headwinds? It wasn't in controlled airspace so they didn't pay any more mind. The time was eleven oh four a.m."

"Moreno was shot at eleven sixteen," Sachs said.

"And at eleven eighteen it turned around and descended outta radar. Two hours and five minutes later, a small aircraft, no transponder, crossed into U.S. airspace and headed toward South Miami."

"That's our boy," Rhyme said. "Thanks, Fred."

"Gooood luck. And forget you ever knew me."
Click.

Wasn't conclusive but like all elements in a case it was a solid brick in the wall of establishing a suspect's guilt.

Nance Laurel got a call. While someone else

might have nodded or offered some facial clues as to the content she listened without expression; her powdered face was a mask. She disconnected. "There's an issue with another case of mine. I have to go interview a prisoner in detention. It shouldn't be long. I'd like to stay but I have to take care of this."

The prosecutor gathered up her purse and headed out the door.

Sachs too received a call. She listened and jotted a few notes.

Rhyme turned from her and was regarding the charts once again. "But I want more," he griped. "Something to *prove* that Shales was at the controls of the drone."

"Ask and ye shall receive." This, from Amelia Sachs.

Rhyme lifted an eyebrow.

She said, "We have a lead to the whistleblower. If anybody can place Barry Shales in the Kill Room on May ninth, it's him."

———

SACHS WAS PLEASED to report that Captain Myers's officers who'd been canvassing the patrons of Java Hut when the whistleblower uploaded the STO had found some witnesses.

Her computer gave a bleat and she looked toward the screen. "Incoming," she said.

Sellitto gave a harsh laugh. "Not a good choice of words in this case, you don't mind."

She opened the attachment. "People buy a lot more with credit or debit cards nowadays. Even if the bill's only three, four dollars. Sure helps us, though. The canvassers talked to everybody who charged something around one p.m. on the eleventh. Mostly a bust but one of them got a picture." She printed out the photo attachments. Not terrible, she decided, but hardly high-def mug shots. "Has to be our man."

She read the officer's memo. "'The photographer was a tourist from Ohio. Shooting pictures of his wife sitting across from him. You can see in the background a man, blurred—because he's turning away fast and raising his hand to cover his face. Asked the tourists if they got a better look at him. They didn't and other patrons and the baristas didn't pay any attention to him.'"

Rhyme looked at the picture. Two tables behind the smiling woman was the presumed whistleblower. White. Solidly built, in a blue suit, an odd color, just shy of navy. He wore a baseball cap—suspicious, given the business attire—but seemed to have light-colored hair. A big laptop sat open before him.

"That's him," Sachs said. "He's got an iBook." She'd downloaded a picture of every model.

The criminalist observed, "Suit doesn't fit well. It's cheap. And see the Splenda packets on the table, along with the stirrer? Confirms he's our man."

"Why?" Sellitto asked. "I use Splenda."

"Not the substance—the fact it's on the table. Most people add sugar or sweetener at the milk station and throw the empty packets out, and the stirrers too. So there's less mess at the table. He's taking his detritus with him. Didn't want to leave friction ridge evidence."

Most objects, even paper, retain very good fingerprints where food is served because of grease from the meals.

"Anything else about him?" Pulaski asked.

"You tell me, rookie."

The young officer said, "Look how he's holding his right hand, palm cupped upward? Maybe he was about to take a pill. Could be a headache, backache. Wait, look, there's a box. Is it? A box at the side of the table?"

It seemed that there was. Blue and gold.

Rhyme said, "Good. I think you're right. And notice he's drinking tea—see the bag in the napkin?—in a coffeehouse? Looks pale. Maybe it's herbal. Not that unusual but a reasonable deduction could be stomach issues. Check antacid, reflux, indigestion medicine boxes that come in two colors."

A moment later Cooper said, "Could be Zantac, maximum strength. Hard to say."

"We don't need definitive answers on everything," Rhyme said softly. "We need direction. So he's probably got a bum gut."

"Stress from leaking classified government documents'll do that," Mel Cooper offered.

"Age?" Rhyme wondered.

"Can't tell," the young officer replied. "How could you tell?"

"Well, I'm not asking you to play a carnival game, rookie. We see he's stocky, we see he's got stomach issues. Hair could be blond but could be gray. Conservative dress. It's reasonable to speculate he's middle-aged or older."

"Sure. I see."

"And his posture. It's perfect, even though he's not young. Suggests a military background. Or could still be in the service, dressing civie."

They stared at the picture and Sachs found herself wondering, Why did you leak the kill order? What was in it for you?

A person with a conscience . . .

But are you a patriot or a traitor?

Wondering too: And where the hell are you?

Sellitto took a call. Sachs noticed that his face went from curious to dark. He glanced at the others in the room, then turned away.

Whispering now: "What?...That's fucked up. You can't just tell me that. I need details."

Everyone was staring at him.

"Who? I want to know who. All right, find out and let me know."

He disconnected and the glance in Sachs's direction, but not directly at her, explained that she was the subject of the call.

"What, Lon?"

"You want to step outside." He nodded toward the hallway.

Sachs glanced at Rhyme and said, "No. Here. What is it? Who called?"

He hesitated.

"Lon," she said firmly. "Tell me."

"Okay, Amelia, I'm sorry. Look, you're off the case."

"What?"

"Actually, gotta say, you're on mandatory leave altogether. You've gotta report down to—"

"What happened?" Rhyme snapped.

"I don't know for sure. That was my PA. She told me the word came from the chief of detectives' office. The formal report's on its way. I don't know who's behind this."

"Oh, I do," Sachs snapped. She ripped open her purse and looked inside to make sure she had the copy of the document she'd found on Nance Laurel's desk the other night. At that time, she'd been reluctant to brandish it as a weapon.

Now she no longer was.

CHAPTER 65

SHREVE METZGER RAN A HAND through his trim hair, remembered his first day out of the service.

Somebody, a civilian, on the streets of Buffalo had called him a skinhead. Baby-killer too. The guy was drunk. Anti-military. An asshole. All of the above.

The Smoke had filled Metzger fast, though he didn't call it Smoke then, didn't call it anything. He proceeded to break at least four bones in the man's body before the relief shot through him. More than relief—almost sexual.

Sometimes this memory came back, like now, when he happened to touch his hair. Nothing more than that. He remembered the man, his unfocused, slightly crossed eyes. The blood, the remarkably swollen jaw.

And the coffee vendor. No, just ram the stand,

scald him, kill him, forget the consequences. The satisfaction would be sublime.

Help me, Dr. Fischer.

But there was no Smoke now. He was in an ecstatic high. Intelligence and surveillance experts were feeding him information about the Rashid operation.

The terrorist—the next task in the queue—was presently meeting with the Matamoros Cartel bomb supplier. Metzger would have given anything to modify the STO to include him as well but the man was a Mexican citizen and getting permission to vaporize him would have meant elaborate discussions with higher-ups in Mexico City and Washington. And heaven knew he had to be careful with them.

Budgetary meetings proceeding apace. Much back-and-forth. Resolution tomorrow. Can't tell which way the wind is blowing...

He received another call about the progress of the UAV, under the command of Barry Shales in the GCS, the trailer outside Metzger's window. The craft had launched not from Homestead, as in the Moreno operation, but from the NIOS facility near Fort Hood, Texas. It had crossed into Mexican airspace, with the Federales' blessing, *unlike* with Moreno in the Bahamas, and was heading through clear weather toward the target.

His phone rang again. Seeing the caller ID he stiffened and glanced at his open door. He could see Ruth's hands through the sliver of view into the ante office. She was typing. She had a small window too and sunlight glinted off her modest engagement and impressive wedding rings.

He rose and slid the door closed, then answered. "Yes."

"Found her," the man's voice reported.

No names or code names...

Her.

Nance Laurel.

"Where?"

"Detention center, interviewing a suspect. Not on this case, something else. I've confirmed it's her. She's there now, pretty much alone. Should I?"

No ending verb to that sentence.

Metzger debated, added pluses and negatives. "Yes."

He disconnected.

Maybe, just maybe this would all go away.

And he turned his attention back to Mexico, where an enemy of the country was about to die. Shreve Metzger felt swollen with joy.

CHAPTER 66

"W
HERE'S NANCE LAUREL?" Sachs asked
the rotund African American woman
on the fifth floor of the New York detention center.

The Department of Corrections officer stiffened
and glanced at Sachs's badge with disdain. Sachs
supposed her voice *was* a bit strident, the greeting
rude. It hadn't been intentional; Nance Laurel simply did this to her.

"Room Five. Box yo weapon." Back to a *People*
magazine. A scandal was breaking among some
quasi-celebrities. Or maybe they were honest-to-
God celebs. Sachs had never heard of them.

She wanted to apologize to the woman for her
bluntness but couldn't figure out how. Then her
anger at Laurel returned and she slipped the Glock
into a locker and slammed the door, drawing a crit-
icizing breath from the lockup mistress. With a
buzz the door opened and she stepped through into

the grim corridor. It was deserted at the moment. This was the area where high-level prisoners— accused of serious felonies—discussed their cases with their lawyers and cut deals with the prosecutors.

The perfume here was disinfectant and paint and pee.

Sachs strode past the first several rooms, all of which were empty. At Interview #5, she looked through smeared glass and saw a shackled man in an orange jumpsuit sitting across from Laurel at a table bolted to the floor. In the corner was another D of C guard, a huge man whose nearly white shaved head glistened with sweat. His arms were crossed and he looked at the prisoner like a biologist examining yet another specimen of toxic but dead bug.

The doors were self-locking; you needed a key to open them from either side so Sachs banged on the door with her palm.

This must have been strident too, since everybody in the room jumped and swiveled. The guard had no gun but his hand dipped toward the pepper spray on his belt. He saw Sachs, apparently recognized her as a cop and relaxed. The prisoner gazed narrowly at Sachs and the look morphed from startled to hungry.

Sex crime, Sachs deduced.

Laurel's lips tightened slightly.

She rose. The guard unlocked the door and let the ADA out, then he locked it again and returned to his watchful state.

The women walked to the end of the corridor, away from the door. Laurel asked, "Have you got something on Metzger or Shales?"

"Why ask me?" Sachs countered. "Since I'm not really in the equation."

"Detective," Laurel said evenly, "what are you talking about?"

She didn't start with the news Sellitto had just informed her of, the suspension. She went chronologically. "You took my name off all the memos, all the emails. You replaced my name with yours."

"I'm not—"

"Anything to help you get elected, right, Assemblywoman Laurel?"

Sachs withdrew the copy she'd made from Laurel's secret files and thrust the sheet forward. It was a petition to put Laurel on the ballot to run for the office of assemblywoman in her district. The assembly was the lower house of the legislature in New York.

The woman's eyes dipped. "Ah."

Busted.

But an instant later she was gazing coolly back into Sachs's face.

Sachs snapped, "You took me off the documents to take credit for yourself. Is that what this case is all about, Nance? 'Your' case, by the way. Not '*our* case' or '*the* case.' Because you wanted big media defendants to make a big splash. Forget Unsub Five Sixteen's torturing innocent women. You don't want him. You want the highest government official you can bag.

"And to make sure that happens you had me running around town digging up all the good things about Moreno I could find. Anything substantive on the case, you co-opted, put your name on it and took credit."

The assistant DA, though, didn't seem the least fazed. "Did you happen to look up my application to go on the ballot?"

"No, I didn't need to. I had this, the petition with the signatures." She lifted the photocopy.

Laurel said, "Those *support* the ballot application. You still need to submit one."

Sachs was pinged by that feeling she sometimes got, a nagging concern, that she might have missed something at a crime scene. Something fundamental. She was silent.

"I'm *not* running for office."

"The petition..."

"The petition was filed, yes. But I changed my mind. I never filed the application to run."

More silence.

Laurel continued, "Yes, I'd wanted to run in the Democratic primary but the party felt I was a little too opinionated for them. I filed a petition to run as an independent. But as time went by I decided not to."

Ping...

Now, curiously, Laurel's eyes were averted. She, not Sachs, seemed the more uneasy. And her shoulders, usually completely upright, sagged. "Last winter I went through a very hard breakup. He was... Well, I thought we'd get married. I understand that those things don't always work out. Fine. But it just wouldn't go away, the pain." Her jaw was set, her thin lips trembling. "It was exhausting."

Sachs recalled her observation from earlier, when Laurel had gotten the phone call in the town house.

She's vulnerable, even defenseless...

"I thought I needed to try something different. I'd run for office, devote myself to politics. I'd always wanted to. I have very strong ideas about this country and government's role. I was class president in high school and college. That was a happy time for me and I guess I wanted to re-create it. But I decided I was a better DA than I would be a politician. This is where I belong."

A nod toward the interview room. "The perp in there? History of sexual assault. He's in here because he groped three high school students. The original prosecutor didn't have time for the case and was going to charge him with forcible touching. Misdemeanor. He couldn't be bothered. I know about people like this suspect, though. Next it'll be raping an eleven-year-old and the time after that he'll kill the girl once he's finished. I took over and I'm going for first-degree sexual act."

"Class B felony," Sachs said.

"Exactly. And I'm going to get it. Running cases like this's my talent, not politics. Stopping rapists and people like Shreve Metzger, who're hiding behind the government and doing whatever the fuck they want, to hell with the Constitution."

An obscenity. She was angry. Sachs suspected this was the real Nance Laurel, rarely visible beneath the buttoned-up suits, the spray-painted makeup, the if-you-don't-mind verbiage.

"Amelia, yes, I took your name off the memos and emails. But that was purely for *your* sake and the sake of your career. It never occurred to me that you'd want credit. Who would?" She gave a shrug. "You know how dangerous this prosecution is? It's a career-ender, if the slightest thing goes wrong. Washington might cut Metzger and Barry Shales loose and let them swing in the wind. But they might also make this their Gettysburg, take a stand against me. And if they do and I lose on the immunity issue, then I'm history. The feds'll pressure Albany to get rid of me, and the attorney general will. In a heartbeat. That'll happen to everybody involved in the case, Amelia."

My *case*...

"I wanted to shelter you and the others as much as I could. Lon Sellitto's not mentioned in any of the memos. Ron Pulaski, the same."

Sachs pointed out, "But one of us'll have to testify in court as experts—to the evidence." Then she understood. "Lincoln."

Laurel said, "He's a consultant. He *can't* be fired."

"I didn't understand any of this," Sachs said. She apologized for her outburst.

"No, no. I should've shared the strategy with you."

Sachs felt her phone vibrate and she glanced at the screen. A text from Lon Sellitto.

A—

Just learned. The suspension came from downtown. Capt. Myers. Thinks you're not up front on health issues. He got your medical records from your private

doctor. I bought you a week to stay on
Moreno case. But need full medical by
May 28th.

So that was it. Laurel had had nothing to do with getting her sidelined. Thank God she hadn't blurted what she'd been thinking earlier. But then: How the hell had Myers gotten her private records? She never made insurance claims through the department. She herself paid for the appointments with her orthopedist—for this very reason: so no one in the Big Building would find out.

"Everything okay?" Laurel asked, nodding at the phone.

"Sure, fine."

At that moment a buzz sounded from the end of the corridor. The door swung open and a man stepped inside, in his thirties, athletic, wearing a dark suit. He blinked in surprise, seeing the women at the end of the hall. Then he started forward, eyes taking in the rest of the hallway and the empty rooms.

Sachs spent a lot of time here. She knew many of the officers and guards. The detectives, of course. But she'd never seen this man before.

Maybe he was the sex pervert's lawyer. But the expression on Laurel's face said that she didn't recognize him either.

Sachs turned back to Laurel. "I do have some news. Before I left we got a lead to the whistle-blower."

"Really?" Laurel lifted an eyebrow.

Sachs explained about the tourist's photos of the tea-drinker who liked Splenda and had a bum stomach. His inexpensive, odd-colored suit. His possible connection to the military.

Laurel asked a question but by then Sachs's instinct had kicked in and she wasn't paying attention.

The man who'd been buzzed in was ignoring the interrogation rooms. He seemed purposefully, but warily, making his way toward the women.

"You know that guy?" Sachs whispered.

"No." Laurel seemed troubled by the detective's concern.

A scenario played itself out in Sachs's imagination, honed by instinct: This wasn't Barry Shales—they'd seen his picture—but could it be Unsub 516? Sachs had been careful with the cell phones but who knew what NIOS was capable of. The man could have tracked her here—or followed Laurel. Maybe he'd just killed the guard out front and buzzed himself in.

Sachs looked for options. She had her switchblade but if this was the unsub he'd be armed. She recalled the terrible knife wounds on Lydia

Foster's body. And he could easily have a gun. She'd have to get him in close before she could use the blade.

But as he approached he slowed and stopped, well out of knife range. She couldn't possibly draw the knife and attack before he opened fire. His smooth face, and cautious eyes, looked from one to the other. "Nance Laurel?"

"That's me. Who are you?"

The man had no interest in answering her question.

With a fast, assessing look at Sachs, he reached into his jacket.

Sachs prepared to launch herself into him, muscles tensing, fingers folding into fists.

Can I get to him in time to grab his hand when it appears, pull my knife out, flick it open?

She crouched and felt a stab of pain. Then got ready to surge forward.

Wondering too if, as before in the alley, her knee would give out again and send her sprawling to the floor, in helpless agony, giving the man all the time he needed to shoot or slash them both to death.

CHAPTER 67

THE MOMENT BEFORE SHE LEAPT, though, Sachs saw that an envelope, not a Glock or a blade, was emerging.

The man noted Sachs's curious pose with a frown then stepped closer and handed the envelope to Laurel.

"Who *are* you?" Laurel persisted.

Still no response to her query. Instead he said, "I've been asked to give this to you. Before you go any further, you should know."

"'Go any further'?"

He didn't elaborate but simply nodded at the envelope.

The prosecutor extracted a single sheet of paper. She read methodically, word by word, to judge from her slow eye movements. Her teeth seemed to clench.

She looked up at the man. "You work for the State Department?"

Sachs's impression was that, though he said nothing, the answer was yes. What was this all about?

A glance at the document. "Is it authentic?" Laurel asked, eyeing the State Department minion closely.

The man answered, "I was asked to deliver a document to Assistant District Attorney Laurel. I have no interest in or knowledge of the contents."

Good use of prepositions, Sachs reflected cynically. Lincoln Rhyme would have approved.

"Shreve Metzger had you do this, didn't he?" Laurel said. "Did he fake it? Answer the question. Is it real?"

No knowledge of, *no interest* in...

The man said nothing more. He turned away, as if the women no longer existed, and left them. He paused at the end of the corridor and was buzzed out.

"What is it?" Sachs asked.

"Didn't some of the intelligence we got from Fred Dellray report that Moreno was seen in or around U.S. embassies or consulates just before he was shot?"

"Right," she confirmed. "Mexico City and Costa Rica. After he left New York on May second."

Sachs's concerns were further allayed when she glanced back and saw the round, dark face of the guard at the door peering in, unharmed and unconcerned about the visitor. She returned to her station and her celebrities.

With a sigh Laurel said to Sachs, "If anybody was thinking that Moreno was going to attack an embassy they were wrong." She nodded toward the letter in her hand. "He *was* looking for an embassy, but one where he could fast-track his renunciation of U.S. citizenship. He did it on May fourth in San José, Costa Rica. The renunciation was effective immediately but the paperwork didn't make it into the State Department database until this morning." She sighed. "When he died Robert Moreno was a Venezuelan citizen, not U.S."

Sachs said, "That's why he told the limo driver in New York he couldn't come back to America. Wasn't because of any terrorist plot but because he'd be non grata and wouldn't be allowed in on a foreign passport."

A phone appeared in Laurel's hand. She looked down at it. Her face had never seemed so wan. Why all the makeup? Sachs wondered yet again. Laurel hit a speed-dial button. Sachs couldn't see which priority but of course it didn't much matter. A 9 is as easy to hit as a 1.

Laurel stepped to the side and had a conversation. Finally she put the phone away and remained for a full minute with her back to Sachs. Her phone rang. Another conversation, briefer.

When she'd ended that call she returned to Sachs. "My boss just talked to the attorney general in Albany. However much Shreve Metzger and his shooter overstepped their authority, there's no interest in pursuing a charge against him when the victim's not a U.S. citizen. I've been ordered to drop the case." She looked at the floor. "So. That's it."

"I'm sorry," Sachs offered. She meant it.

CHAPTER 68

I N THE COOL, DIM SAFE HOUSE in Reynosa,
Mexico, al-Barani Rashid completed the list
of bomb components and pushed it toward
the Fat Man.

That was how he'd thought of the cartel's chief
IED expert when the man had first waddled inside
a half hour ago, dusty and with unwashed hair.
Rashid had given him the name contemptuously,
though accurately—he really was quite heavy.
Then he regretted the unkind thought about his
physique and personal grooming habits; the cartel's man proved to be not only very cooperative
but extremely talented. It turned out he was responsible for some of the more sophisticated
explosive devices deployed in the Western Hemisphere over the past few years.

The man pocketed the shopping list he and
Rashid had come up with and in Spanish said he'd
be back by evening with all the parts and tools.

Rashid was satisfied that this weapon would do the job very efficiently, killing DEA regional director Barbara Summers and anyone at the church picnic within a thirty-foot circle, possibly wider, depending on how many people were waiting in line at the ice cream station, where the device would be planted.

Rashid nodded toward the room where the Mexican hostages were being kept. He asked the Fat Man, "His company has come up with the ransom?"

"Yes, yes, it's confirmed. The family's been told. They can leave tonight, as soon as the last of the money is transferred." He regarded Rashid closely. "It's only business, you know."

"Only business," Rashid said, thinking, No, it's really not.

The Fat Man walked to the kitchen, where he opened the refrigerator and, surprising Rashid, took out not a beer but two cartons of Greek yogurt. Eyeing the Arab, he peeled back both tops and ate one then the other with a plastic spoon, standing in the middle of the room. Then he wiped his mouth with a paper towel, tossed the empties into the trash and sipped from a bottle of water.

"Señor, I will see you soon." They shook hands and he stepped outside, waddling on shoes with heels worn angular.

After the door closed Rashid stepped to the window and looked out. The man climbed into a Mercedes, which sagged port side. The diesel purred to life and the black vehicle bounded down the drive, leaving a dust cloud.

Rashid remained at the window for ten minutes. No sign of surveillance, no neighbors glancing uneasily as they passed by. No curtains dropping back over windows. Dogs stood about unsuspicious and no disembodied barks suggested intruders in unseen places nearby.

From the bedroom suite he heard voices. And then a soft noise he couldn't place at first, uneven, rising, falling in volume and tone. It grew regular and he knew the sound was a child's crying. The little girl. She'd been told she was going home but she wouldn't appreciate that. She wanted to be there *now*, with her stuffed toy, her bed, her blanket.

Rashid thought of his sister, who, with two schoolmates, was killed in Gaza. His sister...not much older than this girl. She hadn't had a chance to cry.

Rashid sipped more tea and examined the diagrams, listening to the mournful sound of the girl, which seemed all the more heart wrenching for being muted by the walls, as if she were a ghost trapped forever in this dusty tomb.

CHAPTER 69

THE PHRASE "KILL ROOM" suggested something out of a science-fiction movie or the operations center in the TV show *24*.

But the National Intelligence and Operations Service's Ground Control Station was a dingy space that looked like a storage area in a medium-sized insurance business or ad agency. It was housed in a fifteen-by-forty-foot trailer and was divided into two rooms. The office area was where you entered from the NIOS parking lot. Lining the wall were cardboard cartons of varying ages, cryptic writing on them, some empty, some containing documents or paper cups or cleaning supplies. A communications center, unoccupied at the moment. Computers. A battered gray desk and brown chair were in one corner and old, unclassified files littered it, as if a secretary had grown tired of finding the right drawer for them and had just given up. A broom, a box of empty Vitaminwater bottles, a broken lamp sat on the floor. Newspapers. Light bulbs. Computer circuit boards. Wires. A *Runner's World* magazine.

For decorations, maps of the Caribbean, Mexico, Canada and Central America, as well as of Iraq, and several OSHA posters warning about the dangers of lifting heavy loads with a bent back and not drinking enough water on hot days.

The place was dim; the overheads were rarely on. As if secrets kept better in hinted light.

You tended not to notice the shabbiness of the office, however, because of the other half of the trailer: The UAV operations station, visible through a thick glass wall.

Men and women like Barry Shales, the pilots and sensor operators, tended to refer to the operations station as a cockpit, which nobody seemed to mind, though the word "drone" was discouraged. Maybe "unmanned aerial vehicle" sounded more sophisticated or sanitized. This term was certainly better—from a public relations view—than what UAVs were called among those who flew them: FFAs, or Fuckers From Above.

Wearing dress slacks and a tie-less short-sleeved blue plaid shirt, slim Barry Shales was sitting in a comfortable overstuffed tan leather chair, which was more like Captain Kirk's in *Star Trek* than a seat in a jet's cockpit. Before him was a three-foot-by-eighteen-inch tabletop metal control board, bristling with dozens of knobs and buttons, switches and readouts, as well as two joysticks. He was not touching them at the moment. The autopilot was flying UAV N-397.

The computer's being in charge was standard procedure at this point in a Special Task Order operation, which involved just getting the bird in the general area of the target. Shales didn't mind being copilot for the moment. He was having trouble concentrating today. He kept thinking about his prior assignment.

The one NIOS had gotten so wrong.

He recalled the intel about the chemicals for Moreno's IED—the nitromethane, the diesel fuel, the fertilizer—that were going to reduce the oil company's headquarters in Miami to a smoking crater. The intel about Moreno's vicious attacks on America, calling for violent assaults on citizens. The intel about the activist's reconnaissance of the embassies in Mexico and Costa Rica, planning to blow them to kingdom come too.

They'd been so sure...

And they'd been so wrong.

Wrong about avoiding collateral damage too. Dc la Rua and the guard.

The primary point of the Long-Range Rifle program at NIOS was to minimize, ideally eliminate, collateral, which was impossible to do when you fired missiles.

And the first time it had been tried in an actual mission, what had happened?

Innocents dead.

Shales had hovered the UAV craft perfectly over the waters of Clifton Bay in the Bahamas, sighted through the leaves of a tree outside with a clear infrared and radar vision of Moreno, double-confirmed it was he, compensated for wind and elevation and fired shots only when the task was standing alone in front of the window.

Shales knew in his heart that only Moreno would die.

But there was that one little matter that had never occurred to him, to anyone: the window.

Who could have thought that the glass would be so lethal?

Wasn't his fault...But if he believed that, if he believed he was innocent of any wrongdoing, then why had he been in the john last night puking?

Just a bit of the flu, honey...No, no, I'm okay.

And why was he having more and more trouble sleeping?

Why was he more and more preoccupied, agitated, heartsick?

Curiously, while drone operators are perhaps the safest of all combat troops physically, they have among the highest rates of depression and post-traumatic stress in the military and national security services. Sitting at a video console in Colorado or New York City, killing someone six thousand miles away and then collecting the kids at gymnastics or football practice, having dinner and sitting down to watch *Dancing with the Stars* in your suburban den was disorienting beyond belief.

Especially when your fellow soldiers were hunkered down in the desert or getting blown to pieces by IEDs.

All right, Airman, he told himself, as he'd been doing lately, concentrate. You're on a mission. An STO mission.

He scanned the five computer monitors before him. The one in front, black background filled with green lines, boxes and type, was a composite of typical aircraft controls: artificial horizon, airspeed, ground speed, heading, nav-com, GPS, fuel and engine status. Above that was a traditional terrain map, like a Rand McNally. An information monitor—weather, messages and other communications reports—was to the upper left.

Below that was a screen that he could switch from regular to synthetic aperture radar. To the right, at eye level, was a high-definition video view of whatever the camera in the drone was seeing, presently daylight, though night vision was, of course, an option.

The view now was dun-colored desert passing underneath.

Though slowly. Drones are not F-16s.

A separate metal panel, below the monitors, was weapons control. It did not have any fancy screens but was black and functional and scuffed.

In many drone missions around the world, especially combat zones, the crew consists of a pilot and a sensor operator. But at NIOS the UAVs were flown solo. This was Metzger's idea; no one knew exactly what was behind it. Some thought it was to limit the number of people who knew about the STO program and therefore minimize the risk of security leaks.

Shales believed, however, the reason was this: The NIOS director appreciated the emotional toll that these missions took and wanted to subject as few people as possible to the stress of STO killings. Employees had been known to snap. And that could have far-ranging consequences, for them, their families...and for the program too, of course.

Barry Shales scanned the readouts. He hit a button and noted several other lights pop on.

He spoke into the stalk mike, "UAV Three Nine Seven to Texas Center."

Instantly: "Go ahead, Three Nine Seven."

"Weapons systems green."

"Roger."

He sat back and was stung by another thought. Metzger had told him that somebody was "looking into" the Moreno task. He'd asked for details but his boss had smiled dismissively and said it was just a technicality. Everything was being taken care of. He had people taking precautions. He didn't need to worry. Shales wasn't satisfied. Any smile from Metzger aroused suspicion.

Shales himself had felt a burst of the same searing rage that he, that *everybody*, knew was the NIOS director's nemesis. *Who* was looking into the matter? The police, Congress, the FBI?

And then, the kicker, Metzger told him that he too should take some precautions.

"Like what?"

"Just remember that it'd be better if there was less...well, 'evidence' is such a stark word. But you get my meaning."

And Shales decided at that moment not to wipe the phone issued to him as Don Bruns. The data—and the emails and texts to and from Metzger—wcre encrypted, but Shales decided it would be a prudent idea for the evidence *not* to disappear. He also printed out dozens of documents and smuggled them out of NIOS.

Insurance.

And the fact he'd felt compelled to take those precautions made him think: Hell, maybe it was time to quit this crazy business. Shales was thirty-nine, he had a degree from the Air Force Academy and a postgrad in engineering and poli-sci. He could go anywhere.

Or could he?

With a résumé like his?

Besides, the idea of no longer helping defend his country was almost unbearable.

But how do I help my country by accidentally killing a famous journalist and hardworking guard while I'm on a mission to assassinate an unpleasant but innocent loudmouth? What about—

"Texas Center to Three Nine Seven."

Like flipping a switch. Barry Shales was all go, "Three Nine Seven."

"You are ten minutes to target."

The operation command center near Fort Hood knew exactly where his drone was.

"Copy."

"Visual conditions?"

A glance to the monitor at the right. "A little haze but pretty good."

"Be advised, Three Nine Seven, eyes on the ground report that the task is alone in target structure. Individual who arrived an hour ago has left."

The task...

"Roger, Texas Center. I'm taking the aircraft," Shales said, disconnecting the autopilot. "Approaching Lucio Blanco International airspace."

Reynosa's airport.

"Friendly nation ATC has been advised of your flight route."

"Roger. Descending to two thousand feet. EAD on."

The engine audio deflectors would reduce the decibel level of the drone's engine to about one-tenth of the regular sound. These could only be used for a short period of time, though, because they tended to make the engines overheat and there was a power loss, which could be dangerous in rough weather. Now, though, the sky was clear and virtually no wind would trouble the craft.

Five minutes later he guided 397 to about fifteen hundred feet above and a half mile from the safe house where al-Barani Rashid was presently planning or perhaps even constructing his bomb.

"In hover mode."

Teasing the joystick.

Shales painted the target safe house with a laser. "Confirm coordinates."

The longitude and latitude of what he'd reported would be matched to those of the stats known to be the target in NIOS's mainframe—just to make sure.

"Texas Center to Three Nine Seven, we have geo match. Target is confirmed. What is your PIN?"

Shales recited the ten digits of his personal identification number, verifying he was who he was supposed to be and that he was authorized to fire this missile at this target.

"Positive ID, Three Nine Seven. Payload launch is authorized."

"Copy. Three Nine Seven."

He slipped up the cover over the arming toggle for the Hellfire missile and pressed the button.

Shales stared at the image of the safe house. Still, he didn't push the launch button just yet.

His eyes took in the windows, the doors, the chimney, the streaks of dust on the sidewalk, a cactus. Looking for a sign. Looking for some indication that he should not launch the deadly package.

"Three Nine Seven, did you copy? Payload launch is authorized."

"Confirmed, Texas Center. Three Nine Seven."

He inhaled deeply.

Thought: Moreno...

And lifted the second cover, over the launch button itself, and pressed down.

There was no sound, only a faint rocking of the screen as the 110-pound missile dropped from the

UAV. A green light confirmed release. Another, ignition.

"Payload away, Texas Center. Three Nine Seven."

"Roger." In the most bland of tones.

There was nothing more for Shales to do now, except watch the safe house disappear in a flash of flame and wash of smoke. He turned to the video.

And he saw the back door to the house open and two people exit into the courtyard between the house and garage. Rashid was one of them. A teenage boy was the other. They spoke briefly and began to kick around a soccer ball.

CHAPTER 70

B ARRY SHALES FELT THE SHOCK like a physical blow.

He cracked a thumbnail jamming the digit into the red button in the middle of the weapons control panel labeled simply *STOP*.

This sent a signal disarming the warhead in the Hellfire. But the missile was still a deadly mass of metal and propellant, streaking at nine hundred miles an hour toward a building with less-than-perfect accuracy. It could easily kill everyone inside even if the explosives didn't detonate.

Shales pressed the autopilot button for the drone itself and overrode the automatic guidance for the missile, taking control of the Hellfire with a small trackball on the weapons panel.

A camera rested in the nose of the missile, not far from the high-explosive payload, but at this speed and with the marginal resolution of the lens you couldn't fly the projectile very accurately. Shales had to rely on the radar in the drone and a feed from Mexican air traffic control to steer the deadly cylinder away from the safe house.

He glanced at the monitor to the right—the drone's camera, which was still pointed toward the soccer players. He noted Rashid pause and look up to the sky. Squint. He would have heard something, seen a glint perhaps.

The teenage boy, about to kick the dusty ball, paused too, regarding the Arab cautiously.

Behind them, Barry Shales could see, a small girl appeared and stood in the doorway of the safe house. She was smiling.

"Texas Center to Three Nine Seven, we read payload path deviation. Please advise."

Shales ignored the transmission and concentrated on trying to steer the Hellfire, twice as fast as any jetliner, away from populated areas in the target zone. It wasn't easy. This part of Reynosa wasn't as dense as to the east but there were still plenty of homes and businesses and traffic. The radar gave a clear image of airliners nearby, which Shales could steer clear of, but the system didn't reveal what was on the ground—and that was where he needed to crash the missile. And pretty damn fast; soon the propellant would be expended and he'd lose control.

"Three Nine Seven? Do you copy?"

Then on the small screen revealing what the nose camera in the missile was viewing, the image faded as it headed into overcast. He was flying blind.

"Jesus Lord..."

Words that Barry Shales, who attended church every Sunday with his wife and young sons, did not use lightly.

"Three Nine Seven, this is Texas Center. Please advise."

He thought angrily: I'm advising you to go fuck yourself.

The haze broke for a moment and he saw that the missile was heading right for a residential development.

No, no...

A tweak of the trackball changing the course farther west.

The haze closed in again.

A glance at the radar. The terrain was mapped out but it wasn't a satellite image, merely a traditional map, and gave no clue as to what was on the ground ahead of the Hellfire.

Only seconds remained until the propellant was gone and the deadly tube would come to earth. But where? In a child's bedroom, in a hospital, in a packed office building?

Then an idea occurred to Shales. Releasing the

missile trackball for a moment, he typed fast on the computer keyboard in front of him.

In the information monitor in the upper left-hand corner, Firefox popped up. This was completely against procedure. You couldn't go online with a commercial browser in a GCS while a drone was operational. But Shales could think of no other option. In an instant he'd called up Google Maps and clicked on satellite view. A photo image of the ground around Reynosa popped up, houses, foliage, roads, stores.

Looking back and forth from the radar panel to the map, lining up roads and other landmarks, he estimated the Hellfire's location.

Christ! The missile was right over another residential subdivision northwest of Reynosa. But according to Google, to the west was a large empty area of beige-and-yellow desert.

"UAV Three—"

Shales ripped off his headset and flung it away.

Right hand back to the trackball.

Gently, gently—man, it was easy to oversteer.

Looking from radar to Google, he saw the Hellfire's path veering away from the houses. Soon the direction was due west, toward what the satellite map promised was nothingness. The nose camera in the missile still showed only haze.

Then the altitude and speed began to drop fast.

The propellant was gone. There was nothing more Shales could do; he'd lost control of the missile. He sat back, wiped his hands on his slacks. Staring at the monitor of the view from the Hellfire's nose camera. He could see only overcast.

The altitude indicator showed: 1500 feet.

670.

590...

What would he see as the Hellfire crashed to earth? Empty desert? Or a school bus on a field trip? Farmworkers staring in horror at what was falling toward them?

Then the haze broke and Shales had a clear view of the missile's destination directly ahead.

However loud and spectacular the impact eighteen hundred miles away was, it registered in the NIOS Kill Room as a simple, silent change of image: from a barren plain of dirt and brush to a screen filled with flickering black and white, like a TV when a storm takes out the cable.

Shales spun back to the drone controls, disengaged the autopilot. He looked at the camera's monitor, still focused on the courtyard of the safe house. The children were still there, the boy, presumably the brother, gently kicking the ball to the girl, who chased after it like a driven terrier. A woman stood in the doorway watching them both, unsmiling.

Jesus Lord, he repeated, not wondering or caring who they were or how they came to be in a safe house that the "impeccable" intelligence had assured was occupied only by a terrorist.

He zoomed out with the camera.

The garage door was open. Rashid was gone. Of course, he would be. The wary eyes earlier had told Shales that the terrorist suspected what was happening.

He scooped up the headsets and placed them on his head. Replugged the jack.

"—opy, Three Nine Seven?"

"Three Nine Seven to Texas Center," he snapped. "Mission aborted at operator's discretion. Returning to base."

CHAPTER 71

D O YOU WANT SOME SCOTCH?" Rhyme asked, from the center of his parlor, near a comparison microscope. "I think you need some."

Looking up from her desk in the corner of the room, where she was packing up files, Nance Laurel swiveled toward Rhyme with furrowed brow, wrinkling a crease into her makeup. He suspected a lecture on the unprofessionalism of drinking on the job would be forthcoming.

Laurel asked, "What distillery?"

Rhyme replied, "Glenmorangie. Twelve or eighteen years."

"Anything peatier?" she wondered aloud, to his additional surprise. Sachs's too, and amusement, to tell from the faint smile on his partner's face.

"No. Try it, you'll like it."

"Okay. The eighteen. Naturally. Drop of water."

Rhyme gripped the bottle and clumsily poured.

She did the water herself. His bionic arm lacked sufficient subtlety. He asked, "Sachs?"

"No, thanks. I'll get something else." She was organizing evidence bags and boxes, which—even in cases that were falling apart—had to be meticulously cataloged and stored.

"Thom and Mel?"

The tech said he was fine with coffee. Thom too declined. He'd grown fond of bourbon Manhattans lately but had explained to Rhyme that drinks that involved a recipe should only be enjoyed on weekends, when no business was likely to intrude.

Thom pulled a bottle of French Chardonnay from the refrigerator in which blood and tissue samples were often stored. He lifted it toward Sachs. She said, "You read my mind."

He opened and poured.

Rhyme sipped some of the fragrant whiskey. "Good, no?"

"It is," Laurel agreed.

Rhyme reread the letter about Moreno's renunciation of his U.S. citizenship. He was as angry as Laurel that this technicality had derailed the case.

"He hated the country that much," Pulaski asked, "that he'd give up his citizenship?"

"Apparently so," Laurel said.

"Come on, boys and girls," Rhyme chided, then sipped some more whiskey. "They won round one.

Or the first inning. Whatever clichéd figure of speech and mixed metaphor you like. But we still have a perp, you know. Unsub Five Sixteen, responsible for an IED in a coffee shop and the Lydia Foster homicide. Those are Major Cases. Lon Sellitto'll assign us to work them."

"It won't be my case, though," Nance Laurel said. "I've been told to get back to my regular caseload."

"This's bullshit," Ron Pulaski spat out, surprising Rhyme with his vehemence. "Moreno's the same person he was when he got shot—an innocent victim. So what if he wasn't a citizen?"

"Bullshit it is, Ron," Laurel said, her voice more resigned than angry. "That's exactly right."

She finished her whiskey and walked over to Rhyme. She shook his hand. "It's been a privilege working with you."

"I'm sure we will again."

A faint smile. But something about the exquisite sadness in the expression told him that she believed her life as a prosecutor was over.

Sachs said to her, "Hey, you want to have dinner sometime? We can dish on the government." She added in a whisper that Rhyme could hear, "And dish on men too?"

"I'd like that. Yes."

They exchanged phone numbers, Sachs having

to check to find out what her new one was. She'd bought a half dozen prepaids in the past few days.

Then the ADA carefully assembled her files, using paper clips and Post-it Notes to mark relevant categories. "I'll have copies sent to you for the unsub case."

The short woman hefted the briefcase in one hand, the litigation bag in the other and with one last look around the room—and no other words—walked out, her solid heels thudding on the wood, then the marble of the hallway. And she was gone.

CHAPTER 72

JACOB SWANN DECIDED, WITH SOME REGRET, that he couldn't rape Nance Laurel before he killed her.

Well, he *could*. And part of him wanted to. But it wouldn't be wise—that was what he meant. A sexual assault left far too much evidence. Minimizing the clues in any murder was hard enough—trying to make sure sweat, tears, saliva, hairs and those hundred thousand skin cells we slough off daily weren't available to be picked up by some diligent crime scene tech.

Not to mention fingerprints *inside* the latex gloves or on skin.

He'd need another option.

Swann was presently in a restaurant on Henry Street across from the prosecutor's apartment in Brooklyn, a four-floor walk-up. He was nursing a very bittersweet Cuban coffee.

Scanning Laurel's abode. Not a doorman build-ing, he noticed. Good.

Swann had decided that *now* he could use a cover crime for the murder: In addition to prosecuting patriotic Americans for taking out vile traitors, Laurel had sent plenty of rapists to jail. He'd looked up her conviction record—extremely im-pressive—and learned that among those she'd put away were dozens of serial rapists and molesters. One of these suspects could easily decide to get his revenge following his release. Or a relative of a prisoner might do just that.

Her own past would come back to get her.

Yes, he'd gotten word from headquarters that the investigation into Moreno's death was over. But that didn't mean it might not surface again. Laurel was the sort who might leave govern-ment service and start writing letters or articles in the papers or online about what had hap-pened, about NIOS, about the STO assassination program.

Better if she just went away. And anyway, Swann had set off a bomb in Little Italy and stabbed an interpreter and limo driver to death. If nothing else, Laurel might be called on to help in the investigation of those crimes. He needed her dead and all her files destroyed.

He fantasized. Not about the sex but about faking

the attack, which he was looking at like a recipe. Planning, preparation, execution. He'd break into her apartment, stun her with a blow to the head (not the throat; there couldn't be a connection to Ms. Lydia Foster, of course), rip her clothes off, make sure her breasts and groin displayed severe striking hematoma (no biting, though he was tempted; that bothersome DNA). Then he'd beat her to death and penetrate her with a foreign object.

He didn't have time to go to an adult bookstore with video booths or a porn theater and scoop up a bit of somebody's DNA to swab on her. But he had stolen some stained and torn underwear, teenager's size, from the trash behind a tenement not far away. Fibers from this garment he'd work under her fingernails and hope the teen had been masturbating at some point in the past few days. Likely.

This would be enough evidence.

He dipped his tongue into the coffee. Enjoyed the intense sensation throughout his mouth; it's a myth that different tastes are experienced in different parts of the tongue: salt, sour, sweet, bitter. Another sip. Swann cooked with coffee sometimes—he'd made a Mexican *mole*-type sauce for pork with 80 percent cacao and espresso. He'd been tempted to submit it for a contest then de-

cided it wasn't a good idea for him to be too
public.

He was running through the plan for Nance Laurel again when he spotted her.

Across the street the ADA had appeared from
around the corner. She was in a navy-blue suit
and white blouse. In her small pudgy hands were
an old-fashioned attaché case, brown and battered,
and a large litigation bag. He wondered if either
was a present from her father or mother, both of
whom were attorneys too, Swann had learned.
They were in the low-rent district of the profession. Her mother, public defender. Her father,
poverty law.

Doin' good deeds, helping society, Swann reflected. Just like their stocky little girl.

Laurel was walking with eyes cast downward
and laboring under the weight of the litigation bag.
Though her face was a cryptic mask, she now gave
off a slight hint of depression, the way Italian parsley in soup suggests but doesn't state. Unlike bold
cilantro.

The source of the somber mood was no doubt the
foundering Moreno case. Swann nearly felt bad for
her. The prosecution would have been the jewel in
her crown but now she was back to a life of sending José, Shariq, Billy and Roy into the system for
crack and rapes and guns.

Wasn't me. No way. I don't know, man, I don't know where it came from, really...

Except, of course, she wouldn't be handling any such cases.

Wouldn't be doing anything at all after tonight. Would be cold and still as a slab of loin.

Nance Laurel found her keys and unlocked the front door, stepped inside.

Swann would give it ten, fifteen minutes. Time for her to let her guard down.

He lifted the small, thick cup to his nose, inhaled and slipped his tongue into the warm liquid once more.

CHAPTER 73

W HAT DO WE KNOW ABOUT the last of our ten little Indians?" Lincoln Rhyme asked absently.

The setback about Moreno's citizenship had defeated Nance Laurel but it had only stoked his hunt lust. "I don't care what Albany wants, Sachs, I want our unsub. Five Sixteen's too dangerous to stay free. What do we know?" He looked over the evidence whiteboards. "All right, we know Five Sixteen was in the Bahamas around the time of the shooting. We know that he killed the student-prostitute Annette Bodel. We know that he set the bomb to eliminate leads to the whistleblower. We know he killed Lydia Foster. We know he was following our Sachs around town. What can we make of that? . . . Sachs!"

"What?"

"The other driver, the one that Moreno usually used? Did you ever get in touch with him?"

"No. Never called back."

This happened frequently when the police phoned, asking for a return call.

Usually this was out of reluctance to get involved.

Sometimes there were other reasons.

She tried the driver once more and shook her head. She placed another call—to Elite Limos, Rhyme deduced. She asked if they had heard from their employee. A brief conversation and she hung up.

"Never called in after he went to see a sick relative."

"Don't trust it. We may have a *third* victim of our unsub. Find out where he lives, Pulaski. Get a team from the closest precinct to his house and see what's there."

The young officer pulled out his mobile and called Dispatch.

Rhyme wheeled back and forth in front of the charts. He didn't believe he'd ever had a case like this, where the evidence was so fragmentary and sparse.

Bits, scraps, observations, 180-degree changes in direction.

Nothing else...

Hell.

Rhyme steered toward the shelf with the whiskey

bottles. He lifted the Glenmorangie and awkwardly poured another hit, then seated the cap on his tumbler and sipped.

"What're you doing?" Thom asked from the doorway.

"What am I doing, what am I doing? Now, that's an odd question. Usually the interrogatory 'what' introduces a sentence in which the inquirer is unable to make any deductions about a situation." A substantial sip. "I think you've wasted a perfectly good sentence, Thom. It's pretty clear what I'm doing."

"You've already had too much."

"That's a declarative sentence and it makes much more sense. It's valid. I disagree with it but it's logically valid."

"Lincoln!" Thom strode forward.

Rhyme glared. "Don't even think—"

"Wait," Sachs said.

Rhyme assumed she was taking Thom's side in the alcohol dispute but when he wheeled around he found her eyes were not on him or the aide but on the whiteboards. She walked forward and Rhyme noticed that she wasn't wincing or limping. She was spry and balanced. Her eyes narrowed. This was her predatory gaze. It made the tall woman frightening and, to Rhyme, appealing.

He set the whiskey down. His eyes rose to the

boards and scanned like radar. Were there some facts he'd missed? Had she made a deduction that had eluded him? "Do you see something about Five Sixteen?"

"No, Rhyme," she whispered. "It's something else. Something else entirely."

CHAPTER 74

NANCYANN OLIVIA LAUREL was sitting on a couch in her Brooklyn Heights apartment, a brown JCPenney slipcover over blue upholstery that had been worn smooth by her family and their friends years and years ago.

Hand-me-downs. A lot of those here. Laurel was tapped by a memory: Her father surreptitiously fishing in the sofa's crevices for coins that had fallen from the pockets of visitors. She'd been eight or so and he'd made a joke of it, a game, when she'd walked into the room unexpectedly.

Except it wasn't a game, and she knew it. Even children can be ashamed of their parents.

Still tasting the smoky scotch, she looked around this home. Her home. Hers alone. In a reflective mood. Despite, or maybe because of, the thread-bare, recycled accoutrements, the sense of the place was comfort, even on a pitiful day like this one. She'd worked hard to make it that way. The walls, coated with dozens of layers of paint, going back to Teddy Roosevelt's era, were a cream shade. For decorations: a silk flower arrangement from a Chelsea crafts fair, an autumn wreath from the Union Square farmers' market, art too. She had paintings and sketches, some original and some prints, all of scenes that had resonated with her personally, horses, farms, rocky streams, still lifes. No idea why they appealed. But she'd known instantly that they did and she'd bought them if there was any way she could spare the cash. Some alpaca yarn hangings, colorful rectangles. Laurel had taken up knitting a few years ago but couldn't find the time or the inclination to complete the scarves for friends' nieces.

What now? she thought.

What now...

The teakettle's whistle was blowing. Had been blowing. Shrill. She was suddenly aware of it. She went into the small space and put a rose hip bag in the mug—navy blue on the outside, white in, matching her outfit, she realized. She should change.

Later.

Laurel stared at the kettle for a full minute. Shut off the heat but did not pour the boiling liquid. She returned to the couch.

What now?

This was the worst of all possible outcomes. If she'd won the convictions of Metzger and Barry Shales, well, that would have made her world. It would have made her *life*. There was no way to describe the importance that this case had taken on for her. She remembered in law school being mesmerized by the stories of the greats of the legal system in America—the lawyers, prosecutors and judges. Clarence Darrow, William O. Douglas, Felix Frankfurter, Benjamin Cardozo, Earl Warren...so many, many others. Louis D. Brandeis she thought of often.

The federal Constitution is perhaps the greatest of human experiments...

There was nothing as marvelous as the machine of justice and she wanted so badly to be a part of it, to make her own imprint on American law.

Her proudest day was law school graduation. She remembered looking out over the audience. Her father had been alone. This was because her mother was arguing a case before the Court of Appeals in Albany—the highest state appellate court—trying to get a homeless man's murder conviction reversed.

Laurel couldn't describe how honored she was that the woman *wasn't* present that day.

The Moreno case was to be her way of validating sacrifices like those. Okay, and of making a name for herself too. Amelia had nailed it right when she'd sussed out the political career track. The ambition remained even if her name ultimately decorated no ballot.

Yet even a loss at the Metzger trial would have succeeded in a way. NIOS's Kill Room would have been exposed. That might have been enough to sink the assassination program forever. The hungry media and more-starved congressmen would have been all over NIOS like flies.

She'd have been sacrificed—her career would have ended—but at least she would have made sure the truth of Metzger's crimes came out.

But now, this? Her boss pulling the case? No, there was nothing good to come of that.

She supposed the whistleblower had vanished and there would be no more identification of other victims in the queue. Sorry, Mr. Rashid.

What was in her future? Laurel laughed at the question. Returned to the kitchen and this time actually brewed a cup of tea. Adding two sugars on the grounds that rose hips were tart. The future, right: an unemployment period she'd spend with *Seinfeld* reruns and dining on one then what the hell a second Lean Cuisine. One glass of Kendall-Jackson too many. Computer chess. Then interviews. Then a job at a big Wall Street firm.

Her heart sank.

She now thought of David, as she often did. Always did. "The thing is, look, you're pushing me for an answer, Nance. Okay, I'll tell you. It's you're kind of a schoolmarm. You know what I mean? I can't live up to that. You want everything perfect, everything right. You correct, you find fault. There, sorry. I didn't want to say it. You made me."

Forget him.

You've got your career.

Except you don't.

On her bookshelf—half law books, half novels, one cookbook—was a picture of her and David. Both smiling.

Below that was a boxed chess set, wood, not plastic.

Throw it out, she told herself.

I will.

Not yet.

All right. Enough of that. Self-pity was what she saw in the most depraved of sex perverts and murderers and she wasn't going to allow it to seep into her soul. You've still got your caseload. Get to work. She—

A noise in the hallway.

A tap, a click, a faint thud.

Then nothing.

Mrs. Parsons dropping her shopping bag. Mr. Lefkowitz juggling toy poodle and cane.

She stared at the TV, then at the microwave, then at the bedroom.

Get out the fucking brief in *State v. Gonzalez* and start editing.

Laurel jumped when the doorbell rang.

She walked to the door. "Who is it?"

"Detective Flaherty, NYPD."

Never heard of him but Manhattan boasted a cop population in the thousands. Laurel peered through the peephole. A white guy, thirties, slim, a suit. He was holding his ID open, though all she could see was a glint of badge.

"How'd you get inside?" she called.

"Somebody was leaving. I rang your buzzer but nobody answered. I was going to leave a note but thought I'd try anyway."

So the bell was out again.

"Okay, just a minute." She opened the chain and the dead-bolt latch, pulling open the door.

And only then did Nance Laurel think, as the man stepped forward, that she probably should have had him slip his ID under the door so she could read it.

But why worry? The case is over with. I'm no threat to anyone.

CHAPTER 75

BARRY SHALES WASN'T A LARGE MAN.
"Compact" was how he was often described.

And his job was sedentary, sitting before flat-screen panels, hands on the joysticks of UAVs, the computer keyboard before him.

But he lifted free weights—because he enjoyed working out.

He jogged—because he enjoyed jogging.

And the former air force captain held the opinion, wholly unsupported, that the more you liked working out the better your muscles responded.

So when he pushed past an alarmed Ruth, the guard dog of a personal assistant, into Shreve Metzger's office and drew back an arm and slugged his boss, the skinny man stumbled and went down hard.

The head of NIOS dropped to one knee, arms

flailing. Files slid off the desk from trying to catch himself.

Shales strode forward, arm drawn back again, but hesitated. The one blow was enough to deflate the anger that had been growing since he'd seen the impromptu soccer match between the task he'd been ordered to blast into molecules and a teenage boy in the courtyard of the safe house in a dingy Mexican suburb.

He lowered his fist, stepped back. But he felt no inclination to help Metzger up and he crossed his arms and watched coldly as the shaken man pressed a hand to his cheek and clumsily rose, collecting the files that had fallen. Shales noted that several manila binders sported a classified stamp that he was not familiar with despite his stratospheric security clearance.

He noted too that Metzger's first concern at the moment wasn't the injury but securing the secret files.

"Barry...Barry." He looked behind Shales and shook his head. Ruth, shocked, hovered, not unlike a drone herself. Metzger smiled at her and pointed to the door. She hesitated then stepped out, closing it.

The man's smile vanished.

Shales walked to the window, breathing deeply. He glanced down to see the fake Maersk container in NIOS's parking lot. A look at the Ground Control Station from which he'd very nearly killed at least three innocent civilians minutes ago re-ignited his anger.

He turned back to Metzger. But the director didn't cower or beg. He gave no response, physical or verbal, except to touch his cheek again and peruse the smear of red on his finger and thumb.

"Did you know?" Shales asked.

"About the collateral in Reynosa? No." As NIOS head, he would have followed the attack in real time. "Of course not."

"I'd launched, Shreve. The Hellfire was in the air! What do you think about that? We were ten seconds away from murdering a young boy and girl and a woman who was probably their mother. And who the hell else was inside, as well?"

"You saw the documentation with the STO. The surveillance program we put in place for Rashid was totally robust. We had DEA and Mexican federal surveillance reports—twenty-four/seven. Nobody had gone inside or come out for a week. Who holes up for seven days, Barry? You ever hear of that? I never have." Metzger sat down. "Hell, Barry, we're not God. We do what we can. My ass was on the line too, you know. If anybody else'd died, it would have been the end of my career. Probably NIOS too."

The airman had shallow jowls around his taut lips and his cold smile deepened them now. "You're mad, aren't you, Shreve?"

He'd meant the word in its sense of "angry" but the way Metzger reacted, eyes narrowing, apparently the NIOS head took it to mean psychotic.

"Mad?"

"That I didn't follow Rashid's car. That I stayed with the missile, guided it down."

A pause. "That scenario wasn't authorized, targeting Rashid's vehicle."

"Fuck authorized. You're thinking I should've let the Hellfire land where it would, while I locked on and fired my second bird at the car."

His eyes revealed that, yes, that's exactly what Metzger had wanted.

"Barry, this is a messy business we're in. There's collateral, there's friendly fire, there're suicides and just plain fucking mistakes. People die because we program in One Hundred West Main Street and the task is actually at One Hundred East."

"Interesting choice of word for a human being, isn't it? 'Task.'"

"Oh, come on. It's easy to make fun of government-speak. But it's the government that keeps us safe from people like Rashid."

"That'll be a nice line for the Congressional

hearings, Shreve." Shales then raged, "You fucked with the evidence for the Moreno STO to take out an asshole you didn't like. Who wasn't patriotic enough for you."

"That's not how it was!" Metzger nearly screamed, spittle flew.

Startled by the uncontrolled outburst, Shales stared at his boss for a moment. Then dug into his pocket and tossed his lanyard and ID card onto the desk. "Kids, Shreve. I nearly blew up two children today. I've had it. I'm quitting."

"No." Metzger leaned forward. "You can't quit."

"Why not?"

Shales was expecting his boss to raise issues of contracts, security.

But the man said, "Because you're the best, Barry. Nobody can handle a bird like you. Nobody can shoot like you. I knew you were the man for the STO program when I conceived it, Barry."

Shales recalled a grinning car salesman who'd used his first name repeatedly because, apparently, he'd been taught at grinning-car-salesman school that this wore down the potential buyer, made him less resistant.

Shales had left the lot without the car he'd very much wanted.

He now shouted, "The project was all about eliminating collateral damage!"

"We didn't run a scenario of firing through picture windows! We should have. It didn't occur to anyone. Did it occur to *you*? We got it wrong. What more do you want me to say? I apologize."

"To me? Maybe you should apologize to Robert Moreno's wife and children or the family of de la Rua, the reporter, or his bodyguard. They need an apology more than I do, don't you think, Shreve?"

Metzger pushed the ID back toward Shales. "This's been tough for you. Take some time off."

Leaving the badge untouched, Shales turned and opened the door, walking out of the office. "I'm sorry if I upset you, Ruth."

She only stared.

In five minutes he was outside the front gate of NIOS and walking through the alley to the main north–south street nearby.

Then he was on the sidewalk, feeling suddenly light of step and aglow with ambiguous satisfaction.

He'd call the sitter, take Margaret to dinner that night. He'd break the news to her that he was now unemployed. He could—

A dark sedan squealed to a stop beside him. Two men flung doors open and were outside in an instant, moving toward him.

For a moment Shales wondered if Shreve Metzger had called in specialists—had arranged for an

STO with the name Barry Shales as the task, to eliminate him as a threat to his precious assassination program.

But the men moving toward him didn't pull out suppressed Berettas or SIGs. The palms of their hands glinted with metal, yes—but they were gold. New York City Police Department shields.

"Barry Shales?" the older of the two asked.

"I . . . yes, I'm Shales."

"I'm Detective Brickard. This is Detective Samuels." The badges and IDs disappeared. "You're under arrest, sir."

Shales gave a brief, surprised laugh. A mistake. Word hadn't filtered down to them that the investigation was over.

"No, there's some mistake."

"Please turn around and put your hands behind your back."

"But what's the charge?"

"Murder."

"No, no—the Moreno case . . . it's been dropped."

The detectives looked at each other. Brickard said, "I don't know anything about any Moreno, sir. Please. Your hands. Now."

CHAPTER 76

I T MAY BE A TOUGH SELL TO THE JURY," Lincoln Rhyme said, speaking of the theory behind a new case against Metzger and Shales.

Amelia Sachs's theory, not his. And one he was quite enamored of—and proud of her for formulating. Rhyme secretly loved it when people—*some people*—outthought him.

Sachs glanced at her humming phone. "A text."

"Nance?"

"No." She looked from the querying eyes of Mel Cooper to Ron Pulaski to, finally, Rhyme. "Barry Shales's in custody. No resistance."

So, they were proceeding now according to Sachs's theory, which she'd come up with from a simple entry in the evidence charts.

— *Victim 2: Eduardo de la Rua.*
    — *COD: Loss of blood. Lacerations from*

> *flying glass from gunshot, measuring*
> *3–4mm wide, 2–3cm long.*
> — *Supplemental information: Journalist,*
> *interviewing Moreno. Born Puerto Rico,*
> *living in Argentina.*
> — *Camera, tape recorder, gold pen, note-*
> *books missing.*
> — *Shoes contained fibers associated with*
> *carpet in hotel corridor, dirt from hotel*
> *entryway.*
> — *Clothing contained traces of breakfast:*
> *allspice and pepper sauce.*

Her thinking was all the more brilliant because of its simplicity: People born in Puerto Rico are U.S. citizens.

Therefore Barry Shales *had* killed an American in the attack on May 9 in the South Cove Inn.

Nance's boss, the DA, had decided not to pursue the case only because Moreno wasn't a citizen. But de la Rua was. Even an unintended death under some circumstances can subject the killer to murder charges.

Sachs continued, "But at the very least, I'd think we could get manslaughter. Shales inadvertently killed de la Rua as part of the intentional act of killing Moreno. He should have known that someone else in the room could have been fatally wounded when he fired the shot."

A woman's voice filled the room. "Good analysis, Amelia. Have you ever thought of going to law school?"

Rhyme turned to see Nance Laurel striding into the parlor, lugging her briefcase and litigation bag once again. Behind her was the detective they'd asked to collect her, a friend of Sachs's. Bill Flaherty. Rhyme had thought it safer for her to have an escort. He was still uneasy that Unsub 516 was at large, especially now that there was a chance of reviving the Moreno case.

Laurel thanked the detective, who nodded and—with a smile toward Sachs and Rhyme—left the town house.

Rhyme asked the ADA, "So? Our case? What do you think? Legally?"

"Well," she said, sitting down at her desk and extracting her files once more, organizing them, "we probably can get Barry Shales on murder two. The penal code provision covers us there." She paraphrased, "A person is guilty of murder in the second degree when he intends to cause the death of someone and he causes the death of a third person. But Amelia's right, manslaughter's definitely a possibility. We'll make it a lesser-included offense, though I'm confident I can make murder stick."

"Thanks for coming back," Sachs said.

"No, thanks to you all for saving our case." She was looking around the room.

Our *case*...

"Amelia came up with the idea," Lon Sellitto said.

Rhyme added, "*I* missed the option entirely."

Sellitto added that he'd been in touch with Captain Myers and the man had—with some reluctance—agreed they should proceed with the new charges. The attorney general had given his tentative approval too.

"Now we have to consider how to proceed," Laurel said, surprising Rhyme by not only unbuttoning but slipping off her jacket. She could smile, she could sip whiskey, she could relax. "First, I'd like some background. Who was he, this reporter?"

Ron Pulaski had been researching. He said, "Eduardo de la Rua, fifty-six. Married. Freelance journalist and blogger. Born in Puerto Rico, U.S. passport. But he's been living in Buenos Aires for the past ten years. Last year he won the Premio a la Excelencia en el Periodismo. That's 'Award for Excellence in Journalism.'"

"You speak Spanish too, rookie?" Rhyme interrupted. "You never fail to astound. Good accent too."

"*Nada.*"

"Ha," Sellitto offered.

The young officer: "Lately de la Rua's been writing for *Diario Seminal Negocio de Argentina*."

"*The Weekly Journal of Argentina*," Rhyme tried.

"Almost. *Weekly* Business *Journal*."

"Of course."

"He was doing a series on American businesses and banks starting up in Latin America. He'd been after Moreno for months to do an interview about that—the alternative view, why U.S. companies *shouldn't* be encouraged to open operations down there. Finally he agreed and de la Rua flew to Nassau. And we know what happened next."

Sachs told Laurel, "Shales is in custody."

"Good," the prosecutor said. "Now, where are we with the evidence?"

"Ah, the evidence," Rhyme mused. "The evidence. All we need to prove is that the bullet caused the flying glass, and the glass was the cause of the reporter's death. We're close. We've got the trace of glass splinters on the bullet and on de la Rua's clothes. I'd just really like some of the shards that actually caused the laceration and bleeding." He looked to Laurel. "Juries love the weapons, don't they?"

"They sure do, Lincoln."

"The morgue in the Bahamas?" Sachs asked.

"The examiner would still have the glass, wouldn't you think?"

"Let's hope. People may steal Rolexes and Oakleys down there but I imagine broken glass is safe from sticky fingers. I'll call Mychal and see what he can find. He can ship some up here with an affidavit that states the shards were recovered from the body and were the cause of death. Or, hell, maybe he could come up himself to testify."

"That's a great idea," Thom said. "He could stay with us for a while, hang out."

Rhyme exhaled in exasperation. "Oh, sure. We've got *so* much time for socializing. I could take him on a tour of the Big Apple. You know, haven't been to the Statue of Liberty in... *ever*. And I intend to keep it that way."

Thom laughed, irritating Rhyme all the more.

The criminalist called up the autopsy pictures and scrolled through them. "A shard from the jugular, carotid or femoral would be best," he mused. "Those would be the fatal ones." But an initial review didn't show any obvious splinters of glass jutting from the pale corpse of Eduardo de la Rua.

"I'll give Mychal a call in the morning. It's late now. Don't want to interfere with his moonlighting job."

Rhyme could have called now but he wanted to speak to the corporal in private. The fact was that he *had* been considering inviting Poitier to New York at some point in the near future and this would be a good excuse to do so.

And, he reflected with some irony, yes, he *did* intend to show Poitier around town. The Statue of Liberty, however, would not be on the tour.

CHAPTER 77

JACOB SWANN WONDERED what had happened.
His plans for Nance Laurel had been interrupted by the arrival of an unmarked police car in front of her apartment in Brooklyn—just as Swann had been about to rise and go visit the ADA, to play out his revenge scenario.

The plainclothes detective had whisked her out quickly—so fast that it was clear something significant was going on. Did it relate to the Moreno case, which supposedly was a case no longer? Or something else?

He was now in his Nissan, headed back home. The answer to the mystery arrived in the form of a text from headquarters. Shit. Shreve Metzger had reported that the case was back on but with a curious variation: Barry Shales had been arrested for the killing not of Robert Moreno but of Eduardo de la Rua, the reporter who'd been interviewing him at the time the bullet had blown the hotel window into a million little shards of glass.

Because de la Rua was a U.S. citizen—*¡Hola, Puerto Rico!*—Ms. Nance Laurel had been reinstated on the case.

Metzger had not been charged but it was possible that he would be soon, accused of at least one or two felony counts; the point of Shales's arrest, of course, was to pressure the drone pilot to give up his boss.

How easy was it to kill someone in detention? Swann wondered. Not that easy, he suspected, at least not without some inside help, which would be extremely expensive.

Swann was told additional services would be needed. He was to await instructions. Tomorrow promised to be a busy day but since the hour was late he doubted any of those directives would involve his going out again tonight.

This was good.

The little butcher man was hungry and had a taste for some wine. A glass or two of Spanish Albariño beckoned, as did some of the Veronique from last night, carefully wrapped up and tucked into the fridge. There wasn't a chef in the world— even those whose eateries boasted three Michelin stars—who didn't appreciate leftovers, whatever they said in public.

VI

SMOKE

CHAPTER 78

C APTAIN SHALES—"

"I've left the military. I'm civilian now."

The hour was early, Friday morning. Nance Laurel and the drone pilot were in an interview room at the detention center. The same floor, as a matter of fact, where she'd been talking to Amelia Sachs when the State Department delivery boy had so successfully derailed the Moreno homicide case.

"All right, Mr. Shales, you've been read your rights, correct?" Laurel put a tape recorder on the scabby table in front of them. She wondered how many invectives, lies, excuses and pleas for mercy this battered rectangle of electronics had heard. Too many to count.

He looked at the device without emotion. "Yes."

She wasn't sure how to read him, and reading defendants was a very important part of her job. Would they cave, would they stonewall, would they offer a modicum of helpful comment, would they look for the right moment to leap from the chair and throttle her?

All of those had happened on occasion.

"And you understand you can terminate this conversation at any point?"

"Yes."

And yet he wasn't terminating and he wasn't crying for his lawyer. She sensed that part of him, a small part, wanted to tell her everything, wanted to confess—though some very thick walls surrounded that portion of his heart still.

She noted something else: Yes, Shales was a trained killer, no different, in theory, from Jimmy Bonittollo, who'd put a bullet into the head of Frank Carson because Carson had moved into Bonittollo's liquor distribution territory. But, practically, there *did* seem to be a difference. Unlike Bonittollo, Shales had a patina of regret in his blue eyes. And not regret because he'd been caught, which was always there, but regret because he understood that Robert Moreno's death was wrong.

"I want to explain why I'm here." Laurel spoke calmly.

"I thought...the case was dropped."

"The case for the death of Robert Moreno is not going forward. We're bringing a case for the death of Eduardo de la Rua."

"The reporter."

"That's right."

His head rose and fell slowly. He said nothing.

"You were ordered by Shreve Metzger to kill Robert Moreno as part of a Special Task Order issued by the National Intelligence and Operations Service."

"I'm choosing not to answer that question."

I didn't ask a question, she reflected. Then continued, "Because you intended to kill Moreno and you did kill him, any deaths that resulted—even if you hoped to avoid them—are murder."

His head turned and it seemed that he took in a pattern of scuff on the wall. It looked like a lightning bolt to Laurel.

And then she realized: Lord, he looks like David! She'd had the same thought when she'd seen Lincoln Rhyme's aide, Thom. But Shales's glance just now had been like an electric shock; the airman was much, much closer in appearance and expression.

Schoolmarm...

Said in the heat of the moment.

Still...

David, her only real boyfriend. Ever.

A deep breath and Laurel, steadied, continued, "Are you aware that Robert Moreno was not, in fact, engaged in a plot to attack the American Petroleum building in Miami? And that the chemicals he imported into the Bahamas were for legitimate agricultural and commercial purposes, to aid his Local Empowerment Movement?"

"I'm choosing not to answer that question, either."

"We've datamined your phone calls, determined your whereabouts, have air traffic control information about the drone, photos of the Ground Control Station in the NIOS parking lot—"

"I'm choosing—" his voice caught. "I'm choosing not to respond." His eyes could not hold hers.

Like David's.

There, sorry. I didn't want to say it. You made me . . .

Instinct told her to back off now. Immediately. Softer voice. "I want to work with you, Mr. Shales. Can I call you Barry?"

"I guess."

"I'm Nance. I want to work something out. We believe that you were a victim in this too. That you weren't given all the information about Robert Moreno that you probably should have been when the STO was issued."

Now a flicker in his eyes.

Which, fuck it all, are just as blue as David's.

"In fact, it's possible," she continued, "that some of the intelligence was intentionally manipulated to make a stronger case for assassinating Moreno. What do you think about that?"

"Intelligence is hard to analyze. It's a tricky business."

Ah, no more name, rank and serial number. No doubt: Shales knows that Metzger fudged the intel and it's been eating at him.

"I'm sure it is. But it presumably is also easy to manipulate. Isn't that the case?"

"I guess it can be." Shales's face was flushed. She believed that veins in his jaw and temple were more prominent than earlier.

Excellent.

Fear was a good tool for persuasion.

Hope was better.

"Let's see if we can work something out."

But his shoulders rose slightly and she measured the level of resistance. Still pretty high.

Laurel had played chess with David. This was one of their Sunday-morning things to do, after breakfast and after, well, what often came after breakfast.

She loved those games. He was slightly better than she. That added to the excitement.

Now, she thought. Now's the time.

"Barry, the stakes are high here. The death of Moreno and the others in the Bahamas are one thing. But the bomb in the coffee shop, the murder of Lydia Foster, that's—"

"*What?*"

"The bomb, the murder of the witnesses." Laurel appeared perplexed.

"Wait. What are you talking about?"

She paused. Then, surveying his face closely, said, "The individual trying to stop our case, the specialist, they're called, aren't they? He killed a witness in the Bahamas and one here in New York. He detonated an IED to destroy a computer holding evidence, nearly killed a half dozen people, including an NYPD police detective. You're not familiar with these?"

"No…"

Bishop to queen's knight three. Check.

She whispered, "Yes. Oh, yes."

He looked away whispering, "Minimal steps…"

She didn't know what that meant.

But Laurel did know that this wasn't an act. Shales, of the pink flesh and eyes impossibly old and achingly blue, hadn't known anything of Unsub 516. Not a single thing. Shreve Metzger had thoroughly deceived him.

Work it…

"Well, Barry, we have proof positive that this man was in the Bahamas around the time of your drone strike. We thought he was your partner."

"No, I work alone. NIOS sometimes has assets on the ground for intel…" His voice faded.

"Who are sent there by Shreve Metzger."

Not a question.

"Sometimes."

"So he's the one who manipulated the evidence in the first place. And has been trying to stop the investigation."

"You have a name?" Shales asked.

"No, he's an unknown subject at this point."

Shales whispered, "Tell me, who's this Lydia Foster you mentioned?"

"Moreno's interpreter here in New York. This unsub killed her. He was eliminating witnesses."

"And the bomb, was that the gas main explosion in the news the other day?"

"Yes, that was the cover story. But it was a bomb. The point was to kill investigators and destroy evidence."

The pilot looked off.

"And two people died?"

"And they were both tortured first."

He said nothing. His eyes focused on a dime-sized ding in the table.

"Barry, you called the South Cove Inn two days before the Moreno assignment. You called from your operational phone, registered to Don Bruns."

If he was surprised at this he gave no reaction.

"I know why you called," Laurel said softly. "It wasn't to confirm Moreno's reservation. The CIA or NIOS's own assets could verify he was going

to be there. You wanted to be sure that he was going to be there *alone*. That his wife and children
wouldn't be coming with him. You wanted to be
sure. So that there was no collateral damage."

The airman's lip trembled for an instant. He
looked away.

Laurel whispered, "That tells me you had doubts
about the assignment from the beginning. You
didn't want it to end up the way it did." She held
his eye, whispered, "Work with us, Barry."

There's a moment in chess, David had told her,
of alarming clarity. You understand that the strategy you've been confidently following is completely wrong, that your opponent has been playing an entirely different game—one of insight and
brilliance, outstripping yours. Your loss might not
be in the next move or the next ten but defeat is in-
evitable.

"He'll see it in your eyes," David had explained.
"Something changes. You know you've lost and
your eyes tell your opponent you understand that."

This is what she observed now with Barry
Shales.

He's going to cave, she understood. He's going
to give me Shreve Metzger! The murderer who
uses national intelligence to kill whomever the hell
he wants to kill.

Checkmate...

His breathing was rapid. "All right. Tell me…
Tell me how this could work?"

"What we can do is—"

A pounding on the door.

Laurel jumped.

A man in a close-fitting gray suit stood at the
window, looking matter-of-factly from her to
Shales and back again.

No, no, no…

Laurel knew him. He was one of the most tena-
cious—and vicious—defense lawyers in the city.
That is, one of the best. But he primarily appeared
in federal court in New York at the behest of associated firms based in Washington, DC. Curious that
he was here, rather than an attorney who knew his
way around the rough-and-tumble state trial court,
which in New York was called the Supreme Court.

The guard opened the door.

"Hello, Counselor Laurel," the lawyer said
pleasantly.

She knew him by reputation. How did he know
her?

Something wasn't right here.

"Who—?" Shales began.

"I'm Artie Rothstein. I've been retained to defend you."

"By Shreve?"

"Don't say anything more, Barry. Were you advised you have the right to an attorney and you don't need to say anything?"

"I...Yes. But I want to—"

"No, you don't, Barry. You don't want to do anything at the moment."

"But, look, I just found out that Shreve—"

"Barry," Rothstein said in a low voice. "I'm advising you to be quiet. It's very important." He waited a moment then added, "We want to make sure you and your family get the best counsel you can have."

"My *family*?"

Hell. That's his game. Laurel said firmly, "The state has no case against your family, Barry. We have no interest in them at all."

Rothstein turned to her and his round, creased face offered a perplexed look. "We've hardly scratched the surface of the case, Nance." He looked at Shales. "You never know the direction a prosecution will take. My theory is to provide for every eventuality. And I'll make sure you and anyone else involved in this prosecution..." His voice grew indignant. "...this *misguided* prosecution is looked after. Now, Barry?"

The pilot's jaw quivered. He looked at Nance quickly then lowered his eyes and nodded.

Rothstein said, "This interview is now terminated."

CHAPTER 79

ORNING SUNLIGHT FILLED Rhyme's town house.

The windows faced east and bands of direct light, filtered through many leaves, fired into the parlor in flickering streams.

The team was gathered here, Cooper, Sellitto, Pulaski. Sachs too. And Nance Laurel, who'd just returned from detention with the disappointing news that Shales had been about to confess and give up Metzger when a lawyer that NIOS or someone in DC had hired arrived and scared him into silence.

But she said, "I can still make the case work. Nothing's going to stop me this time."

Rhyme happened to be glancing at his phone when it rang and he was pleased. He answered. "Corporal, how are you?"

Poitier's melodic voice replied, "Good, Captain. Good. I was happy to get your message this morning. We miss the chaos you brought with you. You must come back. Come back for holiday. And I appreciate your invitation too. I will most certainly come to New York but that will have to be as a holiday as well. I'm afraid I don't have any evidence for you. There was no luck at the morgue. I don't have anything to deliver to you in person."

"No glass shards from de la Rua's body?"

"I'm afraid not. I spoke to the doctor who conducted the autopsy and there were no splinters left in the bodies of either de la Rua or the guard when they were brought in. Apparently they had been removed by the medical technicians trying to save the men."

But Rhyme recalled the crime scene pictures. The wounds had been numerous, the blood loss massive. Some shards must have remained. He now eased close to the whiteboards and examined the autopsy pictures of the victims, the crude incisions, the skull cap placed back after the saw work, the Y incision decorating the chest.

Something was wrong.

Rhyme turned to the room and shouted, to no one in particular, "The autopsy report. I want de la Rua's autopsy report, now!" He couldn't juggle the phone and work the computer at the same time.

Mel Cooper complied and in a moment the

scanned document was on a flat-screen monitor next to Rhyme.

This victim exhibited approximately 35 lacerations in various sites of the chest, abdomen, arms, face and thighs, primarily anterior, presumably caused by shards of glass from a window that was shot out at the crime scene. These lacerations varied in size but the majority were approximately 3–4mm in width and 2 to 3 centimeters in length. Six of said lacerations were in this victim's carotid and jugular vessels and femoral artery, resulting in severe hemorrhaging.

Rhyme was aware of faint breathing on the other end of the line. Then: "Captain Rhyme, is everything all right?"

"I have to go."

"Is there anything more you need me to do?"

Rhyme's eyes were on Nance Laurel, who was scanning quizzically, looking from the autopsy report to the photos to Rhyme himself. He said to Poitier, "No, thank you, Corporal. I'll call you back." He disconnected and wheeled closer to the screen, studying it more closely. Then he turned his attention to the whiteboards.

"What is it, Rhyme?" Sachs asked.

He sighed. When he spun around he looked to Laurel. "I'm sorry. I was wrong."

"What do you mean, Linc?" Sellitto asked.

"De la Rua wasn't collateral damage at all. He was the *target*."

Laurel said, "But, still, Lincoln, we know Shales intended to shoot Moreno. It was the glass shards from the bullet Shales fired that killed de la Rua."

"That's the point," Rhyme said softly. "No, it wasn't."

CHAPTER 80

*U*AV *EIGHT NINE TWO TO FLORIDA CEN-TER. Target identified and acquired. Infrared and SAR."*

"Roger, Eight Nine Two... Use of LRR is authorized."

"Copy. Eight Nine Two."

And six seconds later Robert Moreno was no more.

Barry Shales was in the holding cell, alone, hands together, sitting hunched forward. The bench was hard, the air stifling and sour-human smelling.

Recalling the Moreno task, thinking particularly of the disembodied voices from Florida Center. People he'd never met.

Just like he'd never actually seen the UAV he'd flown on that mission, never run his hand over its fuselage the way he had his F-16. He never saw any of the UAVs in person.

Remote.

Soldier and weapon.

Soldier and target.

Remote.

Remote.

"There seem to be two, no, three people in the room."

"Can you positively identify Moreno?"

"It's... there's some glare. Okay, that's better. Yes. I can identify the task. I can see him."

Shales's thoughts were in turmoil. Like an aircraft in a spin: The horror of learning that he'd killed three innocent men, then being arrested for the murder of one. And then finding that Shreve Metzger had brought in a specialist to clean up after the operation, killing witnesses, setting that bomb.

Which all brought home to him that fundamentally what he was doing for NIOS was wrong.

Barry Shales had flown combat missions in Iraq. He'd dropped bombs and launched missiles and had some confirmed kills, supporting ground operations. When you were in live combat, even if the odds were in your favor, as with most U.S. military ops, there was still the chance that somebody could bring you down—Stingers, AK-47 fire. Even a single bullet from a Kurdish muzzle loader could do it.

This was combat. That was how war worked.

And it was fair. Because you knew the enemy. They were easy to identify: They were the ones who wanted to fucking kill you right back.

But sitting in a Kill Room, thousands of miles away, padded by layers of intel that might or might not be accurate (or *manipulated*), it was different. How did you know the supposed enemy really was just that? How could you *ever* know?

And then you'd go back home, forty minutes away, surrounding yourself with people who might be just as innocent as the ones you'd just killed in a tenth of a second.

Oh, and, honey, get some kids' Nyquil. Sammy's got the sniffles. I forgot to pick some up.

Shales closed his eyes, rocked on the bench.

He knew that there was something off about Shreve Metzger—the temper, those moments when control left him, the intel reports that just didn't seem right, the lectures about the sanctity of America. Hell, when he started a pro-U.S. tirade he sounded an awful lot like the flip side of Robert Moreno.

Only nobody pumped a .420 boattail into the NIOS director.

And to order in a specialist for clean-up, to set IEDs and kill witnesses.

Torture …

Suddenly, sitting in this grim place, wafting of

urine and disinfectant, Barry Shales realized he was overwhelmed. Years of hidden guilt were flooding in to drown him, the ghosts of the men and women in the infamous queue, people he'd killed, were swimming toward him now, to drag him under the surface of the inky blood tide. Years of being someone else—Don Bruns, Samuel McCoy, Billy Dodd... Occasionally, at the store or in a movie theater lobby, when Marg called his real name, he hesitated, not sure who she was talking to.

Just give up Metzger, he told himself. There was plenty of information on his Don Bruns phone to put the NIOS head away for a long time—if it turned out he'd played with the evidence and hired a specialist to eliminate witnesses here. He could give Laurel the encryption code and the backup keyfile and the other phones and documents he'd kept.

A memory of the lawyer came back. He didn't like the man one bit. Rothstein had been retained by a firm in Washington, it seemed. But he wouldn't say which one. When they'd met after Laurel had left, the attorney had suddenly grown distracted, taking and sending several text messages as he explained to Shales how the case was going to proceed. It seemed that his attitude had changed: as if whatever he said or did, Shales was fucked.

It was odd that the man hadn't known much about Shreve Metzger, though he was very familiar with NIOS. Rothstein seemed to spend more time in Washington than here. His advice at this point had been simple: Don't say a word to anybody about anything. They would try to make him cave, Nance Laurel was a duplicitous bitch, you know duplicitous, you know what I mean, Barry. Oh, don't trust a thing she says.

Shales had explained that Metzger may have done some pretty bad things in trying to cover up the case. "Like, I think he might have killed somebody."

"That's not our issue."

"Well, it is," Shales said. "It's exactly our issue."

The lawyer had received another text. He regarded the screen for a long moment. He said he had to go. He'd be in touch soon.

Rothstein had left.

And Barry Shales was brought down here and deposited, alone in the silent, pungent room.

Moments passed, a thousand heartbeats, an eternity, when he heard the door at the far end of the corridor buzz open. Footsteps approached.

Maybe it was a guard to summon him to another meeting. With whom? Rothstein? Or Nance Laurel, who would offer him a solid plea bargain.

In exchange for giving up Shreve Metzger.

Everything told him he should do it. His brain, his heart, his conscience. And think of the torture of living this way: seeing Marg and the boys through a greasy glass window. He'd never see the kids learn sports, never see them on holiday mornings. And they'd grow up enduring the torment and taunting of having a father in prison.

The hopelessness of the situation bore down on him, surrounded him and strangled. He wanted to scream. But the consequences were his own fault. He'd made the decision to join NIOS, to kill people by pushbutton from half a world away.

But ultimately it came down to this: You didn't give up your fellow soldiers. Right or wrong. Barry Shales sighed. Metzger was safe, at least from him. Cells like this one would be his home for the next twenty or thirty years.

He was preparing to give Nance Laurel the news she didn't want to hear when the footsteps outside stopped and the door clanked open.

He gave a brief humorless laugh. The visit was not, it seemed, about him at all. A solid African American guard was delivering another prisoner, who was even larger than the turnkey, a huge man, unclean, hair slicked back. Even from across the room the man's body odor spread out like ripples on a calm pond.

The man looked Shales over with a narrow gaze

and then turned to watch the guard glance at them both, close the cell door and walk off down the hall. The new prisoner hawked and spit on the floor.

The drone pilot rose and moved to the far corner of the cell.

The other prisoner remained where he was, head turned away. Yet the airman had the sense that he was aware of every move of Shales's hands or feet, every shift on the bench, every breath that he took.

My new home...

CHAPTER 81

"YOU'RE SURE?" LAUREL ASKED.

"Yes," Rhyme said, "Barry Shales is innocent. He and Metzger weren't responsible for de la Rua's death."

Laurel was frowning.

The criminalist said, "I . . . there was something I didn't see."

"Rhyme, what?" Sachs asked.

He was watching Nance Laurel's face grow still once more; this was how she responded to pain. Her prized case was again dissolving before her eyes.

Nothing's going to stop me now . . .

Sellitto said, "Talk to me, Linc. The fuck's going on?"

Mel Cooper remained silent and curious.

Rhyme explained, "Look at the wounds." He expanded the autopsy picture, focusing in on the lacerations on the journalist's face and neck.

He then moved another photo next to it: the crime scene itself. De la Rua lay on his back, blood streaming from the same cuts. He was covered with shards of glass. But none of them was actually sticking into a wound.

"Why wasn't I thinking?" Rhyme muttered. "Look at the *measurements* of the lacerations on the autopsy report. Look at them! The wounds're just a few millimeters wide. A glass shard would be much thicker than that. And how could they all be so uniform? I *saw* them but I didn't *see* them."

"He was stabbed to death," Sellitto said, nodding.

"Has to be," Rhyme said. "A knife blade is one to three millimeters in width, two to three centimeters in depth."

Sachs: "And the killer tossed some glass onto de la Rua's body to make it look like he was killed accidentally as collateral damage."

Sipping his sweet coffee, Sellitto muttered, "Pretty fucking smart. And he killed the guard too, the same way. Because he'd be a witness. But who did it?"

Rhyme said, "Obviously. Five Sixteen. We know he was near suite twelve hundred around the time of the drone strike. And remember that a knife's his weapon of choice."

Sachs said, "Well, we also know something else:

Five Sixteen's a specialist. He wasn't doing this for the fun of it. He's working for somebody—somebody who wanted the reporter dead."

Rhyme said, "Right, his boss is the one we want." His eyes were on the chart once more. "But who the hell is he?"

"Metzger," Pulaski said.

"Maybe," Rhyme said slowly.

Laurel said, "Whoever it was knew Moreno was going to be in the Bahamas and that an STO was going to be executed. And when."

"Rookie, you get on the motive issue. You're our Argentinian reporter maven. Who wanted him dead?"

Pulaski asked, "Find out what stories he was working on, controversial ones?"

"Well, yes, of course. And feathers he'd ruffled. But I also want to know his personal life—people he knew, investments he'd made, family, vacation places he went to, real estate he owned."

"You mean everything? Like who he was sleeping with?"

Rhyme muttered, "I'll let you get away with a preposition at the end of that sentence but I won't allow the improper pronoun."

"Sorry. I should've said, 'with who him was sleeping,'" the young officer fired back.

Laughter all around.

"Okay, Ron, I probably deserved that. Yes, everything you can find."

For an hour, then two, Pulaski, with Sachs helping, dug into the journalist's personal life and career and downloaded what articles and blog posts of his they could find.

They printed out everything and brought it to the table in front of Rhyme.

The young officer spread the material out and the criminalist began reading through those that were in English. Then he summoned Pulaski. "Ron, I need you to be Berlitz."

"Who?"

"Translate these headlines." Gesturing to the Spanish-language articles de la Rua had written.

For another hour they went through the stories, Rhyme asking questions, which Pulaski translated quickly and with precision.

Finally, Rhyme gazed up at the whiteboards.

ROBERT MORENO HOMICIDE

Boldface indicates updated information

— Crime Scene 1.
  — Suite 1200, South Cove Inn, New Providence Island, Bahamas.
  — May 9.

— Victim 1: Robert Moreno.

   — COD: Single gunshot wound to chest.

   — Supplemental information: Moreno, 38, U.S. citizen, expatriate, living in Venezuela. Vehemently anti-American. Nickname: "the Messenger of Truth." Determined that "disappear into thin air" and "blowing them up" NOT terrorism references.

   — Shoes contained fibers associated with carpet in hotel corridor, dirt from hotel entryway, also crude oil.

   — Clothing contained traces of breakfast: pastry flakes, jam and bacon, also crude oil.

   — Spent three days in NYC, April 30–May 2.

      — May 1, used Elite Limousine.

      — Driver Tash Farada. (Regular driver Vlad Nikolov was sick. Trying to locate. **Prob. homicide.**)

      — Closed accounts at American Independent Bank and Trust, prob. other banks too.

      — Drove around city with interpreter Lydia Foster (killed by Unsub 516).

- Reason for anti-U.S. feelings:
  best friend killed by U.S.
  troops in Panama invasion,
  1989.
- Moreno's last trip to U.S.
  Never would return.
- Meeting in Wall Street.
  - No record of terrorist
    investigations in area.
- Met with unknown individuals
  at Russian, UAE (Dubai) char-
  ities and Brazilian consulate.
- Met with Henry Cross, head of
  Classrooms for the Americas.
  Reported that Moreno met
  with other charities, but
  doesn't know which. Man fol-
  lowing Moreno, white and
  "tough looking." Private jet
  tailing Moreno? Blue color.
  Checking for identification.
  - **No leads.**
- Victim 2: Eduardo de la Rua.
  - COD: Loss of blood. **Lacerations
    from knife wounds.**
  - Supplemental information: Journal-
    ist, interviewing Moreno. Born
    Puerto Rico, living in Argentina.

- Camera, tape recorder, gold pen, notebooks missing.
- Shoes contained fibers associated with carpet in hotel corridor, dirt from hotel entryway.
- Clothing contained traces of breakfast: allspice and pepper sauce.
— Victim 3: Simon Flores.
  - COD: Loss of blood. **Lacerations from knife wounds.**
  - Supplemental information: Moreno's bodyguard. Brazilian national, living in Venezuela.
  - Rolex watch, Oakley sunglasses missing.
  - Shoes contained fibers associated with carpet in hotel corridor, dirt from hotel entryway, also crude oil.
  - Clothing contained traces of breakfast: pastry flakes, jam and bacon, also crude oil and cigarette ash.
— Chronology of Moreno in Bahamas.
  - May 7. Arrived Nassau with Flores (guard).
  - May 8. Meeting out of hotel all day.
  - May 9. 9 a.m. Meeting two men about forming Local Empowerment Movement in Bahamas. 10:30 a.m.

de la Rua arrives. At 11:15 a.m.
Moreno shot.

— Suspect 1: Shreve Metzger.

    — Director, National Intelligence and
Operations Service.

    — Mentally unstable? Anger issues.

    — Manipulated evidence to illegally au-
thorize Special Task Order?

    — Divorced. Law degree, Yale.

— Suspect 2: Unsub 516.

    — Determined not to be sniper.

    — Possibly individual at South Cove Inn,
May 8. Caucasian, male, mid 30s, short
cut light brown hair, American accent,
thin but athletic. Appears "military."

    — Could be sniper's partner or hired by
Metzger independently for clean-up
and to stop investigation, or working
for cartels.

    — Determined to be perpetrator of Lydia
Foster and Annette Bodel homicides,
and IED attack at Java Hut.

    — Amateur or professional chef or cook
of some skill.

— Suspect 3: Barry Shales.

    — Confirmed to be sniper, code name
Don Bruns.

    — 39, former Air Force, decorated.

- Intelligence specialist at NIOS. Wife is teacher. Have two sons.
- Individual who placed a call to the South Cove Inn on May 7 to confirm arrival of Moreno. Call was from phone registered to Don Bruns, through NIOS cover company.
- Information Services datamining Shales.
- Voiceprint obtained.
- **Drone pilot, who fired shot that killed Moreno.**
- **FAA and Bahamas air traffic control—evidence of drone's flight path and presence in Bahamas.**

- Crime scene report, autopsy report, other details.
  - Crime scene cleaned and contaminated by Unsub 516 and largely useless.
  - General details: Bullet fired through and shattered floor-to-ceiling window, garden outside, poisonwood tree leaves cut back to 25 feet height. View to sniper's nest obscured by haze and pollution.
  - 47 fingerprints found; half analyzed, negative results. Others missing.
  - Candy wrappers recovered.

- — Cigarette ash recovered.
- — Bullet lodged behind couch where Moreno's body was found, **fired from drone.**
  - — Fatal round.
    - — .420 caliber, made by Walker Defense Systems, NJ.
    - — Spitzer boattail round.
    - — Extremely high quality.
    - — Extremely high velocity and high power.
    - — Rare.
    - — Weapon: custom made.
    - — Trace on bullet: glass dust, fiber from Moreno's shirt and poisonwood tree leaf.
- — Crime Scene 2.
  - — **No sniper's nest involved; bullets fired from drone. "Kill Room" is drone command center.**
- — Crime Scene 2A.
  - — Apartment 3C, 182 Augusta Street, Nassau, Bahamas.
  - — May 15.
  - — Victim: Annette Bodel.
  - — COD: TBD, probably strangulation, asphyxiation.
  - — Suspect: Determined to be Unsub 516.

— Victim was probably tortured.
— Trace:
  — Sand associated with sand found at Java Hut.
  — Docosahexaenoic acid—fish oil. Likely caviar or roe. Ingredient in dish from NY restaurant.
  — Two-stroke engine fuel.
  — $C_8H_8O_3$, vanillin. Ingredient in dish from NY restaurant.
— Crime Scene 3.
  — Java Hut, Mott and Hester Streets.
  — May 16.
  — IED explosion, to destroy evidence of whistleblower.
  — Victims: No fatalities, minor injuries.
  — Suspect: Determined to be Unsub 516.
  — Military-style device, anti-personnel, shrapnel. Semtex explosive. Available on arms market.
  — Located customers in shop when whistleblower was present, canvassing for info, pictures.
  — Trace:
    — Sand from tropical region.
— Crime Scene 4.
  — Apartment 230, 1187 Third Avenue.
  — May 16.

— Victim: Lydia Foster.

— COD: Blood loss, shock from knife wounds.

— Suspect: Determined to be Unsub 516.

— Hair, brown and short (from Unsub 516), sent to CODIS for analysis.

— Trace:

   — Glycyrrhiza glabra—licorice. Ingredient in dish from NY restaurant.

   — Cynarine, chemical component of artichokes. Ingredient in dish from NY restaurant.

— Evidence of torture.

— All records of interpreting assignment for Robert Moreno on May 1 stolen.

— No cell phone or computer.

— Receipt for Starbucks where Lydia waited during Moreno's private meeting on May 1. Rumors of drug cartels behind the killings. Considered unlikely.

— Supplemental Investigation.

   — Determine identity of Whistleblower.

      — Unknown subject who leaked the Special Task Order.

      — Sent via anonymous email.

      — Traced through Taiwan to Romania to Sweden. Sent from New York area on public Wi-Fi, no government servers used.

- Used an old computer, probably from ten years ago, iBook, either clamshell model, two tone with other bright colors (like green or tangerine). Or could be traditional model, graphite color, but much thicker than today's laptops.
- **Profile:**
    - **Likely middle-aged male.**
    - **Uses Splenda sweetener.**
    - **Military background?**
    - **Wears inexpensive suit, in unusual blue shade.**
    - **Uses iBook.**
    - **Possibly suffers from stomach disorder, uses Zantac.**
- Individual in light-colored sedan following Det. A. Sachs.
    - Make and model not determined.

Of course, of course...

"I think I've got it. I need to talk to Mychal Poitier again. And, Thom, bring the van around."

"The—"

"The van! We're going for a drive. Sachs, you're coming too. And you *are* armed, aren't you? Oh, and somebody call detention. Have Barry Shales released. The guy's been through enough."

CHAPTER 82

THE SKINNY FIFTY-YEAR-OLD was a lifer in the Department of Corrections.

He was not, however, a prisoner but a guard and had been all his professional days. He actually liked the job, shepherding people through the Tombs.

The nickname of the venue—technically the Manhattan Detention Complex—suggested a place that was worse than the truth. The word went back to the 1800s and was appropriate for a prison modeled after an Egyptian mausoleum, built on an incompetently filled swamp (adding to the aroma and illness that pervaded the place) and situated in the notorious Five Points district of Manhattan— described as "the most dangerous place on earth" at that time.

In fact, the Tombs nowadays was just another lockup, although a damn big one.

Calling into intercoms, using the code word for

the day to open doors, the guard now strode down the hallway to a segregated set of cells reserved for special prisoners.

Like the man he was now going to see. Barry Shales.

Over his twenty-eight years as a guard here he had trained himself to have no opinion about his charges. Child killers and white-collar criminals who'd embezzled from people who probably should be embezzled from…it made no difference to him. His job was to keep order and make sure the system ran smoothly. And also to ease the difficult time these people were going through.

After all, this was not prison but temporary detention, where individuals stayed until bail or transfer to Rikers or, in more than a few cases, freedom forever. Everybody here was presumably innocent. That was how the country worked.

But the man whose cell he was now walking toward was different and the guard *did* have an opinion about him. It was an absolute tragedy that he'd been incarcerated here.

The guard didn't know a lot about Barry Shales's background. But he did know that he was a former air force flier who'd fought in the war in Iraq. And that he worked for the government now, the federal government.

And yet he'd been arrested for murder. But not for killing his wife or his wife's lover or anything like that. For killing some asshole terrorist.

Arrested, even though he was a soldier, even though he was a hero.

And the guard knew why he was here: because of politics. He'd been arrested because the party that wasn't in power had to fuck over the one that was, by making an example of this poor guy.

The guard came to the cell and looked through the window.

Funny.

There was another prisoner in the cell, which the guard hadn't known about. It didn't make sense for him to be here. There was a second empty cell that the man should have been put into. The new prisoner was sitting off to the side, staring ahead blankly. The gaze made the guard feel uneasy. The eyes told you everything about the people here, much more than the crap they said.

And what was with Shales? He was lying on his side on the bench, back to the door. He wasn't moving.

The guard punched in the code and with a buzz the door opened.

"Hey, Shales?"

No movement.

The second prisoner continued to stare at the

wall. Scary fucker, the guard thought, and he was a man who didn't use that phrase lightly.

"Shales?" The guard stepped closer.

Suddenly the flier stirred and sat up. He turned slowly. The guard saw that Shales was holding his hands to his eyes. He'd been crying.

No shame in that. Happened here all the time.

Shales wiped his face.

"On your feet, Shales. Got some news I think you're gonna like."

CHAPTER 83

AT HIS DESK SHREVE METZGER HEARD the siren but thought nothing of it.

This was, after all, Manhattan. You always heard sirens. The same way you heard shouts, horns, the occasional scream, the caw of seagulls. Backfires... Well, staccato reports that were *probably* backfires.

Just the background tapestry of the city.

He hardly paid any mind, especially now, when he was trying to put out the raging forest fire that the Robert Moreno task order had become.

The chaos swirled around him, the tornado of flame: Barry Shales and the goddamn whistle-blower and that bitch of a prosecutor and the people inside and outside the government who had put together the Special Task Order program.

Soon there'd be more tinder adding to the smolder: the press.

Then of course, hovering over it all, was the Wizard.

He wondered what the "budget conference" was deciding right at the moment.

Metzger realized the sirens had stopped.

And they'd stopped right outside his office.

He rose and looked down. At the gated parking lot, where the Ground Control Station sat.

All over with . . .

It sure was.

One unmarked car punctuated with flashing blue lights, one NYPD squad car, one van—maybe SWAT. The doors were open. The police were nowhere to be seen.

Shreve Metzger knew where they were, though. No doubt of that, of course.

A detail that was confirmed a moment later when the guard from downstairs called him on the security line and asked in an uncertain voice, "Director?" He cleared his throat and continued, "There are some police officers here to see you."

CHAPTER 84

L INCOLN RHYME COULD TELL THAT SHREVE
METZGER, looking the criminalist up and
down, was surprised to see him.

Maybe the fact that he was in a wheelchair had
jarred him. But the man would have known that.
The master of intelligence surely had been com-
piling files on everyone involved in the Moreno
investigation.

Maybe the surprise, ironically, was due to
Rhyme's being in better shape than the NIOS head.
Rhyme noted how benign Metzger looked: thin
hair, scrawny physique, thick beige-framed glasses
with a smudge on each lens. Rhyme would have
thought a man who occasionally killed people for
a living would be more grisly and sinister. Metzger
had taken in Rhyme's muscular form, thick hair,
square face. He'd blinked, a cryptic expression
worthy of Nance Laurel.

The man sat down at his desk and turned a

gaze—this one *unsurprised*—toward Sachs and Sellitto. Only they were here; Laurel wasn't. This
was, Rhyme had explained, a police matter, not
prosecutorial. And there was a chance, though
slight, it could be dangerous.

He looked around. The office was pretty bland.
Few decorations, some books that seemed un-
read—their spines uncracked—sat on untidy
shelves. Some file cabinets with very large com-
bination locks and iris scanners. Functional, mismatched furniture. On the ceiling a red light
flashed silently, which meant, Rhyme knew, that
visitors without security clearances were on the
premises and all classified material should be put
away or turned facedown.

Which Metzger had dutifully done.

In a soft voice, a controlled voice, the NIOS
director said, "You understand I'm not saying anything to you."

Lon Sellitto—the senior law enforcer here—
started to reply but Rhyme interrupted with a wry:
"Invoking the Supremacy Clause, are we?"

"I don't owe you any answers."

Breaking his own vow of silence.

Suddenly Metzger's hands began shaking. His
eyes narrowed and his breathing seemed to come
more quickly. This happened in an instant. The
transformation was alarming. Fast and certain

as a snake leaping from quiescence to fang a mouse.

"You think you can goddamn come in here..." He had to stop speaking. His jaw clenched too stridently.

He's had emotional issues. Anger primarily...

"Hey, chill a bit, all right?" Sellitto said. "If we wanted to arrest you, Metzger, you'd be arrested. Listen to the man. Jesus."

Rhyme recalled, with affection, the days when they had been partnered—Sellitto's, not his own, artificial verb. Their technique wasn't good cop/bad cop. But rather smooth cop/rough cop.

Metzger calmed. "Then what...?" He reached into his drawer.

Rhyme noted Sachs stiffen slightly, hand dipping toward her weapon. But the NIOS head withdrew only nail clippers. Then he set them down without clipping.

Sellitto deferred to Rhyme with a nod.

"Now, we have a situation that needs to be...resolved. Your organization issued a Special Task Order."

"I don't know what you're talking about."

"Please." Rhyme lifted an impatient hand. "An STO against a man who appears to have been innocent. But that's between you, your conscience and—presumably—some rather difficult congressional hearings. That's not our business. *We're* here because we need to find somebody who's been killing witnesses involved in the Moreno situation. And—"

"If you're suggesting that NIOS—"

"Called in a specialist?" Sachs said.

Metzger flickered again. He'd have to be wondering, How did they know that term? How did they know *any* of this? He sputtered, "I did not and never have ordered anyone to do that."

Spoken in bureaucratic euphemism.

To do that...

Sellitto barked, "Look at your wrists, Metzger. Look. You in cuffs? I don't see any cuffs. You see any cuffs?"

Rhyme continued, "We know it was somebody else. And that's why we're here. We need you to help us find him."

"Help you?" Metzger replied with a momentary smile. "And why on earth should I help people who are trying to bring down an important department of the government? A department that does vital work keeping citizens safe from our enemies?"

Rhyme offered a sardonic gaze and even the NIOS director seemed to realize the rhetoric was over the top.

"Why should you help?" Rhyme echoed. "Two

reasons leap into my mind. First, so you don't go down for obstruction of justice. You mounted a campaign to stop the investigation. You tracked down Moreno's citizenship renunciation, presumably pulling strings at the State Department. It'd be interesting to see if you followed proper channels for that. We're sure you had Barry Shales, NIOS staff and contractors that you do business with destroy evidence of the STO drone program, you dug up dirt on the investigators. You hacked phones, intercepted emails, borrowed signal information from your friends in Langley and Fort Meade."

Sachs said in a gritty voice, "You stole personal medical records."

She and Rhyme had discussed how Captain Bill Myers had gotten from her orthopedist the files about her condition. They concluded that somebody at NIOS had hacked the records and sent them to Sachs's superiors.

Metzger looked down. A silent confirmation.

"And the second reason to help us? You and NIOS got set up—to murder somebody. And we're the only ones who can help you nail the perp."

Rhyme had Metzger's full attention now.

"What are you saying happened?"

Rhyme replied, "I've heard some people suggest that you're using this job to kill whoever you think is unpatriotic or anti-American. I don't think so. I think you really believed Moreno was a threat—because somebody *wanted* you to think that and leaked phony intelligence to you. So you'd issue an STO and take him out. And that would give the real perp a chance to murder the real intended victim."

Metzger looked off for a moment. "Sure! Moreno gets shot, the others in the room are stunned, scared. The perp slips inside and kills the man he's really after. De la Rua, the reporter. He was writing an exposé, corruption or something, and somebody wanted him dead."

"No, no, no," Rhyme said, though he then conceded, "All right. I *thought* the same thing at first. But then I realized that was wrong." This was delivered as a confession. In fact, he was still irritated he'd jumped to the conclusion about the reporter without considering all the facts.

"Then who...?" Metzger lifted his hands, confused.

Amelia Sachs provided the answer. "Simon Flores, Moreno's bodyguard. He was the target all along."

CHAPTER 85

D E LA RUA WAS A FEATURE WRITER for a business publication," Rhyme explained. "We looked over all his recent articles and found out what he was working on. Human-interest stories, business analysis, economics, investment. No investigative reporting, no exposés. Nothing controversial."

As for the reporter's personal life, well, Pulaski had found nothing that might motivate a killer to take him out. He wasn't involved in shady business dealings or criminal activities, had no enemies and hadn't engaged in any personal moral lapses— there was no controversy about *whom* he was sleeping with (apparently only his wife of twenty-three years).

"So when I didn't find a motive," Rhyme continued, "I had to ask what was curious? I went back to the evidence. And a few minutes later something jumped out. Or, I should say, the *absence* of something jumped out. The bodyguard's missing watch, which was stolen after the shooting. It was a Rolex. The fact of the theft was unremarkable. But why would a bodyguard be wearing a five-thousand-dollar watch?"

Metzger looked blank.

"His boss, Robert Moreno, wasn't rich; he was an activist and journalist. He was probably pretty generous with his workers but paying enough of a salary for any of them to buy a Rolex? I didn't think so. A half hour ago I had our FBI contact profile the guard. Flores had accounts worth six million dollars in banks around the Caribbean. Every month he got fifty thousand cash from an anonymous numbered account in the Caymans."

Metzger's eyes flashed. "The guard was black-mailing someone."

You didn't get to be head of a group like NIOS without being sharp but this was a particularly good deduction.

Rhyme nodded, with a smile. "I think that's right. I remembered that the day of the attack at the South Cove Inn, there was another murder in the Nassau. A lawyer. My Bahamian police contact gave me the lawyer's client list."

Metzger said, "The guard was one of the lawyer's clients, of course. The guard—Flores— left the incriminating information with the attorney for safekeeping. But the man being blackmailed got tired of paying or ran out of money and called up a hit man—this specialist—to kill the guard, kill the lawyer and steal the information, destroy it."

"Exactly. The lawyer's office was ransacked and looted after he died."

Sellitto cast a wry glance at Metzger. "He's good, Linc. He oughta be a spy."

The director regarded the detective coolly, then continued, "Any ideas on how to find out who was being blackmailed?"

Sachs asked, "Who sent you the fake intel about Moreno, that he was planning the attack on American Petroleum Drilling and Refining?"

Metzger leaned back, eyes sweeping the ceiling. "I can't tell you specifically. It's classified. Only that they were intelligence assets in Latin America—ours and another U.S. security organization. Trusted assets."

Rhyme suggested, "Could somebody have leaked bad intel to *them* and they sent it to you?"

The doubtful look faded. "Yes, somebody who knew how the intelligence community worked, somebody with contacts." Metzger's jaw trembled alarmingly again. How fast he switched from calm to enraged. It was unsettling. "But how do we find him?"

"I've been considering that," Rhyme said. "And

I think the key is the whistleblower, the person who leaked the STO."

Metzger grimaced. "The traitor."

"What have you been doing to find him?"

"Searching for him day and night," the man said ruefully. "But no luck. We've cleared everybody here with access to the STO. My personal assistant had the last polygraph appointment. She has..." He hesitated. "...reason to be unhappy with the government. But she passed. There are still a few people in Washington we have to check out. Has to have come from there, we're thinking. Maybe a military base."

"Homestead?"

A pause. "I can't say."

Rhyme asked, "Who was in charge of the internal investigation?"

"My administrations director, Spencer Boston." A pause, as he regarded Rhyme's piercing gaze, then looked down briefly. "He's not a suspect. How could he be? What does he have to gain? Besides, he passed the test."

Sachs: "Who is he exactly? What's his background?"

"Spencer's former military, decorated, former CIA—mostly active in Central America. They called him the 'regime change expert.'"

Sellitto looked at Rhyme. "Remember why

Robert Moreno turned anti-American? The U.S. invasion of Panama. His best friend was killed."

Rhyme didn't respond but, his mind's eye scanning the evidence charts, asked the NIOS director, "So this Boston would have training in beating polygraphs."

"I suppose technically. But—"

"Does he drink tea? And use Splenda? Oh, and does he have a cheap blue suit that's a shade lighter than tasteful?"

Metzger stared. After a moment: "He drinks herbal tea because of his ulcers—"

"Ah, stomach problems." Rhyme glanced at Sachs. She nodded in return.

"With some kind of sweetener, never sugar."

"And his suits?"

Metzger sighed. "He shops at Sears. And, yes, for some reason he likes this weird shade of blue. I never understood that."

CHAPTER 86

N ICE HOUSE," RON PULASKI SAID.
"Is." Sachs was looking around, a little distracted.

"So this is what? Glen Cove?"

"Or Oyster Bay. They kind of run together."

The North Shore of Long Island was a patchwork of small communities, hillier and more tree-filled than the South. Sachs didn't know the area well. She'd been here on a case involving a Chinese snakehead—a human trafficker—a few years ago. And before that she remembered a police pursuit along some of the winding roads. The chase hadn't lasted long; sixteen-year-old Amelia had easily evaded the Nassau County police, after they'd broken up an illegal drag race near Garden City (she had won, beating a Dodge hands down).

"You nervous?" Pulaski asked.

"Yeah. Always before a take-down. Always."

Amelia Sachs felt if you weren't on edge at a time like that, something was wrong.

On the other hand, ever since the arrest was blessed by Lon Sellitto and, above him, Captain Myers, Sachs hadn't once worried her flesh, picked at a nail or—this was odd—felt a throb from her hip or knee.

They were dressed quasi-tactically in body armor and black caps but wore just their sidearms.

They were now approaching Spencer Boston's residence.

An hour ago Shreve Metzger and Rhyme had come up with a plan for the take-down. Metzger had told his Administrations Director Boston that there were going to be hearings about the Moreno STO screwup. He wanted to use a private residence to meet with the NIOS lawyers; could they use Boston's house and could he send his family off for the day?

Boston had agreed and headed up here immediately.

As Sachs and Pulaski approached the large Colonial they paused, looking around the trim lawns, surrounding woods, molded shrubbery and gardens lovingly, almost compulsively, tended.

The young officer was breathing even more rapidly now.

You nervous?...

Sachs noted that he was absently rubbing a scar on his forehead. It was the legacy of a blow delivered by a perp on the first case they'd worked together, a few years ago. The head injury had been severe and he'd nearly given up policing altogether because of the incident—which would have devastated him; policing was a core part of his psyche and bound him closely to his twin brother, also a cop. But thanks largely to the encouragement and example of Lincoln Rhyme he'd gone through extensive rehab and decided to remain on the force.

But the injury had been bad and Sachs knew that the post-traumatic stress continued to snipe.

Can I handle it? Will I fold under pressure?

She knew the double-tap answers to those questions were, in staccato order, yes and no. She smiled. "Let's go bust a bad guy."

"Deal."

They made their way quickly to the door, bracketing it, hands near but not touching their weapons.

She nodded.

Pulaski rapped. "NYPD. Open the door!"

Sounds from inside.

"What?" came the voice. "Who is that?"

The young officer persisted. "NYPD! Open the door or we'll enter."

Again from inside: "Jesus."

A moment passed. Plenty long enough for Boston to grab a pistol. Though their calculations were that he would not do so.

The red wooden door opened and the distinguished, gray-haired man peered out through the screen. He absently stroked the most prominent crease in his dry, creased face.

"Let me see your hands, Mr. Boston."

He lifted them, sighing. "That's why Shreve called me. There's no meeting, is there?"

Sachs and Pulaski pushed inside and she closed the door.

The man brushed a hand through his luxuriant hair then remembered he should be keeping them in view. He stepped back, making clear he was no threat.

"Are you alone?" she asked. "Your family?"

"I'm alone."

Sachs did a fast sweep of the house while Pulaski stayed with the whistleblower.

When she returned Boston said, "What's this all about?" He tried to be indignant but it wasn't working. He knew why they were here.

"Leaking the STO to the DA's Office. We checked flight records. You were on vacation in Maine on the eleventh of May but you flew back to New York in the morning. You went to the Java Hut with your iBook. Uploaded the scan of the kill order to the DA. And flew back that afternoon."

She added details about tracing the email, the tea and Splenda and the blue suit. Then: "Why? Why did you leak it?"

The man sat back on the couch. He slowly reached into his pocket, extracted and clumsily ripped open a pack of antacid tablets. He chewed them.

Reminiscent of her Advil.

Sachs sat across from him: Pulaski walked to the windows and looked out over the manicured lawn.

Boston was frowning. "If I'm going to be prosecuted it'll be under the Espionage Act. That's federal. You're state. Why did *you* come?"

"There are state law implications," she answered, intentionally vague. "Now tell me. Why'd you leak the STO kill order? Because you thought it was the moral thing to do, telling the world that your organization was killing U.S. citizens?"

He gave a laugh that was untidy with bitterness. "Do you think anybody really cares about that? It didn't hurt Obama to take out al-Awlaki? *Everybody* thinks it's the right thing to do—everybody except your prosecutor."

"And?" she asked.

He rested his face in his hands for a moment. "You're young. Both of you. You wouldn't understand."

"Tell me," Sachs persisted.

Boston looked up with burning eyes. "I've been at NIOS from the beginning, from the day it was formed. I was army intelligence, I was CIA. I was on the ground running assets when Shreve Metzger was having keg parties in Cambridge and New Haven. I was key in our resisting the Pink Revolution—the socialists in the nineties and oughts. Hugo Chávez in Venezuela, Lula in Brazil, Néstor Kirchner in Argentina, Vázquez in Uruguay, Evo Morales in Bolivia." He regarded Sachs coldly. "Do you even know who those people are?"

He didn't seem to expect an answer. "I orchestrated two regime changes in Central America and one in South. Drinking in shitty bars, bribing journalists, sucking up to mid-level politicos in Caracas and BA. Going to the funerals when my assets got accidentally on purpose killed in a hit-and-run, and nobody could know what a hero they'd been. Begging Washington for money, cutting deals with the boys from London and Madrid and Tokyo...And when it came time for a new director at NIOS, who'd they pick? Shreve Metzger, a fucking kid with a bad temper. It should've been *me*. I've earned it! I deserve it!"

"So when you realized Shreve had made the mistake with Moreno you decided to use that to bring him down. You leaked the kill order and the intel. You expected you'd be his replacement."

He muttered angrily, "I could run the place a hundred times better than he could."

Pulaski asked, "How'd you beat the polygraph?"

"Oh, that's tradecraft one-oh-one. See! That's my point. This business isn't about pushing buttons and playing computer games." He sat back. "Oh, hell, just arrest me and have done with it."

CHAPTER 87

S CANNING," THE VOICE HISSED through an earbud. "No transmissions, no signals."

The whispering probably wasn't necessary. The men were in a wooded area well out of earshot of anyone in Spencer Boston's house.

"Roger that," Jacob Swann acknowledged, thinking the phrase sounded somewhat ridiculous.

No transmissions, no signals. This was good news. If there had been other officers around to back up Boston's arrest, the chatter would have shown up on Bartlett's scanner. Bartlett, a mercenary, was as dull as a slug but he knew his equipment and could find a microwave or radio transmission inside a lead box.

"Any visuals?"

"No, they came alone. The woman detective—Sachs—and the uniform with her."

Made sense, Swann reflected, only these two and no backup. Boston was a whistleblower and possibly a traitor but he wasn't dangerous in the resisting-arrest sense. He'd kill you with a Hellfire in Yemen or ruin your political career by planting rumors that you were gay in an ardently Catholic South American country. But he probably didn't even own a gun; two NYPD cops would be plenty to bring him in.

Swann moved in closer, through the woods to the side of Boston's house, keeping clear of the windows.

He now checked his Glock, which was mounted with a suppressor, and the extra mags, inverted, in his left cargo pants pocket. On his utility belt, of course, his Kai Shun chef's knife. He pulled down his black Nomex tactical face mask.

Nearby a commercial tree service was chipping a tree they'd just taken down. The roar and grind were loud. Jacob Swann was grateful for the noise. It would cover the sound of the assault; while he and his team had sound suppressors, it wasn't inconceivable that one of the cops inside might get off a shot before they died. He transmitted, "Advise."

"Position," Bartlett said, and the same message was delivered a moment later by the other member of the team, a broad-shouldered Asian American named Xu, whose only substantive comment since they'd rendezvoused had been to correct Jacob Swann's pronunciation of his name.

Xu.

"Like *Shoe*."

I'd change it, thought Swann.

"Scan, interior," Swann said to Bartlett.

A moment later: "Have three souls, all ground floor. Right of the front door, six to eight feet, sitting. Right of the front door, four to five feet, sitting. Left of the front door, four to five feet, standing." Their electronic expert was scanning the house with an infrared sensor and SAR.

Swann asked, "Any visuals, surrounding premises?"

"Negative," transmitted the Shoe. The houses on either side of Boston's were out of range of the infrared but they were dark and the garage doors were closed. This was afternoon in suburbia. Children in school, moms and dads at work or shopping.

Another convenient roar of the chipper.

"Move in," Swann commanded.

The others acknowledged.

Bartlett and Swann were going through the front door. The Shoe, the rear. The approach would be a dynamic entry, shoot on sight. This time Amelia Sachs would have to die, not just join Rhyme in the world of paralysis. If she'd cooperated earlier at least she would have survived.

Leaving his backpack in the bushes, Jacob Swann stepped onto the lawn, crouching. Bartlett was twenty feet away, closer to the house. His mask was down too. A nod.

Fifty feet from the house, then forty.

Scanning the windows. But the attack team was to the side and couldn't be seen from where Bartlett had assured him the occupants were sitting and standing.

Thirty feet.

Looking around the lawn, the houses.

Nobody.

Good, good.

Twenty-five feet.

He would—

And then the hurricane hit.

A massive downwash of breathtaking air slammed into him.

What, what, *what*?

The NYPD chopper swept in fast, dropping, cantilevering to a stop over the front yard.

Swann and Bartlett froze as the lithe aircraft spun broadside and two Emergency Service officers trained H&K automatic weapons on the men.

The wood chipper. Oh, hell. The police had ordered it—to obscure the sound of the helicopter.

Goddamn.

A setup. They knew all along wc were coming.

CHAPTER 88

"DROP YOUR WEAPONS! Lie facedown. Or we *will* fire."

The voice was clattering from a speaker on the helicopter. Or maybe from somewhere on the ground. Hard to tell.

Loud. And no nonsense. The commander meant what he was saying.

Swann noticed that Bartlett complied at once, flinging his own H&K away, lifting his hands and practically falling to the ground. Jacob Swann looked past him and saw that the upstairs window of the house behind Boston's was open and a sniper was aiming into the backyard. He would have the Shoe covered.

The voice from on high: "You, on your feet. Drop your weapon and lie facedown! Do it now!"

A debate.

Swann looked at the house.

He tossed his gun to the ground and got down

on his belly, smelling the piquant scent of grass. It reminded him of Chartreuse, the strident liquor that he used in one of his few desserts—peaches in Chartreuse jelly, part of the tenth, and last, course on *Titanic*'s first-class menu. As the helicopter lowered he gripped the key fob he'd been holding. He pressed the left button once and then the right for three seconds. And closed his eyes.

The explosive in the backpack, which he'd hidden nearby, detonated with more force than he'd expected. It was a diversionary charge only—for eventualities like this, to draw an enemy's attention, get them to turn away momentarily. But this charge, right at the edge of the trees, exploded in a massive fireball, pitching the helicopter sideways a foot or two. The craft wasn't damaged and the pilot controlled it immediately but it had bobbled enough that the gunmen lost their targets.

Jacob Swann was on his feet in an instant, leaping over the prone Bartlett and charging for the house, a smoke grenade in his hand. He flung the compact cylinder through the front window, shattered by the backpack bomb, and leapt through the frame after it.

INSIDE, SWANN SLAMMED into a coffee table, scattering candy bowls, statuettes and framed pictures, and he rolled onto the floor.

The explosion had surprised Boston, Sachs and the other cop and when the smoke grenade bounced into the room they'd scrabbled away for cover, apparently expecting not covering haze but another bang.

Hostages. That was all Swann could think of to buy some time, negotiate his way out. Boston, coughing fiercely, was the first to see him. The man made a halfhearted lunge for his attacker but Jacob Swann drove a fist into the man's throat and doubled him over.

"Amelia," came a voice from somewhere on the other side of the spewing grenade. The young cop's. "Where is he?"

Swann then saw the woman detective, on her side, coughing and squinting as she gazed around her. A Glock was in her hand. Swann went for it— he hadn't had time to collect his pistol outside. He recalled her limping and the occasional wince, recalled too her references to the health problems he'd learned about when he'd hacked her phone. He now saw a frown of pain cross her beautiful face as she tried to rise and draw a target on him. The delay was enough for him to leap forward, tackling her before she fired.

"Amelia!" came the voice from the distance once more.

As they grappled fiercely—she was stronger than she looked—she shouted, "Shut up, Ron! Don't say anything more!"

She was protecting him. When Jacob Swann got her gun he'd fire in the direction of the shouts.

Slamming a fist into his ear, with surprising and painful force, she spat the chemical smoke residue from her mouth and pitched hard into him. Swann hit her in the side and tried to grip her throat but she shoved his arm away and delivered another blow to the side of his head. "Get out, Ron. Go for help. You can't do anything here!"

"I'll get backup." Running footsteps, exiting. A door in the back crashed open.

Swann elbowed her, aiming for the belly, but she twisted just in time to avoid a debilitating blow to the solar plexus. Sachs drove a fist into his side, near his kidney, which sent a burst of pain up to his teeth. Still gripping the wrist of her gun hand, he slugged her hard in the face with his left fist. She grunted and winced.

Thinking again of her injury, he slammed a knee into hers, and she gave a gasping cry. The pain seemed to be intense. It loosened her guard for a moment and his strong hand clawed farther toward the gun in her hand. He was almost to it. Another few inches.

He kicked her joint again. This time she barked a high scream and her grip on the gun slackened even more. Jacob Swann lunged for the weapon.

He touched the grip of the Glock—just as she flung her hand backward, releasing her hold. The pistol spiraled away, invisible in the smoke.

Shit...

Tugging at each other's clothing, trading glancing blows and direct strikes, rolling on the floor, they fought desperately. Smelling sweat, smoke, a hint of perfume. He tried to force Sachs to her feet, which, with her damaged knee, would give him the advantage. But she knew it would be all over then and kept the fight on the ground, grappling and striking.

He heard voices from outside, calling for him to come out. The tactical teams wouldn't risk an entry with the smoke and their star detective inside, invisible through the smoke. Also, for all they knew he'd had an Uzi or MAC-10 hidden on him and would spray the first dozen officers through the door with automatic fire.

Swann and Sachs, sweating, exhausted, coughing.

He leaned toward her as if to bite; when she backed away fast he reversed direction and broke her grip. He rolled away and crouched, facing her. Sachs was in more pain and more winded. She was kneeling on the ground, cradling the joint. Tears filled her eyes from the ache and from the fumes. Her form was ghostly.

But he had to get the gun. Now. Where was it? Nearby, it had to be. But as he moved forward she glared at him, feral, hands turning from fists to claws and back again. She rose to her feet.

She froze and, wincing, reached for her hip, which like her knee also seemed a source of agony.

Now! She's in pain, distracted. Now, her throat!

Swann leapt forward and swung his left hand, open, toward the soft pale flesh of her neck.

And then pain like nothing he'd felt in years exploded up the arm he swung, pain from hand to shoulder.

He jerked back fast, staring at the stripes of blood cascading through his fingers, staring at the glint of steel in her hand, staring at her calm eyes.

What...what?

She held a switchblade knife firmly in front of her. He realized she hadn't been gripping her hip out of pain, but had been fishing for the weapon and clicking it open. She hadn't stabbed him; he'd done it himself—with his furious blow aimed at her throat he'd driven the flesh of his open hand into the sharp blade.

My little butcher man . . .

Sachs backed away, crouching in a street-fighter knife-fight pose.

Swann assessed the damage. The blade had cut to bone between his thumb and index finger. It hurt like hell but the wound was essentially superficial. The tendons were intact.

He quickly drew the Kai Shun and went into a stance similar to hers. There was, however, no real contest. He had killed two dozen people with a blade. She was probably a great shot, but this wasn't her primary weapon. Swann eased forward, his knife edge-up as if he were going to gut a hanging deer carcass.

Feeling comfort in the handle of the Kai Shun, the weight, the dull gleam, the hammered blade.

He started for her fast, aiming low, imagining the slice, belly to breastbone . . .

But she wasn't leaping back or turning and fleeing, as he'd anticipated. She stood her ground. Her weapon too—Italian, he believed—was positioned edge-up. Her eyes flicked confidently among the blade, his eyes and various targets on his body.

He stopped, backed up a few feet and regrouped, flicking hot blood from his left hand. Then moving in fast once more, he feinted with a lunge but she anticipated that and easily avoided the Kai Shun, swinging the switchblade fast and nearly taking skin from his cheek. She knew what she was doing, and—more troubling—there wasn't an iota of uncertainty in her eyes, though evidence of the pain was clear.

Make her work her leg. That's her weakness.

He lunged again and again, not actually trying to stab or slash but driving her back, forcing her to shift her weight, wear down the joints.

And then she made a mistake.

Sachs stepped back a few yards, turned the knife around, gripping the blade. She prepared to throw it.

"Drop it," she called, coughing frantically, wiping tears with her other hand. "Get down on the floor."

Swann eyed her cautiously through the smoke, watching the weapon closely. Throwing knives is a very difficult skill to master and works only when there's good visibility and you have a properly balanced weapon—and you've practiced hundreds of hours. And even striking the target directly usually results in a minor wound. Despite the movies, Jacob Swann doubted that anybody had ever died from being struck by a thrown knife. Blade killing works only by slashing important blood vessels, and even then death takes time.

"Do it now!" she shouted. "On the ground."

Still, a flying blade can distract and a lucky hit

can hurt like hell and possibly take out an eye. So, as she jockeyed to get the distance right, Jacob Swann kept moving side to side and crouching further to make himself a small, evasive target.

"I'm not going to tell you again."

A pause. No flicker in her eyes.

She flung the switchblade.

He squinted and ducked.

But the throw was wide. The knife hit a china cabinet two feet from Swann and shattered a small pane. A plate inside, on a display rack, fell and broke. He was instantly back in stance, but— another mistake—she didn't follow through.

He relaxed and turned back to face her, as she stood leaning forward, arms at her sides, breathing hard, coughing.

She was his now. He'd get the Glock, negotiate some kind of escape. They could use the chopper for a ride out, of course.

He whispered, "Okay, what you're going to do is—"

He felt the muzzle of a pistol pressing against his temple. His eyes shifted to the side.

The young officer, Ron apparently, had returned. No, no...Swann understood. He'd never left at all. He'd been making his way through the smoke, carefully seeking a target.

She'd never been planning to skewer him with

the switchblade at all. She was just buying time and talking, to guide the cop here through the smoke. She'd never intended Ron to leave. Her words earlier meant just the opposite and he'd understood completely.

"Now," the young man said ominously. "Drop it." Swann knew he was fully prepared to send a bullet into his brain.

He looked for a place where the Kai Shun wouldn't get dented or chipped. He tossed it carefully onto the couch.

Sachs eased forward, still wincing, and retrieved it. She noted the blade with some appreciation. The young cop cuffed Swann, and Sachs strode forward, gripped the Nomex hood and yanked it off him.

CHAPTER 89

THE DISABLED-ACCESSIBLE VAN wove through the emergency vehicles and parked at the curb near Spencer Boston's house. Lincoln Rhyme had been at the staging area a few blocks away. Given his inability to wield a weapon, as he'd learned in the Bahamas, Rhyme thought it best to remain clear of the potential battlefield.

Which, of course, Thom would have insisted on anyway.

Old mother hen.

In a few minutes he was freed from the vehicle and he wheeled his new chair, which he quite liked, up to Amelia Sachs.

Rhyme regarded her with some scrutiny. She was in pain, though trying to cover. But her discomfort was obvious to him.

"Where's Ron?"

"Walking the grid in the house."

Rhyme grimaced as he looked at the smoldering

trees and boxwood and the smoke trickling out of the expensive Colonial. Fire department fans had largely exhausted the worst of the fumes. "Didn't anticipate a diversionary charge, Sachs. Sorry."

He was furious with himself for not considering it. He should have known Unsub 516 would try something like that.

Sachs said only, "Still, you came up with a good plan, Rhyme."

"Well, had the desired result," he conceded with some, but not too much, modesty.

The criminalist had never suspected Spencer Boston of anything more than leaking the STO order. True, as Sachs had pointed out, both Boston and Moreno had a Panama connection. But even if Boston *had* been involved in the invasion, Moreno was just a boy then. They couldn't have known each other. No, Panama was just a coincidence.

But Rhyme had decided that Metzger's administrations director would make excellent bait, because whoever *was* behind the plot—the unsub's boss—would want to kill the whistleblower too.

This was the help he'd enlisted Shreve Metzger for. Ever since he'd learned of the investigation last weekend, Metzger had been contacting everyone involved in the STO drone project and telling them to stonewall and dump evidence. These encrypted texts, emails and phone calls were sent to people within NIOS but also to private contractors, military personnel and Washington officials. This was how Unsub 516's boss had known so much about the case. Metzger had been feeding everyone virtually real-time intelligence about what was going on, so passionate was he about keeping the STO program going. The boss, in turn, briefed the unsub.

But who exactly was that person?

At Rhyme's insistence, Metzger had called these same people an hour ago and told them the whistleblower had been identified as Spencer Boston and they should destroy any evidence linking them to the man.

Rhyme suspected that the mastermind behind the plot to kill Moreno's guard would order Unsub 516 to show up in Glen Cove to eliminate Boston.

So the administrations director, along with Sachs and Pulaski, waited inside. NYPD and Nassau County tactical forces took up hidden positions nearby, a helicopter from Emergency Service included. The noisy wood chipper, to cover up the sound of the aircraft, had been Ron Pulaski's idea.

The kid was on a roll.

Rhyme now looked over Unsub 516, sitting shackled and cuffed on the front lawn of Boston's house, about thirty feet away. His hand was bandaged but the wound didn't seem to be too serious.

The compact man gazed back at the authorities placidly, then turned his full attention to what seemed to be an herb garden nearby.

Rhyme said to Sachs, "Wonder how much work it'll be to find out who he's working for. I don't suppose he'll be very cooperative in naming the mastermind."

"He doesn't need to be," Sachs said. "I *know* who he works for."

"You do?" Rhyme asked.

"Harry Walker. At Walker Defense Systems."

The criminalist laughed. "How do you know that?"

She nodded at the unsub. "When I went out to the company to look for the airstrip? He's the one who came to get me in the waiting room and took me to see Walker. By the way, he was really a flirt."

CHAPTER 90

H IS NAME WAS JACOB SWANN, the security director for Walker Defense Systems.

Swann was former military but had been drummed out—if that was what they still called it—for excessive interrogation of suspects in Iraq. Not waterboarding but removing skin from several insurgents. Some other body parts had been removed too. "Expertly and slowly," the report said.

Further datamining revealed that he lived alone in Brooklyn, bought expensive kitchen items and took himself to fine restaurants frequently. He'd had two emergency room visits in the last year. One was for a gunshot wound, which he claimed was inflicted by an unseen hunter when he was out after some venison. The second was for a bad cut on his finger, which he attributed to a knife slipping off a Vidalia onion when he was preparing a dish.

The first would have been a lie, the second probably true, Rhyme guessed, considering what they now knew was Swann's hobby.

Combine those ingredients with caviar and vanilla and you have a real expensive dish that's served at the Patchwork Goose...

A car pulled up near the police tape, an older-model Honda in need of some bodywork.

Nance Laurel, in her white blouse and navy suit, cut the same as her gray one, climbed out. She was rubbing her cheek and Rhyme wondered if she'd just applied more makeup. The assistant district attorney approached and asked if Sachs was all right.

"Fine. Little tussle. But he got the worst of it." A nod at Swann. "He's been read his rights. He hasn't asked for a lawyer but he's not being cooperative."

"We'll see about that," Laurel said. "Let's talk to him. I may need your help, Lincoln. We'll bring him over here."

"Not necessary." He glanced down at the Merits wheelchair. "They tell me it's particularly good on rough terrain. Let's find out."

Without a hesitation the chair sped over the lawn straight to the perp.

Nance Laurel and Sachs joined him. The ADA looked down at Swann. "My name is—"

"I know who you are."

One of her trademarked pauses. "Now, Jacob, we know Harry Walker's behind this. He had you plant fake intelligence to trick NIOS into assassinating Robert Moreno as a cover so you could kill his guard, Simon Flores, who was blackmailing Walker. You were at the South Cove Inn when it happened, waiting for the drone strike. Just afterward, before the rescue workers got there, you broke into suite twelve hundred and stabbed Flores and Eduardo de la Rua to death. Then you went to Flores's lawyer's office in Nassau and tortured and killed him, stole the documents Flores had left for safekeeping—the documents Walker was worried would be made public.

"After my investigation started, Metzger gave Walker updates and names—to destroy evidence and be on guard against the police running the case. But Walker told you to do more than that—to eliminate witnesses and the investigators. You killed Annette Bodel, Lydia Foster and Moreno's driver, Vlad Nikolov—" Laurel glanced toward Sachs and Rhyme. "Officers in Queens found his body in the basement of his house."

Swann merely looked down at his bandaged hand and said nothing.

The prosecutor continued, "You also arranged with some associates in Nassau to kill Captain Rhyme and others working with him down there...And then there was this." She offered a nod around the marred suburban landscape, resembling a combat zone.

The depth of this information, laid out so unemotionally by Nance Laurel, must have taken Swann by surprise but he hesitated only a moment then said in a calm voice, "First of all, as for this incident..." He nodded at Boston's house. "Regarding the weapons, all three of us have Class Three federal firearms licenses and concealed-carry permits valid in the state of New York. Now, in my job at Walker Defense, I'm involved in national security. We came here on a tip that Spencer Boston represented a dangerous security leak. My associates and I were simply going to check that out and discuss the matter with him. Next thing I know, tactical troops were threatening us. They claimed they were NYPD but how was I supposed to know? Not a single person offered me their identification."

Amelia Sachs actually laughed at this.

Laurel asked, "Do you expect me to believe that?"

"Ah, the important question, Ms. Laurel, is will a *jury* believe it? And I suspect they might. And as for those other crimes you mentioned? All speculation. I guarantee you don't have anything on me."

The prosecutor looked at Rhyme, who wheeled up closer. He realized that Swann was intensely studying his insensate legs and left arm. He was truly curious but Rhyme had no idea what he was thinking or what the purpose for the examination was.

The criminalist, in turn, looked the suspect up and down and smiled as he often did at the arrogance of perps. "Don't have anything, don't have anything." Musing thoughtfully. "Oh, I think maybe we do, Jacob. Now, I don't care much for motives, but we have a couple of good ones here, I have to admit. You killed Lydia Foster—and wanted to kill Moreno's driver—because you thought the subject would come up of why Simon Flores wasn't accompanying Moreno on the trip. And that would make *us* wonder why he wasn't here too. And your motive for killing Annette Bodel was that she could place you at the scene in the Bahamas when the shooting happened."

Swann gave a blink but recovered quickly and simply cocked his head in curiosity.

Rhyme paid him no mind and addressed the sky. "Now, for more *objective* evidence: We have a short brown hair from the Lydia Foster crime scene." He glanced at Swann's scalp. "We can do a mandatory DNA swab and I'm sure it will match. Oh, and we're still working on tracing that silver necklace you bought Annette Bodel—to attract the barracuda to hide the fact you'd tortured and killed her. I'm sure somebody will have seen you buy it."

This opened Swann's mouth slightly. A tongue touched the corner of his lips.

"And we found some allspice and hot sauce on the clothing of Eduardo de la Rua. I thought that was from his breakfast the morning of May ninth. But knowing your affinity for the culinary arts, I wonder if you'd been cooking the night before you killed him. Maybe you made dinner for Annette. It'll be interesting to examine your suitcase and clothing and see if there's associated trace.

"And speaking of food: We found some trace in two locations in New York: combine them and apparently you end up with a very interesting dish involving artichoke, licorice, fish roe and vanilla. Did you happen to see the recent recipe in the *New York Times*? I understand the Patchwork Goose is quite the restaurant. And you should know that I have an expert witness to testify about the food."

Rhyme knew Thom would love being thus described.

Swann was completely silent now. In fact, he seemed numb.

"Now, we're looking into whether you had access to a particular type of military IED, which was used at the Java Hut. And saltwater-laced sand was found both there and at Annette Bodel's apartment in Nassau. We'll subpoena your clothes and shoes and see if you happen to have any grains left on them. Your washing machine too. Hm, do we *have* anything else?"

Sachs said, "The two-stroke oil trace."

"Ah, yes, thank you, Sachs. You left some two-stroke oil trace at one of the scenes and I'm sure we'll find the same fuel mixture in your office at Walker Defense or at Homestead Air Reserve Base, if you were there before or after the attack on May 9. Thanks particularly for *that* find, by the way—the oil; that's how we figured out that NIOS was using drones, not flesh-and-blood snipers. Excuse me, UAVs.

"But, I digress. Now, that interesting blade of yours..." Rhyme had seen the evidence bag containing the Japanese chef's knife. "We'll match its tool mark profile with wounds on the bodies of Lydia Foster, de la Rua, Flores and the lawyer in the Bahamas. Oh, and the limo driver too.

"More? Okay. We're datamining your credit card, ATM withdrawals and mobile phone usage." He took a breath. "And we're subpoenaing the Walker Defense Technical Services and Support operation to see whom they've been datamining and spying on. Now, that pretty much wraps up *my* formal presentation. Prosecutor Laurel?"

A trademark pause, which by now Rhyme found

rather charming. She then said in an at-attention tone, "Do you see where we're going with this, Jacob? We need you to testify against Harry Walker. If you do that we'll work something out."

"What does that mean, 'work something out'? How many years?"

"Obviously I can't say for certain but probably we're looking at thirty."

"Not much in it for me, then, is there?" he asked, gazing back at her coolly.

She replied, "The alternative is I don't fight extradition to the Bahamas. And you spend the rest of your life in one of their prisons."

That seemed to bring Swann up short. Still he remained silent.

This wasn't, technically, Rhyme's concern. But he felt he should contribute. "And who knows, Jacob?" Rhyme said, an amused tone in his voice. "Maybe ADA Laurel here might see if you could get a spot in the kitchen in whatever facility you're sent to." He shrugged. "Just a thought."

Laurel nodded. "I'll do what I can."

Swann looked over the smoke-damaged house of Spencer Boston. Then turned back. "When do you want to talk?"

Nance's response was to dig into her pocketbook and extract a battered tape recorder.

CHAPTER 91

B USINESS ISN'T WHAT IT USED TO BE, the arms business, I mean," Swann was telling them. "Walker Defense was having problems, bad problems, with the wars winding down."

Sachs said to Rhyme, "That's right. A lot of the factory facilities were shuttered when I was there."

"Yes, ma'am. Lost sixty percent of our revenue and the company was in the red. Mr. Walker was used to a nice lifestyle. A couple of his ex-wives were too. Along with his present one and she was thirty years younger than him. Without a good income she might not've been too inclined to hang around."

"Was it his Aston Martin in the lot?" Sachs asked.

"Yes. One of his. He's got three."

"Oh. Well. Three."

"But it was more than that. He believed—I believed too—that the company was doing good work, good for the country. The rifle system for the drone, for instance. And that was just one of them. It was important work. We needed to keep the company afloat."

Swann continued, "Orders weren't coming from the U.S. like they used to so Mr. Walker ramped up business in other countries. But there's a huge surplus of arms out there. Not much demand. So he created some."

Nance Laurel asked, "By bribing officers and defense ministers in the armed services in Latin America, right?"

"Exactly. Africa and the Balkans too. Middle East some but you've got to be careful there. Don't want to be found out selling weapons to any insurgents who take out U.S. soldiers. Okay, Simon Flores, Moreno's guard, was with the Brazilian army. Mr. Walker's Latin American operation is based in São Paulo and so Flores was real aware of the bribes. When he left the army he took plenty of proof with him—enough to put Mr. Walker away for the rest of his life. Flores started blackmailing him.

"Flores had met Moreno and liked the work he was doing. Moreno hired him to be his guard. I guess Flores figured it'd be a good cover. He could travel around with Moreno throughout the

Caribbean, buy property, invest the cash, hit the offshore banks—and still get to play soldier as a bodyguard." A glance toward Rhyme. "And, yeah, you got it right. Flores didn't think it was smart to come to our home turf on May first. And Mr. Walker was worried that the subject would come up."

Sachs asked, "And you faked the intel about Moreno?"

"No, it wasn't faked. But *selective*, I guess you could say. I emphasized the fertilizer bomb materials. Then NIOS issued the STO, effective May ninth, and I took a trip down to Nassau to wait for the fireworks. Afterward, we were sure the whole thing would go away but then we heard about your case against Metzger and Barry Shales. Mr. Walker had me do what I could to stop it from going forward. Oh, Metzger didn't know what I was up to, by the way. Yeah, he wanted Walker and all his other suppliers to lose evidence and erase emails but that was it."

"Okay, that's enough to get us started," Laurel said. She nodded to Amelia Sachs. "He can go to detention now."

Sachs had a question first, though. "At Walker, why did you come to get me in the lobby? It was a risk. I might've caught a glimpse of you when you were tailing me."

"A risk, sure." Swann gave a shrug. "But you were good. You derailed me a couple of times. I wanted to see you up close. See if you had any liabilities." He nodded at her knee. "Which I found out. If you hadn't been one step ahead of me in Boston's house, it might've turned out different."

Sachs rounded up a couple of uniforms from the NYPD and they helped Swann to his feet and started to direct him to a blue-and-white transport. He paused and turned back. "Oh, one thing. In my house? The basement?"

Sachs nodded.

"You'll find somebody there. A woman. Her name's Carol Fiori. A British tourist."

"What?" Sachs blinked. Laurel took a moment to process this.

"It's a long story but, anyway, she's in the basement."

"You...she's in your basement. Dead? Injured?"

"No, no, no. She's fine. Probably bored. She's handcuffed down there."

"What did you do, rape her?" Laurel asked.

Swann seemed insulted. "Of *course* not. I made dinner for her is what I did. Asparagus, potatoes Anna and my own version of Veronique—grass-fed veal with grapes and beurre blanc. I have the meat flown in from a special farm in Montana.

Best in the world. She didn't eat any. I didn't think she would. But I gave it a shot." He shrugged.

"What were you going to do with her?" Sachs asked.

"I didn't really know," Swann said. "I didn't know."

CHAPTER 92

THE SITE WAS SECURE, Shreve Metzger had been told, and he piloted his government car from the staging area a few blocks away through the trim streets to the home of his administrations director.

His friend.

His Judas.

Metzger was astonished to see that the man's pleasant suburban house, where he'd had dinner two weeks ago, looked like some of the battlefield locales he remembered from Iraq, except for the lush grass and the Lexuses and Mercs parked on the street nearby. Trees smoldered and smoke dribbled skyward from Boston's windows. The smell would be in the walls for years, even after painting. And forget the furniture and clothing.

Metzger's own brand of Smoke filled him. He thought again for the hundredth time that day: How could you have done this, Spencer?

As with anybody who had affronted him—from rude coffee vendor to someone like this traitor—Metzger felt a mousetrap snap, a nearly overwhelming urge to grab them, shatter their bones, scream, draw blood. Utterly destroy.

But then, thinking that Boston's life as he'd lived it would be over with, Metzger decided that was punishment enough. The Smoke within him faded.

A good sign, Dr. Fischer?

Probably it was. But would the serenity last? Maybe, maybe not. Why did all the important battles have to be lifetime battles? Weight, anger, love...

He flashed an ID at a couple of local uniforms and ducked under the tape, walking toward Lincoln Rhyme and Amelia Sachs.

He greeted them and then learned his administrations director's motive for leaking the STO. The sin arose not from conscience or ideology or money. But simply because he was passed over for the job of head of NIOS.

Metzger was stunned. For one thing, Boston was totally wrong for the senior job. For all his scrawny physique and bland eyes, Metzger was a killer. Whatever makes your own personal Smoke go away defines you.

Spencer Boston, on the other hand, was a diligent and meticulous national security professional, an organizer, a player, a dealer, a man who got things done in the hazy streets of Managua or Rio. Who didn't own a gun and wouldn't know how to use one—or have the guts to do so.

What on earth would he do with an organization like NIOS, whose sole purpose was to end lives?

But ambition doesn't grow from logic, Metzger knew.

He now nodded a tepid farewell to Rhyme and Sachs. He'd hoped to confront Spencer Boston but Sachs had explained that the administrations director had gone to be with his wife and children in Larchmont. He hadn't been officially arrested yet. There was still considerable debate as to what crime, if any, he'd committed. The charges would be federal, not state, however, so the NYPD's involvement was marginal.

Nothing more to do here.

Spencer, how could you...

He turned abruptly toward his car.

And nearly walked smack into stocky Assistant District Attorney Nance Laurel.

They both froze, inches away from each other.

He was silent. She said, "You were lucky this time."

"And what exactly does that mean?"

"Moreno's renunciation of his citizenship. That's why the case got dropped. The only reason."

Shreve Metzger wondered if she held everyone's eyes so steadily. Probably. Everyone except
lovers', he suspected. In this they were the same.
And he wondered where on earth that thought
had come from.

She continued, "How did you manage to pull it
off?"

"What?"

"Did Moreno really renounce? Were those documents from the embassy in Costa Rica legitimate?"

"Are you accusing me of obstruction?"

"You're guilty of obstruction," she said. "That's
a given. We're choosing not to pursue those
charges. I just want to know specifically about the
renunciation documents."

Meaning calls had been made from Washington
to Albany dictating that obstruction charges not be
brought. Metzger wondered if this was a farewell
present from the Wizard. Probably not. A case like
that would look bad for everybody.

"I don't really have anything more to say on that
topic, Counselor. Take it up with State."

"Who's al-Barani Rashid?"

So she had at least two entries in the STO
queue—Moreno's and Rashid's.

"I can't discuss NIOS operations with you. You
don't have a clearance."

"Is he dead?"

Metzger said nothing. He kept his hazel eyes locked easily on hers.

Laurel pressed ahead, "You're positive Rashid is guilty?"

The Smoke boiled and cracked his skin like an eggshell. He whispered harshly, "Walker used me, he used NIOS."

"You *let* yourself be used. You heard what you wanted to about Moreno and stopped asking questions."

Smoke, plumes and plumes of Smoke now. "What's wrong, Counselor? Upset that all you ended up with was a run-of-the-mill homicide? A CEO at a defense contractor orders a couple of hits? Boring. Won't make CNN the way a federal security director's going to jail would."

She didn't rise to the argument. "And Rashid? No mistakes there, you're convinced?"

Metzger couldn't help but recall that Barry Shales—and he—had nearly blown two children to oblivion in Reynosa, Mexico.

CD: Not approved…

An urge to strike Laurel swelled. Or to lash out with cruel words about her short stature, wide hips, excessive makeup, her parents' bankruptcy, her failed love life—a deduction but surely accurate. Metzger's anger had inflicted only a half dozen bruises or welts over the years; his words had hurt legions. The Smoke did that. The Smoke made you inhuman.

Just leave.

He turned.

Laurel said evenly, "And what's Rashid's crime—saying things about America *you* didn't like? Asking people to question the values and the integrity of the country?...But isn't being free to ask questions like that what America's all about?"

Metzger stopped fast, turned and snapped, "Spoken like the most simple-minded, cliché-ridden of bloggers." He reseated himself in front of her. "What is it with you? Why do you resent what we do so much?"

"Because what you do is wrong. The United States is a country of laws, not men."

"'Government' of laws," he corrected. "John Adams. It's a nice-sounding phrase. But parse it and things aren't so simple. A government of laws. Okay. Think about that: Laws require interpretation and delegations of power, down and down the line. To people like me—who make decisions on how to implement those laws."

She fired back with: "Laws don't include ignoring due process and executing citizens arbitrarily."

"There's nothing arbitrary about what I do."

"No? You kill people you *think* are going to commit an offense."

"All right, Counselor. What about a policeman on the street? He sees a perp in a dark alley with what might be a gun. It seems that he's about to shoot someone. The cop is authorized to kill, right? Where's your due process there, where's your reasonable search and seizure, where's your right to confront your accuser?"

"Ah, but Moreno *didn't* have a gun."

"And sometimes the guy in the alley only has a cell phone. But he gets shot anyway because we've chosen to give the police the right to make judgments." He gave a deep, chill laugh. "Tell me, aren't you guilty of the same thing?"

"What do you mean?" she snapped.

"What about *my* due process? What about Barry Shales's?"

She frowned.

He continued, "In making the case, did you datamine me? Or Barry? Did you get classified information from, say, the FBI? Did you somehow 'accidentally' happen to get your hands on NSA intercepts?"

An awkward hesitation. Was she blushing beneath the white mask? "Every bit of evidence I present at trial can pass Fourth Amendment scrutiny."

Metzger smiled. "I'm not talking about trial. I'm talking about unwarranted gathering of information as part of an investigation."

Laurel blinked. She said nothing.

He whispered, "You see? We both interpret, we judge, we make decisions. We live in a gray world."

"You want another quotation, Shreve? Blackstone: 'Better that ten guilty persons escape than that one innocent suffer.' That's what *my* system does, makes sure the innocent don't end up as victims. *Yours* doesn't." She fished her keys from her battered purse. "I'm going to keep watching you."

"Then I'll look forward to seeing you in court, Counselor."

He turned and walked back to his car. He sat, calming, in the front seat, not looking back. Breathing.

Let it go.

Five minutes later he started at his phone's buzz. He noted Ruth's number on caller ID.

"Hi, there."

"Uhm, Shreve. I heard. Is it true about Spencer?"

"Afraid it is. I'll tell you more later. I don't want to talk on an open line."

"Okay. But that's not why I called. We heard from Washington."

The Wizard.

"He wanted to schedule a call with you for to-morrow afternoon."

Didn't firing squads gather at *dawn*?

"That's fine," he said. "Send me the details." He stretched. A joint popped. "Say, Ruth?"

"Yes?"

"What did he sound like?"

There was a pause. "He...It wasn't so good, I don't think, Shreve."

"Okay, Ruth. Thank you."

He disconnected and looked out over the busy crime scene at Spencer Boston's house. The sour chemical vapors still lingered, surrounding the Colonial home and the grounds.

Smoke...

So that was it. Whether Moreno was guilty or not was irrelevant; Washington now had plenty of reason to disband NIOS. Metzger had picked for his administrations director a whistleblower, and for his defense contractor a corrupt CEO who'd ordered people tortured and killed.

This was the end.

Metzger sighed and put the car in gear, thinking: Sorry, America. I did the best I could.

VII

MESSAGES

CHAPTER 93

AT NINE ON SATURDAY MORNING Lincoln Rhyme was maneuvering through the lab and dictating the evidence report to back up the Walker trial and the Swann plea agreement. He noted too his calendar, up on a big monitor.

```
Surgery Friday, May 26. Be at hospital
at 9 a.m.
NO liquor after midnight. None. Not a
drop.
```

He smiled at the second line, Thom's entry.

The town house was quiet. His aide was in the kitchen and Sachs was in her apartment in Brooklyn. She'd had basement problems and was waiting for the contractor. She would also be seeing Nance Laurel later today—getting together for drinks and dinner.

And dish on men too . . .

Rhyme was pleased the women had, against all odds, become friends. Sachs didn't have many.

The sound of a doorbell echoed and Rhyme heard Thom's footfalls making for the portal. A moment later he returned with a tall figure in a brown suit, white shirt and green tie whose hue he couldn't begin to describe.

NYPD Captain Bill Myers. Special Services Division. Whatever that might be.

Greetings were exchanged and the man fell into an effusive tone, with Myers complimenting Rhyme on the resolution of the case.

"Never in a million years would have seen that potentiality," the captain said.

"Was surprised at how it turned out."

"I'll say. Some pretty decent deductions on your part."

The word "decent" only describes that which is socially proper or non-obscene; it doesn't mean fair or good. But you can't change a jargonist so Rhyme kept mum. He realized that silence had descended as Myers took in the gas chromatograph with an intensity that circumstances—and the equipment itself—didn't warrant.

Then the captain looked around the lab and observed that they were alone.

And Rhyme knew.

"This's about Amelia, right, Bill?"

Wishing he hadn't used her first name. Neither of them was the least superstitious, except in this tradition. They never referred to each other by their givens.

"Yes. Lon talked to you? About my problems with her health issues?"

"He did."

"Let me unpack it further," Myers said. "I allowed her some time to finish this case and then have her take a medical. But I'm not going that route. I read the report of the take-down in Glen Cove, when she and Officer Pulaski collared Jacob Swann. The medic's report said that her knee gave out completely after the suspect noticed she was in pain and kicked or hit it. If Officer Pulaski hadn't been there she would have been killed. And Spencer Boston too, and maybe a few of the tactical officers as they did a dynamic entry."

Rhyme said bluntly, "She took down the perp, Bill."

"She was lucky. The report said afterward she could hardly walk."

"She's fine now."

"Is she?"

No, she wasn't. Rhyme said nothing.

"It's the elephant in the room, Lincoln. Nobody wants to talk about it but it's a problematic circumstance. She's putting herself and other people at risk. I wanted to talk to you alone about this. We huddled and conjured up a decision. I'm promoting her out of the field. She'll be a supervisor in Major Cases. And we'll rank her. Sergeant. But I know there'll be pushback from her."

Rhyme was furious. This was his Sachs the captain was talking about in the cheapest of clichés.

But he kept silent.

The captain continued, "I need you to talk her into it, Lincoln. We don't want to lose her; she's too good. But the department can't keep her if she insists on being in the field. Desking her's the only option."

And what would she do post-NYPD? Become a freelance consultant, like him? But that wasn't Sachs's way. She was a brilliant crime scene searcher, with her natural empathy and dogged nature. But she had to be a cop in the field, not lab-bound, like he was. And forensics wasn't her only specialty, of course; if she couldn't speed to a hostage taking or robbery in progress to engage the perp, she'd wither.

"Will you talk to her, Lincoln?"

Finally he said, "I'll talk to her."

"Thank you. It's for her own good, you know. We really do want the best. It'll be a three-sixty for everybody."

The captain shook his hand and departed.

Rhyme stared at the table where Sachs had recently been sitting to work the Moreno case. He believed he could smell some of the gardenia soap she favored though possibly that was just a fragrance memory.

I'll talk to her...

Then he turned his wheelchair and motored back to the whiteboards, examining them closely. Taking, as always, comfort in the elegance and intrigue of evidence.

CHAPTER 94

T HE 110-FOOT GENERAL CARGO VESSEL, chugging under diesel power, plowed through the Caribbean Sea, a massive stretch of turquoise water once home to pirates and noble men-of-war and now the highway of tourists and the playground of the One Percent.

The ship was under a Dominican flag and was thirty years old. A Detroit 16-149 powered her through the water at a respectable thirteen knots, via a single screw. Her draft was fifteen feet but she rode high today, thanks to her light cargo.

A tall mast, forward, dominated the superstructure and the bridge was spacious but cluttered, filled with secondhand navigation equipment bolted, glued or tied down. The wheel was an old-fashioned wooden ring with spokes.

Pirates...

At the helm was squat, fifty-two-year-old Enrico

Cruz. This was his real name, though most people knew him by his pseudonym, Henry Cross, a New Yorker who ran several nonprofit organizations, the largest and most prominent of which was Classrooms for the Americas.

Cruz was alone on the deck today because the man who was to have accompanied him today had been murdered by the U.S. government in suite 1200 of the South Cove Inn in the Bahamas. A single shot to the chest had guaranteed that Roberto Moreno would not make this voyage with his friend.

Cruz and Moreno had known each other for decades, ever since Moreno's best friend, Cruz's brother, José, had been murdered too—yes, that was the right word—by a U.S. helicopter gunship in Panama during the invasion in 1989.

Since that time the two men had worked together to wage a war on the nation that had descended blithely into Panama, his country, and decided that, oh, sorry, the dictator we've been supporting all these years is a bad man after all.

In their campaign against the United States these men differed only in approach. Moreno was outspoken and publicly anti-American, while Cruz remained anonymous, which allowed him to set up the attacks and get the weapons and money where they would do the most good. But together Cruz and Moreno were the backbone of the unnamed movement.

They had engineered the deaths of close to three hundred U.S. citizens and foreigners who kowtowed to Western values: businessmen, professors, politicians, drug enforcement officials, diplomats and their families.

These attacks had been isolated and small, so authorities wouldn't make any connections among them. But what was planned today was just the opposite: a massive strike against the political, social and corporate heart of America. Moreno had prepared for months—renouncing his citizenship, severing all ties to the United States, moving his money from the States to the Cayman Islands, buying a house in the wilderness of Venezuela—all in anticipation of what was about to happen.

And the weapon at the heart of the attack? The ship that now was plowing through the waves.

Cruz, as a native of Panama, had been steeped in the shipping trade for much of his early life; he knew how to drive vessels this size. Besides, nowadays one didn't really need to be more than functional at the helm. A competent crew in the engine room, GPS and autopilot on the bridge were all you needed. That was about it. The computer was doing the donkey's work of getting her to the destination. They were plodding north-by-northwest through the three-foot seas. The day was brilliantly blue, the wind persistent, the spray kaleidoscopic.

The vessel had no name, or did no longer, having been purchased through a series of real but obscure corporations, and was known only by her registration number. There had once been a file on her in a computer in the Dominican Republic, along with a corresponding entry into a registration book, regarding her vital statistics, but they had been, respectively, digitally erased and physically excised.

She was anonymous.

Cruz had thought about informally christening her before they set sail from Nassau—*Roberta*, after his friend, suitably feminized. But then decided it was better to refer to her simply as the ship. She was faded black and gray and streaked with rust. But to him, beautiful.

He now gazed at their destination, the black dot some kilometers away. The GPS tweaked the navigation system to compensate for the wind; new directions went automatically to the rudder. He felt the ship respond. He enjoyed the sensation of such a large creature obeying commands.

The door opened and a man joined him. He had black skin, a bullet-shaped head, shaved shiny, a lean body. Bobby Cheval wore jeans, a denim shirt with sleeves cut off so that it resembled a vest. He was barefoot. He glanced to the horizon. He said,

"Too bad, don't you think? He won't see it happen. That is sad."

Cheval had been Robert Moreno's main contact in the Bahamas.

"Maybe he will," Cruz said. He didn't believe this but he said it to reassure Cheval, who wore a horsehair cross around his neck. Cruz didn't accept the afterlife and knew his dear friend Robert Moreno was as dead as the heart of the government that had killed him.

Cheval, who would lead the Local Empowerment Movement in the Bahamas once it was up and running, had been instrumental in putting together today's plan.

"Any ships? Signs of surveillance?" Cruz asked.

"No, no. Nothing."

Cruz was sure no one suspected what was going to happen. They had been so very careful. His only moment of concern had been earlier in the week when that sexy redheaded policewoman had shown up in the Chambers Street office of Classrooms for the Americas to ask about Roberto's visit on May 1. He'd been surprised at first but Cruz had dealt with some truly despicable people—al-Qaeda operatives, for instance, and Shining Path rebels—and didn't get rattled easily. He'd distracted Detective Sachs with the true story of the "white guy" who'd tailed Roberto, from

NIOS undoubtedly. And distracted her further with some fiction about a mysterious private jet.

A red herring about a blue plane, he thought to himself now and smiled. Roberto would have liked that.

"Is the skiff ready?" Cruz asked Cheval.

"Yes, it is. How close will we get? Before we abandon, I mean."

"Two kilometers will be fine."

At that point the five crewmen would climb into a high-speed cigarette boat and head in the opposite direction. They'd follow the ship's progress on the computer. They could steer remotely if the GPS and autopilot broke down; there was a webcam mounted on the bridge of the vessel and they'd be able to watch the ship approach its destination.

At which the men now gazed.

The *Miami Rover* was American Petroleum Drilling and Refining's only oil rig in the area, located about thirty miles off the coast of Miami. (And named rather ironically; it didn't rove anywhere anymore and its journey here had been straight from Texas, at the meandering rate of four knots.)

Months ago Moreno and Cruz had decided that the oil company would be the target for their biggest "message" to date; American Petroleum had stolen huge tracts of land in South America and displaced thousands of people, offering them a pathetic settlement in return for their signatures on deeds of transfer that most of them couldn't read. Moreno had organized a series of protests in the United States and elsewhere over the past month or so. The protests had served two purposes. First, they'd brought to light the crimes of AmPet. But, second, they lent credence to the proposition that Moreno was all talk. Once the authorities saw that mere protesting was what he had in mind they largely lost interest in him.

And so nobody followed up on leads that might have exposed what was going to happen today: ramming the ship into the *Miami Rover*. Once it hit, the fifty-five-gallon drums containing a poignant mixture of diesel fuel, fertilizer and nitromethane would detonate, destroying the rig.

But that in itself, while a blow for the cause, wasn't enough, Moreno and Cruz had decided. Killing sixty or so workers, ruining the biggest oil rig in the Southeast? That was like that pathetic fellow who suicide-crashed his private plane into the building housing the IRS in Austin, Texas. He killed a few people. Caused some damage, snarled traffic.

And soon, back to business as usual in the Lone Star State's capital.

What would happen today was considerably worse.

After the initial explosion destroyed the rig, the ship would sink fast. In the stern was a second bomb that would descend to the seafloor near the wellhead. A depth-gauge detonator would set off another explosion, which would destroy both the well's ram and annular blowout preventers. Without any BOPs to stop the flow, oil would gush into the ocean at the rate of 120,000 barrels a day, more than twice what escaped in the *Deepwater Horizon* disaster in the Gulf.

The surface currents and wind would speed the oil slick on its mission to destroy much of the eastern coast of Florida and Georgia. And might even spread to the Carolinas. Ports would close, shipping and tourism would stop indefinitely, millions of people would take a huge economic hit.

Roberto had said, "Americans want oil for their cars and their air-conditioning and their capitalist companies. Well, I'll give it to them. They can drown in all the oil we'll deliver!"

Forty minutes later the ship was three kilometers away from the *Miami Rover*.

Enrico Cruz checked the GPS one last time and he and Cheval left the bridge. Cruz said, "Everybody in the speedboat."

Cruz hurried to the gamy forward hold, in which

slimy water sloshed, and checked the main bomb. Everything fine. He armed it. He did the same with the second, the device that would destroy the blowout preventer.

Then he hurried back to the rocking deck. A glance over the bow. Yes, she was making right for the rig. He scanned the massive deck of the structure—easily a hundred feet above the surface. No workers were visible. This was typical. Nobody on oil rigs wasted time lounging on the fiercely hot iron superstructure, taking in the non-view. They were hard at work in the interior of the unit, mostly in the drill house, or asleep, waiting for the next shift.

Cruz hurried to the side of the vessel and climbed down the rope ladder and dropped into the speedboat with Cheval and the others of the crew.

The motor started.

But before they pulled away, Cruz opened his palm and kissed the pads of his fingers. He then touched it to a rusty patch of hull and whispered, "This is for you, Roberto."

CHAPTER 95

THE CLUSTER OF PASSENGERS ON the cruise ship's forward deck was being photographed by Jim from New Jersey, as opposed to Jim from Cleveland or Jim from London (all right, the Brit preferred "James" but since he was on holiday, he was happy to play along with the others).

The group had become friendly in the days since the ocean liner left Hamilton, in Bermuda, and had spent the first tipsy cocktail hour noting coincidences of career and number of children...and given names.

Four Jims, two Sallys.

Jim from California was below, neither the patch nor Dramamine working well, and so he would not be included in the picture.

Jim from New Jersey lined everyone up against what he said was a gunwale, though nobody knew exactly what that was—he didn't either—but it seemed very nautical and fun to say.

"Nobody sing the *Titanic* song."

There'd been a lot of that, especially as the bars remained open late into the night, but the truth was that very few people, men or women, could bring off the treacly song like Celine Dion.

"Is that Florida?" somebody asked. One of the Sallys, Jim from New Jersey believed.

He saw a dim line on the horizon but that was probably just a layer of clouds.

"Not yet, I don't think."

"But what's that? It's a building."

"Oh, that's the oil rig. The first one in this part of the Atlantic. Didn't you see the news? A year ago or so. They found some oil between Nassau and Florida."

"They? Who's they? Everybody always says 'they.' Are you going to take the picture? My margarita's melting."

"U.S. Petroleum. American Petroleum Drilling. I don't remember."

"I hate those things," Sally from Chicago muttered. "Did you see the birds in the Gulf? All covered with oil. It was terrible. I cried."

"And we couldn't get good shrimp for months."

The photog marshaled his subjects into line against the gunwale and tapped down on the Canon shutter.

Click, click, click, click, click . . .

Enough to make sure that there'd be no blinks.

The proof of vacation burned into a silicon chip, the tourists turned to gaze at the sea and conversation meandered to dinner and shopping in Miami and the Fontainebleau hotel and was Versace's mansion still open to the public?

"I heard he had an eight-person shower," said Jim from London.

Claire disputed that.

"Holy shit," Jim from New Jersey gasped.

"Honey!" chided his wife.

But the camera was up once more and by the time the sound of the explosion reached them, everyone had turned and was focused on the massive mushroom cloud rising perhaps a thousand feet in the air.

"Oh, Jesus. It's the oil rig!"

"No, no!"

"Oh, my God. Somebody call somebody."

Click, click, click, click...

CHAPTER 96

"WHAT'S THE DAMAGE ASSESSMENT?"

Shreve Metzger, in blue jeans and a long-sleeved white shirt that was partly untucked amidships, was leaning over a computer monitor, staring, staring at the smoke and haze hovering over the Caribbean Sea, a thousand miles away.

"Gone completely," said a NIOS communications specialist at a control panel beside him, a young woman with hair pulled back in a bun that looked painfully tight. The comspec's voice was unemotional.

The scene on the monitor revealed clearly that, no, there was nothing left, other than an oil slick, some debris.

And smoke. A lot of smoke.

Gone completely...

Lincoln Rhyme and Amelia Sachs, along with Metzger and the comspec, were in the outer office of NIOS's Ground Control Station trailer, on Rector Street in lower Manhattan. In the parking lot.

Rhyme squinted at the bits of wood and plastic and rocking sheen of oil, which had until thirty seconds ago been the 110-foot Dominican cargo ship that Robert Moreno's friend, Henry Cross, aka Enrico Cruz, had guided toward the *Miami Rover*, the American Petroleum Drilling and Refining oil rig off the coast of Florida.

The comspec touched her earphones. "Reports of a second detonation, underwater, Director. About eight or nine hundred feet depth."

A moment later, they could see on the high-resolution monitor a slight bubbling up of the water on the surface. That was all. Rhyme supposed that however large the second bomb had been, intended to destroy the rig's wellhead, he guessed, so much water had quite a mitigating effect.

Rhyme looked through the glass wall dividing the trailer in half: the Kill Room of the GCS. He noted in the dim light the man who had just caused the devastation—and saved the lives of the people on board the rig, as well as much of the east coast of Florida.

Oblivious to those observing him, Barry Shales was at the drone operations station. To Rhyme it seemed like a freestanding airplane cockpit. Shales was sitting forward, apparently quite relaxed, in a comfortable tan leather chair, facing five flat-screen monitors.

The NIOS officer's hands gripped joysticks, though he would occasionally twist or tap one of the other hundred or so knobs, dials, switches and computer keys.

Rhyme noted that somebody had affixed a seat belt to the chair. It dangled to the floor unlatched. A joke, surely.

Shales was alone in the dim room, which was soundproofed, it seemed, presumably so that he wouldn't be distracted by noises from associates— or visitors like Rhyme and Sachs today. Delivering deadly messages from on high undoubtedly required supreme concentration.

The comspec, who also had a live link to the American Petroleum security people on board the oil rig, tapped buttons herself, asked some questions and announced to Metzger, Rhyme and Sachs, "Confirm no damage to *Miami Rover* or blowout preventer. No injuries, except a few ear-aches."

Not unexpected when a massive fertilizer bomb detonates a half mile from you.

As he'd been reviewing the evidence a half hour ago, Rhyme had suddenly realized that some things didn't add up. He'd made a half dozen calls and deduced that an attack might be imminent.

He'd contacted Metzger. Feverish debate in Washington and at NIOS ensued. Scrambling air force fighters required too much authorization from the Pentagon on up; hours would be wasted getting the approval.

Metzger, of course, had a solution. He'd appealed to Barry Shales, who was en route to headquarters anyway to collect his personal belongings—Metzger explained that the pilot had decided to leave NIOS.

Given the horrific consequences if the pending attack was successful and the approaching deadline—a matter of minutes—the former air force officer had reluctantly agreed to help. He'd flown the drone from Homestead to a spot just over the cargo ship and hovered. The ship was apparently abandoned; they'd seen the crew get into a speedboat and flee. When the radio hails, ordering the cargo ship to come about, were ignored, Shales had launched a Hellfire, which struck the forward hold, where Rhyme speculated the fertilizer bomb had been placed.

Bull's-eye.

Shales was now turning the drone in a different direction and began following the small boat that contained the crew, who had abandoned the vessel twenty minutes earlier. Into view on the monitor came the black, long-nosed speedboat, crashing over the waves away from the rig and the explosion.

Rhyme heard Barry Shales's voice over a ceiling-mounted speaker. "UAV Four Eight One to Florida Center. I've got secondary target in range and acquiring lock. Distance from target eighteen hundred yards."

"Copy, Four Eight One. Close DFT to one thousand yards."

"Roger, Florida Center. Four Eight One."

On the monitor, Rhyme could see Henry Cross and the sailors who'd abandoned the vessel and were speeding away to safety. You couldn't quite catch the facial expressions but their body language suggested confusion and concern. They wouldn't have heard the drone or seen the missile, most likely, and would think that some malfunction in the bomb had caused it to detonate prematurely. Perhaps they were thinking, Lord, that could've happened while we were on board.

"Four Eight One to Florida Center. I'm DFT one thousand. Locked on secondary vessel. At their speed they'll be under cover of Harrogate Cay in ten minutes. Please advise."

"Roger. We're hailing now on general frequencies. No response yet."

Shales replied evenly, "Copy. Four Eight One."

Rhyme now glanced at Sachs, whose face revealed the concern he himself felt. Were they about to witness the summary execution of six people?

They'd been caught in an act of terrorism. But that risk had been neutralized. Besides, Rhyme now thought, were they all terrorists? What if one or two were innocent sailors that had no idea what the cargo and mission were?

Suddenly the conflict between Shreve Metzger and Nance Laurel came into stark, wrenching focus.

"Four Eight One, this is Florida Center. No response to the hail. Payload launch is authorized."

Rhyme could see Barry Shales stiffen.

He sat absolutely still for a moment and reached forward, flipped up the cover of a button on a panel in front of him.

Shreve Metzger said into a stalk mike on the desk in front of him, "Barry. Fire the rifle across their bow."

Over the speaker Shales said, "UAV Four Eight One to Florida Center. Negative on payload launch. Switching to LRR mode."

"Copy, Four Eight One."

In the Kill Room, Barry Shales juggled a joystick and squinted at the video image of the speeding ship. He touched a black panel in front of him. A brief delay and, in eerie silence, three sequential plumes of water shot into the air a few feet in front of the speeding boat.

The slim vessel kept going, though everyone on board was looking around. Several of the sailors seemed very young, no more than teenagers.

"Florida Center to Four Eight One. We copy no change in target velocity. Payload launch is still authorized."

"Copy. Four Eight One."

Nothing happened for a moment. But then, with a lurch, the speedboat slowed and stopped in the water. Two of the sailors were pointing to the sky, nowhere near the camera, though. They couldn't see the drone but they all now understood where their enemy was.

Almost in unison they raised their hands.

What followed was comical. The water was choppy and the boat small. They were trying to maintain balance but afraid if they lowered their arms, death from on high would find them. Two fell over and scrabbled quickly to their feet, shooting their hands into the air. They seemed like drunks trying to dance.

"Florida Center to UAV Four Eight One. Copy surrender. Navy advises *Cyclone*-class patrol ship, the *Firebrand*, one mile away, making thirty knots. Keep secondary target dead in the water until it arrives."

"Copy. Four Eight One."

CHAPTER 97

B ARRY SHALES CLOSED THE DOOR to the Kill Room and, ignoring Shreve Metzger, walked to Rhyme and Sachs. He nodded.

The policewoman told him what a good job he'd done at the commands of the drone. "Sorry, I mean UAV."

"Yes, ma'am," he said unemotionally, his bright blue eyes averted. Some of this reserve was perhaps because he was facing two people who'd intended to hang a murder charge on him. On reflection, though, Rhyme thought not. He simply seemed to be a very private person.

Maybe when you have his particular skill you're mentally and emotionally in a different place much of the time.

Shales then turned to Rhyme. "We had to move pretty fast, sir. I never got the chance to ask how you figured it out—that there was going to be an attack on the rig, I mean."

The criminalist said, "There was some evidence unaccounted for."

"Oh, that's right, sir. You're the evidence tsar, someone was saying."

Rhyme decided he liked that pithy phrase quite a bit. He'd remember it. "Specifically paraffin with a branched-chain molecule, an aromatic, a cycloalkane...oh, and some alkenes."

Shales blinked twice.

"Or to put it in more common parlance: crude oil."

"Crude oil?"

"Exactly. Trace amounts were found on Moreno's and his guard's shoes and clothes. They had to pick that up at some point before your attack on May ninth when they were out of the South Cove Inn, at meetings. Now, I didn't think much of it—there are some refineries and oil storage facilities in the Bahamas. But then I realized something else: The morning he died Moreno met with some businesspeople about starting up transportation and agriculture operations there as part of his Local Empowerment Movement. But we'd also learned that fertilizer, diesel oil and nitromethane had been shipped weeks ago to his LEM companies. If those companies hadn't even been formed yet, why buy the chemicals?"

"You put together crude oil and possible bomb."

"We'd known about the rig from the initial intelligence about Moreno's plans for May tenth. Since Moreno was so vocal against American Petroleum Drilling maybe the company *was* a target, after all—for a real attack, not just a protest. I think on Sunday or Monday he went to meet rig workers—maybe to get up-to-date information about security. Oh, and there was one other thing that didn't make sense. Sachs here figured that out."

She said, "When Moreno came to New York earlier in the month, the one meeting he had that he didn't invite his interpreter to was with Henry Cross at the Classrooms for the Americas Foundation. Why not? Most of his meetings were innocent—Moreno wouldn't let her interpret for him if the meeting was about something illegal. But what about the Cross meeting? If it was innocent, what was wrong with Lydia Foster being here, even if she didn't have to interpret? Which told me maybe it *wasn't* so innocent. And Cross told me about this mysterious blue jet that Moreno kept seeing. Well, we couldn't find anything about any blue jets with travel patterns that seemed to match Moreno's. That was the specific sort of thing somebody would tell a cop to lead them off."

Rhyme picked up again: "Now, Classrooms for the Americas had offices in Nicaragua—which is where the diesel fuel, fertilizer and nitromethane were shipped from. There was too much to be co-incidental. We looked into Cross and found out that he was really Cruz and that he and Moreno had a history together. It was Cruz's brother who was Moreno's best friend, killed in Panama during the invasion. That's what turned him against the United States. We datamined Cruz's travel records and credit cards and found he left New York for Nassau yesterday.

"My contact at the Bahamian police found that he and Moreno had chartered a cargo ship a month ago. It left port this morning. The police raided a warehouse where the ship had been docked and found traces of the explosive chemicals. That was good enough for me. I called Shreve. He called you."

"So, Moreno wasn't innocent after all," Shales whispered, glancing at Metzger.

Sachs said, "No. You took out a bad guy, Airman."

The officer looked at his boss. The expression in his blue eyes was complex. And conflicted. One way to read it was: You were right, Shreve. You were right.

Rhyme added, "And this wasn't going to be his only project." He told both men about the intercept Nance Laurel had read to them in their first meeting on Monday.

I have a lot more messages like this one planned...

"Barry," Metzger said. "I'm going to see our visitors out. Then, could I talk to you in my office? Please."

A pause worthy of Nance Laurel. Finally the airman nodded.

Metzger escorted them to the exit, across the parking lot, thanked them warmly.

Outside the security gate, Rhyme took the accessible cutaway in the sidewalk to cross the street to where the van waited, Thom at the wheel. Sachs stepped off the curb. As she did, Rhyme saw her wince, gasp slightly in pain.

She offered a furtive glance his way, as if to see if he'd caught her frown, and then looked ahead quickly.

This cut him. It was as if she'd just lied to him.

And he lied right back; he pretended he hadn't noticed.

Across the street they continued to the van for a moment. Then Rhyme braked the Merits chair to a stop in the middle of the sidewalk.

She turned.

"What is it, Rhyme?"

"Sachs, there's something we need to talk about."

CHAPTER 98

THE PHONE RANG ON SCHEDULE.

Whatever else you could say about him, the Wizard was prompt.

Shreve Metzger, at his desk in a somewhat deserted NIOS this Saturday afternoon, looked at the blinking light of his magic red phone and listened attentively to the trill of the ringer, like a bird, he'd decided. He debated about not picking up.

And never taking a call from the man ever again.

"Metzger here."

"Shreve! How are you doing? Heard about those interesting developments up there, I understand. Long Island. I used to belong to Meadowbrook, did you know that? You don't golf, do you?"

"No."

And squashed a "sir" dead.

The voice grew wizardly once again, low, raspy: "We've been talking about charges against Spencer."

Metzger replied, "We could make a case work...if we wanted to." He removed his bland glasses, polished the lenses and replaced them. Unlike in the United Kingdom, it was not necessarily a crime to release classified material in this country, unless you were spying for another nation.

"Yes, well, we'll have to consider our priorities, of course."

The Wizard was referring undoubtedly to the public relations issues. It might make more sense not to pursue the matter, lest the press get their hands on the story.

Yes, well...

Metzger took out the nail clippers. But there was nothing left to clip. He spun them absently on his desktop. Put them back.

"And good job with that incident in Florida. Interesting that that bad intel turned good. Like magic. David Copperfield, Houdini."

"They're in custody, all of them."

"Delighted to hear it." As if he were sharing Hollywood gossip, the Wizard said, "Now I have to tell you something, Shreve. You there?"

How cheerfully he delivers my death sentence.

"Yes. Go on."

"Got a call from a friend in Langley. A certain individual who was recently in Mexico."

May-hi-co.

"A certain party," the Wizard repeated. "You remember him?"

"In Reynosa," Metzger said.

"That's the place. Well, guess what? He's vacationing outside Santa Rosa, near Tijuana."

"Is that right?"

"Yes indeed. And apparently he still plans on making some deliveries of his specialty products in the near future. The very near future."

So al-Barani Rashid had moved to the West Coast to hide out.

"He was just spotted with some associates but his friends'll be leaving in the morning. And our friend will be all alone in a pleasant little cottage all day tomorrow. And the good news is that the local tourist board is absolutely fine about a visit from us. So, wondering if you could draw up some revised travel plans for our approval. Details are on their way."

A new STO?

But aren't I being fired? he wondered.

"Of course. I'll get right on it. But...?"

"Yes?" the Wizard asked.

Metzger asked, "Those meetings? The budgetary issues?"

A pause. "Oh, the committee moved on to other matters." After a beat the Wizard said sternly, "If there had been issues, I would've mentioned them to you, don't you think?"

"Sure, you would have. Of course."

"Of course."

Click.

VIII

WHEN YOU MOVE...

CHAPTER 99

T HE MORNING OF THE SURGERY.
Rhyme, trailed by Sachs and Thom,
wheeled fast down the hospital corridor to
the Surgical Procedures waiting room where the
patients could visit with their friends and family
until they were whisked off for the knife.

"I hate hospitals," Sachs said.

"Really? Why?" Rhyme found himself in quite
a good mood. "The staff can be sooo charming,
the food sooo good. The latest magazines. And
all the miracles of modern medicine," Rhyme pro-
claimed. "If you'll forgive the alliteration."

Sachs gave a brief laugh.

They'd waited only five minutes when the doctor
strode into the room and shook all their hands,
carefully noting Rhyme's articulating right arm
and digits. "Good," he said. "That is very good."

"I do my best."

The doctor explained what they all knew at this

point: that the surgery should take three hours, possibly a little longer. The stay in the recovery room could be expected to last an hour or so. The surgeon would come find them here, though, right after the operation was completed to tell them how it had gone.

Exuding confidence, the man smiled and headed off to gown and scrub.

The pre-op nurse, a pretty African American woman in puppy-decorated scrubs, arrived and introduced herself, smiling broadly. It's a scary thing, to be knocked out and cut open then put back together. Some medicos didn't appreciate the trauma but this woman did and kept everyone at ease. Finally she asked, "Ready?"

Amelia Sachs leaned over and kissed Rhyme on the mouth. She rose and, limping, accompanied the nurse down the hall.

He called, "We'll be in the recovery room when you wake up."

She turned back. "Don't be crazy, Rhyme. Go back home. Solve a case or something."

"We'll be in the recovery room," he repeated, as the door swung shut and she disappeared.

After a moment of silence Rhyme said to Thom, "You don't happen to have one of those miniatures of whiskey, do you? From the flight to Nassau."

He'd insisted the aide smuggle some scotch on board, though he'd learned that in first class you get as much liquor as you like—or, more accurately, as much as your caregiver is willing to let you have.

"No, and I wouldn't give you any if I did have some. It's nine in the morning."

Rhyme scowled.

He looked once more at the doors through which Sachs had vanished.

We don't want to lose her; she's too good. But the department can't keep her if she insists on being in the field...

Yes, he'd had a conversation with Sachs, as Bill Myers had insisted.

Though the message was a bit different from what the captain had wanted.

Neither a desk job at the NYPD and early retirement and security consulting were options for Amelia Sachs. There was only one solution to avoid those nightmares. Rhyme had contacted Dr. Vic Barrington and gotten the name of the best surgeon in the city specializing in treating severe arthritis.

The man had said he might be able to help; Rhyme's conversation with Sachs on Saturday outside NIOS headquarters was about the possibility of *her* undergoing a procedure to improve the situation…and keeping her in the field. Not *desking* her, to use one of Myers's more pernicious verbs.

Because she wasn't afflicted with rheumatoid arthritis—an immune system malady that affects all the joints—but more common osteoarthritis, she was young enough so that a procedure in her hip and knee could give her a dozen years or more of normal life before a joint replacement would be required.

She'd debated and finally agreed.

In the waiting room now, Rhyme was looking around at the ten or so others here, the couples, the solitary men or women, the families. Some motionless, some lost in intense dialogue not quite discernible, some jittery, some engaging in rituals of distraction: stirring coffee, opening crisp wrappers of snack food, studying limp magazines, texting or playing video games on phones.

Rhyme noted that, unlike the streets of New York, not a soul paid him more than a millisecond of uninterested attention. He was in a wheelchair; this was a hospital. Here, he was normal.

Thom asked, "You've told Dr. Barrington you've canceled your surgery?"

"I've told him."

The aide was quiet for a moment. The *Times* in

his hands dipped ever so slightly. For two people joined by circumstance and profession so inextricably and, in a way, intimately, these two had never been comfortable with discussions personal in nature. Lincoln Rhyme least of all. Yet he was surprised to find himself at ease as he confessed to Thom, "Something happened when I was down in the Bahamas."

His eyes were on a middle-aged couple insincerely reassuring each other. Over the fate of whom? Rhyme wondered. An elderly father? Or a young child?

A world of difference there.

Rhyme continued, "On the spit of land where we thought the sniper nest was."

"When you went for a swim."

The criminalist was silent for a moment, reliving not the horrors of the water but the moments leading up to it. "It was an easy deduction for me to make—that the gold Mercury would show up."

"How?"

"The man in the pickup? Tossing trash into the ditch nearby?"

"The one who turned out to be the ringleader."

"Right. Why did he drive down to the *end* of the spit to dump the bags? There was a public trash yard a half mile away, just off SW Road. And who talks on their cell while unloading heavy bags? He was telling the other two in the Mercury where we were. Oh, and he was in a gray T-shirt—which you'd told me one of the men in the Mercury was wearing earlier. But I missed them, all the clues. I *saw* them but I missed them. And you know why?"

The aide shook his head.

"Because I had the gun. The gun Mychal'd given me. I didn't need to think through the situation. I didn't need to use my *mind*—because I could shoot my way out."

"Except you couldn't."

"Except I couldn't."

A doctor in weary, flecked scrubs emerged and sets of eager eyes dropped onto him like Rhyme's falcon on a pigeon. The man found the family he sought, joined them and delivered what was apparently good news. Rhyme continued to his aide, "I've often wondered if the accident enhanced me somehow. Forced me to think better, more clearly, make sharper deductions. Because I *had* to. I didn't have any other options."

"And now you think the answer is yes."

A nod. "In the Bahamas, I nearly got you, Mychal and me killed because of that lapse. It's not going to happen again."

The aide said, "So I think you're telling me that you've had the last surgery you're going to have."

"That's right. What was that line from a movie, something you made me watch? I liked it. Though I probably didn't admit it at the time."

"Which one?"

"Some cop film. A long time ago. The hero said something like 'A man's got to know his limitations.'"

"Clint Eastwood." Thom considered this. "It's true but you could also say, 'A man's got to know his strengths.'"

"You're such a goddamn optimist." Rhyme lifted his right hand and gazed at his fingers. Lowered the limb. "This is enough."

"It's the only choice you could've made, Lincoln."

Rhyme lifted an eyebrow, querying.

"Otherwise I'd be out of a job. And I'd never find anybody equally difficult to work for."

"I'm glad," Rhyme grumbled, "I've set such a high bar."

Then the subject, and its awkward accoutrements, vanished like snow on a hot car hood. The men fell silent.

Two hours later the door to the operating suites opened and another doctor emerged. Again, all eyes latched onto the green-scrubbed man but this one was Sachs's surgeon and he headed directly toward Rhyme and Thom.

As the others in the room returned to their vending-machine coffee and magazines and text messages, the surgeon looked from Thom to Rhyme. He said, "It went well. She's fine. She's awake. She's asking for you."

THE RECIPES OF JACOB SWANN

Readers wishing to experience Jacob Swann's skills firsthand—culinary, not homicidal—can find a link to recipes for the dishes mentioned in this book, many of them my own variations on classics, at my website: www.jefferydeaver.com.

—*J.D.*

ACKNOWLEDGMENTS

With thanks to Mitch Hoffman, Jamie Raab, Lindsey Rose, David Young and all my friends at Grand Central Publishing—and my cast of regulars: Madelyn Warcholik, Deborah Schneider, Cathy Gleason, Julie Deaver, Jane Davis, Will and Tina Anderson. I couldn't do it without you!

ABOUT THE AUTHOR

A former journalist, folksinger and attorney, Jeffery Deaver is an international number-one bestselling author. His novels have appeared on bestseller lists around the world, including the *New York Times*, the *Times* of London, Italy's *Corriere della Sera*, the *Sydney Morning Herald* and the *Los Angeles Times*. His books are sold in 150 countries and translated into twenty-five languages.

The author of thirty novels, two collections of short stories and a nonfiction law book, he's received or been shortlisted for a number of awards around the world. His *The Bodies Left Behind* was named Novel of the Year by the International Thriller Writers Association, and his Lincoln Rhyme thriller *The Broken Window* and a stand-alone, *Edge*, were also nominated for that prize. He has been awarded the Steel Dagger and the Short Story Dagger from the British Crime Writers' Association and the Nero Wolfe Award, and he is a three-time recipient of the Ellery Queen Readers Award for Best Short Story of the Year and a winner of the British Thumping Good Read Award. *The Cold Moon* was recently named the Book of the Year by the Mystery Writers Association of Japan, as well as by *Kono Mystery Wa Sugoi* magazine. In addition, the Japanese Adventure Fiction Association awarded *The Cold Moon* and *Carte Blanche* their annual Grand Prix award.

His most recent novels are *XO*, a Kathryn Dance thriller, for which he wrote an album of country-western songs, available on iTunes and as a CD; and before that, *Carte Blanche*, the latest James Bond continuation novel, a number-one international bestseller.

Deaver has been nominated for seven Edgar Awards from the Mystery Writers of America, an Anthony Award and a Gumshoe Award. He was recently shortlisted for the ITV3 Crime Thriller Award for Best International Author.

His book *A Maiden's Grave* was made into an HBO movie starring James Garner and Marlee Matlin, and his novel *The Bone Collector* was a feature release from Universal Pictures, starring Denzel Washington and Angelina Jolie. And, yes, the rumors are true; he did appear as a corrupt reporter on his favorite soap opera, *As the World Turns*.

He was born outside Chicago and has a bachelor of journalism degree from the University of Missouri and a law degree from Fordham University.

Readers can visit his website at www.jeffery deaver.com.